Peter Ustinov was _____
He served during the war with the Royal
Sussex Regiment and the RAOC but still
found time to write his first play, *House of
Regrets*, which was produced in 1942. Fur-
ther plays include *The Love of Four Colonels*,
Romanoff and Juliet, *The Unknown Soldier
and His Wife*, and *Beethoven's Tenth*.

His work in the cinema has covered nearly
every aspect of that world: he directed and
acted in the award-winning *Billy Budd:* he was
author and co-director of *School for Secrets*.
As an actor, his roles have ranged from the
Emperor Nero to Hercule Poirot. He has
produced opera at The Royal Opera House,
Covent Garden and at The Hamburg Opera,
and his books include the collection of short
stories *Add a Dash of Pity* and the novels
Krumnagel and *Monsieur René*.

He has worked for many years on behalf of
UNICEF and was awarded The Order of the
Smile for his dedication to the idea of international assistance to children. He received
a CBE in 1975 and a knighthood in 1990.

BY
PETER USTINOV

NOVELS
The Loser
Krumnagel
Monsieur René

NOVELLAS
The Disinformer/A Nose By Any Other Name

SHORT STORIES
Add a Dash of Pity
The Frontiers of the Sea

NON-FICTION
My Russia
Ustinov in Russia

MEMOIRS
Dear Me

The Loser

Peter Ustinov

POCKET
BOOKS

LONDON · SYDNEY · NEW YORK · TOKYO · SINGAPORE · TORONTO

First published in Great Britain in 1961
Reprinted in 1989 by Michael O'Mara Books Ltd
First published in paperback in Great Britain by
Pocket Books, 1994
This edition published by Pocket Books, 1999
An imprint of Simon & Schuster UK Ltd
A Viacom Company

1 3 5 7 9 10 8 6 4 2

Simon & Schuster UK Ltd
Africa House
64–78 Kingsway
London WC2B 6AH

Simon & Schuster Australia
Sydney

A CIP catalogue record for this book is available
from the British Library

ISBN 0–671–03323–9

Typeset by Palimpsest Book Production Limited,
Polmont, Stirlingshire
Printed and bound in Great Britain by
Caledonian International Book Manufacturing, Glasgow

For
Moura Budberg

In gratitude

PROLOGUE

HANS WINTERSCHILD was born on the 17th of October, 1920, in the little town of Langensalza, on the border separating Prussia from Thuringia. His father, Friedrich Winterschild, looked down at the little, writhing shape, with its moss of silver hair and its searching fists, and knew that his prayers had been answered. Kissing his wife tenderly on her moist forehead, he murmured, 'Mutti, you have given me a boy.'

For many generations the family had been one of moderate importance in the town, the father of Friedrich Winterschild even having stood unsuccessfully for mayor at the turn of the century. Friedrich himself, now in his late fifties, had commanded a local artillery regiment, serving for four years on the Western Front and rising to the rank of full colonel before his guns were confiscated and destroyed as a bitter consequence of the Armistice. His wife, born Wilhelmina von Weza-Babersbeck, had given the family the thin glazing of aristocracy after which it hankered for so long. 'If my mother had been the von instead of my wife,' Colonel Winterschild used to say, 'there would have been no question of the artillery. It would have meant the cavalry, and useful introductions to the General Staff.' He failed to recognize the fact that, since Germany was deprived of an army, these niceties would have meant nothing in any case. To him, the armed forces were one reality, and life another. They did not have to be reconciled to one another in the realm of possibility.

Their children had come with difficulty. There was a daughter, Hannele, now twenty-two and a predestined spinster. She rather embarrassingly preserved the sweet ways of childhood by teaching movement and mime in a kindergarten. She was seldom without a whimsical smile, and grew older visibly at her father's knee, never having left the nursery in spirit. The other daughter, nick-named Mopsel, had married a man called Helmut Bollmann, who had about him all the aggressive, wounded majesty of one who carried the weight of Germany's sorrows on his shoulders. Nature had given him a voice of unparalleled stridency, and a tumbling eloquence. When both were in use, no power on earth could interrupt him.

Now, in the aftermath of the war, a boy had

been born to the aging couple, who was to give their later years a marvelous and unexpected warmth.

CHILDREN ARE told that pride comes before the fall, that the fall is the automatic consequence of pride. It follows that pride is bad. Bad for the individual. Paradoxically, they are also taught that what is bad for the individual is imperative for the masses. A child who is reprimanded for placing himself on a pedestal is at the same time encouraged to place his country there, his country right or wrong. It is when pride is hurt that it becomes dangerous, and arithmetic can prove that a nation's pride is more of a problem to the world than the pride of one man.

Few could have foreseen how ugly the First World War would become. Jean Jaurès in France foresaw it and was assassinated for his clairvoyance. Generals on both sides agreed that the war would be over 'by Christmas.' Had it indeed ended by Christmas 1914, there can be little doubt that the repercussions would not have been much more terrible than they had been in 1870. A moment of degradation would have been suffered by one side or the other, either Berlin or Paris would have been occupied momentarily, Germany would have ceded part of German West Africa to France, part of German East Africa to Britain, or else Madagascar and Bermuda might have passed temporarily to Germany in the game

of colonial checkers fashionable at the time, and
the invasion of Mexico would have remained the
high point of General Pershing's career.

The use of cavalry, the red trousers of the
French and the glinting spikes of the German
helmets all proclaimed that it would be a civilized
war, a chivalrous war, a seasonal trial of strength
in the best traditions. The public, who were never
averse at that time to waving a flag outside a palace
and rushing thoughtlessly to the recruiting offices,
slowly began to realize that the sides were evenly
matched, and in their intense disenchantment
began to break the age-old rules of the contest. Since there was no hope of winning, it
was imperative not to lose. Not only would
defeat entail degradation of a kind and on a scale
unknown before, but it was becoming clear that
some sort of terrible precedent would have to be
set, the consequences of which loomed black and
unfathomable. A conflagration of such magnitude
could hardly end with the surrender of a sword
and a hasty abdication.

When Germany finally gave up, her delegates
were forced to pretend that they expected the
same degree of clemency which Napoleon granted
to the defeated, and when such consideration
was not forthcoming they feigned horror at the
realization that the Reich was the first country
in history to suffer punishment on a calculated,
modern scale. They were perhaps not entirely
wrong in feeling sorry for themselves, since they

were, in a sense, the victims of a communal guilt, a guilt of people on both sides who had entered the war light-heartedly to settle the affairs of kings, and who had survived to be responsible for the affairs of men.

Colonel Winterschild had experienced all the bitterness of the surrender, more especially since he had allowed himself four years of confidence and hope, an extravagant span of time for anyone but a hardened patriot. When peace came, he was sincerely and deeply shocked by the severity of the sentence imposed on a land which, in his eyes, had not been guilty.

His moral problems became more palpable when the inflation reduced his pension to a pittance. Food was as scarce as money, and he used to stare at the young Hans playing in his playpen, and mutter that if the child grew up a weakling, it would be the fault of those pagan nations which had nailed Germany so callously to the cross.

After the verdict of Versailles the myth spread that the defeat had come about by some mean trick rather than by exhaustion. When others had half forgotten the war, the Germans were still refighting the battles on the sand tables of their imagination. Never did they ask themselves the question 'Why did we do it?' but always, 'What went wrong?'

Also, after the cohesive, the reassuring feeling of life under a form of Imperial dictatorship, the

new multi-partied system of democratic government, composed largely of sincere men trying
desperately to make ends meet, seemed not only
ineffectual but worse, a calculated Allied plan to
keep Germany weak. Against suspicions of this
kind, a parliament, still in its crawling infancy,
had no chance whatever of survival in the long
run. The selection of Hindenburg as Reich's
Chancellor betrayed both a hankering for the old
Imperial glories and a defiant vote of confidence
in one so closely identified with the local triumphs
of both the Army and the Empire as to give body
to the hope that all was not lost and the last battle
was yet to be fought.

On Hans's tenth birthday, the colonel hung a
picture of Hindenburg over his son's bed.

I

HANS WAS good at school. He recognized his duty to his parents from an early age, and took to heart the immense hopes which were invested in him. School is the place where not only knowledge but prejudices are inseminated into the unformed mind, and since Hans was born with a sense of discipline after the generations of solid if unspectacular service which had made the name of Winterschild respected, it follows that he drank from the fountain of learning without ever questioning the taste. He knew that Germany had been wronged throughout history, that Frederick the Great had brilliantly struggled against encirclement, the devious conspiracy of those jealous of German military prowess, that Blücher and not Wellington had won at Waterloo, and that the end had come in 1918

not as a result of the defeat of German arms,
but because of a disgraceful collapse of the home
front. He knew all this because he had been
told it, and his father confirmed the teacher's
theories by long rhetorical statements after dinner
dealing with the German soul, permeated with
a rampant self-pity. 'We have God's interests
at heart,' the colonel loved to cry. '*Gott mit
uns!*'

The boy's early years were spent in charming
and tactful deference to the colonel's increasing
mysticism. With a genuine filial piety, Hans
would respectfully listen to and inwardly digest
the romantic gospel.

Every evening Helmut Bollmann would come
to the house, and boast about the prowess of
German Olympic runners, about the superiority
of German racing cars, about the unsurpassed
soldierly qualities of the German nation. The
old man liked to hear these tales. Even when
Bollmann extended his theorizing over more dis-
putable ground, such as the urgent need for
pogroms, the colonel could not find the energy
to disagree. He would mumble something vaguely
for his own satisfaction, and then relapse into his
usual pensive and dimly appreciative silence.

Hans and his mother were quite grateful for
these lengthy monologues; they were uttered with
the weight of a frenzied conviction, which is pleasant in uncertain times. Mopsel used to watch her
husband, her blue eyes hypnotized by his fluency,

and her evident belief in him strengthened Hans in his own devotion to the cause.

One evening Helmut was late. Mopsel sat by herself, knitting the endless white garments which were the price of her faith.

'Where is Helmut tonight?' asked Frau Winterschild, knitting something small and white herself in dutiful anticipation of the recurring inevitable.

'He will come,' answered Mopsel, secretly. In due course there was a noise on the stairs, harsher than usual, more clipped.

Helmut entered, and for the first time they saw him in uniform.

'What is that?' asked the colonel. 'Have we departed from the traditional cut of our military clothes? Have you joined the Army?'

'This is the uniform of the *Schutzstaffel*, the *Waffen SS*,' said Helmut, who seemed intoxicated.

'A new technical arm?'

'Yes,' cried Helmut, 'a new technical, moral, and patriotic arm. The Reichstag is on fire.'

The colonel took his pipe from his mouth. 'You're joking,' he said.

Helmut smiled. 'I am not joking.'

The colonel grumbled. 'Some stupid idiot of a tourist with a lighted cigarette, I wouldn't be surprised.'

THE UNCERTAINTIES of day-to-day existence were reflected at school. Occasionally the lessons would be interrupted momentarily as truckloads of Brownshirts would drive past the windows, yelling the words *'Deutschland, erwache!'* in unison. It was hardly a dignified pastime for self-respecting men, and yet these frustrated creatures found a meaning to their weaponless existence in this hoarse exhortation for Germany to awake. Only Herr Waechter, the Latin teacher, had the courage to demand the attention of the boys whenever the hecklers threatened to drown his lessons. If a boy found himself too transported by the demonstration in the street to sit down at once, Herr Waechter made the culprit translate *'Deutschland, erwache'* into Latin. This translation was all the Latin some of the boys knew, or would ever know.

As time passed, there was no further need to awaken Germany. Adolf Hitler rose to power, and made such a noise that further sleep was out of the question. Unable at first to risk any conflict with an organized power, and yet compelled to keep the minds of his listeners not only active but militant, in anticipation of the great day of reckoning, he began practicing on the Jews the methods which would soon be applied to everyone else. The internationalism of the Jews made them suspect as being, of one accord, party to a huge conspiracy to defraud those who live honestly by the land. They became the convenient symbol of the epoch, the equivalent of 'Wall Street' in the parlance of Communists.

It is, of course, relatively easy for nations to maltreat their own nationals, since they invariably claim that the horror of public opinion elsewhere is but an interference in internal problems. However, such activities are almost without exception the result of a frustrated inability to do harm on a more generous scale. Unable to attack Czechoslovakia without requisite arms, the young warriors attacked the Jews with sticks and torches.

One day Herr Weinstein, the physics teacher, was removed. In a prepared statement the principal of the school, Dr Kress, told the boys that Herr Weinstein had been relieved of his duties because he was a Jew, and that such rendered him incapable of teaching physics. From now on physics was a German preserve. Dr Kress was an elderly man, and there was something about the difficulty he experienced in reading his own writing which betrayed his conviction that he was talking nonsense. At all events, he did not look up, but left the school auditorium, his head bent.

Soon afterwards Herr Waechter left. In another prepared statement, Dr Kress informed his pupils that Herr Waechter was not in tune with the spirit of the times and had therefore asked for a leave of absence in order to serve his country elsewhere. Dr Kress's voice broke slightly on the word 'elsewhere,' and he drank two glasses of water before leaving, spilling some of it on the floor.

There was no great surprise when Dr Dülder, the new principal, read yet another prepared statement shortly afterwards, declaring in a firm yet querulous voice that Dr Kress had reached the age of retirement and that at his own request there would be no silver collection for a farewell gift. Gratuitously Dr Dülder added, 'If you wish to show your appreciation, you may give your contributions to the National Socialist Winter Help Scheme, the *Winterhilfe*. This fund will, of course, bear Dr Kress's name.'

Dr Dülder began his regime by declaring a half holiday. 'I am only allowing you this half holiday,' he said sternly, 'in order to become acquainted with the school, and to hold conferences with all the teachers individually and collectively. For the rest of the year, you will work harder than you have ever worked before. I will see to that. I will tolerate no slacking. Germany will tolerate no slacking. Is that clear? The emphasis will be not only on intellectual attainments but on physical training, for we must look our geopolitical destiny in the face, and when the time comes, and we hear our name in the roll call, we must and will answer in a clear, uplifting, powerful voice: "Present!"'

Tschürke, the school bully, an overgrown, hir-sute fellow of sixteen, who was held back in a class two years his junior by his surpassing ignorance, cried, 'At last! That's talking!' when Dr Dülder had left, and then added slyly, 'Come on, let's take the old man by surprise.'

Everyone was frightened of Tschürke, not only because of his size but because he kept a rusty hypodermic needle in his desk, which was used without mercy on those with minds of their own. Now the class waited shyly for Tschürke to explain himself. He took his time. Slowly he took the needle from his desk, while the boys looked at each other furtively.

'Maybe our geo-whatever-it-is destiny is staring at us already, and saying "Look at the bunch of slackers from the Immanuel Kant Gymnasium. They have half-a-day off, and what do they do? Go home and have a good time, eating ice cream, and don't give a thought to the Fatherland." Any questions!'

There were no questions.

'You know old Feldmann, where we buy our candy? What's the matter with you all? Too scared of Tschürke and his hypodermic to answer?'

'Of course we know Feldmann' . . . 'We're not scared' . . . 'Who doesn't know Feldmann?'

'Well,' said Tschürke quietly, 'I've found something out about Feldmann. He's a Jew.'

Half an hour later, a yellow Star of David had been painted on Feldmann's window, and shortly afterwards the window was broken, sweets pouring first into the street and then into the pockets of the young hooligans. Some of the younger passers-by stopped to help in the work of destruction, while older people tended to cross the road, or just look on with a sullen, troubled interest.

Hans took part in the orgy, trying his best to look determined and enthusiastic, in spite of the fact that his heart was hammering against his ribs. He stole no sweets. Most of the boys became slightly hysterical once it became clear that their work of destruction would not be stopped by the police. This produced a strange sense of anti-climax, since the destructiveness possessed none of the devious thrills of lawbreaking but was evidently considered no more than a public-spirited chore, like sweeping the pavements after snow. Only Tschürke seemed to enjoy himself, but then he was older. It was he who actually entered the shop and dragged the wretched Herr Feldmann into the street, kicking him and sticking him with the hypodermic. Frau Feldmann opened a window, and screamed hysterically. A few members of the small crowd which had collected looked up and laughed, but the majority had the natural gravity of those who see another human being in distress. Nobody protested, however. Feldmann was punched, slapped, and had his shirt daubed with the paint which Tschürke had thoughtfully brought along.

Suddenly a youth rushed from the shop, under the canopy of Frau Feldmann's loudest scream. It was a boy of about ten, who picked up a piece of broken glass and charged the nearest of the tormentors, who happened to be Hans. Heedless of Herr Feldmann's sudden yell, the boy dug the glass into Hans's arm.

Here the police intervened on the outskirts of the crowd, and they now ran forward and took the weeping Jewish boy away. When Tschürke tried one last vicious kick, one of the policemen hit him across the back with his truncheon. There was no reading the thoughts of the police.

The crowd dispersed while Tschürke shouted imprecations at the policeman and the timid Feldmann followed his captive son to the police-station at a certain distance, mumbling softly. The little boy never once looked back as he walked away between the two lumbering *schupos*.

Hans, who felt no pain, suddenly found himself looking into Tschürke's eyes.

'That little bastard hurt you?' asked Tschürke.

Hans stared at Tschürke, then at his bleeding arm, then, head down, he bolted for home. Very pale, he entered the parlor, nonchalantly.

'My God, what has happened to you?' cried his mother.

'Nothing.'

'Nothing? Look at your arm!'

His arm was covered with blood.

'Did you meet with an accident?' asked the colonel.

'A fight.'

'Quick, I'm going to call Dr Heyse,' said his mother, crossing to the telephone.

'Mutti, Mutti, a little blood, and immediately you call an ambulance,' grumbled the colonel affectionately. He belonged to a generation for which a little blood was rather manly.

'A little blood?' she replied. 'I was a nurse that last time, remember. That was done with a knife or something sharp. Hullo, Dr Heyse—'

As she spoke, Hans sank heavily into an arm-chair, his forehead beaded with cold sweat.

'Hans, where have you been?' rapped the colonel, rising as suddenly as his son had sat.

The wound was superficial. Dr Heyse, who had been with the family for years, said that he thought the slight fever which Hans had was probably due to some emotional shock, or even the result of the fact of having been stabbed. They talked in Hans's presence, but he just stared ahead of him.

'But it was not done with a knife, you say,' repeated the colonel for the fiftieth time, sitting on the edge of his son's bed, and putting his hand on the quilt around where he imagined the boy's knee would be.

'No,' replied Dr Heyse, 'as I told you, my guess is a piece of broken glass.'

'Glass?' repeated Frau Winterschild tonelessly.

'How did it happen? Who did it?' asked the colonel, feeling out of touch with the boy.

'What do we know about our children these days?' asked Dr Heyse, when no reply was forthcoming. 'When they are born we think we know them, just as I thought I knew this fellow here when I brought him into the world for you, but look at him now. What goes on in their heads these days? You know, I heard that a group of young ruffians attacked a Jewish shop early this afternoon. Broke the windows.'

The colonel sat up, and opened his mouth to speak, then smiled in relief.

'That's not possible, Hansi was at school this afternoon. In any case, he would never lend himself to such foolish actions.'

Dr Heyse fixed Hans intently, and the boy could not resist returning the glance briefly.

'"Foolish"? What a strange adjective you use, Colonel.'

'Why strange, Doctor?'

'So mild.'

'What adjective would you use?'

'Despicable perhaps. Loathsome. Shameful.'

'I must say, I can't see what the poor Jews have done,' said Frau Winterschild. 'Frau Leventhal is really most charming. Unless you have been told you'd never know she was a Jewess. Herr Frankfurter is another one. A real gentleman, but then his family have been here for so long.'

'You say that you can't see what the poor Jews have done, Frau Winterschild,' said the doctor, still staring at Hans out of the corner of his eye. 'Allow me to inform you of part of their activities. As a medical man, I can safely testify without exaggeration that German medicine owes its international reputation to doctors of Jewish origin.'

'Oh, surely not,' the colonel replied, slightly affronted.

'I am not speculating,' the doctor went on, staring at Hans, 'but only telling you cold facts. Even if I was violently anti-Semitic, I would have to tell you the same facts. And that is why I think that for a bunch of youth to go looting Jewish shops is a crime, not just a foolish activity. It is a crime like maltreating a dog, because the poor Jews as you chose to call them have no recourse. The police no longer intervene. It is so easy. And once it is easy, it is the work of boys deficient in honor, the work of cowards.'

Hans suddenly began shaking like a leaf.

'Now you know where your son has been,' said the doctor evenly, taking his hat in his hand.

'Doctor, you have gone too far,' the colonel said stiffly. 'Whatever happens, it will be our fault. We have no sense of values left. What are we to tell our children?'

The doctor left, and Frau Winterschild clung to her son in an embrace which embarrassed the colonel, who forgot to accompany the doctor to the front door.

'Wilhelmina, leave him alone. He's almost a man!'

His demand was unheeded.

'Did you go there of your own free will?' asked the colonel.

Hans hesitated. He couldn't admit he had been forced to go out of fear of a bully with a hypodermic needle. It was better to have courage. He nodded.

'Why?' rapped the colonel.

'I wanted to go,' Hans whispered.

'Did a lot of boys go?'

Hans nodded.

The colonel momentarily ran out of questions. He was confused. The whole thing was outside his experience. He even began to find it a little aggravating to be put in such a position. He almost asked whether the expedition had been organized by the school, because if it hadn't been, how had it occurred during school hours, but he was restrained by the fear that such a question might sound a little ludicrous. He fell into a momentary torpor, and then, like many military men confronted by an incomprehensible situation, he began to feel an urgent desire to command respect. He tapped his foot nervously.

'Who wounded you?' he asked at length.

'A man,' lied Hans.

'A man? What sort of man?'

'A man.'

'A Jew?'

'I . . . I think so.'

'Aha!' said the colonel, as though everything were clear.

'Leave us alone,' implored his wife. Both offended and relieved, the colonel left the room.

HELMUT BOLLMANN came to dinner that night.

Hans drank a little consommé, in bed, and his
mother came to take away his plate, to kiss him
good night, and to turn out his light.

'Feel better, my angel?' she asked.

'I feel fine.'

He no longer needed her, and now he felt a
little ashamed of his behavior, so that he resented
her sugary solicitude. She smiled sadly, as at a
child abruptly grown up. 'Sleep well.'

'What did Helmut say?'

'Oh you know, politics, politics. They're not
for me.'

'Politics are very interesting,' he said.

'Of course they are, my darling,' she whispered.

He shut his eyes. Once the lights were out, he
opened them again, and stared at the ceiling.

Of all the activities of the day only one thing
remained with him burningly, and that was his
humiliating acceptance of Tschürke's leadership.
The destruction of the sweetshop hadn't been
much fun. Anyone can break a pane of glass with
a stick. Some of the boys had greedily stuffed
their pockets with sweets, but he had not come
to steal, nor would he ever have come for that,
Tschürke or no Tschürke. The maltreatment
of Herr Feldmann hadn't made any sense. If
Feldmann had defended himself it might have
been a little more even, but as it was, the middle-
aged man with the resigned face and downcast
eyes had merely joined the class freakishly for

one afternoon and fallen victim to that wicked, stabbing hypodermic.

Intrinsically what had happened to Feldmann was not much worse than what had happened to all his schoolmates at some time or another, to himself even. Tschürke, who had been in the same class for over two years, liked to consider himself as the grand master of this conveniently low order, and each new graduate was compelled to pass through a degrading ceremony of initiation, entailing every kind of base act.

Hans suddenly remembered Frau Feldmann's screams, and heard again the sharp note of her despair, jagged and unmusical. Oh, if his mother had seen him, blindfold and bleeding at his initiation, she would have screamed too, and how! There was nothing to it; all women screamed when things got a little tough. It was their form of expression, the feminine equivalent of the masculine shout.

It was, of course, unfortunate that he should have been stabbed by a child. It would have been more honorable to be stabbed by someone larger and older than himself. Still, the stab was on his upper arm over halfway to the back. It was very nearly a piece of treachery.

What had made the young Jew do it? Had his father, the colonel, been attacked by a group of hooligans, Hans told himself that he too might have lunged hopelessly but heroically, with his fists though, not with a piece of glass. You can kill with a piece of glass. But then, there was no question of the colonel being attacked, because he was German. Feldmann was a Jew, therein lay all the difference. He accepted his fate because he knew he was a Jew. Who ever heard of a Jew fighting? Who ever had even heard of a Jew angry? Such phenomena were virtually nonexistent. All the same, Hans could not liberate himself from the thought of it, and the more he succeeded in convincing himself that all had been normal, the more urgently the doubts crowded in on him. The fact remained that if he hadn't obeyed Tschürke, none of it would have happened.

The voices of the colonel and Helmut Bollmann suddenly grew in volume. A slit of light appeared under his door. Dinner was over. They were going into the sitting room for some coffee. The sharp staccato of Bollmann's hobnailed boots on the cold tiles was a brave, true sound, especially when set off against the shuffling of the colonel's slippers. The hall light went out; electricity was dear. The voices died to a murmur. The men were alone to kick the world around, while the women washed the dishes.

Hans waited a moment, then rose. His arm throbbed painfully as he stood. Quietly he opened the door and tiptoed silently into the corridor. From the kitchen he could hear the noise of dishes and the gossip of the women. Silently he kneeled by the sitting room door and listened.

The colonel, unsure of himself, was spluttering.

'Whatever you say, it seems incredible that a group of boys can do such a thing during school hours. I don't call that education.'

Bollmann laughed patronizingly.

'Of course, it is part of education, Colonel. I respect you because of your soldierly qualities, but I must point out to you that times have changed, and it behooves men to change with them. The entire geopolitical question, to say nothing of the racial-historical field, are entirely new areas of education and of study.

'In the old days, a youth interested in banking would learn about business and finance without for a moment considering the racial-historical aspects of it. But with the coming to power of National Socialism, the studies of such brilliant minds as Gauleiter Stompfl and Professor Schleiff, to say nothing of Volksgenosse Rosenberg, have revealed the hidden panorama of Judaeo-Levantine activities in the world of finance. My friend, it is as though a picture with which you were familiar had been sent to be restored, and the restorer, while clearing it, had discovered another picture painted underneath – a vile, odious picture. The hidden panorama of the worldwide Jewish conspiracy extends like a vast web over the entire financial structure of civilization, stifling all opposition with its subtle system of preferential treatment for its own members, financing wars for its own sinister convenience, and employing a communal language, the so-called Yiddish corruption, for its

internal communications. Half the bankers of
America know it, half the commissars of the
Kremlin know it, and they are in constant touch
with one another. Under the façade of international politics, a still more lethal organization is
endlessly at work, the Rothschilds and their breth-
ren, with no devotion to anything but money.
Disraeli, they say, was a British patriot. Why, he
even duped the British intelligence service! Who
owns the shares in the Suez Canal? Gentile names
perhaps, but in the service of Judaeo-Levantine
interests, using the tricolor and the Union Jack
as a front. Take the case of Dreyfus—'

'Dreyfus was innocent,' said the colonel.

'Innocent!' roared Bollmann. 'For once the
conspiracy came to light; and when honorable
French officers attempted to ventilate the shocking state of affairs these same Judaeo-Levantine
interests forced the hand of the French government, threatening it with bankruptcy, and the
culprit was reinstated.'

'Have you proof of this?'

'Proof? It's common knowledge in the party!
Do you think our inflation was necessary? Was it
economically inevitable? No, sir. It was engineered
by these same internationalists.'

'But why?' asked the colonel, now really interested.

'In order to provoke us into breaking our agreement, and rearming. They wanted chaos here in
Germany, followed by revolution and a second

war. It was in their interest for the arms race to be resumed, so that they could assist us financially, and then when we had become strong enough to threaten other countries, they could assist those other countries. That is the whole sinister scheme of the conspiracy, to maintain a parity of strength, so that sales are good to both sides.'

'What a shocking state of affairs,' said the colonel.

'Yes, but we cheated them,' Bollmann went on, a cold smile in his voice. 'They did not reckon that the revolution would be a National Socialist one, that we would take the law into our own hands, make our own arms by tightening our belts, without their help, and pluck this disease from our intestines. It is our duty to liberate not only ourselves but all mankind.'

'So, in other words, you are not shocked by the fact that Hans takes part in the destruction of a Jewish shop.'

'Shocked? It demonstrates the fact that he is a devoted pupil and a fine son.'

'Well, an emporium I could understand, or a bank, but a sweetshop?'

'Who can tell where the head of the serpent is? In such a devious conspiracy, it is to be expected that the head is hidden in the most unexpected place. No, dear Colonel, we have been duped for over a thousand years. To be on the safe side, we must destroy it all, without sentimental considerations.'

'All the same, it is hardly honorable to attack a small shop.'

'Is it honorable to make thousands of small shopkeepers starve by arranging an inflation?'

'No.'

There was a pause.

'Colonel,' Bollmann resumed in a kindlier tone, 'sooner or later the work will have to be done. Why wait? It only serves to lessen our efficiency. When the time comes, we will need all our fanatical bravery, all our unique discipline and soldierly qualities. It will be too late then to worry about the weeds in our own garden.'

'I agree,' said the colonel, and added in a last flush of gallantry, 'but you must admit, the Jewish contribution to German medicine—'

'What!' roared Bollman. 'Zero. Less than nothing. Rüttelberger discovered Salvarsan, the world thinks it was Ehrlich. Why? Once the international conspiracy can arrange the financial structure of society, isn't it a little thing for it to arrange for reputations to be made and lost? For centuries German medicine and German science have been victimized by the Judaeo-Levantine cartel. It is time for us to shout the facts from the rooftops.'

'But Dr Heyse told me—'

'Who?'

'Dr Heyse.'

'Yes? What did he tell you?'

'He told me that the Jewish contribution to German medicine had been incalculable.'

'Thank you very much for reporting the matter.'

'I don't want to cause any trouble—' said the colonel, nervously.

'None. None at all, I assure you.'

There was another pause.

'So you think I shouldn't move Hans to another school.'

'Colonel,' replied Bollmann evenly, 'if you object to your son doing his sacred duty toward Führer and Fatherland, remove him by all means, only don't be surprised if you lose all respect in the neighborhood.'

'There is no need to be offensive.'

'We must throw niceties to the wind!' cried Bollmann. 'If you are so easily insulted, you will find that there is very little room for you in the new Germany. Facts are facts, sir. Once it is our duty to destroy the freemasonry of Judaism as the first step on the road to realizing our geopolitical destiny, then let us do it, with a grim hand and a cold eye. There is no other way. The end justifies any means. From today on, anyone who is not a hero is a coward.'

The lights went out in the kitchen. The women were on their way to rejoin the men. Hans tiptoed back into his room, and lay awake all night.

HANS COULD have gone back to school the next

morning, but he pretended to feel ill, and sat in his room meditating on the profundities which he had overheard. Nobody had ever talked to him directly like that. He was seized with a desire to grow up, to grapple with the problem of geopolitics, whatever it was. The secret of existence evidently lay in the fact that nothing was as it appeared to be. To a child, a smile is a smile, inviting recognition, a sign of friendship. To an adult, it is probably just the opposite, a warning of imminent deceit. Growing up is nothing more than understanding this.

He was too embarrassed to ask the meaning of 'geopolitics.' Somewhere along the line he had been inattentive when it was being explained to him. One thing was sure, though, and that was that geopolitics were desirable, since Germany had them and no one else did, not even the Judaeo-Levantine conspiracy. Perhaps in the light of this it would have been more humane to have explained to Herr Feldmann exactly why his shop was destroyed. After all, even a Jew deserves an explanation. It would have made the whole exploit less infantile, more serious and adult.

'Herr Feldmann,' he would have explained had he been Tschürke, 'unfortunately you are a Jew, and therefore part of the worldwide Judaeo-Levantine conspiracy. For all we know, the head of the serpent is right here, in your sweetshop. Whatever you say, you cannot prove to our satisfaction that it is not. Since our aim is the total destruction of that which stands in the way of our geopolitics, we must regretfully destroy your shop. We regret this, since you have been very good to us in the past – on the surface, that is. Only you know the deceit which lay hidden beneath your apparent kindness. Now we are old enough to know that some deceit must have been hidden there. I'm sorry, but there is no other way. Facts are facts in the new Germany.'

That was the way to do it. Tschürke was a swine, a cruel, unthinking swine.

Hans's plans were carefully laid. The next day, a Thursday, he still stayed in his room. When his mother was about to call Dr Heyse, thinking that her boy was concealing some graver malady, she was interrupted by the colonel speaking from the other room.

'What is it, Friedrich? Don't disturb me now. I'm just calling Dr Heyse on the telephone.'

'Dr Heyse is dead,' said the colonel, appearing in the doorway, a newspaper in his hand.

'Dead?' echoed his wife, replacing the receiver reverently.

'It's here, in the paper. He took poison.'

'When?'

'Last night.'

'But why did he do it? He was so calm, so logical,' Frau Winterschild cried, suddenly emotional.

A terrible thought crossed the colonel's mind, but he dismissed it violently. His face flushed, he replied as evenly as he could. 'I haven't the faintest idea.'

To Hans, the news of Dr Heyse's suicide meant very little. He had known him as a doctor, but was not old enough to have known him as a friend. In any case, three masters at school had gone, and no questions asked. It was becoming normal not to ask why, or where.

Later in the day, Frau Winterschild couldn't resist calling Frau Heyse to find out all the details of the tragedy. Colonel Winterschild was afraid to ask her what she had found out, but she volunteered the information.

'I must say poor Agnete is taking it very well,' she said, 'but all she would tell me was that yesterday he was in good spirits, then towards evening he received a phone call which seemed to depress him. A quarter of an hour after his death, the Gestapo came to arrest him.'

'What a tragedy,' said the colonel.

The next morning, Friday, Hans declared himself ready to go back to school. The colonel said he was glad. Just before leaving, Hans reminded his father rather agitatedly that it was the day for his pocket money. The old man dug in his purse, and gave his son a mark.

'Not too much chocolate,' the colonel admonished.

Without a word Hans ran into the street, and

on, breathlessly, to the hardware store, where he bought a pocketknife, with a marlinspike. He arrived at school ten minutes late.

At half-past eleven there was the usual fifteen-minute break. Tschürke wandered over to Hans amid general interest, and asked, 'How's the arm, soldier?'

'How's the back, coward?' replied Hans, slightly shocked at his own daring.

'What was that?'

The other boys looked at each other in amazement. Two or three of the more timid ones left the schoolroom to go into the yard.

'It seems our young hero has decided to be impertinent,' said Tschürke slowly. 'Well, since you find bloodshed so inspiring, let's give you another taste of it.' And, taking his time, he opened his desk and produced the famous hypodermic needle. 'Come here. It's time for your injection.'

Hans stood his ground.

'Not only impertinent, but disobedient,' growled Tschürke, advancing.

Hans drew his knife, and opened his marlinspike.

'That's unfair,' said Tschürke, 'a knife against a needle.'

'I know, that's why I will use a marlinspike,' replied Hans, 'it has no sharp edge, only a point, like your needle.'

'I advise you to change your mind,' said

Tschürke, uncertainly, 'and to submit to a little operation. It will hurt much less.'

'Come on,' whispered Hans through clenched teeth.

They circled round each other, the boys giving way before them. Abruptly Tschürke feinted, pretending to come in high, but suddenly attacking low. He knew, in his unpleasant mind, that there is nothing like an attack below the belt to make even the bravest of males cringe. He did not reckon with Hans's mood, however. As soon as Hans saw the direction of the lunge, he struck downwards, piercing the back of Tschürke's hand. With a howl, the bully drew his hand to his stomach, letting the needle fall to the ground. Hans stepped on it, crushing the glass, and then rushed at Tschürke. As they fell to the ground, he stabbed and stabbed again blindly. Tschürke yelled that the contest was now unfair, but Hans had a one-track mind, and a job to do.

'Get up! Get up at once!' It was Dr Dülder, shouting. 'What is this, a school or a menagerie?'

Sheepishly the two boys rose to their feet, panting. Tschürke was bleeding from hand and face, and blood from a wound on his scalp was trickling down his temple.

'Get yourself attended to,' yelled Dr Dülder, 'and you, Winterschild, follow me to my office.'

For a full five minutes the principal ranted, and then, when he had calmed down a little, he demanded an explanation.

'Well, sir—'

'Stand at attention when you talk to me!'

'With your permission, sir, for a long time now Tschürke has bullied the class.'

'Do you think it is very attractive to tell tales?'

'No, sir, that is why I decided to rectify the position myself. I did not come to you and tell you. You asked me.'

'No impertinence now! Tschürke is not very bright, but we can't all be brilliant. His father is a high official of the State Railways. This is very awkward. I must know the reason for the fight.'

'When you first came here, sir, the other day, you gave us a half holiday. Tschürke, who used to bully the class with a hypodermic needle—'

'A hypodermic needle? That can be very dangerous. What did he do with it?'

'He used to pretend to inject us with it if we didn't obey him. Well, the day of the half holiday, he made us all go out and wreck Feldmann's sweetshop.'

'You objected?'

'No, sir. I objected to the manner in which it was carried out. It was done thoughtlessly, without taking into consideration the geopolitical and historical justification of such an act.'

Dr Dülder was frankly taken aback.

'The geopolitical justification for wrecking a sweetshop?' he asked.

'Yes, sir, with your permission. It is not enough

to wreck a shop because you know you will not be punished. It is necessary also to understand the geopolitical side of the question. Tschürke only thought of wrecking the shop because it was fun to break a window. He had no thought of why he was doing it.'

'Since when do boys of your age concern yourselves with questions of a philosophical order?' asked Dr Dülder.

'Even if we don't all, we should, sir.'

'Hm. You don't object to wrecking a Jewish shop, and yet you object to the spirit in which it is done. Is that right?'

'Yes, sir. I object when it is done thoughtlessly, as I said sir, without due regard for the geopolitical ... how should I put it ... the geopolitical things.'

'For God's sake shut up about geopolitics!' shouted Dr Dülder. 'Don't use a word you don't understand.'

'You yourself said that our geopolitical destiny is looking us in the face, sir, and that when our name is called, we should answer "Present!"'

Dr Dülder passed his hand hopelessly over his forehead.

'You remember everything, don't you? I sometimes forget that I am talking to infants. I am glad you told me about the hypodermic needle, however. That gives me something to go on.'

'Please, sir.'

'Yes?'

'You are wrong when you say that I use words I don't understand. Herr Feldmann is a Jew, and is therefore part of the worldwide Judaeo-Levantine conspiracy which brought about a great deal of misery with Disraeli and Dreyfus.'

'Dreyfus?'

'Yes, sir, when he was falsely acquitted at the time. Also German doctors had their inventions stolen by Jewish doctors, as part of the Judaeo-Levantine conspiracy.'

'And all that, I suppose, is part of the geopolitical aspects of wrecking a sweetshop?'

'Precisely.'

Dr Dülder was half amused now.

'Winterschild,' he asked, 'have you chosen a career yet?'

'I will go into the Army like my father.'

Dr Dülder smiled.

'You can fight. You have proved that. You also know what you are fighting against. Only leave the wrecking of the shops to the weaklings. When the time comes, there will be greater things for you to fight.'

'Yes, sir. Thank you, sir.'

'And Winterschild.'

'Yes, sir.'

'You may borrow this book. I had a hand in its compilation. It is called *Aspects of Racial Purification in the Era of Geopolitical Consciousness in our Eastern Provinces.* I warn you, it is not light reading, but you are obviously a serious-minded boy, and there's nothing wrong with you but your youth. Your ideas are right, but raw. In mentioning Disraeli and Dreyfus you are but scratching the outer shell of a problem incredible in its complexity and weight. If ever you have a question, do not hesitate to ask. And no more fighting, please. Nurture your muscles for tomorrow.'

II

HANS PROGRESSED well as a leader now that Tschürke was discredited, and he dominated without need of his marlinspike. He read the book which Dr Dülder had given him several times without understanding it; the act in itself showed great fiber and tenacity. Unable to understand it, he did the next best thing, which was to learn sections of it by heart. He could, at will, produce the exact percentage of mixed marriages in Pomerania in the first quarter of 1935. Mixed meant Jewish-Aryan, of course.

The destruction of Jewish property Hans left to his elders, organizing instead discussion groups within the school in which all phases of the current geopolitical problems were tentatively discussed in anticipation of *der Tag*. There was not much time for any awakening of sex, since an interest in a girl's origins rather than an interest in the girl tends to make courtship a little stiff. He went to dances, certainly, but after a few opening remarks he would find himself explaining his ideas about the future, not of the girl or of himself, but of the Reich. The girls who tolerated this were hardly of the kind to lure him onto a convenient couch.

His feet were large, and he was a clumsy dancer. Yet at the same time he liked girls and watched them with real interest, as potential mothers, with their curious grace of movement so foreign to a man. He could hardly notice the dress of an attractive girl without guessing at the form beneath. This used to bring a blush to his cheek. Statues also commanded his attention. There was a little water sprite in the Public Gardens, kneeling in her *fin-de-siècle* way and holding a water lily in the palm of her hand with an expression of unbearable sweetness on her face. Her breasts were firm and hard, her neck quite lovely, and the small of her back almost alive with its delicate lateral curves and the ripple of her spine. He could tolerate a wife like that, who never spoke and who found such pleasure in a mere water lily. He lavished whatever emotion he had on her, and only went to parties because he was invited.

As time passed, and he noticed more and more of his contemporaries necking and making dates with girls, he began to brood. Invariably he came to the conclusion that he was destined to lead rather than to follow, and that his natural aptitude entailed grave responsibilities, separating him from the normal run of men. The Führer had found that his love for Germany was in itself a marriage. Hans believed that he too might have to choose between an alliance of the flesh and a monastic alliance of the spirit. Still, the subject was never quite closed. It would reclaim his attention almost every day, and if his conclusion was always the same, it would reopen whenever some gay wisp of a girl passed his way, leaving an ephemeral backwash of perfume behind her as she giggled on the arm of her consort.

Laughter as such irritated him, and yet the laughter of women was fascinating in its tremulous excitement and obscure promise of delight. There was something pleasantly indecent and irresponsible about it; an element of flattery and an invitation were contained in it. The girls seemed to bend towards the men, leaning more heavily on them, when they laughed – as though they were ready, for two more jokes, to throw caution aside. He was jealous of men who could make women laugh.

Occasionally his mother would say, 'Why don't you ask Hannelore Eckschmidt to come for supper? She's a nice girl, and quiet.'

He hated this solicitude. Why should he be content with a quiet girl, or even a nice one?

When the colonel replied, as he always did, 'All

in good time, Mutti – these things will happen when they will,' it only made matters worse.

The whole problem of women was infinitely annoying, and a bore. And yet . . .

'YOU MUST understand, Mutti,' the colonel would say when they were alone, 'that Hans is a little slow to develop. Mentally he is very far in advance of his age, physically he is a splendid specimen, but he is by so far the youngest of our children that he had to spend too much time alone, or with us. He is still shy with girls, and reserved. Some girls like that, but usually because they too are shy and reserved. Courtships of people who are temperamentally suited in this way can last many years. My cousin Otto married his childhood sweetheart when they were both in their forties. Neither could bring themselves to pop the question. When she eventually did, Otto wept like a baby, and yet in all other respects he is entirely normal, the director of a slaughterhouse, and very successful in his field.'

'The boy has a heart of gold, and he will make someone very happy,' Frau Winterschild would reply.

In the Hitlerjugend, Hans won rapid promotion, and he enjoyed it, since all his febrile energy was spent in road building, singing in unison round a campfire, and other hearty exploits in field and forest. He was tanned by sun and wind, and his virginity caused him no torment.

In the spring of 1939 he entered the Wehrmacht with excellent recommendations, and was sent a telegram of congratulation by Helmut Bollmann, which he cherished. No time for women now, except on one memorable occasion when he was compelled to join four friends in an avowed search for compliant females. The trail led into the seamy quarter of St Pauli, in Hamburg, where Hans was stationed. Every archway, every portal of the narrow streets was alive with commerce. There were loiterers catering to every taste, and those who shouted the loudest during the day for the regeneration of the Aryan race seemed now the most concerned with their baser desires. The Gauleiters and Gruppenführers, who proclaimed on paper and platform that the Jewish defilers of Aryan women merited immediate sterilization, gravitated to the half-light of this Nordic sook to find the mincing boy of their dreams.

There was a kind of horror in this market place which decreed that nobody recognize a friend, or even an enemy. Just as the firing in the trenches stops for Christmas, so all affairs of the day were forgotten here to a profaner end. The stout official of some ministry could be seen hugging a coy hermaphrodite under a street lamp, but the sight would not be remembered under the angry eagle of his office wall.

With his particular temperament, Hans saw nothing ridiculous in the balding satyrs clawing members of any old sex in the shadows; he saw nothing but the horror of it, like some impassioned pastor of an Ibsen drama. Nor did he see that the difference between night and day was not so extreme; that the daily obsession with breeding, with stud farms for the perfect specimens of Aryan stock, with *Mutterehrenringe* – rings for accomplishment in the realm of maternity, to be worn proudly on a prescribed finger, with a detachable center containing the endlessly changing number of the offspring vowed to the altar of the Fatherland – was the growing omen of the sexual insanity of an entire nation. To think endlessly of health is to be obsessed with disease. And here they were, in St Pauli, the minor prophets of the New Order, paying homage to the old, rotting by night in the dirt which they sought to eradicate during office hours.

Hans allowed his friends to do the negotiating, while he stood frozen on the sidewalk. Before he knew what was happening, he found himself with a repellent harridan, who smiled at him suggestively, flicking her eyelids like a doll.

One of the soldiers noticed his look of alarm, and, drawing him aside good-naturedly, explained that none of the girls were much to look at but that their terms were extremely reasonable. Twenty marks. 'Soldiers can't be choosers,' he said, and laughed. As they all mounted the rickety stairs of the house before which the ladies had been lying in wait, stairs which smelled of damp and polish and last year's cabbages, Hans hung back.

'What's the matter, sweetheart?' asked the cut-price Venus.

'I don't feel well.'

'Big boy like you, don't feel well? Don't give me that,' and she whispered winningly, 'I know, Anna knows, it's always the big ones that are timid. Come out and buy me a drink before we go by-byes.'

Hans agreed willingly. As they walked to a dive, she gave him a luscious foretaste of what awaited him behind closed shutters. He began to surrender to an inner panic. They entered a bar, and the expensive Anna ordered champagne, patriotic champagne, Ribbentrop's champagne. Eighty marks. Four times the price of copulation.

Unsubtly she tried to provoke him. She had no talent. She began to lean on his arm, to let her hand wander. He pushed her away. She was atrocious, with her dark hair like a wire brush.

'You're a brute, I can see that. A hard man, who means to get his way. I'm frightened of you.'

'No need to be frightened of me,' Hans mumbled.

All of a sudden, she lost patience.

'What's the matter with you?' she cried.

'Nothing,' he barked back.

'You're not a pervert, are you? D'you want to kiss my shoes?'

Hans thought he hadn't heard right.

'Are you a naughty boy with bad marks at school?'

'What?'

'I am an Oriental queen. You will be my slave, my dog!'

She must be mad.

'You like men, that's the trouble with you, isn't it?'

This Hans understood, and rose to his feet, shaking with anger. In his transcending desire for revenge at the insult, he imitated the Helmut Bollmann he knew and admired.

'How do you allow yourself such insolence!' he roared. 'You ought to be ashamed of yourself! As the New Germany which we are pledged to build is ashamed of you! When the whole of our nation is bent on work, on creation, on the forward march with inflexible will and heads held high, women like you still attempt to corrupt our people! Damn you and your kind! Damn you!'

This outburst produced immediate applause from the other men who were sitting with whores in the dark. In real alarm at this unforeseen resurgence of morality, Anna fled. The tone of the entire establishment changed. The men looked around as though reveille had sounded prematurely, and they suddenly saw the wretched prostitutes for what they were. For one dizzy moment, Hans was the Führer of his own little Reich. His exit was slightly spoiled, however, when the angry manager met him at the door with the check. He didn't have eighty marks. Two men he had never seen before rose from their tables and paid the difference.

'We can't do too much for the Army,' said one.

'That's right,' said the other, 'I was shot through the hip the last time.'

It was conscience money.

Hans was met with looks of complicity at the barracks.

'What happened to you?' asked one friend.

'He's a lone wolf,' said another.

'I had a great roll in the hay,' said the third, 'did you?'

'It was marvelous,' Hans replied.

SOMETIMES, AT night, after a hard day of drill, Hans would lie and think while the air was filled with contented snoring. He began to fear the hours of darkness, when a man is alone with himself. He was far from home. The security of boyhood was vanishing like a waving hand in a crowded station; he could hardly see it any more. And yet now, because the sergeants and the corporals were asleep, he could remember, and that was cruel. He enjoyed drill, march, countermarch, all sorts of innocuous but complicated sleight of hand with the rifle, and he enjoyed the rough talk of the noncommissioned officers, because they were emancipated from fear and from timidity. They must be, to command such language. He was getting on well, he knew that. After a bit more training, he would be an officer, with a right to shout if he felt it was necessary. But for the moment, they must not hear him sobbing in the night.

Oh, it was childish, but all he was really doing was giving expression to the tenderness within him. He wished to perform noble acts which were not necessarily violent. He was as solemn as Parsifal when given the chance. First of all he wished to repay his parents in some way for their great kindness to him. Of motherhood he was fearful and suspicious, but he had the art of muttihood at his entire command. He knew how to write postcards which would give pleasure, and he kept two photographs in his wallet, one of his mother in a mood of sunlit serenity, holding a reluctant cat up to her cheek, the other characteristically of his father as a much younger man, in uniform, stark and intolerant at the request of a military-minded photographer. He never forgot an anniversary and he knew the difference between a bronze wedding and a silver one. He was what parents call a good son.

Yet now all kinds of physical forces were at work within him which he hardly understood, forces which were bullying his simple, strait-laced mentality. Soon the facts of life (learned remarkably late in life during an embarrassing talk with the colonel) would have to be faced. Evidently the colonel must have gone through the same crisis in his youth, otherwise he would hardly have experienced the stuttering difficulty in transmitting this vital information to his son. All the colonel had insisted on at the time with an almost frightening doggedness was that it was 'natural.' What was? This agony of doubt? This anguish of a body somehow enriched, yet without means of expression? The colonel hadn't specified. He had merely said 'it.'

His dreams began to crowd with women – noble, soft, warm, undulant Gretchens who were as ignorant as he. Occasionally the vile doxy from Hamburg would invade his serenity, and he would wake up with a start. If only women had the mentality of men it would be easy, but they were different. How different? Did they all, even the blue-eyed, prim ones, carry within them some of the elements of that unfortunate Anna, with her incomprehensible questions and her odious insinuations? Was there a certain amount of capriciousness, of insincerity in every woman as part of her make-up? Certainly men, especially soldiers, made cynical remarks about women. There must be a reason for this.

Hans learned to joke about women, he learned the facile way of doing it – 'Oh women, you know what they're like, one minute . . . the next . . .' – simply by imitation. He also learned very quickly that when his comrades expressed a desire for a woman they no longer referred to their target by any name but by a specific part of the body. He entered into the rough spirit of the badinage, and frequently said that he yearned for that particular anatomical feature without the remotest idea what he was talking about. His reputation as a good sport rose.

It could not go on forever. Several times he trembled on the brink of a great decision, only to retract timidly in the last moment. With every failure, his anguish became more acute. Just as a real crisis was approaching, Adolf Hitler himself came to the rescue. The all-seeing, the kindly light which led, invaded Poland, and, in doing so, compassionately took Hans's mind off the problems of his late adolescence.

He was home on leave when the telegram arrived informing him of the urgent recall. He had already spent the first two days of his home-coming pacing the house agitatedly to the distress of his mother, who had baked a variety of small cakes to divert him from the endless newscasts, but without success. The news was becoming worse by the minute, and the commentator's voice was exultant. As one incident after the other occurred on the Polish frontier, involving intolerable affronts to the honor of the German nation, it became clear that war could no longer be averted.

Germany at that moment was like the Heidelberg student who has practiced his saber work all day, and who sits in a beer cellar impatiently waiting to be insulted. To the polite request of another student, 'Is this seat taken?' the answer prescribed by the protocol of counterfeit honor is 'How dare you indulge in such insolence?' Hans accepted this mood without questioning it. He identified himself with Germany in a milky mysticism, and felt personally affronted by the very existence of Poles in the world.

'How long will our patience endure?' he cried on the second afternoon of his homecoming. 'Another family of German origin has been molested by those Polish swine, and we do nothing.'

The colonel's spirit had been somewhat enslaved by the self-assured philosophizing of Helmut Bollmann, but he still strove valiantly to give his opinions a patina of wisdom, as befitted his distinguished elderly appearance.

'The Poles are not a nation,' he said, 'and it was a mistake, one of the many mistakes of Versailles, to encourage them to stand on their own feet. Their failure was preordained, of course. All those people, Poles, Czechs, Lithuanians – there are some more up in that corner whose names I forget – Bulgarians, Rumanians, Hungarians, they all live in the German *Sprachgebiet*, the zone of German linguistic predominance. They are impure and inferior people of borrowed tradition, whose historical function is to be subservient to us, and to be a buffer against the Mongols.'

'That doesn't help the present situation!' snapped

Hans. 'What we cannot rectify by words, we must rectify by force.'

His mother hardly recognized him. Not a cake eaten, the cakes he used to love as a boy. While the men listened to the radio, she sat in the kitchen, a lace-edged handkerchief to her mouth.

When the telegram eventually arrived, Hans became much more considerate of his mother. He allowed her to help him into his equipment, and kissed her on the forehead. His parents came to the station in spite of his appeal to them not to.

'It is fitting that we should come,' said the colonel. 'When I left him in '14, my father was at the station. It was the last time I saw him. Grand old man.'

The implied tragedy of this *faux pas* appealed to the colonel, and when his wife tearfully asked him not to say such things, he replied that life is what it is, and that if it wasn't, it wouldn't be life, or words to that effect, which under the circumstances seemed almost unbearably profound and noble.

The station was full of activity, a steaming, hissing, hooting jungle, with military music to enchant the ear and to make of the great milling loneliness a communal ecstasy. All trains seemed to be outgoing, and to be filled with men, men singing the old songs of death and transfiguration in the trenches just off key with baleful, campfire insistence. The marches blaring out of the inter-com system were the artifice, the bright buttons, the sunlight caught on a million ardent boots in parallel rivulets; the songs of the men were tinged with reality, muddy, footsore, sad and bleeding. The two had nothing in common, but neither would give in to the other. Here was a foretaste of the chaos that is battle, of the unreal orders from the staff, the encouragement of generals casually dictated in comfortable offices, and the eternal winter of reality, the dull pain of survival in ignorance and in exposure, forgotten, lost. Frau Winterschild, being a woman, responded to this conflict without understanding it, and wept.

The colonel walked and stood erect as never before, because he was in civilian clothes, and that was working against him. There was some-thing subtly militant about the way he held his umbrella, the ferrule upwards, at a consistent angle to the ground. His feet fell on the concrete platform in time with the march, his head turned sideways towards the train as though passing a Kaiser in salute. Imperceptibly at first, his free arm began swinging across his body, his fingers held together in the leather glove. His mouth was turned down at the corners in devotion to a cause he did not question, since the music was enough. Ah, youth!

Frau Winterschild kissed her son, and told him incoherently that she would pray for him. The colonel extended his hand as though to a stranger.

This was the warmth of soldiers who happened to be father and son. In the last minute, the father gave the son a flask which had been given him by his father, and so on: a dented silver flask.

'It saved my life,' he said, 'A bullet . . . here . . .'

'Be good.'

'Write.'

'Yes.'

The climax was passing. Trains always leave slightly later than they should. 'All aboard!'

Long after the train had passed out of sight, Frau Winterschild went on waving.

'Come, Mutti,' said the colonel, tenderly.

When they arrived home, Frau Winterschild returned to the kitchen, and, in the sanctuary of her own dominion, wept her eyes out. The colonel walked about the house agitatedly, unable to settle to anything. He couldn't get the tune of the march out of his head.

It was a source of great disappointment to Hans that his battalion took no part in the Polish campaign. All he did was to sit fuming in a little café at Leverkusen in the Rhineland, and write long letters to his father in a style so florid and so emotional that one could easily suppose him to have been a witness of the horrors of Warsaw.

'He is getting on rather well,' said the colonel to Frau Winterschild.

Then, one evening in the early spring of 1940, the battalion moved by night to Bocholt, near the

Dutch frontier. There, after intolerably enervating delays, it launched an attack in support of a great mass of armor, and found itself consigned to occupy the town of Appeldoorn without having fired more than a few shots.

Sitting in a military canteen a few days later, the exasperated Hans wrote his father a violent account of the Dutch holocaust, which ended with the words, 'There are no Dutch left.'

The old man read the letter out to his wife, and added, 'He will soon be a captain.'

'Yes, but all that loss of life,' said Frau Winterschild sadly.

'Yes . . . yes,' sighed the colonel, with genuine sorrow, 'but that is inevitable in war.'

Six months later, Hans was transferred to a battalion stationed near Lille, in France. He wrote to his father about the crushed spirit of the French, at the same time telling him about the warfare then being waged against the underground movement. These letters arrived at Langensalza heavily mutilated by the censorship. The colonel, in his answer, implored his son to be careful of indiscretion.

Another few weeks passed, and Hans's regiment entrained for Austria, where it was reformed prior to the attack on Yugoslavia. Once again, when the assault was launched, the armor virtually crushed all opposition, and the wiping up was done by crack troops specially trained to impart death before the arrival of more conventional, more cumbersome units.

Depressed, but undismayed, Hans kept up his correspondence with his father, and even from the calm beauty of the Greek coast he managed to garnish his writings with a deal of indiscriminate warlike superlatives. The effect this continuous stream of battle evocations had on the colonel was simply one of bewilderment that promotion had not yet come his son's way, while Frau Winterschild began to wilt under the continuous threat of 'the worst.'

'They ought to give the poor boy a rest,' she would wail, 'nothing but blood and death – that's all he writes about.'

'And still not a captain,' grumbled the colonel. 'I suppose not enough have yet died.'

'Friedrich,' said Frau Winterschild, pained.

'Such is war,' sighed the colonel, once again with perfect sincerity. 'Cannae, Waterloo, Tannenberg, it's all the same . . .'

In May 1941 Hans at last got his wish and was transferred to a unit with a considerable reputation, 'The Nibelungen' Regiment, stationed in Poland. On June 22nd, after a textbook artillery preparation, his unit moved forward into Russia, and on the 24th, at the head of his platoon of young Vikings, he was one of the first to enter Brest-Litovsk.

Now he experienced battle under all conditions, and soon became inured to it, living, like his comrades, only for the day. This sense that death might be around the corner led them to behave with the shamelessness of animals. To men enslaved by a cynical and unimaginative philosophy, death is an end and not a beginning.

They raped the girls because it was manly, and they were always at pains to prove their manhood to each other. This forced them to pretend that an organized platoon assault on a defenseless creature of unknown personality, stretched hideously on the floor, gave them considerably more pleasure than it actually did. In nearly all of them, as they performed their shameless ritual to the bawdy yells of their comrades, the natural instincts were already deeply impregnated with disgust, so that the repellent act of rape became a trial of strength, like leaping through flames. It was, in the final analysis, a victory of the nerves and stomach over the terrible possibility of adverse criticism by friends, and had very little to do with lust.

Every now and then, during a lull in the battles, they would be examined for disease by a dispassionate doctor; and when, now and then, one of them would have to report for treatment, he would go with a sort of pride, the envy of his winking and sniggering mates. He had proved something or other to everyone's satisfaction.

For nearly a year the men in Hans's unit behaved as soldiers tend to do under the conditions of war and occupation, far more lenient,

approachable and gentlemanly when alone than
in the mass. The winter imposed its own strain
upon good nature, and there were outbursts of
looting and spiteful, meaningless murder. Hans
himself, having been commissioned very soon
after the outbreak of actual hostilities, was no
longer under any obligation to behave as one of
the boys; on the contrary, he was encouraged
to be an officer and a gentleman, and therefore
to take his pleasures behind locked doors. He
was appalled by the behavior of his men, which
reminded him too forcibly for comfort of the
excesses practiced by Tschürke in the classroom.
Since the Army is but an extension of school, a
paradise for those unwilling to grow up, there
was every justification for this feeling, and he
yearned to burst in on these orgies, arresting
everyone in sight and taking the ringleaders to
his office as Dr Dülder had done in the past.
Wiser counsel prevailed, however. Older officers,
those who had campaigned before in lost causes,
explained to him indulgently that a good leader
of men must know when to relax his grip on
the reins. Reality and the blueprint had nothing
in common when the snow was up to a man's
navel, and when every tree, every shadow, every
undulation of the ground seemed to be alive with
hostile vigilance.

Hans began to spend as much time as possible
alone, thinking. It was difficult for his temperament to accept without revolt the tarnishing of

a dream. At times the older officers seemed to him subtly treacherous in their apathy. They appeared to be hanging back, taking the Führer's gospel with a pinch of salt, dismissing a thing as impractical before having put it to the test, with no justification except experience. At other times, he resented his own youth, which made him strain for the authority which came so naturally to the well-lined faces, with their unforced elegance and spare haughtiness. His impatience for glory, for a chance to shine, was tempered with a deep, inexplicable lassitude, a sensation of being lost in a vast emporium of similar uniforms, a field-gray ocean in which all identity was lost, all achievement shared.

Beneath this malaise, which could be explained to some extent by rational thoughts, a romantic geyser was bubbling, a turbulence which haunted his sleeping hours and which often made him bring his hand to his burning forehead. He thought he was ill. Sometimes he talked to himself, just for the pleasure of hearing a voice saying what he wished to hear. The voice assumed different characters according to his mood. It might exhort an imaginary army to deeds of incredible heroism, or else it might speak with great tenderness to no one in particular, shedding an overflow of love into a pillow gripped and pushed out of shape with febrile fingers. He was conscious of his body. When he lay on his mattress, he felt its shape and knew its possibilities. It was yearning for company. It was mature.

There was no question of advance or retreat that winter. Nature had her will of the earth, and mocked at the fragility of supermen. The snow fell silently, with an insulting grace. The snouts of hibernating cannons pushed into the air, but barely. A man could be seen breathing half a mile away. It was neither good nor bad to be alive. It didn't matter.

The village of Pleshchanitza lay just within the German lines; an untidy agglomeration of baleful houses. The population faced the occupation without emotion. They were neither strikingly dignified in their comportment nor were they in any way servile. The cold neutralized what emotion there was. If the local German commander issued a decree, it was more or less adhered to, but it was as difficult to enforce an order as it was to accede to it. The winter was a mutual enemy, and soon each side was content to ignore the other in the long, white, whistling night.

There was a woman in the village, a certain Valeria, who had been a nurse, or an entertainer, exactly what was not clear, but she was not a native of the place. She had not retreated quickly enough, and now she lived in the house of the mayor, sharing her room with some five or six other unexplained refugees. Her eyes were watery and embarrassingly suggestive, eyes of the sort a man will turn away from because their invitation is too scandalous to be responded to in public. A mop of yellow hair falling in ringlets over her forehead, a tiny twitching nose, flared at the tip, and a mouth gathered into a puckered rosette, flanked by delicate grooves like quotation marks, to say nothing of the two beauty spots, one on her upper lip, the other high on her cheek, all conspired to give her a look of clumsy fatality, of weary yet insatiable lust. She had about her all the tawdry artifice of the stranded actress, who believes that life is a ladder of men, a fabric of cynical impermanencies. She smelled of cheap perfume and tobacco, and sang gypsy songs to keep her spirits up.

Hans had noticed her casually, but had regarded her without interest, as a piece of driftwood among many others. One day she turned up at the hut he used as his platoon headquarters. She was wearing a thick quilted coat which gave her no recognizable shape, and a ludicrous knitted Balaklava helmet. The guard at the door admitted her because he understood no Russian, and because he was timid. Hans was writing some report at his desk, and when she entered he hardly looked up.

She spoke in a deep, caressing contralto voice, but there was no knowing what she wanted. Hans glanced up and met the gaze of those obscene eyes, with the brilliance of a slight goiter in them. He looked down, blushed, and

pretended to examine a document. In German
he asked what she wished. The flow of Russian
went on – an appeal, judging by the inflections,
but expressed reasonably and with a degree of
resignation at the outcome. He looked up again
because he was compelled to. The woman was in
her forties, and raddled by experience, but her
eyes were like prison windows, hands stretching
out through the bars. He frowned and looked
down at his papers.

She came close to him, and picked up a printed
form on his desk. He asked her angrily what she
was doing, and felt her thigh against his shoulder.
People, when they touch each other in error,
usually leap away with profuse apologies, so eager
are they that their involuntary gesture should not
be misunderstood. She did not retract an inch,
but seemed to hug his shoulder as an animal will
find comfort from a post.

In answer to his brusque inquiry, she smiled,
let her eyelids half sink, sunshades over an entic-
ing shop, and talked on endlessly, reasonably,
poutingly. He also took protection in talk, and
countered with a string of carelessly chosen,
hesitant sentences. Since he knew she couldn't
understand, he just said anything, and hit the
desk lightly and rhythmically with a pencil to
emphasize the point he was making, but his mind
wandered off the subject, away from sense and
grammar. He became aware of the pneumatic
warmth of that thigh, and realized that he had

made no gesture of withdrawal either. He glanced up, and there was an amused triumph in her face. He cleared his throat. She showered his desk with faded photographs. A handsome man with the hard criminal look associated with pictures in passports. Herself, shielding her eyes against the sun while sitting cross-ankled on a swing, no feature visible except a sidelong dimple and the three-petaled flower of her mouth. Herself in a striped bathing suit, prudishly skirted yet pornographically wet, showing the nipples, castles seen from the air in the late afternoon, throwing long shadows. Herself and the man, both in bathing suits, he with portholes of nudity at his sides, in the fashion of the '50s, and a groin heavy with fruit. What was the point of showing him these pictures? Better days?

Once again she picked up a form and made a gesture of writing. Hans told her it was impossible to have a form filled, any form, without a previous application for an appointment, and a suitable period would have to elapse for screening – oh, he didn't really know what he was saying or why, he was playing for time, playing for something. The thigh throbbed on his sleeve, the same thigh as the cello curve on the photograph, a thigh which would shake with African motions as it moved. She picked up the photographs, and related them to the official form. What now? Was she applying for some concession on behalf of someone else?

He looked at her. She was the embodiment of sex, sad and hot. He swallowed. So dry was his throat that he coughed, an intolerable itch settling in his gullet, unreachably. She began hitting his back, and as the spasm passed, and he sat panting with watering eyes, her hand lingered, climbing slowly to the back of his neck, where a nail drove a furrow with diabolical subtlety into the roots of his hair. He shuddered deeply, and looked at her. She knew what she was doing.

'Come,' she probably said. Hans rose. The hypocrisy helped him. She spoke as though she knew of something worthy of investigation, something the Germans ought to know about. He could pretend he was on the trail of some criminal activity. In spite of her troubled face, her inflections were conversational. She held the form in one hand, the photographs in the other, and beckoned urgently with her jaw at the houses through the window. He joined her at the window, and looked out penetratingly at a view he knew by heart. She crossed to the door. He followed. They went into the slush.

'I'll be back presently if anyone should ask,' he snapped at the sentry, and added gratuitously, 'a very serious situation . . .'

He followed Valeria between the walls of snow piled on either side of the road. She did not look back, and he suddenly felt there was a halter round his neck, with a chain leading to her hand. They stumbled on the snow turning to icy water as it crowded into their boots. She led him right into the wall, across it, and to the back door of the mayor's house.

As he entered, he spoke in his most official voice.

'Now, once and for all, what do you want?'

She ignored him, and locked the door leading to the other rooms.

'Is this a trap? Are you a partisan?'

She kicked off her boots, and placed them by the great tiled stove in the corner. Then she removed her woolen stockings, placing them with her boots. She moved her toes in a slow arpeggio, as though to revive them, and shot him a gypsy look, crammed with destiny. He blushed and stamped his foot. He sounded like a horse in a stable. She took her coat off, and her cap, and shook the curls free. One of them landed over her eye, and she looked at him through it.

'I don't understand why you brought me here,' he said. She picked up the hem of her dress, and grumbled that the snow got in everywhere. There was an uneven line of moisture round it. Turning her back on him, she undid a few buttons, and then pulled the dress over her head. He could find no words, nor could he move away. She didn't turn round, but just stood there in her old salmon slip. There were freckles on her back. Her head hung as though in contrition, as though already sinned against. The hips were massive. The play of light on the shiny artificial

silk emphasized the contours of her body, a pink
landscape of sunlit heights and bits of smoothness
and the sudden shade of valleys. Statue-still she
stood, and he began to tremble, damn her. He
took a step, with a crunch of gravel brought
indoors. Her spine stiffened slightly at the sound
of it. There were blue veins at the back of her
knees. He stared at her back, the flakes of gold
on the field of cream, and smelled the warmth
and the cheap scent. His boots were in pools of
water, his feet were cold. He stepped closer. Her
head drew back a little, the neck jutting forward.
Her eyes were probably closed. He could hear
himself breathing, feel the thunder of his pulse.
His nose touched her hair, hard it was, rough,
and it tickled. The tobacco joined the scent again,
taking away the curse of its jam-like sweetness,
adding sour Latakia and aphrodisiac smoke. His
nose sank to rest on her scalp, his face lost in the
yellow jungle. He placed his cold hands on her
shoulders, and felt the shock through her. His
fingers toyed with two thin strands of material;
he dragged the moment out. Then the slip sank
to the floor. In a violent movement, she turned,
and her mouth, so small and pouting, became
enormous. His mouth disappeared into a cavern
of pulsating moisture, and one after another the
buttons of his tunic sprang open as a frenetic
insensitive hand clawed at them.

He felt his chest pressed against the vast
welcoming autumn breasts, and they rolled to

the floor in a confusion of disheveled clothes. The floor was cold and wet, above all hard, and it played havoc with the senses. The heat of bodies and the coldness of the monastic tiles, the wind wailing under the door, shrieking, the woman shrieking too, but louder with less breath, the patient ticking of a clock which had no eyes to see with; he was lost in warmth, but his liberated feet were freezing. Gasping, he felt a spring within him tightening, tightening to breaking point, and then howlingly the release, a roar of rivers, a galloping and prancing and an avalanche of pebbles, and then, unexpectedly, the sound of silence, and a cocoon of peace.

He looked at the woman. She was ugly now. Her eyes could no longer focus, her breath was stale, she had some gun-metal fittings he never noticed before, and nicotine stains. Her forehead glistened. She was old. Her mouth was small again, and through the contentment came a look of gratitude. She examined the details of his face with a mysterious detachment. Undefinable thoughts were passing through her mind, intimate, vaguely amusing, affectionate ones. He felt out of it, and yet content just to watch her thinking. It was quiet now. When the body is hungry, it must eat its fill.

On the short walk back, he wondered what she was after with her photographs and her form for filling. He stopped thinking of it when he realized what had happened to him. Stopping dead in the slush, his hands deep in his pockets, he suddenly shouted: 'I am a man!'

He had never felt so good in his life, physically. The dreary village looked clean, washed. The world was new. A young girl passed down the street, carrying a pail. Hans looked at her in such a way that she blushed, and ran a few steps. He smiled almost cruelly in the knowledge that he held the key to every door. When he returned to his billet, he put the sentry on a charge for having dirty boots, and sent a soldier out to buy him a cigar in the mess. Sitting idly at his desk, he puffed away and watched the blue smoke curling voluptuously like the arm of an Arab dancer. Women. Delicious sex. After a few minutes, he rose abruptly, and vomited. Cigars and fornication were too much for one day. There was a war to win. Be serious.

On February 14, 1942, when the Nibelungen Regiment formed part of von Busch's 16th Army in the north, the Russians launched a savage attack, and Hans had his first real taste of defeat. Ten days later, the entire German 16th Army was surrounded, and it was only by dint of extraordinary tenacity that his tattered regiment broke out of the trap.

It was soon after this disagreeable surprise that the German administration decided that sufficient men had now been killed to warrant Hans's promotion to acting captain. He received the news with pleasure, but without effusiveness, since he considered his promotion overdue. A couple of weeks after his promotion, he was wounded in the leg, and learned in hospital that he was now a lieutenant again.

In November 1942, after a period of rest at a depot in Germany, Hans was once again transferred to a regiment of the line, engaged in the desperate fighting north of Stalingrad. He was quick to discover that the morale of his new unit was extremely low, owing not only to the fact that it had been in the line far too long without relief, but also to the unfortunate personality of the commanding officer, who was a drunkard and desperado of the worst order. This man, who was gradually becoming unhinged owing to the continuous and intense gunfire, was found groveling on the floor a few days after Hans's arrival, in a degrading kind of fit. The second-in-command was such a hopeless military robot that he stood stiff as a ramrod, awaiting orders from the creature howling his fright on all fours, but who had a special designation on his epaulet. With characteristic lack of *savoir-faire*, the Russians selected the very morning of this lamentable occurrence to overrun the German positions. It was Hans's moment, and he took it bravely. The details of the actual engagement are the business of the historian, but Hans arrived at his base a couple of weeks later at the head of twenty-five men, all that was left of the battalion.

He was promoted to captain again, and awarded a magnificent order with a jeweled pendant and a garland of oak leaves. The Fatherland was becoming generous in adversity.

For another year and three months he fought in various parts of the Eastern front, always conducting painful retreats, which was not what he was trained for. By 1944, his hair was white in places, while his right eye had contracted a nervous habit of winking incessantly. He would often fire at nothing in particular with his revolver, for his world was peopled by fleeting shadows who seemed impervious to bullets, but who had to be shown that he was not afraid. Life was for him the arduous, the sly business of remaining on the raft while the others fell noiselessly into the water; there were times when the struggle seemed futile, and when the water beckoned.

It was in this mood, half desperate, half calm, glacial yet fretful, that he endured his last action in the East. It had been an uncommonly mild winter, but not nearly mild enough for the Spanish volunteers who were holding a position along the river Volkhov, on the flank of Hans's regiment. These legionaries found it temperamentally impossible to acquire the lethal apathy of their Teutonic hosts (had they not already defied the strict orders imposed by the Germans against fraternization in Warsaw by marching through the streets with inflated contraceptives tied like balloons to their bayonets?). The Spanish colonel had on several occasions refused to obey the commands of the German divisional commander, wording his refusals with all the acerbic felicity of a grandee. Whenever the exasperated General Ritter von Horstwald ordered a new local counterattack, the Spaniards retreated to 'prepared positions,' by which they meant an agglomeration of houses. This was not done out of cowardice, for these Spaniards were very tough and stubborn soldiers, but, to quote the words of one of their officers, 'Every step backwards is a step nearer Spain.' It was well known to the medical services of the German Army that the only troops on whom the anaphrodisiacs so carefully prepared by learned authorities had not the slightest effect were these angry Latins.

The Russians, true to form, sent a hundred tanks against the Spanish lines as a prelude to their winter offensive in the region, only to find that, by a brilliant intuition, their enemy had already retreated well out of reach, and had no intention of entering into any dangerous argument with the Soviet hordes until they reached the Pyrenees. There, they would have laid down their lives with passion.

General Ritter von Horstwald was not as gifted in the psychology of battle as was his skillful subordinate, and so with a singular lack of imagination he had failed to retreat even a centimeter, with the result that his flank was

wide open to the caprices of a famous Armenian
tank commander, who took full advantage of the
opportunity so handsomely presented.

In a trice Hans found himself and a handful
of hopeless men, doubtfully reinforced by some
hastily armed over-age Luftwaffe personnel, surrounded in what is known as a 'pocket,' but
which looked to Hans more like an open field
bereft of any cover. Here he determined to die
gloriously. With his right eye winking unrestrainedly, he exhorted his soldiers to come with him
and meet a Hero's End, an offer they ungratefully
declined. In a frenzy of exalted mystical emotion,
he advanced alone into the open, firing a tommy
gun at nothing as he went.

General Ritter von Horstwald arrived on the
scene at that moment. He was an impetuous
and intensely disagreeable man, bitterly jealous
of Rommel, whom he never ceased to attack as
a boor and an upstart. He was at pains to point
out that the myth about Rommel being a soldiers'
general, always in the thick of the fighting, was a
gross exaggeration, and that he, Egon Willibald
Ritter von Horstwald, never asked his troops
to do anything that he himself would not do.
True to his ancient quarrel, he had now braved
the threat of encirclement by throwing in every
reserve, with himself in the van of the assault.

'Who is that?' he roared, as he launched his
two hundred and twenty pounds over the closed
door of his Volkswagen.

'Captain Winterschild,' stammered a wretched Luftwaffe corporal, emerging from a shrub.

'And what is he doing?' screamed Ritter von Horstwald, sweat streaming down his porous face.

'He's gone to find something,' said the unhappy corporal.

'Find something? You swine, you know very well what he's gone to find! The Hero's Death! *Des Heldens Tod!* And why aren't you with him? All of you?'

The corporal couldn't find any words, so the general borrowed a revolver and shot him dead.

'Let that be a lesson to you all!' he shouted. 'And now fetch him back.'

Nine or ten horrified soldiers, preferring the uncertainties of the open field to the certainty of death in their modest cover, began running toward Hans, who was now a small figure in the distance. They presented a melancholy sight as they ran, the one with flat feet, the other with ulcers, the third with chronic gout, and so on.

'Run!' bellowed the general, firing between them. '*Ach*, what can one do with troops like that? Why don't you answer me?'

'Nothing,' said a quaking aide-de-camp.

Just then a motorcyclist slid to a spectacular standstill in the slush with a message from the corps commander, General Hanuschek. It ordered an immediate retreat.

'And with generals like that!' roared von Horst-wald. 'General, soldiers, they are all betraying Germany, eternal Germany, *das ewige Deutschland.* All of them. Give me a battalion, one battalion of men like that young man out there in the field, and I will stand before Moscow in a week.'

It was the eternal cry of the frustrated commander throughout history. 'Give me a handful of men who—': the carrion squawk after he has used up his ration of hundreds of thousands, and proclaims that his own mistaken tactical whims are the fault of the instrument, not of the user. Hans was brought in, howling about blood and destiny. It was decided that he deserved both promotion and a rest, consequently he was made a major, awarded some more oak clusters, and sent forthwith to Monte Cassino.

III

HANS QUICKLY discovered that the sound of Communist bullets and democratic bullets was, for all practical purposes, identical. he found his new brigade commander, General Grutze, sympathetic, in spite of his squat and repellent features, owing to the fact that he asked interminable and affectionate questions about Ritter von Horstwald, who was, it appeared, one of his greatest friends. Hans's other colleagues irked him almost as much as he irked them. Colonel von Leideberg, his immediate superior, was a soldier of the old school, a regular who had been saved from retirement by the dearth of capable leaders, but for a long while nobody had asked his opinion, which he had always been so burning to give. He had grown now into a pale and silent man, who looked older than he really was; and who resented any interruption of the flow of bitter memories on which he fed. Grutze he loathed as a party man who had usurped his legitimate position on the ladder to a field marshal's baton, while Ritter von Horstwald, whom he had never met, sounded to him like a traitor to his class, so much more treasonable than treachery to a gentlemanly foe.

Major Prince Kaertner-Tschetterwitz was an Austrian fop whose pastime, apart from the endless playing of selections from operettas on any available piano, was the looting of perfume shops. He was supposed to be an intelligence officer.

Captain Jahn was a gaunt and silent young fellow who lacked personality to an alarming degree; Captain Brehmig was a sour man, once again too old for the front, who picked quarrels with a heavy ingenuity; Captain Scherff was an innocent youngster who hated the war because it had interrupted his examinations for a history degree. His subject had been the political structure of Ostrogoth society.

Faithful to his destiny, Hans began his duties at the front on the very day when, accompanied by an air raid of unprecedented proportions, the Americans and Poles made a concerted attempt to overrun the German positions. Hans was in the thick of it, roaring his orders in a tone which Captain Brehmig evidently resented, for when the attack had died down he approached Hans, who was squatting in a trench, and said, 'You take this war too seriously, Herr Major, there is really no need to shout quite so loud.'

Hans blinked at the newcomer suspiciously, and then snapped, 'I give my orders in my own way.'

'That's what they all say,' answered Brehmig.

'What do you mean?'

'Yours is an unlucky job.' Brehmig was smiling, his gold teeth glinting in the late sunset. 'The last one was Major Braun. We didn't like him, because he shouted as though his pants were on fire. He had just come from Russia, you see. Only he shouted so loud, the Poles over there heard him, and shot in the direction of the sound.' He shrugged his shoulders. 'We had to send a telegram to Frau Braun, and they put in the papers that he had found the Hero's End. Apparently to be a hero you must attract attention to yourself by shouting.'

'Are you insulting me?' shouted Hans.

'Not at all,' answered Brehmig, smiling. 'I'm just telling you the little bedtime story I tell my sentries so that they'll sleep well.'

'Listen to me,' said Hans, white with anger and stiff with formality. 'Your duties here are simple. You are here to obey my orders, and, if necessary, to die at your post. That is all. Gratuitous joking at the expense of the Hero's End will not be tolerated. Is that understood?'

'My duties are clear, Herr Major, but they must not be confused with my pleasures, which are to knock a little of the stuffing out of you cocksure lads from the Russian front. You know everything, don't you? Tell me, have you ever seen so many planes as you saw today?'

'This is an outrage!' shouted Hans. 'I shall report you to the colonel.'

'Ah,' smiled Brehmig, 'if you only knew what he feels. *Auf Wiedersehen*, Herr Greenhorn. See you in the graveyard if not before' – and before Hans could issue a dramatic order for him to take his leave, the sarcastic Brehmig crept away.

'Is he drunk?' said Hans abruptly, turning to the foolish Captain Jahn, who was trying to read a letter from his doting mother in the failing light.

'What, Herr Major?' said Jahn.

'I asked you if that officer was drunk,' snapped Hans.

'Drunk? No, I don't think so—'

'Stand up!' shouted Hans, suddenly furious.

'There's no room,' answered Jahn, surprised.

'Stand up!'

Jahn struggled slowly to his feet, and stood, stooping, under a small canopy of earth.

'Come out of there!'

'But it's very dangerous,' said Jahn, quite reasonably.

'Did you hear me?'

Hans was beside himself with incredulity that a German soldier should mention the word 'danger.'

'Now, answer me. Was that officer drunk?' said Hans, quietly.

A machine gun broke the silence. Jahn ducked instinctively.

'*Stillstehen!* screamed Hans.

Jahn began to realize as he stood shivering, his head and torso exposed to a seeming infinity of landscape, the real menace of his new commander.

'No, Herr Major. He's like that. He's . . . well, he's Brehmig, we all know him.'

'Know him?'

'Yes. He's a bit . . . well, odd. We've all been here so long.'

'You've been *here* so long! *Junge, junge,* you can talk. And what about us, in Russia?'

'It must be much the same, Herr Major.'

'Much the same?' Hans permitted himself a laugh.

Another burst of machine-gun fire broke into the conversation; a stream of tracers rushed into the earth like a distant train flashing into a tunnel.

'You may take cover,' said Hans, sitting down himself. 'Listen, in Russia we . . .'

In Russia we lay in frozen ditches while the Red tanks rolled over us, shedding their boiling oil on us. That was war such as the world has never seen, wrote Hans to his father. *Only the heroism of our soldiers, shamefully betrayed by Spaniards*

*and other alien riffraff, allowed us to maintain
our positions for so long. What other nation could
have withstood the murderous onslaught of the
Asiatics? Dear Papa, if one may be permitted to
criticize the policy of our Führer, who has otherwise done what no man in the history of the
world has ever done, then one would say that
he had insufficient faith in the German soldier,
in that he ought to have allowed us to beat the
Russians alone, without the encumbrance of foreign
mercenaries, who were always more trouble than
they were worth. (Please don't tell Helmut Bollmann
of my opinions. You understand what I mean, but
would he?)*

*Here, in Italy, it is quite a little war, and
given the soldiers we had in Russia, men like
General von Horstwald (whom the troops called
'The Eagle of Odessa'), then we would have put
the Anglo-Americans into the sea a long time ago.
Unfortunately our troops here, apart from General
Grutze, who is an alter Kämpfer, do us no credit.
The men are of variable quality, but the officers
singularly lack fanaticism. Never mind, we will
pull through.*

'It is quite a little war in Italy,' said the colonel
to Frau Winterschild, 'and the troops are bad.
Austrians, I wouldn't be surprised. A pity. Never
mind, Hansi says we'll pull through.'

'A little war?' asked Frau Winterschild. 'Perhaps, but it's quite as easy to be killed in a little
war as in a big one.'

'Don't think of such things,' said the colonel.

AT BRIGADE headquarters, a derelict farmhouse quite a way behind the lines, General Grutze paced the floor before a map of Italy, which hung from a hook in the wall. Colonel von Leideberg sat at the table like an angry sphinx. Another colonel, a man called Wohlholtz, gazed out of the window. A third colonel, Breithand, beat a tattoo with his fingers on the lid of a shattered upright piano. Hans stamped his foot in time with some imaginary march rhythm. Feathers were flying.

'It is unthinkable, unthinkable, that German officers can be so uncooperative,' ranted Grutze, and suddenly stopped pacing. 'Since when does a general have to appeal to his officers to attack? I order you to attack!'

'Where?' asked Breithand.

'Where I have indicated!' shouted Grutze.

'Do you mean the divisional assault which you mentioned in the direction of San Ambrogio, Herr Generalmajor?' said Wohlholtz, turning from the window.

'What else have I been talking about for the last half hour?'

'There are three things against it,' said von Leideberg, breaking the silence.

'Trust you to find things against it,' cried Grutze.

Von Leideberg, once he had started, was not

easily put off. 'The first is that the terrain you have selected is passable only to monkeys—'

'Monkeys without equipment,' interrupted Breithand.

'The second is that it is ridiculous to waste our already limited strength on local engagements of doubtful aim and predestined failure. The third is that an attack on a divisional front is the business of a divisional general, and not of a brigade general.'

Grutze practically burst with anger. His face became an unpleasant violet and a torrent of words claimed simultaneous attention on his lips. At the sight of a brave commander so betrayed, Hans forgot himself, and blurted out a startling accusation.

'There is a fourth point,' he gasped, as he leaped to his feet, 'and that is victory – victory as can only be achieved by German soldiers in the face of the seemingly impossible. I have come from Russia, and I can tell you that such a situation could not have arisen there. In Russia, gentlemen, we are fighting a war, we attack where and when we can, and often we attack when reason tells us to do the opposite!'

'And look at the result,' said the phlegmatic Breithand.

'Results are achieved, not looked at,' said Grutze, who liked coining phrases which he imagined would be remembered after his death.

To make sure, he told all his friends all the phrases all the time.

'In Russia, they are retreating faster than we are,' said Wohlholtz.

'We are not retreating at all,' said Grutze, 'but this stalemate is intolerable. We must and shall advance. it is from now on treason to think of further retreat. Argument with me is useless. We shall attack due south and retake San Ambrogio, recrossing the Garigliano, and exposing the enemy flank to the assaults of our reserve battalion, which, under your command, Colonel Breithand, will retake Cervaro, I said, *will retake Cervaro*. Do I make myself clear?'

There was a pause. Breithand looked at his fingers, and moistened his lips.

'You do not answer.'

Breithand rose slowly, and said, 'Herr Generalmajor, I wish to be relieved of my command.'

'I see,' replied Grutze curtly. He was not slow to recognize the intended insult of being perpetually called Herr Generalmajor instead of just Herr General by all his officers. 'And to what may I attribute your request, Herr Oberstleutnant? Could it be cowardice? I ask for the purpose of making my report.'

Breithand stood there as if slapped in the face.

'My two Iron Crosses are a sufficient answer to that insult, Herr Generalmajor,' he said, controlling himself with difficulty. 'I wish to be relieved of my command because I am a soldier, not a murderer.'

Grutze lost his temper. 'What are you suggesting?' he screamed.

'I have evidently made myself clear,' answered Breithand, 'and I now ask formal leave to retire.'

'Not granted!' yelled Grutze. 'Not granted, do you hear? Oberst Wohlholtz, you will command the troops which will attack Cervaro.'

There was another pause.

Wohlholtz raised his eyebrows, and thought for a moment.

'Well?' said Grutze.

Wohlholtz, a man of slacker fiber, answered slowly and reasonably. 'My duty is clear,' he said, 'but I ask leave to suggest that tempers here have become perhaps unnecessarily frayed. While not associating myself in any way with the attitude of my gallant brother in arms, Colonel Breithand, I would feel happier if at the outset of such a – how should I put it – such a momentous step—'

'What is the meaning of all this ridiculous diplomatic language?' said Grutze. 'I want a clear yes or no.'

'It is not as simple as that,' suggested Wohlholtz.

'Yes is an extremely simple reply,' answered Grutze, with heavy humor. 'No you will find more complicated.'

Von Leideberg rose suddenly, and said, with supreme disdain, 'I am sick to death of amateurs.'

Grutze went violet again. 'Explain yourself,' he said, almost voicelessly.

'I am an old soldier of '14–'18,' said von Leideberg. 'I knew von Falkenhayn, and served under Mackensen and Liman von Sanders—'

'I have neither time nor inclination to listen to your autobiography,' said Grutze.

Von Leideberg ignored the interruption. 'Those were men who knew what they were doing,' he went on, 'men who were betrayed by politicians, but men who never allowed themselves to become the tools of these selfsame politicians. They finished their war, deserted but undefeated. They were experts. Here, gentlemen, we are busy defeating ourselves, because it is half the business of soldiering to know when to advance and when to retreat, coldly, dispassionately, without considerations of the Hero's End and other melodramatic silliness.'

Grutze looked at Hans.

'Major Winterschild, I order you to take over the command of the reserve battalion, and to attack Cervaro under my command.'

His eyes staring at the ceiling as though he could see a truth denied the others, Hans declaimed, 'Where you lead, Herr General, I follow.'

'The conference, gentlemen, is over,' said Grutze, with savage satisfaction.

Just then the door opened and the divisional commander, General Wonniger, entered,

accompanied by his aide and Captain Brehmig.
He was on a surprise visit. Brehmig had seen the
Volkswagen approaching, and had saluted. The
general had stopped the car, and had talked to
Brehmig for a time. He was a great believer in
talking to everyone and anyone, in order, as he
called it, 'to feel the pulse of my soldiers.' This
Wonniger was a shrewd and cultivated man, still
fairly young, a great one for the ladies.

'Good afternoon, gentlemen,' he said, as the
officers stiffened to attention. 'I must apologize
for having interrupted a conference. Tell me,
have you reached any interesting conclusions?'

Grutze talked with determined servility. 'I have
a plan, Herr General, which it was my intention
to submit for your consideration.'

Wonniger laughed charmingly, and as he was
lighting a cigarette, he said, 'Come on, let's hear
it, Grutze, in these hard days we can never have
enough plans.'

Grutze crossed to the map with authority. 'My
plan is one, Herr General, which I had envisaged
as an operation on a divisional scale. I believe
that there is no more detrimental factor to the
morale of the German soldier, with his inborn
love of activity and victory, than a stalemate.
Consequently I believe that it is time to advance,
and teach the Americans and those rebellious
Poles a lesson.'

'Go on,' said Wonniger, amused.

'My idea is to launch a divisional offensive in

a southerly direction, aimed at San Ambrogio and the Garigliano, but with a surprise attack developing behind it, and swinging to the east in the direction of Cervaro, thereby isolating the enemy troops before Cassino.'

Wonniger smiled.

'What is your reaction to this plan, Wohlholtz?' he asked.

Wohlholtz wished that he hadn't been asked first. He cleared his throat noisily. 'Well, on the face of it,' he said, 'it is a plan which is, I suppose, theoretically fairly sound, although there are, in my opinion, many things which stand, more or less plainly, against it.'

'Colonel Breithand?' said Wonniger.

'I have already made my position clear,' answered Breithand, 'by asking to be relieved of my command, Herr General.'

'Good gracious me,' said Wonniger. 'Colonel von Leideberg?'

'In my opinion, Herr General, the plan is of highly unorthodox and indeed unprofessional conception. The German soldier is well known for his fighting qualities, but he is not a chimpanzee. Far from it. The mountains in the suggested area are of such difficulty that even if they were not insuperable to a modern army, they would preclude any possibility of surprise being effected.'

Wonniger looked at Hans.

'Major Winterschild, Herr General,' said the

angry Grutze, 'who has just joined us from the Eastern front.'

'Is that so?' said Wonniger. 'And what are your views, Major Winterschild?'

Hans stood proudly erect and answered, with the appropriate fanaticism, 'In Russia we learned that anything is possible, Herr General.'

'Even defeat,' said Wonniger, whimsically.

Breithand laughed.

'Defeat? No, sir,' replied Hans. 'There has never been any thought of defeat.'

'Since when?'

'Since the beginning of operations, Herr General.'

'You surprise me. Tell me, are conditions still very bad?'

'Conditions are bad, but that is only a challenge to our troops, which will be overcome, in spite of the Spaniards, Herr General.'

'You had Spaniards?'

'Yes, Herr General.'

'Bad?'

'Hopeless, Herr General.'

'I had a couple of Rumanian divisions. I too was on the Eastern front – left there three months ago. The Rumanians fought remarkably well,' added the General gratuitously. 'They were very near Rumania. I am afraid that in one or two instances we let them down rather badly. Now, Grutze, I want a talk with you. I think we can dismiss our friends. We must make absolutely sure that when we are compelled to retreat from Cassino, our withdrawal to the Arno doesn't become a rout.'

'Our withdrawal to where?' asked Grutze, horrified.

'The Arno. Florence. A matter of about six hundred kilometers,' answered Wonniger, quietly.

Then Hans noticed that Brehmig was smiling at him.

ALL WILL crumble, Hans wrote to his father, *unless certain gentlemen who shall be nameless until after our victory are quickly dealt with in a manner which tradition prescribes for traitors. I cannot mention what I know, dear Father, because we can rely upon the integrity of nobody in these times. Indeed, it is difficulties of the type we are encountering at the moment which show up the weaklings from the heroes. Perhaps the time has come to mention something of what I write about to H., for it is painful for one who has the Führer and the Fatherland always in mind to see how subtle and yet how deadly are the betrayals which I have seen at work. Finally, with love and kisses to Mutti, Mopsel and Hannele, and a big hug to you, I send you all my solemn assurances that defeat is impossible.*

'There seem to be some difficulties at the front – he even wants us to mention them to Helmut,' said the colonel to Frau Winterschild.

'He is alive, thank God,' answered Frau Winterschild.

'Still, he ends the letter with a guarantee that
defeat is impossible. I believe him, and I trust him
more than the friends you meet at the butcher's.'

'Frau Oehlmann's boy is a major, and of course
he couldn't say what he really thinks, but Frau
Oehlmann tells me that, reading between the
lines, one can see that the situation is very black,'
said Frau Winterschild, who was resigned to the
worst and had no wish to be stoked up with any
illusory optimism.

'My son is a major also, and I believe him,'
said the old man, stubbornly, filling his pipe.

'Whatever happens,' added his wife, 'they will
blame the home front. They always say we who
worry without much news are letting down the
boys at the front.'

NOTHING MUCH happened until the second week
in May, except that General Wonniger wrote a
confidential letter to a friend on the General
Staff, advising the immediate removal of Grutze,
whom he described as 'thoroughly incompetent,
the worst kind of political general, headstrong,
vain, and monstrously stupid.' Grutze also wrote
a confidential letter, addressed to an important
party member with the rank of Undersecretary,
advising the immediate removal of Wonniger,
whom he described as 'a downright swine, effeminate, smirking and deterimental to our ideals.'

Colonel von Leideberg wrote a third confidential letter, this one addressed to Field Marshal
von Witzleben, who had lands adjoining the
Leideberg property. He advocated the removal
of both Wonniger, whom he called unbelievably
young, and Grutze, whom he called a name
of soldierly vulgarity. Old Colonel Winterschild
duly wrote off to Helmut Bollmann, confiden-
tially of course, seasoning his son's vagueness
with concrete proof which he invented. Bollmann
never replied. Witzleben wrote back to Leideberg,
'Ah, my dear friend, if these were all our troubles!'
The Undersecretary wrote to Grutze promising
an immediate investigation, which never, in fact,
took place. The staff officer wrote back to
Wonniger, congratulating him on his zeal, and
asking 'What can we do?'

The battles of words were interrupted by an
Allied effort which had about it all the uncomfortable savor of finality. Hans could exhort as
loudly as he wished, Grutze could bellow his
orders of the day to his heart's content. The
legions at their disposal were illusory.

By May 16th, that portion of the vaunted
Gustav Line south of the river Liri was overrun.
On the 17th, General Wonniger, in obedience to
the army commander, ordered a general retreat.
On the 18th, Polish soldiers planted their red and
white flag in the ruins of Monte Cassino abbey,
while the British entered the little town. Other
units of the 8th Army succeeded in cutting the

Via Casilina on the line of the German retreat towards Rome.

General Wonniger handled his part of the withdrawal expertly enough, and his rear guards, led by Grutze, who rushed hither and thither, tears streaming down his face, acquitted themselves well. The situation was further aggravated, however, when on the 23rd the Allies attacked from their beachhead at Anzio, on the German right flank. They used so many planes that the sky seemed to be rocking, like an ill-fitting slide in a magic lantern. Every window, every windshield for miles around vibrated with the noise of chattering teeth, and nerves were unsteadied.

As Hans led his men in their slow retirement, a British or American plane would appear quite casually and unmolestedly rake them with cannon and rocket fire, as though it were running affectionate fingers through the earth's hair.

'*Wo sind unsere Flieger?*' shrieked Jahn, who was at the end of his tether. Brehmig grimly told him exactly where the Luftwaffe was.

On May 25th, more than eleven hundred German vehicles were put out of action on the roads, and Captain Jahn was killed in action.

On June 1st, Captain Scherff, the expert on the Ostrogoths, who rarely talked, disappeared. Missing, believed killed.

On June 4th, at half-past seven in the evening, the Allied advance guard entered Rome.

IV

By July 20th, the position was to some extent stabilized. True to General Wonniger's information, the bulk of the German army was now stretched roughly between Marina di Pisa and Florence, on the line of the Arno. Allied pressure after the fantastic advance was not, at the moment, very intense. Hans had seen heavy rear-guard action, especially in the hills of Tuscany, where the land was particularly adapted to defensive engagements, and now, after six weeks of grim warfare, he found himself in the little village of San Rocco al Monte, some miles northeast of Florence. Grutze's entire division was, for the moment, out of the line.

Hans had set up his headquarters in a farmhouse only about a hundred yards north of the village, on the road to Borgo San Lorenzo. The house was owned by a farmer called Signor Buonsignori, who was a massive block of a man, an ex-mayor, terror of his family, genial host to the stranger. His hospitality did not, however, extend to the point where he was actively glad to welcome a joyless and blinking German officer who sat so consistently brooding at a table, his head cupped in his hands. Already the enforced sojourn had been punctuated by one unpleasant incident. Signor Buonsignori had a dog, a charming and bewildered-looking cross between a Dalmatian and a setter, very obviously intimately related to all the other dogs in the village, and called Folgore – Lightning. This dog, who was as friendly as he was intelligent, had ambled across to where Hans was sitting and had tried to ingratiate himself with the new visitor by squeezing his nose under Hans's hand, an invitation to be stroked. He got a vicious kick for his pains. It must be said that Hans was very far from being himself, and regretted his action as soon as he realized what he had done. After this he made every effort to be friendly with the dog, but Folgore just looked at him with the resentful stare of an offended child and slouched away, leaving Hans only the enigma of an expressionless tail.

Signor Buonsignori knew very well that something had passed between the intruder and his dog; there was always an atmosphere in the room when they were there together. He said nothing, but made a private noise to reassure Folgore, who agitated his tail slowly in recognition and then sat down near the large table in order to ignore Hans at close quarters.

Unfortunately the Buonsignoris had a piano, a veteran, dating practically from the days of Austrian oppression. This meant that Prince Kaertner-Tschetterwitz was almost permanently at the yellowing keyboard, singing all the parts in the most cloying Viennese operettas. His bass was a hoarse whisper, his tenor a bit of stretch, his soprano a shrill shriek, his contralto really quite beautiful. Brehmig also used to come and join in the choruses with brash gusto. He was, for some reason, always staring at Hans, as though to break him down.

Buonsignori knew very well that something dreadful was bound to happen sooner or later.

'They are already defeated,' he said to his wife, after the intruders had been there for only one day, the 19th of July to be precise. He was undressing for bed as he said this, in as far as he ever undressed in these mad times. He took his trousers off, untied his bootlaces, and lifted a floorboard to examine a rifle hidden there.

'So long as we don't become involved,' said Elena, his wife, already in bed.

Signor Buonsignori made a noise both inviting fate to do its worst and defying it to do anything whatever.

The situation in the village was complicated enough without the added nuisance of Germans in the house. Everyone knew that Colonello Garetta, hero of Caporetto, who lived in retirement in the Piazza Vittorio Emmanuele II, was in active touch with 'certain people.' Everyone knew that the 'certain people' were the remnants of the 806th Battalion of the Gran Sasso division, dispersed among the forests and the olive groves, and that these renegade soldiers were in their turn in active touch with 'other people.' Everyone knew that the 'other people' were partisans operating from the hidden heights of Monte Calvo, and that they were in active touch with 'a man in an apron.' Everyone knew that 'the man in the apron' was the village general-store keeper, Signor Filigrani, who had done a term for Communism, and that he got his money from 'a stiff collar.' Everyone knew that 'a stiff collar' was the squire of the region, Conte Remigio Fabbri di San Rocco Tomazuoli, who was nevertheless an old friend of 'the bald one.' Everyone knew that 'the bald one,' who had been the podestà of the village, a Fascist of the March on Rome days, the local mechanic and only garagist for kilometers round, was Signor Bacca, who used to play chess once a week regularly with 'Old Plumes.' Everyone knew that 'Old Plumes' was Colonello Garetta, hero of Caporetto, who lived in retirement in the Piazza Vittorio Emmanuele II, and was in touch with 'certain people.' Everyone knew, everyone was sworn to secrecy, and everyone talked their heads off.

No sooner had the stout Elena resigned herself to sleep than one of their infants began to scream.

'Which one is that?' said Signor Buonsignori, scratching his stubbled head with two fistfuls of thick fingers.

'Maria Pia,' answered Elena, who had no ear for conventional music but was a magician in segregating the various stridencies of the very young.

'Better go and soothe her,' said Signor Buonsignori. 'We don't want our guests shooting through the floor.'

But Elena was already halfway up. 'I'll bring them all in here,' she said.

'Then we shall get no sleep at all.'

'Will we anyway?'

PRINCE KAERTNER-TSCHETTERWITZ heard the child crying, and his watery blue eyes lost their concentration. Without stopping his rendering of a difficult quartet, he looked upwards with the threatening expression of a prima donna who had detected a snorer at the back of the hall. Brehmig smiled, and said to Hans, 'We set out to conquer the world, and to create our own rules, and yet here we are, we have eighteen bullets between us, and we are prevented from using them by international law, which we are beginning to respect as we are forced back to our own frontiers.'

Hans looked up as Brehmig had anticipated.

His right eye, shot with blood, was blinking with the speed of a machine gun.

'Who asked your opinion?' he said.

'Grant me the fundamental liberty of saying what I think, Herr Major,' pleaded Brehmig, mockingly. 'Please, please.'

Hans's irritation had grown to a bitter hatred, largely because he had no idea of how to deal with Brehmig's complicated subversiveness.

'I would use my bullets on you,' he said, 'with the greatest pleasure.'

'Hurrah!' cried Brehmig. 'We will reconstruct old Heidelberg here, miles from home, because our hearts are breaking. We will shoot each other's hearts out in the traditional manner, in order to put an end to the intolerable pain. Our Austrian exquisite will be the umpire, for lack of a real bloodthirsty German. We will find the Hero's End in the boudoir, and the papers at home will ring our names with black, and say, "It had to be."'

'Children, children,' implored the prince, 'why can't you think of nice things, like the lovely times we had before the war, when Vienna was Vienna, and there were still Jews to be rude to. The great mistake of persecuting the Jews has become painfully clear to me. Nowadays we have to be rude to one another.'

'Go to bed,' said Brehmig. 'You won't have the energy for the next retreat if you don't look after yourself.'

'You are disgusting,' said the prince. 'Listen to this – Offenbach.'

'A Jew,' said Brehmig.

'A genius,' said the prince.

THIS IS intolerable,' grumbled Signor Buonsignori, his arms full of squealing babies.

'For God's sake don't complain,' implored Elena. 'I'm sure I heard the clink of bottles. They're bound to have found the *grappa*. Heaven alone knows what mood they'll be in.'

Then a stone fell against the window. Very excited, Buonsignori deposited the babies on the bed quilt and rushed to pull aside the curtains.

'*Dio*, what now?' moaned Elena, on the verge of tears. A dark figure stood in the street.

'Psss, Febo!' (Signor Buonsignori's name was Phoebus.)

'*Che c'è?*

'*Vieni alle Vecchie Piume, urgentissimo.*'

'*Ma—*'

'*E imperativo.*'

And the dark figure vanished silently.

Signor Buonsignori turned back into the room, biting his fingers.

'You are not going out,' said Elena.

'*E imperativo*,' answered Buonsignori.

'But how will you leave the house with all those Germans downstairs?'

'It will take greater obstacles to stop me.'

'And you will leave me with all the children, *isolata, abbandonata?*'

'I must obey the order of the Consiglio Superiore de la Guerra di San Rocco.'

'You and your Consiglio Superiore de la Guerra. What do they do all the time? Sit in the bushes waiting for the Allies to arrive, and being fed out of our meager rations.'

'No criticism,' said Signor Buonsignori, lifting a menacing hand. 'They are the potential heroes of the nation. I must go and take my place in their ranks.'

'But not at one o'clock in the morning!'

'Time means nothing to the Consiglio Superiore de la Guerra di San Rocco. Comforts must be put aside. Every man must be at his post when the hour finally strikes—' as he struggled into his trousers.

'Good night,' said Signor Buonsignori, as he kissed his babies good-by. '*In tempo di guerra,* one never knows if . . .'

Elena was crying at the sight of so much heroism as her husband tiptoed grimly out of the room.

Prudently, Signor Buonsignori decided not to try to leave the house unobserved. He began whistling for Folgore before he entered the room occupied by the Germans.

'Going out?' said Brehmig.

'The dog wishes to relieve himself,' answered Buonsignori, 'Folgore, *vieni, vieni.*'

The Germans turned to look at Folgore, who was still fast asleep.

'The dog is asleep,' observed Hans, 'and anyway, you know perfectly well that it is forbidden to walk in the streets at night.'

'I beg you to believe me that I know my dog better than he knows himself,' answered Buonsignori, 'and I can tell you that even if he seems to be asleep, he very badly wants to relieve himself. He is so well trained that he never asks for anything. As for walking in the streets, I am convinced that our brave allies would not deny a poor Italian dog the opportunity of relieving himself in a civilized way. Folgore, Folgore, *vieni far pipi.*'

They all looked at Folgore, who stretched, yawned, and relapsed into a hopeless relaxation in order to begin a new dream.

'It is clear to me,' said Hans, humorlessly, 'that the dog in question does not want to relieve himself, and that your desire to go out at this time of the night is highly suspicious.'

'I tell you,' insisted Buonsignori, 'that the dog is so intimidated by the sight of so many, albeit welcome, strangers in this house, that his reactions to even the most commonplace desires are a little confused. Folgore, *vieni, sporcaccione.*'

Folgore opened a yellow eye, and closed it again.

'Good God,' said Hans, with undue agitation. 'I have had wolfhounds, boxers and Doberman pinschers in my life, and I can tell you that I know when a dog wants to relieve itself and when it doesn't, and I can tell you categorically that all this dog wants is to be left alone.'

Buonsignori's inventive powers were stimulated by his rising temperature.

'Listen to me, Signor Maggiore!' he shouted. 'I have known Folgore ever since he was an embryo. He has grown up in this house. All dogs are different, like human beings. They are creatures full of complexes. Some of them are easily embarrassed, and they don't like asking to be let out in company. There are men like that too. Men to whom the natural functions of life are an excuse for shame, for blushing, and who would rather die than be seen relieving themselves. I ask you to believe that Folgore is like that, and beg you to respect his difficulties, as I have respected them. These are things one does not talk about, they are things one understands! Folgore, *piccolo, vieni, vieni.*'

Folgore looked up, and wagged a feeble tail.

'You see!' said Buonsignori, triumphant.

'I see nothing at all,' snapped Hans, 'except that you wish, for some reason, to leave the house at night.'

'I have left the house at one o'clock in the morning ever since I became conscious of Folgore's problems,' barked Buonsignori. 'I respect my dog, because I expect him to respect me. Without mutual respect, it is no joy to go hunting. There.

If you deny me the right to go out with my dog, I warn you that at about three o'clock he will start howling, and when Folgore howls, then there is no answer.'

'Except perhaps bullets,' drawled Brehmig.

'Bullets?'

'You Italians have no idea of the strength of the German military machine, and of its sensitivity,' said Brehmig, smiling. 'It is not always the passive weapon which bends nations to its will. It can be as selective, as poetic as the hands of a great surgeon. A bullet into a dog would delicately solve a problem which would baffle less gifted organizations, just as a fly, hovering over your head at lunch, could be shot out of the sky. We have snipers specially trained for such badinage.'

'Stop talking nonsense!' stormed Hans.

'Nonsense? My dear Hansel, we live in desperate days, and we can't afford to take risks. Much better shoot everyone than ask questions. We have arrived beyond the point of foolish discrimination. Shoot Herr Buonsignori for wanting to go out. Shoot Frau Buonsignori for no reason at all. Shoot the dog because it exists. It is much safer.'

'Get out, but return in five minutes,' said Hans.

'You're losing your grip,' whispered Brehmig.

'You leave the house at your own risk, is that understood?' said Hans.

'Naturally. *In tempo di guerra . . .*' replied Buonsignori.

By this time Folgore had dozed off again, and had to be dragged whimpering to the door. Buonsignori muttered his apology to the dog as they went, excusing himself on the grounds of his terror that the Germans might change their minds.

'I forbid you to talk about shooting dogs,' said Hans to Brehmig after Buonsignori had gone.

Brehmig smiled. 'You foolish boy,' he said, 'I only wanted to stop you making an ass of yourself. I only wanted you to let him go.'

'And now perhaps we may continue,' simpered the prince, applying himself once again to the keyboard.

Upstairs the children yelled unrestrainedly.

BUONSIGNORI RAN down the empty street, clinging to the houses, Folgore cantering at his heels. Once a German soldier passed, moaning his loneliness to the stars in a sentimental ditty, recollected from childhood. Buonsignori threw himself into a doorway with a desperate hiss at the dog. Folgore was, however, too tired to hear, and sidled over to the soldier, sniffing at his footsteps. The soldier was too absorbed to notice.

Sweating ice, Buonsignori jog-trotted on till he reached the Piazza Vittorio Emmanuele II. Here he sheltered for a moment under the war memorial, on which a collection of angels were struggling for ascendancy. Then he walked quickly on, holding Folgore by the collar. Folgore was going to be a damned nuisance, that was quite clear, because by now he had woken up to such an extent that the wafting and contradictory odors of the night began to hold an irresistible fascination for him. Still, he was the only valid excuse. One must be grateful, *in tempo di guerra* . . .

Buonsignori knocked on the door of the house where 'Old Plumes' lived. 'Old Plumes' himself appeared, and implored silence with a noisy and effusive gesture. They entered the hallway.

'Old Plumes,' Colonello Galeazzo Garetta, was an old officer of *Bersaglieri,* hence the nickname. His vast head, covered with a porcupine brush of snow-white hair, was held straight upright by a neck of immense caliber, grooved like an elephant's knee. His face, tanned by desert and sirocco, carried an expression of mingled determination and disgust. A short, straight nose with huge, disdainful nostrils passed like an aqueduct into a horny forehead, separating two gray eyes notable for their anger and their melancholy. A ruthless mouth sheltered under the generous umbrella of an iron-gray mustache.

'News of the utmost importance has just reached us. By us, I mean, of course, the Stato Maggiore del Consiglio di Guerra Superiore di San Rocco. But first—' he held out a hand for shaking.

Buonsignori responded, and Folgore leaped up on the man he had, since birth, come to regard as an uncle. After all, did the Colonello not own his half-sister, Papavera, a disgruntled, mottled bitch with an infinity of breasts trailing on the ground.

'Why did you bring your dog?' asked Old Plumes.

Buonsignori explained his ruse with a degree of pleasure, but Old Plumes was not impressed.

'Some other excuse should have been found,' he said. 'Come, we must fetch "the apron" and "stiff collar," and then meet "certain people." There is no time to lose.'

'But I can't be out longer than five minutes,' said Buonsignori, paling.

'Once you are out for five minutes, you might as well be out for five hours,' answered Old Plumes.

'Impossible – then there are the *bambini*.'

'Are you a soldier, yes or no?'

'Yes.'

'Very well then, means must be found to re-adjust your domestic position. I will not entertain contradiction. *Avanti!*'

'But the dog?'

'It will stay here.'

'But—'

'The nation calls to us. Even now, the muffled voices of the dead urge us on, calling out in their agony from the fragrant fields they now inhabit:

"Succeed, where we, through no fault of our own, failed." Shall we turn a deaf ear to their clarion note?'

'No,' said Buonsignori, reasonably. Old Plumes was a man of few words, but when they flowed they were lusciously selected, and brooked no kind of half-measures. The two men shook hands, and left the house by the stables at the back.

In the vestry of the church, Signor Filigrani was talking in a hushed voice to Don Diomiro, the priest, who was, even at this desperate hour, busily trying to convert the lost but gallant Communist lamb to the Catholic fold. Filigrani, a thin man with an unforgiving face, greeted Old Plumes, and then reprimanded him for being late.

'It has given me more time to work upon the Christian conscience of our poor, courageous son,' smiled Don Diomiro, a youngish man with burning black eyes and one black eyebrow stretching from temple to temple.

Old Plumes was annoyed. 'In military matters,' he said, 'expedience must always remain the slave of efficiency. I came when I could, but I determined to wait until the arrival of Febo Buonsignori for reasons which are my own, and which will remain my own until the meeting of the Consiglio Superiore.'

'Come,' said Filigrani, and the three men left silently as Don Diomiro crooned a blessing.

In the grounds of a disused convent they

picked up the count, a bachelor in his late forties, who was sitting on a stone bench with two servants, drinking beef tea from a Thermos bottle. Filigrani immediately asked why servants had been brought on an expedition in which mobility might be essential, and the knowledge of which was in any case confined to the elite. The count frowned, twisting the hundreds of lines on his proudly doleful face into vertical channels. 'In the army,' he said, 'I was given a batman. It was my privilege as an elevated servant of the state. Now I am a private citizen. Surely you will not grudge me a couple of batmen, provided I agree to pay their salaries.'

'The days of such luxuries are past,' remarked Filigrani.

The count remarked testily that he could offer nobody any beef tea, as he had drunk it all himself. The little procession then wound its way into the landscape in search of 'certain people.'

MEANWHILE, IN Old Plumes's house, Folgore began to moan pitifully as the tantalizing aromas of the countryside crept cruelly through the open window. Downstairs, on her mat, Papavera rolled over in her sleep. She was having a nightmare about herself being locked in a strange house while the tantalizing aromas of the countryside crept cruelly through the open window. The moaning of her half-brother gave a horrible reality to these imaginings. For a moment she hovered between the terrifying reality of the dream and the unnatural calm of awareness, and then sat up with a look of bald annoyance. There was no doubt about it. She was awake, the objects in the room were sniffable, the breeze was bullying the curtains. The moaning of the dream had, however, accompanied her into the unruffled, workaday room. The phenomenon called for immediate investigation. Pushing her way through the half open door, she climbed the stairs, her head held low, the white of her eyes showing. The intrepid Folgore noticed the approach of a strange perfume from an unexpected direction, and looked towards the door, one paw held under him in readiness.

Growling, Papavera peeped around the corner. She was like the aging mistress of an influential man, determined to fight for her ephemeral rights. Folgore tried to plead with her, running the whole gamut of canine argument from counter-growl to wary lick of affection, but it was no use. The fight was on, and it was pursued with intense bitterness for about three minutes, at the end of which Folgore, humbled and terror-struck, struggled like a stricken worm through the slightly open window and fell in an uncoordinated mass to the ground.

Papavera barked her victory to the neighborhood, while Folgore howled his protest against unprovoked and unwarranted aggression as he limped painfully home.

*   *   *

'WHAT THE hell is going on out there?' said Hans, going to the window.

'The dogs of hell are heralding a German victory,' laughed Brehmig, who had found the bottle of *grappa*, and who was therefore quickly acquiring a justification for his extraordinary method of conducting a conversation.

'*Dio, Dio, Dio*,' groaned Elena, as she prayed that nothing untoward had happened.

Just then there was scratching on the door. Hans put an unfinished letter into his pocket, and then crossed the room. Folgore wagged his tail for a second, but preferred not to enter when he saw Hans.

'Where's your master?' asked Hans.

Folgore lay down outside.

'He's covered in blood,' said Hans.

'He's learning from us,' said Brehmig.

A shot rang across the valley, echoing and re-echoing against the hills.

'*Dio, Dio*,' whispered Elena, crossing herself and the five weeping children.

'What was that?' said Hans, very much the soldier.

'A shot,' said Brehmig, smiling.

WHAT HAD in fact occurred was that while the patriotic procession was searching the olive groves for its contacts, a figure had suddenly emerged from behind a tree and challenged the count's butler, of all people, with a request for the password. The butler had been brought as a convenience by the count, not as a fighting body, and so he had replied proudly, with credentials which he had imagined to be worth ever so much more than some cabalistic phrase, 'I am the personal butler of His Excellency Count Remigio Fabbri di San Rocco, who are you?' – only to be shot in the arm.

The count was naturally furious, and demanded to see the commander of 'certain people.' It meant being without a butler for the period of convalescence, and so none of the consolations proffered served to stem the tide of anger. Buonsignori spoke about '*le fortune della guerra*,' Old Plumes about a '*sacrifizio all'altare della gloria*,' Filigrani told the count to pull himself together, but it is not so easy to calm a man whose family have supplied a couple of popes, a dozen or so *condottieri*, and at least thirty brigands, and have splashed the pages of history with both blood and godliness.

The commander of the remnants of the Gran Sasso division was a certain Captain Val di Sarat, a Piedmontese with red hair, a short red beard, and bright blue eyes. He held out his hand to the count, but the count declined to return the gesture. Val di Sarat laughed.

The 'other people,' attracted by the noise of the butler being shot, jumped to the conclusion that a battle of considerable dimensions was about to begin, and so set in motion military operations on a large scale against an imaginary enemy.

After several hillocks had been overrun successfully against no resistance, the scampering advance guards of the 'other people' came brusquely into contact with the vigilant outposts of 'certain people,' and another series of shooting incidents was narrowly avoided by nothing less than a miracle, for the knowledge of the password, a complicated lyrical phrase by the poet Carducci, had only been roughly digested. Those who, when asked to produce the phrase, found they had forgotten it, were saved by those who, when they asked for it to be produced, had also forgotten it. In fact, any bit of poetry would have done, and anyone silly enough to come out with a sentence as pedestrian as 'I am the count's butler' fully deserved to be shot. It showed lack of imagination, a punishable offense in Italy.

When they were all sorted out, and the leaders had repaired to a derelict hut, the conference began.

The important news had come by grapevine from nobody knew quite where, but it was evidently correct. Filigrani, as chief of the *partigiani*, vouched for its authenticity. It was that Hitler had been killed that very day while attending a conference, and that German troops everywhere were mutinous.

'A government of generals has been set up,'

said Filigrani. 'Our problem, comrades, is to forget our differences and to study how best the present situation can benefit our arms. I hereby open the conference, and any suggestions are welcome.'

Then, with admirable impartiality, he turned to Elviro Robusto, his deputy at the helm of the partisan detachment, and asked him to lead off the discussion. Robusto, a one-eyed giant who had fought with the Garibaldini in Spain, began his speech, which had been carefully edited by Filigrani a couple of hours before.

'Comrades, soldiers, friends, it is my opinion as deputy commander of the partisan shock brigade that the Germans, who are now already dispirited and in a state of utter confusion throughout this, our sacred Italy, will by tomorrow morning, that is, this morning, be in no fit state to resist our onslaught, and that therefore we ought to attack them in the open with every means at our disposal, thereby crowning Italian arms with yet another glorious achievement, and forestalling the forces of the Anglo-American troops who will arrive in due time and claim that they have liberated us. Comrades, it is my belief that the region of San Rocco al Monte should and must be liberated by Italians. Forward to the common victory.'

'Colonello?' said Filigrani.

Old Plumes was a royalist. By that he didn't mean to say that he had any great affection for the reigning monarch, but rather that he had a deep respect for the sanctity of his own uniform.

'Among the dicta I learned at Caporetto, and subsequently at Vittorio Veneto, is "*Pazienza, sempre pazienza.*" "Never show your hand unless you know it yourself." "When tempted to advance, always ask yourself if it would not be prudent to retire first, and of course, vice versa,"' he said, and then he looked fixedly at both Filigrani and Val di Sarat, and there was a glow of affection about his eyes, the kind of soldierly affection so easily pushed to the point of brutality. 'When I looked at the men at our disposal,' he continued, 'there arose in my heart a wave of pride which I can only describe as paternal. You will forgive me, I am a rather older man than you.'

There was an appropriate pause of awe while Old Plumes wiped his dry eyes with a handkerchief.

'And I said to myself,' he went on, his hoarse voice quivering with an emotion which he recognized as his master, 'I said, may not through some commander's whim, may not good strong blood be spilled in vain; may not the report about the death of the archenemy Adolfo Hitler be either premature or else a piece of cunning mendacity designed to draw us into a trap? Gentlemen, gentlemen, let us be wary, wary and watchful, and when the hour strikes, then let every man be at his post! Then let us go forward, under the banners which the dead have immortalized with their sacrifices and which the living will perpetuate by their supernatural bravery!'

It was hard not to clap, but Filigrani was a little removed from life by his arid convictions. 'Count?' he said.

'I believe,' answered the count, 'that when people talk about waiting for the hour to strike, they mean in fact that it would be advisable to enter the fray when the issue is already decided. They really mean, let us wait for the hour to strike, let us allow a respectable time to elapse after it has struck, and then, with shouts of joy, let us capture the already captured.'

He silenced the outburst of criticism with a magnificent gesture.

'I speak with the authority of ten centuries of administration behind me, and am guided always by the intimate papers of Lodovico I and the political sonnets of Ermenegildo degli Occhi Bruni, an ancestor, as all of you know, on the side of my lamented mother. I can tell you that our national genius is one of reaction, not of initiative – in military matters, that is. We are a nation of individuals. In peace time, this has its advantages, in that we have given the world painters, poets, architects, mechanics, explorers, on a scale unapproached by any other nation. In time of war, however, it has its disadvantages. We still produce excellent heroes, who go to their death in one-man torpedoes, and in other desperate single operations. When we are in a

mass, however, we frankly lack excellence. Every
nation has some kind of constitutional tragedy.
Ours is the lamentable fact that when there are
many Italians together they invariably fight more
effectively against each other than they do against
the enemy. It therefore came as no surprise to me
that in an operation of characteristic brilliance my
butler should be the victim. In the light of this
achievement, I advocate even greater prudence
than does Colonello Garetta. I advocate the
immediate identification of that heroic hour
which is destined to strike with the moment
that the first Allied troops pass through the
village. Let us be as shrewd as we have been
throughout history; let us win our victory when
all chance of defeat has been removed by less
subtle allies.'

There was an outcry of pros and cons, silenced
by the count himself, who added, 'The Germans
act without thinking; we talk without acting. As
a consequence, we will win the war. Gentlemen,
in time of war it is terribly dangerous, under any
circumstances, to act.'

Captain Val di Sarat was less cautious, but then
he was less experienced. His blue eyes twinkled
as he spoke, a cherry-wood pipe held between
his teeth.

'I would agree with Signor Conte,' he said, 'if
I had a brace of popes and a platoon of *condottieri*
and a life of undisturbed peace to back me up,
but I have nothing of the sort. I spring from

the ranks of the adventurers who have graced
or blemished our history, it depends which way
you look at it, in those glorious days before we
suffered the terrible misfortune of becoming a
united nation. True to my personal tradition,
I have been a motorcycle ace, a lumberjack, a
futurist painter, a Fascist legionary, a gangster,
a society photographer and a bridge engineer,
to say nothing of the time when I practiced
as an abortionist in Shanghai. Now, I am a
soldier, living like a bandit, and determined
that I will bring the same genius into play. It
is possible, Signor Conte, as long as we don't
pretend that we are soldiers. The partisans have
already fallen into that trap, the old Italian trap
of illusory power. They have eighteen men, and
they call themselves a shock-brigade. Typical of
that damned mentality which has made us so
ridiculous in Albania and other places. Imagine,
if I were to call the twenty-one men at my
disposal the Fifty-first Italian National Army
of Liberation, or the *Divisione Giulio Cesare!*
Yes, you smile now, because I make it sound
ridiculous, but if I seriously called my little body
of men by such a name, you'd be believing it in
half an hour. Your imaginations would create a
division, a corps, an army for me, just as your
imaginations created forty million bayonets for
Mussolini. Well, let us not pretend that we are
soldiers. We are robbers, no more, no less, and
as robbers we will succeed. I was in Chicago, and

I can tell you that we made excellent robbers, the best there are, and – funny thing – we never killed unnecessarily, like the real Americans, or the Syrians, or the Mexicans, because we were sure of ourselves. I therefore am in favor of harrying operations against the Germans on an increased scale. Our aim: to rob, and to inspire a feeling of mistrust. I know these are the feelings of my men, because I have consulted them.'

At this point, Filigrani quite unnecessarily threw the debate open, with no result, as they had all volubly interrupted each other throughout.

It was about the time that Old Plumes was propounding a hideously ingenious plan which had been in his mind all along, whereby Buonsignori would signal with lanterns from his window about the activities of the Germans (a plan which Buonsignori vigorously resisted), that a motorcyclist arrived in the village and handed Hans a message.

With trembling lips, Hans announced to his two colleagues that an attempt had been made on the life of the Führer.

V

'My Warning to Helmut Bollmann has gone unheeded,' said Hans softly.

'Now we have found an excuse for all our defeats,' said Brehmig.

The prince stopped playing, and asked if this would mean the end of the war.

Hans lost his temper. 'The Führer is alive!' he shouted. 'Now suspicions will turn to facts, and the guilty will be shot. The cancer will be ripped from the body of the nation! No mercy will be shown—'

Suddenly he stopped dead, and a look of unusual cunning came into his eye.

'I knew I was wrong to let that Italian go out,' he said, and turning to Brehmig, he added, 'It was your fault that he went, and I shall not forget this.'

Brehmig calmly drained yet another glass of ferocious *grappa*, and answered, 'You are the commander, and you are responsible for all our decisions.'

The prince was at a loss to understand what was going on.

'You baffle me, all of you,' he said wearily. 'What on earth has an attempt to assassinate Adolf Hitler got to do with an Italian taking his dog for a walk?'

'Fool,' snarled Hans. 'You are supposed to be an intelligence officer and look at you. Why didn't they make you entertainment officer. Idiot.'

'I protest,' said the prince, rising energetically and placing his monocle in his eye, which made him look more surprised than ever.

'Protest! Now he protests!' jeered Hans. 'Listen, you nincompoop, the valleys are bursting with partisans—'

'One or two unprincipled men.'

'One or two unprincipled men! Bursting with them, I say. It's a nation-wide organization. And why should Buonsignori leave the house with a ridiculous excuse at one o'clock in the morning?'

'His dog—'

'His dog came back fifteen minutes after he had left, torn and bleeding. Where had he been? What could be the reason? Barbed wire? Or what? And why isn't Buonsignori back yet? And what was that shot? One of the soldiers killing rabbits?'

'A general finding the Hero's End,' said Brehmig.

'You persuaded me to take no notice of it at the time,' Hans went on, 'and I listened to you because I did not see things clearly. You said one of our patrols might have seen something suspicious. I am as much to blame as you—'

'But Buonsignori hasn't been away so very long,' said the prince. 'And why shouldn't the dog come back before its master? It knew the way.'

'Not so very long?' cried Hans, running to the windows and tearing the curtains aside. 'Look at that! It is four o'clock in the morning! Three hours!'

And indeed the landscape was bathed in the deep blue light of dawn, not yet illuminated by the faint orange streak which had formed like a feather on the horizon.

'Gracious, how time does fly when one is playing music,' said the prince.

'Put out the light,' ordered Hans.

In the eerie morning light the three officers looked at one another, and knew that something had gone wrong.

Hans crossed to the door, and called out '*Feldwebel!*' After a moment, a sleepy corporal arrived.

'Did you trace where that shot came from?'

'No, Herr Major, the patrols reported nothing untoward.'

'Call the guard, and wake up all the soldiers.'

'Now?'

'Yes, now, and stop yawning.'

'Yes, Herr Major.'

'We are going on a little expedition into the valley.'

THE NOCTURNAL meeting was breaking up. The Italians had decided nothing, but were in the best of spirits. There had been a great ventilation of the soul, and a resolution had been passed binding them to 'unceasing vigilance.'

As they were engaged in epic handshakes, one of the partisans thought he saw something move in the far-away olive groves. Old Plumes was informed, and adjusted a pair of binoculars to his straining eyes. For a moment it seemed an illusion, but then, at the intersection of the graticules, a figure appeared, creeping about cautiously.

'You have younger eyes than I have,' whispered Old Plumes, giving the binoculars to Val di Sarat.

Val di Sarat could make out a little more detail than Old Plumes, and his face broke into a mischievous smile.

'*Ragazzi*,' he said softly. 'Here is the best reason for having called the conference.'

Then a distant voice could be heard shouting '*Drei Mann durch dem Wald!*' and all doubts were dispelled.

'How subtle they think they are,' said Val di Sarat.

Old Plumes's eyes narrowed. The hour had undoubtedly, inevitably, and somewhat embarrassingly, struck; the banners were unfurled and flapping; the voice of the dead implored in an irresistible chorus.

'I will take command,' he said. 'Signor Conte, you will be chief of staff, and your valet will be headquarters runner. Buonsignori, you will be my deputy, in command of the reserve. Captain Val di Sarat, you will take the right wing. Filigrani, you will take the left wing.'

There was no argument. Solemnly, and with utter simplicity, Old Plumes embraced Val di Sarat and Filigrani, and then gave the curt order, 'Spread out. God bless our arms.'

The silence was maintained for about five minutes, interrupted only by the casual croaking of the frogs and the endless gossip of the cicadas.

Then a soldier's voice from much closer to them said, '*Junge, Junge, ist es kalt!*'

He was answered by another unseen voice, saying, '*Es ist doch blödsinnig, hier finden wir keine Partisanen.*'

'*In dieser Kälte wird doch kein Italiener aus dem Bett kriechen,*' and there was a laugh.

'It was on this very spot that Cesare Borgia and Ermenegildo degli Occhi Bruni met in mortal combat nearly five hundred years ago,' whispered the count.

'Who won?' whispered Buonsignori.

'Neither of them. That's my whole point,' whispered the count.

'Ssssh,' whispered Old Plumes.

By this time, one could almost see it growing lighter, as though nature had allowed itself the license of the theater. Old Plumes knew that contact could not be delayed much longer. Disengagement was out of the question.

His two commanders made a surprising contrast as they lay in their positions, awaiting the first shot. Filigrani, the civilian who imagined himself a soldier, wore a mask of efficient hatred on his face, while Val di Sarat, the soldier who imagined himself a highwayman, smiled with the unsophisticated abandon of a happy boy, which only faded momentarily when a rifle shot rang out on his rival's flank.

Then there was another short silence. Everyone lay still, but the dawn had now burst into early day. Hans, his face contorted with fury, fired a submachine gun at no particular target, hoping to draw the enemy fire.

'*Pazienza,*' said Filigrani to his enraged men. The silence was renewed.

Hans fired again, and this arrogance was too much for Elviro Robusto, who put his blind eye to the sights of his rifle and answered the challenge. The battle was on.

'*Vorwärts!*' shouted Hans, breaking cover, firing as he went. A handful of men followed him, but two of them rose only to fall with grotesque gestures to the ground.

'No subtlety,' growled Brehmig, watching his commander, and then ordered his men to fan out, in order to take the partisans in the flank.

Filigrani had foreseen this obvious maneuver, however, and had sent four of his calmest and most reliable men crawling through the under-growth in the depths of the valley, so that they could in their turn take the outflanking Germans in the rear.

'*Vorwärts!*' shouted Hans again, but this time he was addressing his order to the prince, who was in command of a detachment of Val di Sarat's wing and had been watching develop-ments with characteristic prudence. The prince disliked intensely the feeling of being exposed. In moments of danger, his gregarious instincts came very much to the fore, and so he gathered his men and began to converge on Hans. Val di Sarat laughed quietly as he saw the oafish Germans galloping across his front with all their bulky equipment bouncing and wriggling on their bodies.

Old Plumes had no need to issue an order. Val di Sarat knew very well what to do. Without firing a single shot, he took his men discreetly up through the olive groves, to occupy the positions the Germans had just vacated, and so cut their communications with the village.

'Go away – keep to your side!' screamed Hans,

his voice breaking in rage, but it was no use. In a trice, the prince was alongside him. Too late to argue.

'*Vorwärts!*' The Germans swept down the olive groves in desperate rushes. Old Plumes didn't like fighting uphill, but on the other hand he had the advantage of a protective embankment, while the Germans were easy targets. It was only in in-fighting that the tables would be turned. This Hans realized, and was consequently making every effort to rush the Italian line frontally.

As soon as the Germans were uncomfortably close, Old Plumes exhorted his men, and their rifles blazed away without much aim, but it was the best substitute for artillery that could be improvised on the spur of the moment. Hans came on relentlessly, at any cost. Ten of his men were dead, ten more wounded, but his leadership was by now quite unreasonable.

'Only two more groves,' he shouted, 'and then we have the swine. Not one will remain alive. *Vorwärts!*'

'*Fuoco!*' shouted Old Plumes, brandishing a revolver.

The prince fell, wounded in the ear. Then Brehmig appeared on the flank, and hand-to-hand fighting began between the Germans and the partisans.

'Hand grenades!' cried Hans.

'Val di Sarat!' yelled Old Plumes.

Filigrani's four men emerged from the bushes and took Brehmig in the rear.

'Never mind!' shouted Hans. The hand grenades flew through the air and landed among the Italians. Buonsignori, in a flaming temper, picked one up and flung it back. The majority exploded, but the firing did not die down. Old Plumes, his face streaming blood, sent six bullets flying from his revolver, killing a German, and chipping the bark of an olive tree. The count's valet threw himself on a grenade, and was blown to pieces. The count seized an abandoned rifle, and blazed away disdainfully.

Then Val di Sarat set up a murderous barrage from behind the Germans, and at close quarters. Nineteen men were aiming to kill. The other two had been dispatched to the village, and as a result ox carts were streaming away by the other road, crammed with belongings, salvaged from the houses at miraculous speed.

Hans looked round madly. '*Zurück!*' he cried, as wild tears gathered in his eyes.

The confused Germans ran along the unprotected olive groves towards Brehmig's flank, trying to disengage themselves by recrossing the road on the crest of the hill, and so get back to the village. Val di Sarat's men accompanied them on a higher level, and accounted for five more victims.

Of fifty-five Germans, there were now only eleven left, including Hans and Brehmig. As

they staggered across the main road to the
north, Val di Sarat could see a distant cloud
of traveling smoke.

'Retreat!' he shouted into the valley. 'They are
bringing up armored cars! Take the wounded and
what prisoners you can! Don't get flustered, we
will cover your movement! Kindly signify that
you have heard me!'

Old Plumes had fainted from his wounds,
so the count cried out, 'We have heard you
and thank you for your information. It will be
acted upon!'

'And establish contact with the civilian refugees!' shouted Val di Sarat.

'Indeed!' shouted the count.

Hans heard the brazen voices, and retarded his
retreat. He walked back onto the road, slowly,
palely, and overwhelmingly insulted.

'Where is the major?' asked Brehmig.

'Look, over there!' gasped a German soldier.

Val di Sarat turned round to find Hans facing
him across the road, and smiled.

'Retire!' he called to his men. They obeyed
him reluctantly.

Hans aimed his revolver at Val di Sarat, fired
and missed.

Val di Sarat laughed loudly. 'So Your Excellency has romantic notions of single combat?'
he said. 'Very well, an Italian soldier will not
be proved wanting when it is necessary to teach

an ally a lesson.' So saying, he drew his revolver, and shot Hans's cap from his head.

'Your turn,' he laughed.

Hans fired again, his aim blinded by his tears. He missed.

'I wish you to pick up your cap,' said Val di Sarat. 'Protocol insists that a soldier must be properly dressed.'

Stiffly, Hans bent over to pick up his cap. No sooner had he adjusted it than Val di Sarat shot it off again. Enraged, Hans emptied his revolver at the form before him, and then said, 'You bastard, shoot me.'

'No,' answered Val di Sarat, with a twinkle, 'but I should like to keep your cap as a souvenir.'

Mortally offended, Hans stooped to pick it up, only to have it shot out of his hand.

'Try again, next time you may be lucky,' said Val di Sarat.

Unable to bear the humiliation, Hans turned and threw himself down on the ground, beyond speech, beyond thought.

As the first German armored car turned the distant corner into the long stretch leading to the village, Val di Sarat bounded across the road, seized the cap, and vanished into the valley. In the comparative safety of the woods, he examined his trophy, and saw, written inside, 'Winterschild, Hans, Major.'

'What was their commander like?' asked Old

Plumes, as he lay on an improvised bed. He was keen to know what manner of man he had defeated.

'He never stopped blinking his right eye,' answered Val di Sarat.

GENERAL GRUTZE emerged like a figurehead from the turret of the leading armored car. He halted the column by a gesture of his gloved hand and raised his goggles to his forehead to examine with greater precision a sight he could scarcely believe. German troops were climbing painfully up through the olive groves. Here a wounded man was being helped by a colleague, there a private was seated in an attitude of dejection on a kilometer-post, one bare foot hanging limply from a trouser leg held high off the ground. No one made any effort to acknowledge the presence of a general. Grutze looked round to find an officer. Brehmig reached the road just as the general was clambering from his turret.

'Captain!'

Brehmig was shivering slightly.

'Captain, are you in charge?'

'I don't know, Herr General.'

'You don't know?'

Habitually Grutze would have begun ranting at such an unsoldierly reply and yet now he was disconcertingly calm. It was vaguely unnerving. Brehmig broke the silence.

'We had some casualties. Killed. Damned Italians.'

Grutze nodded slightly, but looked away into the olive groves.

'Winterschild!'

Hans heard his name, but didn't react.

'Winterschild!'

It was Grutze's voice. Hans still didn't react, but in the absence of a coherent mind, his training took over and he began stumbling up the hill, climbing over the walls of gray stone as best he could. Grutze smiled at him like a father when at last he reached the road, and returned his salute, with an economy of gesture reserved for those in high authority. It was unbelievable, sobering. The general even produced a small silver flask, and some little goblets which fitted over each other like thimbles.

'Here, I will drink a little cognac with my officers.'

Time was being lost. Hans pulled himself together.

'Do you wish me to pursue the partisans?' he stuttered.

'There is no hurry,' Grutze replied.

It had to be sarcasm, especially spoken before a squadron of armored cars with idle guns.

'I will go alone, if necessary, if you order it,' Hans suddenly cried.

'Where to?' asked Grutze.

'In pursuit of the partisans.' Surely he had no

need to explain. Or had the general taken leave of his senses? In the army, it is safer to understand no nuances, to take everything at its face value, and explain the obvious as though it were original.

'Fill them up. We must finish the flask. Prosit!'

When a field officer is concerned with his men's good health, it is no time to argue.

'Prosit, Herr General,' said Hans.

'Prosit,' said Brehmig.

The soldiers were frowning.

'It is good cognac, don't you think?' asked Grutze. 'In all respects I find German cognac equal, if not superior, to the French.'

'I'm no expert,' said Hans.

'In any case they're both better than the Italian *grappa*,' Brehmig remarked. Grutze laughed heartily, and filled the goblets, for the last time, attempting to be meticulously equitable with the final drops.

'To our victory!' Hans proposed, seeking to bring the conversation back along more traditional lines.

'To our victory?'

'To our victory!'

Grutze closed the flask, stacked the goblets and placed all the objects carefully in their leather container.

'May I make an observation, Herr General?' Hans asked.

'By all means.'

'There is still time to catch the partisans. They mauled us in a manner which . . . which cries out for revenge.'

'Who are our enemies?' Grutze asked. 'The partisans or the Italians?'

'I don't understand, Herr General.'

Grutze spoke slowly and meticulously.

'Under the German occupation of Europe,' he said, 'we have shown as much clemency for the uniformed soldiers of the defeated as we have shown ruthlessness for those who oppose us in civilian guise. The strength of partisans is that they vanish without trace into the population after they have done their dirty work; their weakness is that they expose the entire population to danger by their recklessness. Once they use the protection of civilian clothes, are we to be blamed for automatically assuming that every civilian is a partisan? I asked you who our enemy is, the partisans or the Italians? The answer is immaterial. For our purposes the partisans and the Italians are from now on one and the same thing.'

'Surely all the more reason for chasing them,' said Hans, whose cheeks were burning with the brandy.

'You keep looking into the valley to find your enemy. He won't run away. He's here. There's no hurry.'

'Where?'

'Here.' Grutze pointed at the village. And

he borrowed a submachine gun from one of his men.

'See who's the best shot,' he said, and fired a burst near an earthenware pot on a balcony. 'I am aiming at the neck of that pot. Your turn.'

Hans was given a gun. He fired and missed. Brehmig fired, and destroyed the pot.

'A little low,' cried Grutze, 'but you were the best of us three.'

An albino cat ran out into the street. Grutze laughed, and fired round the cat, which darted hither and thither. The men joined in the laughter, as the antics of the cat were amusing. It crawled into a grating.

'It was too quick for us.' Grutze took his defeat in good part. A woman appeared briefly at a window. There was more laughter.

'Together!' cried Grutze.

A triple burst shattered the window. There was more laughter.

'That'll teach you to be nosy, mother,' a soldier cried. The general smiled appreciatively. The quality of folksy humor was a yardstick of morale. There was no doubt in any mind what they were here to do. This was just the badinage which preceded the act. As with love, so destruction needs careful psychological preparation. A drink or two, in intimacy. Then a slap, a tickle, a fondling of the senses. Then, the heightening rhythm of the act itself.

After a moment of silence as solemn as that

which proceeds the first endless exploratory kiss, a silence in which nothing moves but the eyes, Grutze called out, 'In parade step, forwards!'

The three officers advanced at a slow march as one man, followed, as though on some grotesque hunt, by soldiers with reloaded guns. Grutze cried out the tempo as they fired, and as they fired so the step grew quicker, in spite of itself. He could no longer call, the act had its own pulse, it was each man to himself, to his own delirium, linked to the others only by a sense of his part in the orgiastic rite. Faster, faster on the road to exhaustion, the bullets spattered wastefully from the red-hot barrel of each steel phallus.

AN HOUR later, smoke could be seen rising from the village.

Val di Sarat frowned. 'It was only to be expected,' he said.

'My dog,' said Old Plumes.

Then the sentry saw a little white-clad figure running desperately through the forest, stumbling, appearing and reappearing, terrified. He kept silent until he saw that it was a boy, and then he called to him. The boy, wide-eyed with terror, fell into the arms of the sentry, and wept his heart out. When he had calmed down, they took the boy to Old Plumes, who said, 'Why, it's Cavaleschi's boy, the blacksmith . . .'

The boy told a dreadful story.

A dog, one of Folgore's vast family, had been

the first to perish. It had dropped like a sack, and
the sand around it had become red. Then Signor
Biati's grandmother, who was too old to move,
had been shot in her rocking chair. Then a baby,
which had given itself away by crying fitfully in
an attic, had been silenced. Signor Tommani,
who ran the post office, and who had refused
to leave with the others, came grimly to meet
the Germans, a primitive shotgun in his arm.
'*Evviva l'Italia!*' he had shouted as he died in
the roadway, riddled with bullets. Dr Zuoli, the
physician, had been crushed by his horse as he
tried to gallop away. The Germans had shot the
larger target. There must have been other deaths,
according to the little boy, as the machine guns
were stuttering almost continually while he ran
away. Behind the officers, the soldiers, weary and
dispirited, had begun their systematic arson in
obedience to orders, hence the pillars of smoke
which were beginning to build Greek temples in
the air above San Rocco.

'Describe the officers,' said Old Plumes, with
a feeble attempt at military bearing, but the little
boy relapsed into a nervous fit when Signora
Cavaleschi, his mother, came running from the civilian encampment among the trees, and reclaiming
her child, almost smothered him in her welcoming breast, uttering mingled consolations
and imprecations, scolding him for being so
nearly dead.

Later on, in the midday heat, two rough men

came through the woods and were halted by the sentries. They muttered a prearranged phrase, and were brought in to Old Plumes.

'Are you the commander?' the elder of the two asked.

'I am Colonello Galeazzo Garetta, President of the Consiglio Superiore della Guerra di San Rocco al Monte,' said Old Plumes.

The two newcomers saluted. The elder spoke. 'I am Andrea Deodato, member and delegate of the Comitato della Liberazione di Castelbravo degli Angeli.'

The two men shook hands.

'But Castelbravo degli Angeli is nearly thirty kilometers away,' said Old Plumes.

'We are arranging to disperse the population of San Rocco al Monte over ten or fifteen villages, as far away from here as we can manage. Your action was heroic, but regrettably premature,' explained Deodato.

Old Plumes was, not unnaturally, extremely annoyed at this criticism, and insisted that all the other secret fighting organizations had lamentably missed the bus.

The other delegate, a partisan called Scala, from the Divisione Partigiana del Val d'Arno, had gone straight to Filigrani. The two men had exchanged the clenched-fist salute, and were now talking animatedly.

Soon a plan was fixed, and the movement arranged for the twilight. In case the Germans should attempt any mopping-up operations among the twisting byways of the Tuscan countryside before the time set for the evacuation, a detachment of neighboring partisans was infiltrating into the region, prepared, in an emergency, to cover the withdrawal with fire. But there was little chance of trouble. There are few landscapes more sensible to the needs of their inhabitants than the grandiose Apennines, composed of so many strange and intimate compartments, volcanic undulations intermingled with sudden valleys jealous of their secrets.

There was little left to do before nightfall, apart from the burying of the single partisan, a badly wounded man who had died about ten o'clock, quietly and decently, surrounded by his family. With a proper sense of occasion, Old Plumes invited the two representatives of other patriotic organizations to be present at the ceremony.

'You will be witnesses on behalf of Italy,' he said.

The grave was dug, and the body lowered into it. The family had wept so greatly that they had no tears left, and just stood, like a little cluster of ghosts, at their breadwinner's vanishing feet.

'Luigi Guicciardini is a name which is known to us,' said Old Plumes, with an indescribable dignity, 'and it is a name which we will never forget. We must condole with his family, and with them deplore his evil fortune, because, my friends, the lifeless body which all of us

have just seen for the last time might, but
for the direction of a bullet, have been that
of Giosuè Filigrani, of Febo Buonsignori, of
Signor Conte, of any one of us here. Death
unites all classes. To death, there is no wealth,
no intellect, and no nobility. Identity is lost
for ever. We remember Luigi Guicciardini as
a smiling face, as a manner of speaking, as a
personality. The corpse we have just buried was,
in that sense, not Luigi Guicciardini at all, but
a convenient symbol which, I repeat, any one of
us here could have furnished. My friends, San
Rocco al Monte has found its unknown soldier.
May he rest in peace.'

After a short prayer, the gathering dispersed,
and the two delegates gravely took their leave.

The Germans did not do much more that
day than send a couple of fighting patrols out
into the unknown beyond the battlefield, both
of which terrorized the innocent farmers of the
neighborhood, stealing a bit, shooting a bit, and
then losing their bearings among the treacherous
hillocks, and returning to base much later than
they were expected.

They buried their dead without ceremony, sent
Hans to hospital, and left the burning village
when the flames became too hot.

At five o'clock in the afternoon, a German
artillery-spotter plane flew low over the countryside, but saw nothing among the trees. Old
Plumes decided that the dispersal would begin

at seven-thirty, or rather at 1930, as he liked to call it.

At about seven, Val di Sarat strolled about the encampment as though looking for something. He stumbled over the recumbent form of the prince, who was the only prisoner of war the patriots had taken, and apologized. The prince, convinced for the thousandth time that he was about to be shot, began hysterically to stammer his loathing of the Nazi regime.

'I'd give you a cigarette if I had one,' laughed Val di Sarat, while the prince moaned his relief.

Eventually Val di Sarat spotted the young Cavaleschi boy, playing among the trees, and joined him in his childish make-believe. He was fighting a battle of epic proportions with twigs, and imitating the brash sounds of the cannonades as he systematically destroyed both armies in his imagination. With the resilience of his age, he had already superficially forgotten the horrors of a few hours ago, and was translating his experiences into a romance.

Val di Sarat was good with children. He first pretended to be a tank, but this impersonation found no place in the symmetry of the child's fantasy, so he abandoned that and contented himself by breaking up more twigs for the battle. After he had thoroughly ingratiated himself with the child, he knelt down and grasped his little friend rather roughly round the waist.

'So you are a soldier like me, *bimbo*,' he said.

'Yes,' admitted the child.

'Hm. Then can you tell me as one soldier to another, what did the three enemies in the village look like?'

The boy, reminded and alarmed, looked as though he might cry.

'Soldiers are forbidden to cry,' said Val di Sarat sternly.

'I don't remember,' said the boy.

'Soldiers are forbidden to forget.'

'One was small and fat.'

'*Bravo*, you shall have a medal for that information.' Val di Sarat was smiling, as usual. 'And the others, what did they look like?'

'One didn't look like anybody I know,' said the child.

'*Bravo*, another medal. And the third?'

'The third, he was the one who shot most.'

'Yes, and what did he look like?'

'I didn't like him.'

'Why not?'

'He never stopped blinking.'

And for the first time all trace of humor drained out of Val di Sarat's face.

VI

THE STORY of San Rocco al Monte soon became
known as an example of the Italian capacity for
martyrdom in comprehensible and fundamental
causes. It was only when the reason for death was
tinged with doubt, only when the cessation of life
seemed even in the minutest degree unnecessary,
that the Italians preferred surrender, and the
hazardous joys of survival. It would be unfair
to their inherent bravery to say that they cling
desperately to life; fairer to say that life clings
desperately, and lovingly, to them.

Old Plumes regarded the ruin of the thirteenth-
century village as an unavoidable evil of war,
and had none of the squeamish sorrow of the
art historian. 'It might have happened before;
it might have happened later,' he said. 'It is,
however, our destiny that it happened in our

time, and that we had at our disposal a worthy sacrifice to burn on the altar of liberty.'

'Did you fight yesterday for liberty, as Old Plumes has said he did?' asked Val di Sarat of the count, 'or did you fight because you find joy in battle, as I do?'

'I fought,' said the count, 'for my lands, just as Ermenegildo degli Occhi Bruni fought for them centuries ago, and like him, I have temporarily lost them. Never mind, I am undefeated. I still have castles farther north. And, my friend, I take leave to say that while most of our dead gave their lives for Italy, for their humble homes, my valet gave his life for me, and my butler, when he received his wound, asked my permission to retire temporarily from the battle. That is true nobility.'

'It is servility of the most odious variety,' said Filigrani suddenly.

'*Ragazzi*, we have a long period of peace to come after the defeat of the Germans,' declared Old Plumes. 'Let us keep our private war until then, otherwise it will mean fighting on several fronts at once, which is military and moral folly.'

THE NEXT day, the Germans, bringing up every available man, embarked on a punitive expedition, which found nothing except the remains of the encampment. They retired to their base as the distance was already reverberating with the thunder of artillery. Meanwhile, in the narrow vestibule of a small mountain church, about twenty-five kilometers to the west, Val di Sarat sat with the prince, and chatted amicably.

'If you do not answer my questions satisfactorily, I will have no alternative but to take you out and shoot you,' he said.

The prince had so often thought that his fate would inevitably be the firing squad that it was almost a relief to hear the dreadful threat pronounced, quietly and unemotionally. Now there was some basis for discussion.

'You would not shoot me in a church,' he heard himself saying.

'No, I would take you out,' answered Val di Sarat, 'although all sense of values has really been destroyed in these matters. Your soldiers have burned down the church of San Rocco, so it is a little ridiculous for you to suggest that your death in here would be particularly sacrilegious. After all,' he said, indicating the flagstones of the nave, 'you would be in good company. There are four or five dead here already.'

The prince thought the joke in bad taste, and said so. Val di Sarat expressed the opinion that the whole war was in pretty bad taste, and that he personally was not vain enough to believe that he could elevate its tone by a single honorable act.

'Such as?' asked the prince.

'Such as shooting you a decent way away from the church,' answered Val di Sarat.

'What do you want from me?' said the prince, chilled by this levity.

'The identity of your regiment.'

'108th Infantry Regiment, Wehrkreis Darmstadt.'

Val di Sarat took notes. 'Now about this fellow Winterschild.'

'How do you know his name?'

Val di Sarat told of his tourney, spicing the tale with permissible embroidery.

'Then there is no need to tell you that he is a fanatical Nazi,' said the prince.

'Or a fanatical German?'

'You do not offend me by saying that. I am Austrian, and a mortal enemy of the Prussian mentality. Winterschild is about twenty-four years old, comes, I believe, from Langensalza in Thuringia, is a highly nervous character – I don't know much more about him, except that he said once, I remember, that as a young fellow who had just undergone his baptism of fire, he had been forced to rape a girl in a village.'

'Forced to?' laughed Val di Sarat. 'How? By *esprit de corps*?'

The prince looked pained.

'I beg your pardon for another lapse of taste,' said Val di Sarat, trying to look grave. 'Do go on.'

'He told me about this incident,' said the prince, 'and told me how much his own behavior had disgusted him, later on, although at the time it had uplifted him. It was really rather tragic, if anything is tragic any more in these days. He said – and I am sure he was quite sincere – that he would never marry as a consequence. He felt, in a sense, unclean – paradoxically, there is an absurdly moral, even puritanical, side to this kind of man. But, with all his puritanism, he is still, first and foremost, a soldier. I remember him jokingly saying that love for him would have to be something he could buy.'

'Jokingly?'

'Yes, but it wasn't a joke.'

Val di Sarat made some more notes, and remarked, in an unusually quiet and sympathetic voice, 'You're quite right, it is rather tragic. For an Italian, very tragic. Now tell me the names of the other officers.'

'There was only one, Brehmig.'

'And how does he look?'

'Impossible to describe. Completely insignificant.'

'No particular distinguishing marks?'

'None.'

It was useless to continue the interrogation, because the count had arrived, looking more noble than ever now that he was dressed as a humble peasant. He had heard that the captive was an Austrian prince, and was dying to know what had happened to Elly von Balinsky, who was going to marry Count Elfensiedel in 1938,

but didn't, and how the Czaparcitch family had
resolved their little morganatic troubles with the
royal house of you-know-where, and wasn't Bidi
de Hoszonyi-Hoszvos far too intelligent and
wasn't she unfortunate to inherit her mother's
torso. Aristocracy, like death, recognizes no frontiers.

WHEN COLONEL Winterschild opened a letter,
and began reading '*Dear Papa, if I should ever
shoot myself . . .,*' he put it away, and relit his
pipe by plunging the crumpled envelope into
the fire.

'Why don't you use a match?' asked Frau
Winterschild, when she saw the charred pieces
of paper floating onto the floor, dislodged by her
husband's puffing.

'Absent-minded,' replied the colonel.

'I thought that was a letter from Hansi you
had received.'

'So did I, but it wasn't.'

'Who is it from?'

'What? You wouldn't know him . . . man
called . . . Enzinger . . . used to be . . . well, my
orderly . . .' And, so saying, the colonel went to
the bathroom, and locked himself in.

Dear Papa, if I should ever shoot myself,
you would know that such a desperate
act was forced on me by circumstances
beyond my control. Once again Germany

lies bleeding, betrayed by her weaker sons and daughters. Now nobody can tell what the end will be. All is black. I long for you and Mutti, to tell you — and yet it is not manly to complain. There comes a time when the bullet is the only language heart and brain can understand. Servitude does not interest me. You, dear Papa, have taught me to be proud. We are alone, as we always have been alone, against the world, which I have grown to hate. It is the idea I am willing to die for. The people here do not share my view, and I can only despise them. If only all Germans had the courage of the Führer's convictions! Ah, but what's the use? It is too late. Now only personal honor remains. There, I shall not be found lacking. I, like you, dearest Papa, am only interested in what lies beyond mere duty. So long as we have this belief, then not even death can part us. Remember me.

The paper had been crumpled on arrival. Hans had even forgotten to sign his name. There were no loving greetings to his mother. This was a farewell between men, and women would weep later. The colonel went slowly into the garden, and hid the letter under the earth of a plant.

'What are you doing out there in the freezing

cold?' shouted Frau Winterschild from a window.

'Coming, dear,' called the colonel, and thought, '*Ach*, women, how little they understand.'

HANS WAS released from hospital after two days of 'observation,' during which time he never saw a doctor, except for the old fellow who came along on the second day, and said, 'You're leaving us, old man. I'm sorry, but we need this bed for a hopeless case. In these days, I'm afraid nobody's ill. You are either alive or dead.'

It was clear by now to General Wonniger that the Allies were exerting every effort to reach Florence, and to save that historic city by the very speed of their advance. Consequently, he threw the 108th Regiment into the town, having learned in Russia exactly how much easier built-up areas are to defend than open country. He tried to delay as long as possible the decision to blow up the famous bridges, because he was a person who understood that men are replaceable, but the fruits of their occasional genius, never. As luck would have it, he was saved from having to make the decision by the fact that on the eve of the battle he was arrested for complicity in the attempt on Hitler's life, and was never seen again. The command now passed to the odious Grutze, who was promoted to Lieutenant General by the personal intervention of the Führer, and who determined to destroy everything he could see in gratitude. On the 24th, the Hitler salute became obligatory for the German Army. Ten days later, the battle for Florence was to open.

There was a nightclub in Florence called the *Uccello Rosso*, the Red Bird, as drear as all its competitors, the world over. This club was, at the time, the favorite haunt of German officers. The barman had obediently learned the language of the occupation, which pained him by its dissonance, but he registered nothing except patience and resignation. Occasionally he would exchange a hooded, secret glance with one of the hostesses, who sat at empty tables looking prematurely old and depressingly hopeful. It was during the lull before the fighting for the city began that Hans was dragged there by Brehmig.

'What is really wrong with you,' Brehmig had said, 'is that you need a woman. Look at you, you're becoming as hysterical as an old spinster. One minute you're shouting about victory, and the next you're sniveling like a little girl. That sort of behavior has its roots in only one trouble.'

They wandered to the bar, greeting one or two of their officer acquaintances with the new salute. The officers dutifully interrupted their petting in order to reply, and the hostesses tried hard not to giggle.

'Look over there,' said Brehmig, after they had ordered their drinks and had exchanged a few stereotyped wisecracks with the barman. The object of his scrutiny, a large lady stripped off an opulent Tintoretto canvas, was preening herself, conscious of the two newcomers. The barman shrugged at her behind their backs. He had not made up his mind about them.

'She has dyed her hair,' said Hans.

'Good heavens, since when are we so particular?' laughed Brehmig. 'I suppose you prefer that undisguised Levantine sitting over there?'

'I don't like any of them very much,' said Hans, but he was lying, because he had caught sight of a girl who, exceptionally, was making no effort to claim his attention. She was not very tall, in fact not particularly striking in any way, but she was remarkable for her attitude, which was at once pensive and resentful.

A frighteningly squat lady peeped through some curtains, and smiled at the two officers in a manner reminiscent of the more repellent Chinese porcelain effigies.

'Do the gentlemen have any particular type of lady they prefer?' she enquired.

Brehmig teased her, but she was impervious to anything but flattery, and accepted the implied insults at their face value, rolling her eyes with incredulity and pleasure.

'Nevertheless, let us look further afield,' said Brehmig.

Disappointed, but devoted to the business she had so painstakingly built up, she pointed at the artificial blonde, who smiled aggressively.

'Rosanna is a Venetian,' she said, 'and there

is no need to tell you gentlemen, who are so
well versed in history, that Casanova was a
Venetian. Luisa, over there' – and she pointed
at the woman whom Brehmig had referred to
as the Levantine – 'Luisa is a Neapolitan, and it
is known throughout Italy that the Neapolitans
are notorious for their passion. Carlotta, over
there, behind the column, you can just see the
back of her head, Carlotta is a Roman. Rome is,
to the rest of Italy, celebrated for its decadence
and its venality. Marta, who was here a minute
ago, and who will be back any second, is from
Milan, a blonde girl from the north, very partial
to homesick officers.'

Then they all looked at the solitary figure in
the corner.

The procuress immediately lost her temper,
and advanced on the wretched girl. A scene
ensued, which ended as quickly as it had begun
when Hans sat down by her side. The procuress
lifted her eyes to the sky, for she was deeply
religious at times, and went back to stimulate
Brehmig's imagination.

The girl and Hans sat in silence for a while.
'Why, in God's name, did you pick on me?' said
the girl at length.

Hans, who had mastered pidgin Italian, as
well as most foreign soldiers did, asked her
her name.

'Teresa.'

'My name is Hans.'

'I didn't ask you.'

Hans looked at her closely. She was undoubtedly a very curious girl, not by virtue of the mask, but of the torment beneath. A small, very delicate face it was, with a fine little nose, both pretty and arrogant. The lips were full, the cheek soft and young, and the hair, brown with a tinge of red, hung down in a sweet disorder. The impression of pastoral innocence was, however, belied by the eyes, which were as large and dark as chestnuts. They had about them the fervor of revolution.

'What are you so angry about?' asked Hans.

She didn't answer. Hans felt like giving it up until he saw the terrible neckless harridan just waiting for the moment to deliver the *coup de grâce*. This time Teresa broke the silence.

'Why don't you go?' she said.

'Because I intend to stay,' answered Hans.

'Funny.' She laughed, emptily, and then looked at him for the first time. A searching look, full of misgiving.

'D'you want to go to bed?'

'I suppose so,' said Hans, feeling a little foolish.

'Then why don't you go with one of the others? I'm not your type. I'm not the German officer type.'

'I'm quite capable of forming my own opinions,' replied Hans stiffly, because he objected to an institution as august as the German officer caste being categorized.

Teresa laughed, to the exasperation of the procuress, who began muttering audibly. Hans now became stubborn. He was determined to see this thing through.

'You may as well resign yourself to the fact that I am staying here,' he said, 'and you had better tell me the usual ritual in these places. I am unacquainted with it.'

She looked at him bitterly, and said, 'First you buy me the most expensive drink in the place. Then, when I've drunk it, you buy me another. And then another. Then I ask a friend over, and we drink some more. Then I have a sandwich, for which you are grossly overcharged. Then I drink some more. Then a girl comes over with some flowers. I look coy, and you buy me one. Then I drink some more, and – if I'm drunk enough by then, we shall see.'

'We will not see anything,' said Hans sharply. 'I am not easily cheated, and if I am going to be forced to give you a whole lot of things you don't really want, and which I don't really want to give you, then I shall regard it as an investment, and you can resign yourself to that as well.'

'Why do you always blink?' asked Teresa.

'Because I have been fighting since 1941, practically without leave.'

'And that makes a man blink?'

She was trying to be deliberately infuriating, and for a moment Hans wished he were in Brehmig's shoes. Brehmig was now seated at another table, laughing and joking with the ample Venetian; kisses were being exchanged, stories told. For a moment, Brehmig caught Hans's eye, and pulled a long face, as if to say, 'You silly fool, always taking the more difficult road.'

'She's pretty, isn't she?' said Teresa.

'Divine,' said Hans, acidly.

Teresa laughed again.

The barman arrived.

'Can I have a bottle of the most expensive champagne,' asked Hans, 'and a couple of sandwiches and a corsage, I'm in rather a hurry.'

'Two bottles of champagne,' said Teresa.

'Three bottles of champagne,' said Hans, 'and a glass of milk for me.'

'One bottle of champagne,' said Teresa.

The barman went away, shrugging his shoulders as always.

'May I tell you something very personal?' asked Hans.

'There is nothing personal you can tell me,' she said, softly, 'because I am a creature without personality. I am a convenience for homesick soldiers.'

Who had put such complicated ideas into her head? She had said the words as though she had learned them.

'How old are you?' asked Hans.

'Twenty-seven.'

'Nonsense.'

'Well, then, don't ask me. A lady doesn't readily give her age.'

'You're nineteen.'

'Thank you.' She pretended to be coy.

The champagne arrived, and when the cork was extracted, a little gasp of exasperation was all that was forthcoming from the neck of the bottle. The liquid was flat and sweet, and the sandwiches were a travesty, each composed of two stale slices of bread enclosing a moribund lettuce leaf, while the corsage was a weary flower bristling with unnecessary pins, which Teresa returned to the barman once Hans had paid for it.

Over the way, Brchmig began singing old German folk songs with soldiers' words, which the Venetian attempted to harmonize. Other German officers helped her out from various parts of the room.

As Hans sat and looked glumly at the too familiar scene, Teresa spoke to him in a much quieter voice than ever before.

'You are different from the others,' she said.

This time Hans did not reply.

Teresa drained her glass without enjoyment, took Hans by the arm, and said, 'Shall we go?'

Hans was pleased to leave the place at any cost, but as he rose he was the automatic butt of coarse jests from Brchmig and the others, who had joined forces and were well on the way to a joyless orgy.

Hans helped Teresa with a sparse fur coat, and they went out. The night was very light, and infused with a latent excitement. The sky was occasionally lit brilliantly by stabs of summer lightning, and now and then the distant burble of artillery broke the unearthly stillness in the shadow of the Duomo. As they crossed the square, they could hear their footsteps too, echoing and re-echoing against the marble façade. A soldier thought to challenge them, but when he saw that they were only an officer and a lady, he passed back to his lonely reverie.

Their walk took them past a row of stern, great statues, petrified in unending and withering criticism of the specks of flesh and blood whose heads passed so unheeding on a level with their cold stone toes. Hans took no notice of the wind-swept critics. He was too wrapped up in a strange turbulence which had assailed him. Teresa took no notice either. She knew them too well, and they were just landmarks to her.

They passed into narrower byways, and left the statues to their nocturnal colloquy, unheeded and majestic, symbols of a city which stood aloof from the petty ebb and flow of mortal conquest, and which had given men, as souvenirs, greater things by far than feats of arms.

Before a dingy doorway, Teresa stopped, and fumbled for a key.

'Do you really want to go in yet?' asked Hans, suddenly.

'Of course,' said Teresa, 'it's very cold out here.'

It wasn't.

They climbed a creaking staircase until they came to a room which gave onto a little balcony. The room was sparsely furnished, and smelled of the oil used in cooking. The floor, which was made up of tiles in a quasi-Moorish pattern, deflected the light of the moon, and seemed to glisten like still water.

'Don't put on the light,' said Hans.

'Why on earth not?' asked Teresa, crossing the room by instinct, and pulling the curtains.

'I'd rather you didn't.'

'There,' said Teresa, switching on the naked bulb, which hung on an improvised string over the cracked sink.

'Why do you always do the opposite of what I ask you?'

'I'm independent.' Teresa began to unbutton her dress.

'What are you doing now?' said Hans.

'If you don't keep me too long I can go back to the club, and probably drink some more champagne with another officer,' she said. She took her dress off.

'But you haven't asked me for any money yet.'

'Who knows, I may not ask you for any,' she replied, and kicked off her shoes.

'I don't understand you at all,' he confessed.

'I don't understand myself,' she said lightly.
'I just go through the motions of living, like a
machine.'

'But do you enjoy that?'

'I should be blinking by now, like you, shouldn't
I?' By now she had removed her blouse.

Hans rose abruptly. He felt no desire.

'Please don't talk like that, and please don't
undress,' he said, sharply.

'You are a strange fellow.' She looked at him
without surprise, and then undid her brassière.

Half naked, she looked more like a child than
a woman. Supported by a very thin white neck,
narrow little shoulders, and a modest, undevel-
oped body, her grave face lost its authority
She suddenly appeared a helpless waif. Hans
looked at her for a moment with a kind of
pity, and then, as she began to discard her
final garments, he went furiously to the light
and turned it off.

There was a pause in the pitch darkness, and
then she spoke in a voice choked with fear.

'What sort of man are you? You're not a
murderer?'

Hans didn't answer. It was a cruel revenge,
but she deserved it. No woman – woman? – girl
had a right to torment a man like that, to be so
deliberately insubordinate.

She listened hard for the approach of stealthy
footsteps, and then said in a frightened little
whisper, 'I'm sixteen.'

'I believe you,' said Hans.

'I swear it's true,' she cried.

'I've just told you that I believe you,' said Hans. 'You're so used to lies, you don't trust any straightforward remark.'

'What are you going to do to me?'

'Nothing.'

'Then please put the light on.'

'No.'

'I said please.'

'I heard you.'

'I shall scream.'

'I shall prevent you.'

Hans threw open the curtains and the window, and turning saw her prudishly covering her nakedness with her coat. She had lost her composure.

'Come here,' he said, 'and don't be afraid.'

She was shivering with fright.

'You'll throw me out of the window,' she stuttered. Hans laughed lightly.

'Don't be silly,' he said. 'Up to a minute ago I was frightened of you.'

Timidly she came towards him, her bare feet patting the tiles. He took her by the shoulders, and looked into her face, turned to pale blue by the moon.

'Yes, you're sixteen,' he said softly, 'and I am twenty-four. But you're lucky. You look sixteen. I look thirty, don't I?'

'I can't see you without the light on.'

Hans laughed. 'You certainly stick to your guns. Cunning as they make them.'

'I'm cold,' she said.

'Then put your clothes on.'

'But what are we going to do? Shall we go back to the club for another drink?'

'No.' Hans turned her towards the landscape, towards the tops of the sleeping houses. 'Look at what you shut out because you were so eager to return to your trade,' he said. 'I bet you never look at it properly, even during the day.'

'What?' she asked.

Hans taxed his untrained imagination to the uttermost as he searched the undemonstrative serenity for a few words of poetry.

'Over there, the mountains are losing them-selves in the clouds; the flashes of light, that's their artillery; the stars twinkling up above; the moon—'

'Please don't be romantic,' she interrupted, deeply distressed.

Hans thought for a moment, but prevented her from turning away from the panorama.

'He was killed, I suppose,' he said at length. She moaned gently. 'He was a soldier, I suppose, a pawn in this gigantic game of chess, like I am, and he too had killed, as I have.'

She pulled at his lapels in an effort not to break down.

'I have killed because that is what I was told to do,' Hans went on with gathering agitation.

'You are clinging to a man who has done his duty, Teresa, by committing murder, endlessly, endlessly, for five years, and by causing the hearts of those he has never seen to break!'

A part of him was staggered to hear such words being uttered by a German officer, who had always despised the emotions as an embarrassment to grandiose ideals, but the words continued to fall from his lips in an ordered profusion, as though he had had them in his mind for years.

'Do you know what I have done?' he said, in an impassioned voice. 'I have been guilty of rape, of arson, of plunder, of looting as well as of murder. In Russia, Holland, Yugoslavia, as well as Italy. And the terrible thing, Teresa, is that I was not alone. I was not even the worst. It was a habit. A habit!'

Then he grew calmer. It was the lofty, the epic side of his nature which reclaimed his attention.

'And because of a whim, a matter of a moment, you have changed your life, and have locked all this glory from your vision. This calm infinity which seems to say "Nothing matters. You do not travel forwards. You do not travel backwards. Rush hither and thither as you will, you are standing still, and awaiting our pleasure."'

As Hans uttered all the complicated words of his tirade in German, she didn't understand everything, but all the same, a Tristanesque monologue was not exactly what she had bargained for, and now she was both miserable and mystified.

'Take me back to the club,' she said.

'Who was he?'

'No, no, please not.'

Hans was adamant. Confessions, sorrows, defeats, victories, successes, errors, had to be on a vast, and therefore honorable scale. There was no room for annoyance, it had to be fury. There was no room for little dramas, they had to be tragic. There was no room for pleasure, it had to be ecstasy.

'Where was he killed?'

'No, no, no, no!' screamed Teresa, throwing herself on the bed in an uncontrollable paroxysm. Her thin back rose and fell with the rhythm of her unrestrained weeping.

Hans, torn between his new-found cosmic unleashing and the rigid code to which he would still no doubt adhere in less impassioned moments, became once again the wooden officer, and sitting himself beside Teresa's heaving form, he said, 'Let us change the subject, what do you say?' As this had no effect, he recited a melancholy poem in German.

It was natural exhaustion which finally calmed her down, and not, as Hans imagined, his histrionic powers. Slowly she looked up at him, and he would have believed her at that moment if she had told him that she was not sixteen, but ten. Instinctively he took her into his arms, and kissed her on the forehead. She clung to his rough uniform for warmth, and gazed, expressionless, out of the window.

They sat there, gently rocking backwards and forwards, without so much as exchanging a whisper, for the best part of an hour, and at the end of that time Hans Winterschild, thrice mentioned in dispatches, holder of the Ritterkreuz with oak clusters and pendants, hero of the National Socialist movement, recognized the strange fact that the silence had been more eloquent than even his most poignant words, and that he was therefore in love.

Not far away, in the heart of another range of hills, Captain Val di Sarat received the interesting information that the 108th Infantry Regiment, Wehrkreis Darmstadt, had moved from San Rocco al Monte to Florence.

VII

Hans Left her when she fell asleep in his arms.
He laid her gently on her bed, and covered
her with a blanket. He thought he'd leave
no money, until it occurred to him that this
might be interpreted by her as an attempt to
get something for nothing. He left a few notes
on the rickety table by her bed and muttered
two lines from a medieval poem by Albrecht von
Johansdorf in a hushed voice. He had learned the
poem at school.

Mich macht der Tod ihrer Liebe wohl scheiden . . .
Anders Niemand: das habe ich geschworen . . .

He left silently, his cheek burning with a sense
of occasion.

Outside in the street, he was inclined to

dawdle. So many conflicting thoughts crowded his mind.

What right have I to fall in love? What guarantee is there that I am in love? That I know anything about love? That my destiny allows me to weaken, to become sloppy and feminine? ... No, if this is indeed love, then it must be glorious. It must be worth fighting, worth dying for, and probably it will be my fate to perish in battle with words of tenderness on my lips.

This time he stopped before the statues, and drank in their haughty disapproval. Under the billowing canopy of clouds, the allegorical figures with Roman senators' faces seemed to stir in their eternal hibernation.

'They must be very old,' thought Hans, with an undefinable emotion, a bewildering blend of exultation and sorrow. He felt at once part of it all, part of a mystery with no discernible beginning or end, and at the same time outside it, below it and above it, its omnipotent master and its infinitesimal slave. It was as though a dimension had suddenly been added to his life, and he was the prey to sensations against which his instincts could provide no spontaneous reaction. All he was sure of was that he had no wish to return to his headquarters immediately.

A lazy soldier passed, clinging to the wall, and Hans opened his mouth to call the shuffling recreant to order, but said nothing. 'Typical,' he thought, 'of what our army has come to,' and walked on. He knew in advance that the sight of Brehmig, a smile spread unevenly over his insignificant face, would be more irritating than ever now.

Hans, in his effort to grapple with the pressing problems of the heart, was falling into the trap, peculiar to the German spirit, of trying to experience all sensations at once. He wished to be cruel and tender, victorious and humble, right and openminded. The human brain will not respond logically to such a crushing emotional load, and so it is diverted into meaningless cosmic mysticism, which, being unselective, is a kind of folly.

He arrived at headquarters determined to cover up his problems by an increased devotion to duty. Nobody must ever know that, confronted by aged statuary, a landscape only tinged with the sounds of war, and a sleeping girl, he had passed through a mild crisis of the spirit. It was the reduction of the general to the particular which had caused the trouble. He would probably never have noticed the girl in a large crowd, and if his orders had been to shoot that crowd, he would have done so without compunction, unmoved. But this damned Teresa, sweet Teresa, was alone in this instance; she had cried over some private grief which was none of his business, and such was his compassion that he would have given her his last penny, his last crust of bread.

The next morning he performed his routine duties, inspecting defenses, giving instructions, and so forth. He saw Brehmig at lunchtime, and reacted coldly to the affectation of overwhelming exhaustion which colored the whole of his deputy's conversation.

'But tell me about yourself,' said Brehmig, 'you picked a rum one.'

'She didn't look much, but she was magnificent,' lied Hans.

By evening, there were no immediate signs of battle, so Hans went into the street.

Brehmig called after him, 'Where are you going?'

'I thought I'd drop in at the Red Bird,' he said.

'What, again? Two nights running? Damn it, how you've changed – to think I had to drag you there yesterday! D'you want me to come with you?'

'Not particularly.'

'That doesn't sound very companionable.' Brehmig joined him. 'I tell you what,' he said. 'Let's swap tonight. You take the Venetian and I'll take your—'

'No!' said Hans, far too emphatically.

Brehmig looked at him with quizzical surprise, and they walked on in silence.

When they entered, the Venetian lady was busily engaged in toying with the mustache of a lieutenant. The lieutenant, in spite of his delight, dutifully rose when he saw Brehmig, and began to look for another partner. Hans sat down by Teresa, who seemed to be annoyed with him for some reason.

'Don't you say good evening?' asked Hans.

'Why did you leave the money?'

Hans felt momentarily embarrassed. He had not wished to leave it, he said, owing to his extreme exaltation at the time. Nothing could have been further from his wishes than to detract from such a rare evening by striking a note which might be interpreted as sordid.

Teresa laughed rather disagreeably. 'I wasn't thinking of the tone of the evening,' she said. 'I was thinking that I hadn't given you anything to deserve payment.'

'You gave me more than you think.'

'Next thing you'll be saying that you're in love with me.'

Hans cleared his throat, and said, 'Perhaps.'

Teresa looked at him incredulously, tried to laugh again, but relapsed into a tortured stillness.

'I'm glad you didn't laugh,' said Hans, trying to look light-hearted, because Brehmig was smiling at him.

'I can't laugh any more,' answered Teresa.

'Why not?'

'I no longer find anything funny. And then I'm not a person.'

'Why do you keep saying that?' Hans was irritated.

'I have my reasons. And I know all about the love of soldiers.'

The barman came for orders.

'A bottle—' began Hans.

'No. Nothing,' said Teresa. 'I don't feel well. I think I shall go home.'

'May I walk with you?' asked Hans.

'If you wish. I can't prevent you,' replied Teresa.

'Nothing?' said the barman, dangerously.

'Nothing,' said Teresa, looking straight at him, unafraid.

'Not even a flower?'

'Nothing.'

They rose and went out, to the fury of the neckless lady, who had been watching the reiteration of the previous night's scene with misgiving.

'That young Winterschild is fantastic,' said Brehmig to the Venetian.

As HANS and Teresa walked across the Piazza del Duomo, it seemed to them as though the gunfire was louder than on the previous night, but it may have been only imagination, stimulated by their reflections on the shortness of life. When they reached the narrow streets, Hans suddenly changed his direction, and Teresa followed him without talking. Against her will, the enforced calm of her attitude to life, so easy to maintain under the painful circumstances of the occupation, was beginning to thaw. As they reached the river, and stood silently looking over the water and the great hill of Fiesole, she felt helplessly sixteen, wanting comfort, longing to find refuge again in the idealism of youth.

Why did this oppressor take such an interest in her? She had seen them all in such a disgusting light, drunken, perverted, animal, and yet here was one of them who could so easily have had his will of her for a few coins, and who still preferred to talk hesitatingly, creating an atmosphere which was somehow touching and embarrassing, and who was willing to put her on a pedestal which she refused to accept. The best of the others had been painfully polite. They had accepted the bargain she had proposed, and fulfilled their contract to the letter. They had been honorable, even on occasion gallant. One of them had kissed her hand on leaving, and she had imagined, as she lay in her tumbledown room, that she was a great courtesan. But this fellow was not polite. He was brusque, often rude, yet he lacked the intolerable confidence of his colleagues, and when he held her hand, it was not a gesture of experience, but gentle, as though he was belatedly discovering the shimmering uncertainties of a first love. Perhaps he too had been the victim of some unspeakable injustice, and had learned compassion in that way. His eyes, now that she looked at them, were cold, but not cruel. But perhaps to her all eyes of such a glacial clarity and intense lightness would look cold. Italian eyes, even blue ones, were different. That blink, about which she had been so callous, might be the aftermath of a tragedy as awful as hers, and the coldness might be the permanent result.

His hand was warm. There was blood coursing through his veins. Spread over the battlefield, it would be indistinguishable from the blood of any other man, Italian or German. As he took her hand, and pressed it to his tunic, she could feel the distant but solid beating of his heart.

'Your hands are cold,' he said.

So he had noticed.

'Here, take my gloves.'

But she preferred to be cold, and feel the warmth of his hand. Why? If she gave way now to her emotions, and allowed herself to tell him how touched she was at finding herself the object of such inexplicable affection, could she ever quite regain the drugged despair which had made her so impervious to anything but the vague desire to keep alive? Could this be anything but another disillusionment in any case? A few days, and the Allies would be here. That meant good business – Americans, British, French, whoever got there first. This could be nothing but an interlude.

'After the battle,' thought Hans, 'we will move forward, to Rome, to the tip of Italy.' A veteran deserves some respite. Leave would surely be granted when victory was once again in sight. There would be no need to tell parents about this. Leave is a luxury, and they know it. It would be spent here, as a prelude to a long life packed with domestic joy, crowds of children and the hero's pillow. The cynicism about love in Poland and Russia had been just the exuberant errors of inexperience. It was his duty to love, and someone else's duty to love him, otherwise his creative powers would be squandered, and he would pass into venerated old age without issue, a traitor to the blood in his veins. The German nation must flourish, and, in a sense, death was a betrayal of the race. The fittest must survive, and the soul of a German is not averse to romance. Had not Germany produced the greatest romantic poets and the greatest romantic musicians in the world?

But these generalizations didn't explain the agitation in the breast, the flutter in the diaphragm. Brown eyes, they were, as large, as deep as oceans. The pupils, dilating and contracting like heartbeats searched his eyes desperately, and then flew with the restlessness of butterflies over his face, never settling. Her hand moved to the back of his head, and he felt his skull cupped in warmth. What was she thinking?

What was he thinking? What was he thinking? Their mouths met, and the famine was over.

When they opened their eyes, it was already light. They looked at one another, and had known each other since before the cradle; they would know each other beyond the tomb. They were safe. A part of existence was explained.

'*La bella Fiorentina, la bella Fiorentina,*' crooned Hans, rocking her. This was a time for mild trivialities, a sort of resignation, a glimpse into the serenity of old age.

She smiled gratefully. 'Why do you call me a *Fiorentina?* she said. 'I don't come from Florence.'

'Does it matter?' he answered.

'No.'

And then, as there was nothing more important to talk about, Hans asked her where she did come from.

'A little village, some kilometers to the north,' she said. 'You may have heard of it, San Rocco al Monte.'

He frowned for a moment. It seemed so long ago, and he had found something so very much more important.

The next evening, he went dutifully to the Uccello Rosso skillfully avoiding Brehmig. It had been useless to persuade her to give up her mode of life. He had nothing to offer, and she had to eat. For the first time he admitted the possibility that a further retreat might be inevitable.

As he entered the garish room, he saw to his alarm that there was someone else sitting with Teresa, a man in a uniform covered with braid. It was Grutze. He stiffened as the general looked at him, and tried to smile, but found himself unable to. He caught also Teresa's agonized glance, and after a moment of hesitation he crossed to the bar and ordered himself a drink.

He had evidently become the object of discussion. A few words, uttered in that brash voice which he found himself suddenly loathing, floated across the room.

'Type of German officer . . . heroic fighter in Russia . . . upstanding . . . initiative . . .'

He ordered another drink. Teresa seemed to be remonstrating in hushed tones. Then Grutze's voice bellowed in German. 'Good God, a creature like you shouldn't feel so deeply. I've told you so often, you are a necessary evil. Without you, society would be impossible, *come si dice in italiano?* Like a soldier, you cannot afford a heart.'

Hans walked out in a stupor, unable to feel anything. At his headquarters, he locked himself into his room, and for the first time since the war, wrote a long letter to his mother.

The following night, he revisited the club as early as possible. Teresa was not there. All he noticed apart from her absence was the triumphant expression on the face of the neckless lady.

After two hours of searching among the grim side-streets, where every second doorway whispered a starved invitation, he found the house he thought he remembered. Entering the hallway, he was challenged by a couple of German sentries.

'It is forbidden to go up, Herr Major,' said one of them.

'Why?'

'We are not allowed to reveal the reason.'

'Who issued your orders?'

The two sentries looked at one another sheepishly.

'If you don't tell me,' snapped Hans at his most military, 'I shall have you both arrested.'

'The orders of Generalleutnant Grutze,' said the second sentry, finding pleasure in momentarily lording it over a major.

'Is he up there?'

'No . . . that is, in a way,' stammered the first sentry.

Hans, in a fury, said, 'I have an urgent message for him from Oberst von Leideberg.'

'I am sorry, Herr Major,' said the second sentry. 'We have our orders, and I shall have to go up and announce you to the general if the message is really urgent. Shall I do that?'

Hans put his hand on his revolver holster, in blind rage, and then walked into the night, frozen by an overwhelming hatred.

Fighting began the next morning, and on the night of the 10th the Germans, harassed by Italian snipers, evacuated Florence. Hans did not see Teresa again before the retreat.

A WEEK or so later, Val di Sarat and the remnants of his division crossed into the Allied lines, and a short time afterwards the ruins of San Rocco al Monte were liberated. The priest had evidently perished in the flames of his own church, and now the charred murals by the anonymous masters of the Florentine school stood fading under the open sky, just the picture to stimulate the war correspondents' imagination. Two British journalists made a memorable broadcast about it, and an American author, one Hooper Boyt, began writing a book which was later to be selected by book clubs on both continents as the most graphic account ever written of a community's sacrifice. Mr Boyt, a hard-drinking and energetic fellow with yellow hair like a stunted cornfield and rimless glasses, had already written the famous *Thus Angry the Dawn*, about the Spanish Civil War, and the best-selling *They Are the Law*, about unscrupulous businessmen in the deep South, and now his publishers were agitating for a speedy immortalization of the martyr-village. Consequently he arrived in a jeep a few hours after the first troops, and after a respite of ten minutes a typewriter was stuttering in a corner of the Piazza Vittorio Emmanuele II.

VIII

THE COUNT entertained Mr Boyt at lunch, and, while four servants supplied their every need, standing around like waxworks when they weren't actually needed, he explained to his guest that he was rather short-staffed owing to the misfortunes of war. The palace, standing some way away from the village, had not been gutted by the enemy, who had found it too useful as billets for their rude soldiery. Now the poor count, rid of the invader, had to contend with an invasion of homeless villagers, who were camping in every part of the palace apart from his intimate suite of rooms in the right wing.

'We have all made grave sacrifices,' said the count, lighting an American cigar which Mr Boyt had generously offered him. 'Think of it – eighty head of working oxen, thirty-six horses, a cellar of unparalleled wine, the spoliation of quite forty per cent of my crops, and the death of a devoted manservant are only part of my crushing misfortunes,' and, looking disdainfully at the anemic ash of his cigar, he added, 'to say nothing of my cabinet of Havanas.'

Mr Boyt, who was making furious notes, looked up to say, 'Just go on talking, Count, that's the way I like it.'

Fatal it was to invite the count to talk.

'It is impossible to capture the essence of San Rocco,' he said, 'without understanding the history of my family, for without our family the village would not exist physically, and even had it, unthinkably, existed physically, it would not have existed morally or spiritually.'

He rose, and crossed to the family tree which was painted on the wall, each of its many leaves boasting a proud name. Taking a pointer of blown glass which reclined on a red velvet contraption of great age, he flashed it upwards with an elegant fencing motion until it rested on one of the topmost leaves, and said, casually. 'In our church, there were murals by Botticelli, now unhappily erased or destroyed. Those murals would never have been painted had it not been for the initiative of one man, my relative Alcide, Marchese di Romontano, whose name is inscribed on this leaf. Here, on this leaf, we have the name of Ermenegildo degli Occhi Bruni, of whom you, as a writer, will no doubt have heard.'

'I'm afraid not,' said Boyt. 'When did he live, eighteenth century?'

A squall of pain spent itself on the count's face, and he replied, 'He was a friend and enemy of Cesare Borgia.'

'A long time ago,' remarked Boyt, sagely, adding, in a more urgent tone of voice, 'but I want to hear more about this recent battle you had. Were you in it, sir?'

'Sir?' thought the count. 'At long last this barbarian has perceived my nobility,' and said, in profound disgust, 'Was I in it? My dear man, where is the traditional place of a nobleman? At the head of his fiefs, of course. Under my guidance, they gave battle as the *bravi* and *confalonieri* of old, lances gleaming, the proud purple, yellow and red of the Counts of San Rocco gracing their shields, the two-headed dolphins dancing over their helmets.'

'Do you mean, sir, that your men were actually dressed up in medieval costume for the occasion?'

'No, of course not. I am talking of history, the only topic of interest left to a gentleman in these drab days. You insult me by suggesting that I would expose my soldiers to unnecessary dangers by exercising my *droits de seigneur* in modern battle. They were dressed decently, but in no way exceptionally.'

'I didn't mean to insult you, sir,' said Boyt, smiling. This crank was great material.

'But you did,' answered the count. 'However, I will overlook the implications of quixotic lunacy implied in your remark, and explain to you that the engagement followed in broad outline the unfortunate battle of Montaperti, of which you certainly have heard.'

'No, sir. Can't say I have. Was it on the Fifth Army front?'

The count buried his irritation in the folds of his face, and answered, 'It was fought on September 4th, 1260, and was remarkable for an ingenious use of cavalry by Manfred of Sicily.'

'I'm afraid that's way out of my province,' laughed Boyt.

'I see nothing risible in that fact,' answered the count, 'nor is there anything particularly droll in a skillful cavalry enfilade, executed in this instance by mobile infantry under the local leadership of a Piedmontese gentleman, Captain Val di Sarat, whose mother was, incidentally, an Ubaldini from Capua. The enemy were lured into a trap, and attacked with unusual abandon, on their exposed flank. It was a perfect plan, perfectly executed by soldiers with faith in their squire.'

Old Plumes's account was somewhat different. As he and Boyt strolled through his ravaged vineyards, he told of his determination to wait until the hour had struck, and then to launch an attack with the *élan* of which only Italian troops were capable. 'As I stood with my small force along unfavorable lines,' he explained, 'there were three courses left open to me, the course of dishonor, the course of prudence, and the course of glory!' He allowed a suitable time to elapse, so that these weighty words could sink into the skull of the American, and took care to talk very slowly, so that the full meaning of the strange language of honor could have its effect on this representative of a nation far too young to know the routine of elegant, courteous homicide.

'The course of dishonor, by which I mean the dastardly act of surrender, is unknown to me. The course of prudence – in other words, headlong flight – is alien to my nature, and to the nature of my soldiers. Arithmetic shows that, having disposed of two out of three alternative courses of action, there is only one course of action left, the course of glory!' It was then that Old Plumes noticed, to his horror, that Boyt was taking no notes.

'Do you retain everything in your head,' he asked.

'I am looking for facts, sir,' said Boyt, smiling.

'I am giving you facts,' retorted Old Plumes tartly.

'You mistake me, sir. I'm a writer. I do my own embroidery. Perhaps you have read *Thus Angry the Dawn?* No? Well, it was a big seller. I just went round with a lot of little guys in Spain, and joined all their fragmentary evidence together in my own style, the way I know how.

Today it's translated into sixteen languages and a great movie with Chesney Bartram as Don Balthazar and Sigrid Tollefsen as Aïsha, the Moorish girl. You'll just have to trust me, sir, to do you justice.'

'I am not thinking of myself,' lied Old Plumes, 'but of my country and of our glorious dead.'

'I am sensible of my duties towards them, sir,' said Boyt gravely. Innumerable pamphlets had warned the United States forces of the extreme touchiness of all foreigners, and of their hatred of both criticism and advice. Boyt not only took these pamphlets very seriously, but had, in fact, written most of them.

'Very well,' said Old Plumes warily, 'I will continue with my report. I occupied, as I said, disadvantageous ground halfway down the ravine. The Germans approached in a nor'nor-easterly direction, masking their intentions behind a fan of scouts. Their intentions, I feel constrained to add, were not clear even to themselves, as they had no conception of where we were. My dispositions were as follows. The center lay in the hollow at the bottom of Todeschini's olive grove. My right was stretched in the direction of Sabrone's farm, and was composed of a portion of a celebrated Italian division, the Gran Sasso, under my deputy, Val di Sarat. My left, under the somewhat inexperienced guidance of Filigrani, the Communist, was deployed in the general area of the old Franciscan monastery.

'Battle was joined on my left wing, where Filigrani imprudently entered in premature contact with the enemy against my orders. The German right wing attacked with automatic weapons at their disposal. A superficial knowledge of ballistics is enough to show that they had the advantage over us, armed as we were with weapons only capable of firing a shot at a time. The Germans counterattacked my forces with unpremeditated violence, and they were joined in their onslaught by the German left, which converged in an effort to destroy our center, and therewith the head of the body, as it were . . . Seizing my opportunity, I sent my right in a large arc to encircle the exposed German flank. By dint of superb heroism, the center held its ground, inspired by the example of its officers, or rather, officer, for I was the only one present with experience of battle. At the exact moment I gave the signal and my right attacked the Germans with characteristic fury. A counterattack by the center at the point of the bayonet sealed the fate of the enemy, who retired in the most distressing confusion to his strong-points, there to wreak his impotent vengeance on a defenseless village, which will stand forever as an eloquent memorial to the undying majesty of our dead!'

'Don't you intend to rebuild it?' asked Boyt.

'Of course,' replied Old Plumes, with considerable annoyance. 'I was speaking metaphorically.'

Before taking his leave, Boyt asked Old Plumes how many soldiers were involved on either side.

'Germans, between five and six hundred. Italians thirty-five.'

'But the count gave the figures as about a hundred Germans, and about fifty Italians,' protested Boyt.

'The count,' answered Old Plumes, 'is both physically and mentally shortsighted.'

Filigrani, interviewed in the ruins of his shop, which could boast no merchandise, but was already crowned with a limp red flag, told a somewhat different story.

'It must be made clear that the brunt of the fighting was done by the partisan shock brigade. The rest of our forces were composed of depressed and devitalized troops of the old Italian army, badly led and ill-equipped, and of deadheads like Old Plumes and the count. Our shock brigade, inspired by the glorious example of the Red Army, entered the battle against the Fascist hyenas at precisely the right moment, and, in spite of the feeble resistance of the colonel's party, and the deplorable deflection of the regulars, who did not fire a shot until the action was virtually over, we outsmarted and outfought the enemy hordes.'

'But Colonel Garetta told me that in his opinion you opened fire too soon,' said Boyt.

'If he had his way, we would never have fired at all,' answered Filigrani, contemptuously.

'He said he organized an outflanking movement.'

'There was no question of outflanking movements. It was a question of the attempted treachery on behalf of men who were not upheld by a great idea. They only condescended to enter the fray when the heroes of our May Day Shock Brigade had already decided the issue.'

'And how many men were involved on either side?'

'Not counting the ineffective, there were twenty-one Italians, and close to a thousand Germans.'

Boyt looked unblinkingly at Filigrani.

'I find that impossible,' he said.

'There is all the difference in the world between improbable and impossible,' answered Filigrani, haughtily.

'Very well, I will qualify my statement, and suggest to you that it is improbable,' said Boyt.

'What may appear improbable to you, coming as you do from the commercial, cynical land of exploiters, is nevertheless quite probable to those impregnated with the spirit of dialectic materialism.'

It was useless to argue.

Buonsignori, leaning against the cluster of angels in the Piazzi Vittorio Emmanuele II, disagreed with the count, whom he called a rude name suggesting sexual deficiency; Old Plumes, whom he called a rude name suggesting gaseous self-importance; and Filigrani, whom he called a string of names not only suggesting, but categorically stating, every vile thing under the sun.

'The credit for the victory,' he said, 'belongs to everyone' — but then qualified his magnanimity by naming as exceptions to the rule practically all the inhabitants of the village. 'The count,' he explained, 'is a man so immersed in the past that the present just seems to him a perpetual foretaste of a revolting future. He is no accurate judge of any event after 1500, although, to give him his due, before that date his comments carry with them an eyewitness authority. Old Plumes won a brilliant cluster of diplomas at the Military Academy, and you must realize that any man capable of doing that is a bit of a gasbag, and is guaranteed to lose any battle in which he is engaged, as he is still the virtual slave of the old buffers who gave him his diplomas. As for Filigrani, he is one of those angry souls who has invested his bitterness in the bank of Communism, and draws thence a handsome dividend of nonsense. If you listen to his account of the battle, you may as well go to the fountainhead of all truth, and telephone the Kremlin. They will tell you all about us, as I believe we all have the honor to be filed.'

It was a pity that so much of the irony of Buonsignori's remarks was missed by Mr Boyt, who was extremely serious by nature, and therefore a highly successful writer. However, the searing flames of his imagination were beginning to give not mere warmth but positively and eminently commercial heat to the episodic stories.

'Tell me the truth about the Italian regulars,' he said.

'If it had not been for them!' Buonsignori shrugged his shoulders. 'They saved the situation for us.' And he went on to tell of Val di Sarat's theories of banditry as opposed to soldiery, and of the extraordinary single combat on the crest of the hill. He also took care to give a spiced account of his battle of wits with a room full of Germans about poor Folgore's calls of nature.

'But who is this guy, this officer, who shot it out with the German?' asked Boyt, sweating with schoolboy excitement.

'His name was Val di Sarat.'

'What did he look like, a big guy, dark, handsome?'

'Not very tall, but with a red beard the color of carrots, and eyes of blue, *chiari, chiari, chiarissimi.*'

'That's no good,' muttered Boyt, 'he's got to look different.'

The afternoon brought him the welcome news that his proposed book had already been bought by Olympic Pictures, sight unseen. A nine-page cable to this effect arrived from Boyt's old boon companion and fellow gin-rummy addict Malcolm Zitherman, or, more correctly, Colonel Malcolm Zitherman, the President in Charge of

Production at Olympic, at the moment engaged in advising the United States Government on how to shoot pictures.

The colonel was one of those fortunates in the army who had never known any other rank but the one he held, and who, benefiting from the opulence of American organization, flew restlessly from California to places very near the front and back again in the four-engined transport plane set aside for him. He was a man inordinately jealous of the shades of past producers, and his search for immortality had already led him to name a large white building on the Olympic lot, a building in which captive writers stared at the ceiling while awaiting inspiration or instructions, the Zitherman Building.

It was entirely in character that his fragmentary experiences of combat should now have convinced this born leader that he had witnessed things denied to others, and, wishing to give the public, for their entertainment, the benefits of his vision, he now determined to shoot Boyt's book on the spot. 'You can never reproduce the actual conditions of battle in the studio,' he wrote in his economically worded cable. 'Those days are past. From now on we have to be out there and ready before history is made. This will be tough to organize, but I will make it my personal business to push this through. I am flying to Washington today, and expect to see the Chief of Staff at my earliest convenience. I already

had General Watson to lunch at Romanoff's
and he gave me his personal assurance we can
expect every cooperation. I ran *Thus Angry the
Dawn* for the General and Mrs Watson and he
expressed the personal opinion that the picture
was quote great for America unquote. Kindest
personal regards . . .'

Zitherman dropped a practical hint in the
middle of his dreams that a vehicle was urgently
required for the gorgeous Norwegian contract
artist Sigrid Tolletsen. Boyt's thoughts were suitably canalized.

Meanwhile the battles raged with a stubborn
and desperate fury. Val di Sarat, suitably dec-
orated, had reluctantly abandoned his life of
pleasant gangsterdom and was now a major in the
Divisione Cremona, one of the Italian formations
fighting with the Allies. Deep in his kitbag,
his trophy, Hans's cap, lay hidden. Its owner
was fighting along the Mugello range, north of
Florence, and was contesting every inch of the
ground with a cold, functional determination.
The façade of fanaticism was there, but the fact
that genuine zeal was lacking could not be hidden
from such a diabolical observer as Brehmig.

'It is the duty of every officer to lay down his
life for his country,' said Brehmig one day, in harsh
imitation of the mass-produced Gauleiter, and to
his surprise the mimicry drew from Hans a hollow
smile of recognition. Brehmig went on. 'The playing
of the music of Felix Mendelssohn-Bartholdy, that

Jewish note-perverter, that hook-nosed harmony-defiler, that leering chord-debaucher, is strongly prohibited.'

Hans laughed. 'And,' he said, 'in order to prevent the music of Felix Mendelssohn-Bartholdy from being played, we must trample over the whole world at immense loss of life, destroying his scores.'

'Hans,' remarked Brehmig softly, 'you've changed.'

'War changes everyone.'

'Into animals, my dear boy, but something else changes animals into human beings.'

'What?' asked Hans, blushing in spite of himself.

Brehmig began to sing a sentimental song.

'Answer me,' insisted Hans.

Brehmig altered the words of the song. '*La bella Teresa, ich hab' dich so ungeheuer gern,*' he crooned.

'Don't be ridiculous.'

'Ridiculous? Not at all,' insisted Brehmig. 'I thought I was in love with a laundress in Palermo, and I daren't admit it to my brother officers. They found out, and my love affair was over, trampled to death by jokes.'

'What are you trying to prove?'

'Nothing,' said Brehmig, smiling, 'I never try to prove anything. What's the use? We have our orders. But it just seems a little, shall I say, paradoxical, that our number-one Party boy, who told us that he would never fall in love in the spiritual sense, should now tumble into a morass of introspection about a Florentine tart. I suppose, though, that you had farther to fall. Your fall is there by rendered more obvious to the perspicacious observer.'

'You don't know what you are talking about,' said Hans, who had nearly given himself away when Brehmig called Teresa a tart.

Brehmig grew serious. 'Listen,' he said, 'a solider has only room in his make-up for desires of the flesh. Leave the heart out of it.'

'Why?' asked Hans, suddenly proud of his love. How it was lasting!

'Why?' whispered Brehmig. 'Then you do admit that you are in love?'

'My father was in love with my mother.'

'And you are in love with a tart.'

'Shut your mouth!'

Brehmig stretched himself lazily and reflected on how he seemed to have an incredible capacity for annoying his more successful juniors.

'My dear Hans, we are all doomed men, from the meanest private to the proudest general. It is quite unpleasant enough to be waiting for the end, but don't let's add to our complications by allowing sincerity to rear its head.'

'The subject is closed.'

'As you wish, Herr Major, as you wish. But mark my words, you will ruin the slender chances of survival you have by bringing your heart into your work.'

'Just now you said that we were all doomed,' said Hans, with a revival of interest. He liked to talk about after the war. 'Now you talk about survival.'

Brehmig smiled. 'I never lose hope entirely,' he said, 'and if there is only one survivor, I intend to be it.'

Hans frowned. 'What do you intend to do?' he asked.

Brehmig shrugged his shoulders enigmatically.

On August 15th, Allied forces invaded the south of France. On August 23rd, Paris was freed. On September 3rd, Brussels was lost to the Germans. Hope rose to a fever in the Axis camp when the first V-2 rocket hit London on September 8th, but the fact didn't seem to have much effect on the operations in the field. However, sustained by the hopes of a miracle, the Germans in Italy fought doggedly. It was surely only a matter of time. On December 16th, the great German effort in the Ardennes began, but on the same day the important town of Faenza in Italy fell to the Allies. Grutze was here, there and everywhere, exhorting his troops to supreme efforts. They survived 1944, but early in 1945 the Russians crossed the Reich frontiers, and on the 7th of March the Rhine was breached by the Americans.

'They are letting our army in Italy down,' Grutze would howl, in his pre-mortal anguish, but all his blustering could not prevent the 8th Army from landing between Lake Comacchio and Ravenna on the 2nd of April, nor the 5th Army from commanding the Ligurian littoral from Monte Folgonita three days later. Although the ardent Nazis drank a toast to celebrate the death of President Roosevelt on the 12th of April, they had to bow to the fact that the Allies forded the Santerno River on the same day.

On the 16th, the Americans entered Nuremberg, the scene of so many happy rallies, and Grutze paced the ground, his eyes bloodshot, screaming like a wounded animal. On the 21st, the Second Polish Corps seized Bologna, and Grutze had to be restrained from counterattacking by himself. The humiliation of a Polish military achievement after the decisive German victory of 1939 was too much for him. Three days passed in the most frenzied fighting, and then Ferrara, Spezia and Modena fell within hours of each other. The Po was crossed. A few hours later the Russians and Americans linked up in Germany. Another few hours, and Mantua and Parma had gone the way of all cities. Another few hours and Verona had been written off. The north was seething with revolt. The Italians were in control of Genoa, and wrestling with Milan. More humiliation. Another few hours, and the French, pulverized in 1940, entered Italy

from the west and seized Ventimiglia. Another
few hours and Brescia and Bergamo fell. The
Americans reached the Swiss frontier at Como.
Mussolini and most of his cabinet were captured
and shot by their compatriots. Hitler married Eva
Braun, now that Mussolini's death had made him
a widower. There was talk of surrender in Italy.
Two delegates were in discussion at Caserta.
Venice fell. Hitler consummated his wedding
with fire, and Grutze had no voice left. Another
few hours, and New Zealand troops in Italy
made contact with Yugoslav partisans. Graziani
commanded the Fascist Republicans to lay down
their arms. Berlin surrendered to the Russians. At
noon on May 2nd hostilities in Italy ceased.

At that moment, Hans was in Savona. He did
not wait to say good-by to any of his colleagues.
Brehmig had vanished the night before. The
soldiers were sitting about in sullen groups. He
went into the harbor, which bore the marks of
severe bombardment, and entered a small grocery
shop. There he held up the terrified owner at the
point of his revolver, and stole a suit of clothing.
He was just about to leave when he noticed a
bicycle wheel protruding from behind a large
sack. Forcing the owner to remove the sack, he
took the bicycle, and threw his uniform down
as payment. He then pedaled away furiously in
a northwesterly direction, away from the Gulf
of Genoa, towards the peak of Cadibona. He
was eager to keep away from the obvious coast

road, and then, once he was inland, to make his way back into the center of Italy, and Florence. The bicycle became worse than useless among the sharp gradients of the Cadibona pass, so he discarded it, and continued on foot, waving at several truckloads of singing Italians who passed him on the way. Once such a wagon, decked with red flags and bristling with small arms, slowed down to give him a lift, an offer which he wisely declined, urging it cheerily on its way with ebullient gestures.

Towards nightfall he entered a lonely farmhouse, and demanded a meal. The kind people looked suspicious, for the Ligurians at the best of times are rather uncommunicative compared to most other Italians, but he shrewdly told them that he was '*Inglese — prigioniero*,' and they welcomed this blond ally from the North.

'*Tedeschi finiti!* German finish!' they said with great laughter and clapping. He joyously agreed with them.

'Yes, yes,' he laughed. '*Sì, sì!*' and everyone laughed.

They gave him a couch for the night by the splendid expediency of accommodating five members of a copious family in the same bed. The next morning they gave him wine and bread for his journey from their humble reserves, and the dogs barked him out of the grounds, their tails wagging, in a perfect understanding of their master's effusive hospitality.

He reached the village of Dego by eleven in the morning, and turned east, along the road to Pontinvrea, which he bypassed about two hours later, and he settled down to a healthy meal on the flank of the Fiovo peak when the heat of the day began to tire him. He slept till wakened by the sudden cool of the early evening, and then set off by way of Sassello towards the main road leading from the coast to Alessandria. The brilliant night dropped imperceptibly, like a gauze, over the mountains, and as he saw the distant peaks, cold and silent under their coronets of restless stars, he rejoiced in the lightness of his steps, which were taking him back to his beloved. Strange it was, to be lost in a landscape undisturbed by the shudder of guns, the sulphurous odors of battle, strange to be alone in such a luxury of space. The air, cool and yet without a sting, rushed into his lungs, and gently slapped his face until his cheeks were ice. When he felt the soil with the back of his hand, it was still warm from the sun, pure, unfertilized with blood.

What, then, was the meaning of conquest? Why struggle for a landscape, why die for a panorama, which was ever changing, an ocean of land with a million facets? What was the point, when a man alone could feel a freedom, a delirious loneliness divorced from nationality and the sordid details of possession? Ah, but there were mineral resources, the hard substances and the oily nectar hidden by a jealous soil. Metals must be dragged from the earth, fashioned by mortal genius in the shape of other mineral manipulations, and returned to the unforgiving earth as contortions of rust. That was the elaborate, the remote dicing of high politics, the gargantuan meal served in a sauce of blood, the game of endless checkmates, invented not by wanderers in immensity, but by people who couldn't spare the time; men correctly dressed to paddle in deep carpets and sit at golden desks, stiff-collared acrobats who jumped at conclusions and never missed.

Yet here was a world, impersonal and luxuriant, nobody's world, everybody's world. There was a pattern of hills and valleys, a geography of fields and rivers, scarred by roads, pimpled by houses, which was claimed by men who sentimentally called it sacred, men who claimed the body because they thrived upon the skin. But this world was deep. It recognized no language, and kept its secrets well. Men could kill men for its land, but it was an elusive mistress; it hid its strength on the wedding night, and forever.

How foolish, how pathetic the maneuvers of soldiers suddenly appeared, the passion of fragile flesh imprisoned between the dense infinity of soil and the free infinity of sky, the agony of beings able to hurt nothing but themselves, the butchery of perishables.

Hans, feeling like a speck of dust in this

immensity, understood nothing of the reasons
of his recent life. The nightmare of the Eastern
campaign, so crushing at the time, was now
compressed into a few graphic impressions – it
might have been a film he had seen. Of the
monotony there was no trace. Boredom was an
emotion which the mind could not recollect
faithfully. The pain of his wound, the lonely walk
into a gale of death, the eulogies of the Ritter von
Horstwald – they were experiences which might
have happened to someone else, and, being badly
told, he had remembered them as recorded facts,
and that was all. As for his complicated training,
the free-masonry of military leadership, he could
remember none of it, like the actor who dreams
that he is about to walk onto the stage in a
costume he does not recognize and to cues he
does not understand.

The Führer, a little while ago as real a conception as an absent lover, was already a Wagnerian
myth. Brehmig, last talked to forty-eight hours
previously, was a name which evoked a face
half lost among other half-lost faces. Childhood, parents, schools, brothers, sisters, they
were vague hurdles, vague signposts. Nothing
was real except the moment. Even the landscape
changed as he moved forward, mountains slid
sideways to conceal hills, the moon dropped
lower to conceal valleys. The moment, and
the radiance of the spirit, that was all there
was. The radiance, the heart he had left, held

in tender trust in Florence, the radiance, his eloquent emptiness.

The next morning a couple of American jeeps flashed past him in a cyclone of dust, and he decided that the time for being British was temporarily over. He therefore became a Yugoslav prisoner, and glowed inwardly at his daring and at his utter freedom of choice.

Lunch was begged near Mornese, but it was not satisfactory, as the farmer had lost a son in Greece, and regarded the whole Balkan peninsula as a hotbed of lethal extremity. 'Worse than the Italians, even worse than us,' he said, as he sent Hans packing with a slice of salami.

Hungry, with nothing but the taste of garlic in his mouth, Hans reached the main Genoa-Tortona road before the twilight. Three miles to the east, in the village of Casella, he saw a military motorcycle, parked outside a café. He examined the machine with the kind of envy of the racing fanatic, and cautiously switched on the ignition. The flickering of the needle told him that the tank was almost full. No one was looking.

QUICKLY HE straddled the machine and found that the rakish handlebars were absurdly close to his body, pinning him to the saddle like the antlers of a charging stag. It seemed to have been constructed in the '20s, and yet it gleamed with modern chrome. He tried to start it, but it reacted grudgingly and noisily. He twisted the handlebars desperately in order to coax the engine to life, but his wrists were compelled to operate at such a curious angle that he couldn't get the feel of the mechanism. He cursed out of a sense of guilt. One more try.

'*Sind sie verrückt?*' A German voice asked him if he was mad.

Hans looked up and saw a hunchbacked dwarf in Tirolese costume smiling at him, a savage gaiety in his intense blue eyes. Hans was lost for words, and thought of running.

'Don't move,' said the dwarf, plunging his huge right hand into the pocket of his leather shorts. He produced a small key, inserted it into the top of the carburetor, and turned it.

'Now it should work. Try it.'

Hans kicked the starter, and the engine spurted into uncertain life.

'It's cold,' said the dwarf, 'you can drive if you wish, but I hardly think you'll find the position of the handlebars very comfortable.'

'I was only interested in the motorcycle,' Hans muttered.

'Don't lie,' replied the dwarf, still smiling. 'Get on the pillion seat.'

'Where arc we going?'

The only answer was the roar of the motor.

It was cold at the speed they were going. The dwarf was so small he afforded Hans no protection against the wind. Hans began to feel irritated by this minute figure huddled before him. His self-assurance was almost inhuman, as was his ability to humiliate without taking advantage of his ascendancy. He cornered like an ace, and seemed to be traveling at immense speed. The rush of air was such that Hans could breathe only by turning his face sideways. Where were they going?

A roadblock brought them to a standstill. As the officers approached, the dwarf said quietly, 'Don't lose your head.' Hans saw from his profile that he was still smiling.

'*Documenti*,' said the officer.

The dwarf dug into the inside pocket of his gray and green jacket, and produced some papers.

'You are Dr Eugenio Pichl?'

'Yes.'

'What do you do?'

'Engineer, attached to the Ministry of the Marine in a civilian capacity. No interest in politics.'

'Did you ever serve in the armed forces? – oh, I'm sorry. Where do you live?'

'Merano.'

'And who's your friend?'

'My foreman, Lorenzo Brechbühler.'

'Also from Merano?'

'Naturally.'

'All right, on your way.'

Hans wanted to ask some questions, but

it was impossible over the harsh rasp of the motor. The scenery became flatter, and the roads straighter. After a time, Hans caught sight of arrows pointing to Milan. They were going in the wrong direction. Annoyed, he tapped the dwarf on the back. Half-turning, his face still smiling diabolically, the dwarf roared over the wind in his deep bass voice:

'D'you need good luck as badly as that?'

IT WAS nightfall by the time they reached Merano, with its chalky pinkness glowing like the phosphorescent numbers on a watch in the cool mountain darkness.

'Come in,' said the dwarf, as he opened a creaking wooden door onto a warm hallway. The heads of deer plunged from the walls in great profusion, their innocent eyes half-alive in the flickering light from the huge fire, which pulsated hungrily on the walls. A solid-looking girl appeared, her hair braided tidily in the Tirolese fashion. Her clothes did so little to help her unsubtle figure that it was impossible to know whether she was pregnant or whether nature was just growing impatient for her to fulfil those functions for which she, of all people, was evidently intended.

The dwarf put his arm around her waist, and lifted her off the ground with apparent ease, cackling with pleasure, while she flirtatiously feigned fear.

'This is Martha,' said the dwarf, by way of introduction, 'and she is not my wife. I am single.'

His grotesque smile seemed to give some corrupt color to this statement, which Hans couldn't fathom.

'Perhaps I should introduce myself, or is it too late in the day for that?' the dwarf went on. 'After all, we have shared a motorcycle for some hours, but although it is an admirable means of conveyance, it is hardly conducive to conversation.' He looked at Hans intently, and extended his hand. 'My name is Eugen Pichl.'

Hans shook hands, and felt his fingers imprisoned in an instrument of medieval torture. The pressure became intolerable, and Hans bent his body in an effort to find relief. The smile on Pichl's face was one of effort rather than good nature.

'Strong, eh?' he grunted.

'Oh, he loves showing off,' said Martha casually.

'Mind what you say!' warned Pichl, playfully.

'I'm black and blue all over,' Martha went on, with sickening coyness.

'D'you hear that?'

Pichl let Hans's hand go, and Hans looked at his fingers. They resembled a pale block of toffee, which could be broken, finger by finger.

'What's your name?'

'Hans Winterschild.'

'Rank?'

'Just a moment,' said Hans. 'Are you German or Italian?'

'*Südtiroler* – one of the damned,' Pichl replied, grandiloquently. 'One of those sacrificed by Hitler to his allies – our passports are Italian, our language German, our hearts and our culture Tirolese. Martha, some wine. Serious conversation is impossible without wine.'

The wine was dark and stained the tongue and hung on the breath. It was worse than garlic. Since the taste was better than the aftertaste, Hans drank more and more, and as he drank, he talked of war.

Martha sat and listened quietly, her hands folded on her lap. A younger girl came in during the evening, together with a school friend. Pichl pulled the two girls beside him as Hans talked, and fondled them absent-mindedly. One was Martha's sister Trudl, the other's name Hans didn't catch. A sort of peace seemed to settle over Pichl as Hans talked of Russia – more particularly Russia, it was farther away, and he could tell his tale without the encumbrance of factual accuracy. Not that he embroidered, but he could make drama out of the mournful winters with that bleak understatement which heroes employ in order to make their achievements more incalculable to mere laymen.

When he finished, Pichl stared before him, his eyes half-closed in a voluptuous enjoyment of some private thoughts. There was a silence during which all the girls looked at each other and smiled shyly.

'You know,' murmured the dwarf at length, lighting a clay pipe more folkloric than functional, and fumigating the timbered room with a smoke which made Hans swallow, 'you know, all my life I have had everything I want. Toys? I had mountains of them, because I was malformed. My every whim was satisfied. My parents, obsessed by some obscure guilt for having engendered me, ate out of my hand. My teachers at school thought me brilliant because they pitied me, and believed I should be encouraged more than a normal boy.' He laughed. 'I took advantage of them. I took advantage of everybody.'

The women smiled again. This time he noticed them smile.

'Women have never been a problem either. Don't ask me why, but they have always flocked to me.'

The women looked curiously at Hans, as though members of some secret cult who took refuge in pleasures which society would condemn, if it ever had the imagination to conceive of them. There was a silence while Hans lowered his eyes out of an embarrassment which was instinctive rather than logical.

'Why do you blink?' snapped Pichl.

Hans looked up, annoyed. 'I can't help my blink any more than you can help your shape.'

'Nonsense,' Pichl shouted, his eyes wide and imperious. 'A blink is a nervous complaint. What happened to me has nothing to do with my nerves. I hate nerves. They are indications of surrender to outside pressure. They are signs of weakness.'

Hans grew angry, but could find no words to express his feelings.

'Yes, sir,' Pichl went on, 'you are weak.'

The girls looked like a jury.

'Where were you going when you tried to steal my motorcycle?'

'I didn't steal it.'

'You didn't succeed in stealing it. Where were you going?'

'Florence,' Hans cried.

'Florence?' Pichl whispered in surprise. 'And why should a German officer on the run decide to go to Florence?'

'Private reasons.'

'Private? A soldier without an army, without a government, has private reasons to go deep into enemy-held territory?'

'I don't see why I should have to answer all these questions,' Hans said, rising to his feet. 'Who are you? What do you want with me?'

'Never mind. Germans help each other.'

'But you are not German—'

'How dare you say that!' cried Pichl, dropping his playthings from his lap, and standing up. 'That you have suffered a great deal I am willing to concede, but that does not mean for a moment that you knew what you were fighting for!'

This accusation was too much for Hans, who began to rave, his high voice consistently drowned by that of Dr Pichl, who commanded more volume and more breath. It was only after a quarter of an hour of rhetoric and counter-rhetoric that they discovered that they were both in agreement as regards Germany's traditional position at the helm of things. In order to make up the quarrel, Pichl offered to shake hands again, an offer which Hans declined to the dwarf's amusement.

'You're a good sort after all,' he said, slapping Hans on the back as though felling a tree. 'But young, and highly strung.' He grew graver, grimmer. 'I said that I had enjoyed my life, but one aspect of it is unknown to me – I grope towards its image like a blind man who only has a sense of what light might be in the cavern of his mind. I am strong, I am healthy, I have a violent disposition, and yet I have never known what it is to be shoulder to shoulder with a file of anonymous comrades, with that mystical relationship which exists between boot and paving stone hammered out in a wrenching rhythm, echoing among the houses, the surrender of personality to a primeval and unquenchable force, the heartbeat of an army, carried by fife and bugle towards the unstable frontiers! Yam, pam, pam – und, yam, pam, pam.' Singing the Badenweiler March, the tune which sparked

the Führer's eye with turbulent ambition, which
made him toss and throw his head like a horse
troubled by the bit, Pichl marched the length of
the room, countermarched, and marched again,
his legs thrown high, his arms swinging across his
body. In the uncertain shadows of the firelit room
his hunched back resembled the knapsack of the
infantryman, his huge head with its long fair hair
covering where the neck should be, looked like
a helmet.

It was a sacrilege of the religion in which Hans
had been brought up, and he shuddered, but by
now without real emotion.

VAL DI SARAT was called to Rome with the
utmost urgency. The summons had come from
his uncle, Colonel Ubaldini, a stout and swarthy
Neapolitan, his mother's brother. Ubaldini was,
at this vital period, a high official of the reconstituted Carabinieri, and he wished to question
his nephew about the possibility of joining the
ranks of his guardians of the peace, and more particularly, to acquire scraps of evidence about the
Germans responsible for the sack of San Rocco.

'My boy,' he said, sweat gleaming at every
pore, his team of chins leaning on each other
heavily in their exhaustion, 'my dear boy, you
are now thirty-five years of age, it is time you
chose a career. In Italy, to be a hero is not
enough.' (Ubaldini, being a Neapolitan, was very
intelligent. He was also highly respectable and

slightly disreputable, a blend of qualities which would seem impossible anywhere but in Naples.) 'In Italy, a hero must consolidate his position by a clever use of the many impressive titles which are always at the disposal of the industrious. Unfortunately, owing to your somewhat unbalanced career in Chicago and elsewhere – oh, I am not blaming you, my boy – you were doing your duty as an Italian ambassador abroad, I have no doubt, and that in itself is a function which must command our respect. Unfortunately, however, it prevented you from acquiring a degree, and as a consequence you are unable to boast even a single prefix to your name. You are not an *avvocato*, you are not a *dottore*, you are not even an *ingeniere*, and therefore it is my sorry duty to tell you that you are in a minority in Italy. Please don't interrupt me. You see, here success is mainly a matter of visiting cards. Visiting cards are the most valuable of documents, worth more to the man of quality than passports, identity cards, or any of the other frivolous credentials which weigh down our wallets. Look at my visiting card.'

He showed Val di Sarat a card on which was written Commendatore Avvocato Dottore Ingeniere Ubaldo Ubaldini, and, crossed out in the mildest pencil, an exalted Fascist rank.

'There,' he said, 'is the story of my success.'

'What about the Fascist rank?' asked Val di Sarat.

'That deletion is a sacrifice which I have

had to make temporarily owing to the existing situation.'

'But aren't you frightened of being shot?'

The colonel smiled, and shook his head. 'No. The Italian desperado will not easily shoot a man with so many degrees. He feels his inferiority too painfully, and has too great a respect for high words. During the last week before the arrival of the Allies, I dressed in civilian clothes and joined in the search for myself. The Communists shot three stout men in the belief that they had finally caught me, just as they shot four bearded men in the belief that they had caught the Duce's friend, General Terruzzi. I am only a colonel, and worthy of only three mistakes. Terruzzi, like me, is still alive. The newcomers have not been in power since the March on Rome. They lack experience and authority, and they need us much more than we need them. Titles, my boy, are titles in this blessed country, and Fascist titles are quite as good as any others.'

Val di Sarat's blue eyes twinkled, because scruples meant very little to him in a world which was in any case corrupt; what pleased him was audacity. His admiration for this uncle increased by leaps and bounds as each new impertinence was revealed.

'Uncle, you would have survived even in the time of Alexander VI,' he said, with great tenderness.

'Easily,' answered Ubaldini, contemptuously,

'because those Borgias were so unutterably silly not to have succeeded in evading the consequences of their folly. Alexander died of the plague, admittedly, but in that he was like the boxer who is saved from being knocked out by the bell. The act of God did not prevent him from being defeated on points in the eyes of history. Cesare spent himself in his youth, and therefore missed the best years of his life. Lucrezia was the wisest of that brood. She squandered her ration of suffering at an early age, and thereafter spent the rest of her life in the pursuit of good works, colorless perhaps, and yet a pleasant change from the round-dance of bedmates who had replaced each other with the regularity of saints on a cathedral clock. No, no, they lacked philosophy, my boy.

'Look at me. My private life is impeccable. I have taken precautions against a broken heart by taking a mistress both older and uglier than my wife. I must add that my wife is immensely and continually flattered by the consideration I show her, and our relationship is as happy as any matrimonial tie ever is. Try not to marry, my dear boy, but if you have to because of rumor – I know of no other reason – then marry a beauty and deceive her with women distinctly inferior in every way. This will be regarded as a physical necessity and not as an insult. Altogether, except in the questions of titles and self-preservation during popular insurrections, it is safe to do

what the majority don't do. My instincts lead
me to live the life I lead. If crime does not pay,
it is only because I am in the police. Rest assured
that the police wouldn't pay if I was in crime.
Of course, the instincts which lead a man to
be a detective and those which lead him to be
a criminal are identical. The majority of those
obsessed by this particular kink choose crime, in
the belief that it is both better paid and easier.
They are fools because they are in the majority,
and in the majority because they are fools. Being
a policeman, my dear fellow, is far easier and far
safer than being a criminal, and it can be far
more lucrative.'

'D'you mean to say you accept bribes?' asked
Val di Sarat, with mock surprise.

Ubaldini looked distinctly dangerous for a
moment. 'Of course not. Never suggest such a
terrible thing,' he gasped. 'There is a world of
difference between making money a condition for
your cooperation, and doing your duty normally,
thereby drawing a handsome reward in gratitude
for your decisions. Now, will you join me in my
important work?'

Val di Sarat grinned pleasantly. 'No,' he said,
'I feel no attraction for either crime or the law in
such restrictive circumstances. Italy is too small,
as indeed was Chicago. I prefer banditry and
detection in the open spaces, where other people
can't get hurt. Anyway, I have experienced a
belated call to the sea, and I will probably

satisfy my wanderlust now that patriotic duties are over.'

'Nonsense,' said Ubaldini, 'will you ever grow up? When you were a child, you wanted to be a locomotive engineer.'

'I still want to be one,' sighed Val di Sarat, sincerely, 'but the job needs such training.'

'Incorrigible. Stupid. You are squandering a career of brilliant possibilities. However, I can see that it is no use arguing with you for the moment. You look so atrociously happy. Will you at least help me to track down the criminals of San Rocco? An arrest or two must be made soon, otherwise they will only shoot the wrong people, and we have had enough of such mistakes. Since other nations have produced war criminals, it would be insufferable if Italy were left out of the running again.'

'Have you any clues?' asked Val di Sarat.

'None. Except that the unit responsible for the crime was the 108th Infantry Regiment from Darmstadt. What have you got there?'

Val di Sarat had produced the cap. 'This,' he said, 'is the cap of the commanding officer.'

'Brilliant. *Brilliantissimo*. But, my dear boy, it is so full of bullet holes that it is surely doubtful whether he survived.'

'I did not do honor to Italy in Chicago without learning something in return,' smiled Val di Sarat. 'When I left this man, he was alive.'

'Most creditable,' said Ubaldini, and read the name inside. 'Winterschild?'

'From the town of Langensalza, in Thuringia. The other officer's name was Brehmig. I have it from the prisoner we took, an Austrian prince.'

The colonel seized the telephone, his brown eyes furtive.

Ubaldini borrowed Prince Kaertner-Tschetterwitz from an American prisoner-of-war compound and subjected him to a merciless cross-examination under a battery of lights, at the end of which he had the wretched victim half demented with exhaustion, without incidentally having found out anything he didn't know already. Then the first clue showed up, unexpectedly, and without effort. The Carabinieri in Savona reported that there had been a holdup in which a German officer had entered a shop, stolen a suit of clothing and a bicycle, leaving his own uniform with a cynical disregard for personal safety and a beastly kind of generosity. This uniform had been marked with the name of Winterschild.

'Will you go to Savona?' asked Ubaldini.

'What is the point?' said Val di Sarat, his interest awakened by the sport of it. 'He may have gone in any direction, west into France, north towards Milan, or east into Italy.'

'Why should he go into France?'

'It is the least obvious direction to take.'

'Let us examine the map.'

Savona is astride the great coastal road connecting Rome with the French frontier. They quite rightly guessed that a man in Hans's position would scarcely ride west, even in the hope of trying to confuse potential pursuers. The immediate hazards were too real. To a lesser degree, eastward flight into Italy along one of her main arteries appeared foolhardy.

'That leaves one alternative,' said Ubaldini, 'the road to the north. In my experience, I have noticed that the escaping criminal invariably tries to disappear into the hinterland. It is only when he knows he is being pursued that he goes to earth in a big city. If I were escaping, I would go north, and then, at the first opportunity, I would take a subsidiary road. Here—' and he pointed at the network of small stone and sand highways marked 'mediocre' on the map.

A phone call from Savona announced that the bicycle had been found abandoned on the Cadibona pass by a Carabinieri patrol.

'As I thought,' said Ubaldini.

'Just a moment—' Val di Sarat seized the telephone from his uncle and asked the barely audible officer on the other end whether the shopkeeper had noticed anything peculiar about the culprit.

'Yes,' shouted the distant officer, 'he seemed to have a defect of the eye. He blinked.'

'That's our man,' said Val di Sarat, replacing the receiver. 'I'll go to Savona at once.'

Accompanied by a grim sergeant, Ottoni, who had just walked from captivity in Bulgaria, and a

dreamy little officer, Garin, who was pining for
Venice and its lingering decadence, Val di Sarat
left for Savona in a borrowed jeep. Ottoni worked
the hysterical siren with singular devotion to duty
for five hundred kilometers.

When they arrived, the chief of Carabinieri
at Savona was pacing his office, baffled by new
and contradictory information. A farmer living
near Dego had admitted to an inquiring patrol
that he had given hospitality to an English
prisoner of war with a curious blink. A family
near Mornese admitted to having given a slice
of salami the thickness of a blade of grass
to a Yugoslav prisoner of war with an ocular
oddity. After that, everyone for miles around
had miraculously given hospitality to blinking
men of all nationalities. The Italian desire to be
helpful often leads them to admit to the untrue
out of a sheer desire to please. This they now
did, with the usual results.

Val di Sarat studied the map. 'If we admit
the first report to be truthful,' he said, 'before
participation in this chase became popular in
the neighborhood, then it looks possible that
he is heading northeast towards Pavia, with the
eventual hope of reaching the Austrian frontier. That would seem to be a logical course
of action, and yet I have my doubts. Warn
Pavia.'

'Pavia is already warned,' said Barrello, distinguished Carabiniere of Savona, with the robust

satisfaction of the functionary who has successfully read into his superior's mind.

The next information did indeed come from
near Pavia. A truck was stolen by a fair-haired
man with a blink. The Carabinieri of Pavia were
watching for numbers, and repaint jobs. Val di
Sarat, Ottoni and Garin mounted their jeep and
set off north, their siren wailing. Halfway to their
destination they were overtaken by a motorcycle,
ridden as only an Italian can, and stopped. News
had reached Savona that the truck had been
found, and the thief had turned out to be a
local thief, somber as the night, and blinkless.
Muttering and downhearted, the three avengers
returned to Savona, their siren silent. A report
followed that a local train had been stolen miles
to the northwest, in the mountains.

'Is this worthy of investigation?' asked Barrello,
who attached immense importance to everything.

'No,' said Val di Sarat, and fell asleep in
his chair.

A little later, a baby carriage was stolen only
four kilometers from where Hans had been
last reported. Barrello woke Val di Sarat up
in order to ask for instructions. Val di Sarat
said a few impolite words, and then went to
sleep again.

Since there was no report made on any attempt
to steal a motorcycle in Casella, the police soon
lost the scent, and Val di Sarat returned to Rome.

His uncle laughed aloud to see his nephew so disconsolate.

'It is always the young who are depressed at failure. I know, however, that the road to success is paved with little failures, just as that to experience is paved with errors. That you failed to find this blinking criminal today means but one thing, that you will succeed in finding him tomorrow. Sooner or later, he will make a mistake, even if it is only to relieve himself against a wall where such activities are expressly forbidden, and he will be apprehended. In 1929, a bandit killed a high Fascist official in Calabria – there was nothing political about the killing – unless you can call a man's desire for the wife of a blackshirt political – some people would. We knew nothing about the man, except that the forefinger of his right hand was missing. I waited a long time to catch him.'

'How did you do it?' asked his nephew.

'I knew that sooner or later war was inevitable. Our entire economy was geared for it. Had it come in 1935, we would have done very well. Alas, we lacked the final degree of self-confidence to declare it when we were ready – and we waited slavishly for the Germans to be ready. By then, we were already out of date.' He sighed deeply. 'Be that as it may, I waited till 1940 to catch my man. Compared to me, the elephant is absent-minded. I issued instructions to all recruiting offices to hold all men rejected for military service because they lacked the member in question. In December 1940, two days before Christmas, we caught him in Padua. He had become the director of thirty-two companies, among them a couple of country banks.'

'Are you sure it was the right man?'

'Almost positive.'

'Where is he now?'

'In prison.'

'But why do you tell me all this?'

'Bedtime stories are good for the morale of young policemen. Get some sleep. You've had a trying time.'

Val di Sarat turned at the door. 'Then we'll catch him in 1960,' he said.

'If we're lucky. But we'll catch him.'

PICHL FORBADE Hans to leave the house, on the grounds that it was too dangerous. He was not even to go into the garden.

'Wait till all this blows over,' he counseled.

'But I must go to Florence.'

'Florence, Florence, what's in Florence? A girl? Why can't you take your pleasures where you find them, as I do? That's the trouble with all you wholesome specimens, you allow yourselves to grow sentimental, and become as confused mentally as I am in body. I can see clear. I despise you. Idiots.'

It was hard to argue with Pichl. He was both lucid and extremely noisy. Even someone with a bright inner light forever burning before the shrine of his convictions, like the Führer, would have found it hard going against the brassy intellect of this gnome.

'Sooner or later I'll find something for you. The world can't live without Germans and their know-how. Remember that.'

He seemed to know some secret, and his words, when he was not in wine, were more than merely reassuring, they were an anchor. Hans, prematurely aged in all but his emotions, surrendered as willingly, as gratefully even, to the peremptory domination of Pichl as he had when he was young and fresh to the bugle calls of duty.

Naturally there was much about his host which displeased him, but as he came to know him better over the weeks, it seemed as though the horrid playfulness of the little man were a natural adjunct to the serious explosions of conviction and his moments of somnolent brooding. To Hans he became a fully rounded character, a hero even, a superman who had ridden roughshod over the obstacles which life had cruelly placed in his way, and emerged a creature, who, while not untouched by the bitter price of his victory, had nevertheless acquired a scandalous gaiety and an indomitable will.

There were times when Hans thought of Teresa – usually at night, for even Pichl had to sleep – and then he began to resent the fact that the great adventure of escape which had started so promisingly had now been so strangely denied him. He had dreamed of incredible adventures, labors even, which would befall him on the way to his beloved, as they had to the heroes of antiquity, trials which gave triumph its value.

Oh, Teresa wasn't much. He had only known her for a fraction of time, and yet in the vast emptiness of his soul she was everything. He could reconstruct every detail of their meetings, the arch of her eyebrows, with one or two coarser hairs which had wandered out of line, the curve of her neck up to an ear which was always cold, the dark line touchingly, carefully, badly drawn under her eye to emphasize her knowledge of the hard ways of the world.

As the months wore on, Hans surrendered to apathy. There was nothing to do. He helped Martha about the house, Martha or others he didn't even bother to get to know. Whenever the doorbell rang, he hid. He had been told to by Pichl, and he had no alternative but to believe that it was necessary. Every evening, Pichl organized games which were trials of strength, games he always won. He would lift tables, chairs, people, and throw them around the room, and every now and then, intoxicated by the mountain wine, he would shout orders and obey them himself, running forward under fire, tumbling into cover, capturing the enemy at the point of the bayonet. There was nothing about military life he didn't

know, down to the precedence of decorations and
the precise functions of every ancillary arm. And
every night Hans would speak aloud to Teresa,
and curse himself weakly for having fallen under
this strange spell of indolent obedience to the
commands of yet another leader.

One day in August a German arrived, a surly
fellow, big and glowering. He spent one evening
there, having his hand pulverized in fun, and left
the next morning.

Pichl looked at his watch.

'In eight hours' time, he will be there.'

'Where?' Hans asked.

'Never mind.'

'But why not me? I got here first.'

Some time later, another came in the middle
of the night, riding pillion on Pichl's motorcycle.
A man by the name of Schauer, or Sauer. He was
so timid he hardly opened his mouth to speak.
When he shook Pichl's hand, he screamed. Pichl
showed no mercy on him from that moment
on, and made his two days at the house a
misery with every kind of practical joke and
low trick.

'Where has he gone?' asked Hans angrily after
he had left.

'Is there no end to your inquisitiveness?' cried
Pichl.

'I am bored here!'

'Better bored than dead.'

'Why can't I go?'

'Because you have no money and no clothes,' said Pichl coldly.

'I saw you give both to the man who just left.'

'So now you listen at doors?'

'It's time I left,' Hans insisted doggedly.

'Listen, you numbskull,' said Pichl, 'if the stories you told me are true, you seem a fairly competent officer. Your concept of what it is to have German blood in your veins is correct. You know that it entails not only pride, but responsibility as well. You are a cut above this riffraff I import over the frontier. You can be of value to the movement.'

'What movement?'

'For the moment I can't tell you. One day – we'll see how we go. All I can say now is that you have your own soldierly and fanatical qualities to blame for your retention here. That, and your blink.'

'My blink? What's my blink got to do with it?'

'My dear boy, you're far too easy to identify.'

THE THIRD German to arrive was a talkative, rough man who had once been a light heavyweight contender. His career had left its mark on him, and he bobbed and ducked as he talked, as though his nervous system were forever leading him to sidestep the blows of yesteryear.

During his initiation, he almost managed to twist
Pichl's arm off, but after an orgy of grunting it
was he who sank to one knee in submission. Both
men were in ill humor, the boxer because of his
humiliation at the hands of an elf, Pichl because
his arm hurt abominably.

'The man's mad,' the boxer confided to Hans.

'What's he asked you to do?'

'I'm not talking about that, I'm talking about
his parlor tricks.'

'Yes, mad, cracked. You did very well.'

'If he hadn't taken me by surprise, I tell you,
I'd have made dripping of him.'

'I bet you would. Where are you off to
tomorrow?'

'Christ knows. They'll tell me there.'

'Where?'

'Caffé dell' Orologio. Is that a town?'

'No, that's a café.'

'Oh.'

'Where is it?'

The boxer consulted a bit of paper. 'La Spezia.'

When the doorbell rang some days later, at
three in the morning, Hans got out of bed,
and hid. Martha happened to be staying the
night, and answered the door. Four Carabinieri
pushed past her, but couldn't prevent her from
screaming. They caught Pichl as he was about
to leap into the garden, and were badly mauled
before they overpowered him. Other militiamen
entered and began a house search. Hans watched

them through the rafters of the attic floor, and knew that, in time, they would find the way up.

For the moment they were in Pichl's room. They made journeys to the front door carrying files, ledgers and other loose documents. When they had finished there, they moved noisily to the kitchen, and the servants' quarters. Silently Hans removed the floorboard, and slid down the ladder into his room. From there, he walked as quietly as he could into Pichl's room, which was down the corridor. The little pair of leather trousers still hung tidily over the back of the chair. Digging into the back pocket, Hans found the key to the motorcycle. He dropped into the garden and ran furiously to the garage. The door was open, and a Carabiniere was examining the machine with interest. Police the world over have a tendency to carry away as much as possible in evidence, and Hans therefore rushed at the man hoping to take him off his guard. The Carabiniere turned before Hans could reach him, and the two men fought in the darkness, among the grease guns and the laths and the jerry cans. A hard blow knocked the Italian against the wall, and he sank slowly to the floor, but as he sank, he switched the light on with his back. With blood streaming from his mouth, he looked up and saw Hans standing over him, blinking. Hans picked up a wrench and brought it down mercilessly on the Carabiniere's skull. Nervously, he filled the tank of the machine from a jerry can, inserted the key in the carburetor, and roared into the night. The sudden noise brought the other Carabinieri to the windows of the house.

Ubaldini heard of Pichl's arrest with casual satisfaction, but grew more attentive on the telephone when told that a man had got away. He asked whether anyone had seen this man, and smiled comfortably when he was told what the unfortunate Carabiniere could remember of his assailant. He called his nephew, and said, 'What did I tell you? And after only six months. The fellow blinked.'

Ubaldini mused for a moment after he had replaced the receiver, then gave instructions for the course of the motorcycle to be plotted, but that on no account was it to be molested. 'You never know what he may lead us to,' he said.

Several hours later, the motorcycle was seen to enter La Spezia down the tortuous Bracco Pass, and twenty minutes after that, it was found parked in a small street in the city. Its tank was empty.

IT WAS raining when the screaming jeep arrived, and the little squads of police were cursing the November sky as well as their damned profession. Cicci, the officer in charge of the search, was a bright fellow, without much imagination but with a pleasant sense of the ridiculous once a situation was thrust upon him.

'We never think how silly it is,' he said to Val di Sarat, 'when we chase one man with a battalion of men, especially as only the other day one such man was terrorizing battalions of us. Mussolini was an optimist, worse luck. He didn't realize that Italy could only be a great military power if it was the size of the Americas, with the population of China and India combined.'

'God forbid,' said Val di Sarat. 'There are too many of us as it is. But you are quite right about Mussolini. If only he had been a pessimist how immensely prosperous we should now have been.'

'Yes,' added Garin, 'there's absolutely no point in entering a war unless you are going to win it.'

Ottoni looked at the glowering clouds.

'Water's wet in any language,' he said.

The exits to the town were sealed, and the fleet of little boats tied to their moorings was placed under constant surveillance. The little party, with an escort of armed men, began their investigations in the dockside cafés.

'The rain may help us,' said Val di Sarat, 'it will serve to localize people.'

A policeman arrived in a state of great excitement just as they were investigating the first café, to announce that a German had been caught. While he did not conspicuously blink one eye, he very conspicuously blinked both. Val di Sarat gave instructions for the search to be suspended until his return, and accompanied the policeman to headquarters. The man they had captured was not Hans, but a German on the run.

'Did you come here on a motorcycle?' asked Val di Sarat.

'No. On foot,' replied the German.

'He's lying!' cried a police officer, with a menacing gesture.

Val di Sarat waved the officer aside, and asked him whether the German had any documents.

'He had several documents.'

'What do you mean?'

'He had blank identity cards for several people.'

'Genuine?'

'Forged.'

Val di Sarat frowned.

'What's your name?' he asked the German.

'Schubert.'

'You realize that things may be easier for you if you help us. Suppose you give us your real name.'

'Schubert.' ⸻

'SCHUBERT'S LATE,' said a man in a dockside café.

'Perhaps we ought to go,' said the other man, nervously.

They both stopped to listen to the padrone, who was holding forth to his entire clientele. The law in Italy is perpetually hampered by

the fact that rumor travels much faster than
the police.

'We will certainly have a visit tonight,' he said,
'they are looking for a German with a blink.
I heard it from Giovanotto, who runs errands
for Donadei, the police doctor. This German
murdered several women in the north, so it
seemed. A thoroughly desperate character.'

The two men looked at one another, and
then the first glanced into one of the mirrors
which were supposed to invest the tiny room
with palatial proportions. He deemed it unsafe
to turn around for the moment. The Italians
were busy elaborating on the slender evidence
supplied by the errand boy, and making of it
a really worth-while story.

In a corner the man saw a figure slumped on
the table in either exhaustion or drunkenness.
There was something in the shape of the head
which seemed familiar. Strange.

'Where are you going?' asked the second man,
alarmed.

'Don't panic,' said the first man quietly, in
German. He crossed the room, and sat at the
same table as the slumped figure.

'Winterschild,' he said softly.

The mention of his name galvanized Hans into
action. The man put a restraining hand firmly on
Hans's arm. Their eyes met.

'Scherff!' said Hans.

'Yes. Not too loud.'

'But I thought you were dead.'

'No, my dear major, you are talking to a deserter. Isn't that dreadful? Do you wish to move to another table?'

Hans looked at him, worn out, apathetic.

'No,' he said.

'Funny. I thought you'd be dead by now. Your face had a Hero's End written all over it at the time I knew you.'

'No. I'm alive, and on the run.'

'Are you the man they're looking for?'

Hans nodded.

'How did you know where to come? Pichl?'

Hans nodded again. 'They caught him.'

Scherff grunted, 'It's all in the game.'

'I haven't eaten for more than a day,' Hans said.

'I'm expecting a man with identity cards at any moment – that is, if you don't mind being helped by a man who ran away in order to finish his exams.'

'How can you help me?' asked Hans, with misgivings. 'They'll find me sooner or later. Is it true that they're searching the port?'

'I don't know,' said Scherff, 'but whether these rumors are true or not, it is essential to move quickly. You will get an identity card, and I will give you some money, enough for the fare to Rome.'

'Rome? Why Rome?'

'Don't ask any questions. You will go by

autobus. The trains are not reliable yet. When you are there you will report at Via dell' Aspromonte 15. Tell them that Müller sent you.'

'Müller?'

'I am now Müller. Scherff is, as you know, dead. It was very tragic.'

'But what is all this, I don't understand.'

'You must trust me.'

The man at the other table was making urgent signals, pointing to his watch.

'Who is that?' asked Hans.

'Schneider. 342nd Panzer Grenadiers. That's not his real name. He's leaving for the Argentine.'

'When?'

Scherff smiled. 'Now,' he said.

'But how?'

'He went to Rome, like you. We found him in Genoa.'

'But what is this organization?'

'We are Germans,' said Scherff grimly, 'and whatever happens we were comrades once, and suffered together. Come on. We can't wait for Schubert. He may have been caught. You'll have to risk going without an identity card.'

They rose, and went to the door.

'*Buona sera,*' said Scherff.

'*Sera,*' answered the padrone, and explained to his friends, 'They are Swedish sailors employed on that Spanish ship in the harbor.'

Scherff saw the group of policemen far away

down the street. The reflections of their flashlights caught the glistening cobbles, and their
arguments were audible even over the hissing
rain.

'Come on,' he said, and led the way to
a landing stage. Suddenly a capstan came to
life, and challenged them. It was a Carabiniere
who had been sitting despondently in the dark,
waiting to be relieved.

'Swedish sailors,' said Scherff.

'*Documenti.*'

Scherff began to fumble among his pockets,
singing incoherently and swearing as though
slightly drunk. Schneider was his main worry.
The man was so nervous that there was a grave
risk he would give them all away. Already his
teeth were chattering noisily, and his eyes were
desperate. The Carabiniere smiled.

'*Ubbriacchi?*' he said.

'Drunk? Yes, drunk as lords. What else is there
to do in this stinking town?' answered Scherff.

'La Spezia? *Cattiva.*' The Carabiniere was eager
to run down the town so that the foreigners
should be made to feel at home.

'*Cattivississimo,*' drawled Scherff, and the Carabiniere laughed. '*Documenti niente, perduto, sul
bastimento.* They're on our ship.'

The Carabiniere stopped laughing. 'I'd let you
pass normally,' he said, 'but tonight it's more
than my job's worth.'

'Why?'

'They're looking for a German—'

He stopped talking, because he had seen Hans. Hans blinked. The Carabiniere slowly placed a whistle between his teeth. Schneider gasped. Hans noticed that the whistle was on a lanyard. The Carabiniere was preparing to blow, his finger on the trigger of the tommy gun strapped round his chest, its muzzle in the air. In a flash, Hans lunged out, caught the lanyard, and pulled with all his might. The Carabiniere cried out in pain as the whistle wrenched his teeth, but the cry was stifled by Scherff, who clamped his hand over the poor man's mouth. Hans ran behind him and pulled him backwards by the tight strap on his forearm. The Carabiniere fell to the ground, where Hans, with a brief apology, knocked him unconscious.

'Into the water?' said the neurotic Schneider, who had done nothing.

'Don't be an idiot,' said Scherff. 'We'll take him with us.'

They half carried, half pulled the limp body of the Carabiniere into the little rowboat, moored at the bottom of the steps.

'Don't use the motor yet,' said Scherff. 'Schneider, you watch the policeman.'

The boat slid into the darkness, with Hans and Scherff at the oars. When they were a little way out, and beginning to feel the ruthless swell of the sea under them, in spite of the protective

embrace of the harbor moles, Scherff relaxed and
told Hans to do likewise.

'We mustn't frighten these Spaniards. They're
not averse to helping us, but the sight of a
Carabiniere dead to the world may worry them.
Winterschild, we'll leave the harbor and drop you
and our Italian friend a little way outside Spezia
– on the road to Lerici. It's very rocky, but we'll
have to risk it.'

'But they're waiting for me on the ship,' cried
Schneider. 'They leave tonight.'

'Shut up!' cried Scherff. 'Winterschild, you'll
wait for me there, and I'll rejoin you when I've
delivered Schneider. Spezia's too hot for us for
the time being. I'll go with you as far as Leghorn.
And–' he smiled – 'I have an idea.'

'We'll all be drowned,' shouted Schneider, over
the whipping gale.

'Start the motor instead of talking!' Scherff
shouted back.

As soon as they left the harbor, they were
drenched by icy waves as high as houses, which
lingered threateningly over them before subsiding
into dizzy dives, and disappearing into the body
of the ocean. It was as though a giant were toying
with them, infinitesimal figures in the palm of his
restless hand.

Schneider's brow was wet with cold sweat,
foam and rain. 'We'll all be dead,' he intoned,
with a strident monotony.

Scherff laughed, and Hans, for his part, had

rarely felt better. The Italian came to, and silently crossed himself.

For ten minutes which seemed an hour the boat was flung hither and thither, until it began to drift in spasms towards the bleak rocks of the coast, at moments hurrying forward, at moments spinning on its axis.

'Switch the engine off!' yelled Scherff, but Schneider was past caring.

'Switch the engine off!' yelled Scherff again. The Italian had to do it.

Seizing an oar, Hans tried grimly to stave off disaster. Scherff shouted to him not to be a fool. Missing the rocks by inches, the boat cycloned into a shallow cove, where the waves, their grandeur shattered by the curl of land, contented themselves by muttering and stuttering among the pebbles.

'Sand!' cried Hans.

The boat ran aground, and fell helplessly onto its side. The sea tried angrily to suck it back out of the lap of safety, and then spewed it up again with a roar of disgust.

The four men leaped into the water. Scherff attempted to cling desperately to the boat, but Schneider ran silently ashore, and fell into a stupor of relief on the wet stones.

'Bring him back!' shouted Scherff.

The Italian, forgetting entirely whose side he was on, seized Schneider and propelled him forcibly through the nagging water. The boat

spun, and Scherff was carried from deeper water
into the shallows, where slippery rocks repelled
his feet, and back again. Hans rejoined them,
and coiled himself round the prow in the vain
hope that his weight would serve to anchor the
boat. They were like four men trying to hold a
rebellious bull for branding. If they let go, they
would all be lost.

At last Scherff struggled aboard, and nearly
capsized the craft in his struggle with Schneider,
who was resisting help with the lunatic strength
of a drowning man. The engine sputtered into
life, inaudible above the weather. The only
indication of its health were the puffs of blue
smoke it coughed into the blackness.

'You're mad to go back!' shouted Hans.

Scherff, shivering and drenched from head to
toe, laughed, and gave Hans a flashlight.

'Wish me luck!' he shouted back as the boat
turned to meet the waves. Often there was
nothing visible but the panic of water, and then
for brief seconds the whiteness of the boat would
show, a flutter of a handkerchief seen from the
corner of the eye, only finally to vanish.

'Look at that!' said the Italian, as the wind
dislodged the froth from the waves, and sent it
chasing away like shoals of sparkling fish into the
sky, there to be beaten to death by the rain.

'It's a bad night,' answered Hans, who didn't
want to talk.

'My tooth aches.'

'I'm sorry.'

THE HOURS went by in miserable silence. Every now and then Hans flashed the light towards the sea, until the bulb was orange from exhaustion. It seemed as though the dawn should have come hours ago.

The Italian, frozen, suddenly and quite reasonably became very angry, and told Hans that he had absolutely no right to detain a Carabiniere in the pursuit of his duty.

'The penalties are severe,' he said.

'So are the penalties for continuing to annoy me,' replied Hans lightly, but his negligent manner only served to irritate the Italian further.

When at last a shape could be seen swirling in the dark, the Italian was brazenly attacking the cursed Germans for all their foul works, and Hans was no longer bothering to reply. Desperately he shook the flashlight and it responded, a sleepy sun through fog. The boat, balancing for a moment on a spire of water, charged the beach in a headlong rush, only to be savagely gored by an ambushing rock. There was a noise of wrenching, audible even above the weather, and the boat disappeared from sight.

Characteristically, the Italian forgot everything once again in his errand of mercy, and plowed into the surf. Hans shouted instructions, but the Italian, mindful of his pride, shouted other instructions back to Hans. Waist-deep in water, their mouths and nostrils invaded by brine, they were hurled against each other, then apart, then against each other again. On one of these collisions, both noticed in the confusion that there were now three struggling bodies in the water.

'Get back!' shouted Scherff, belching salt water.

All three were washed onto the shore like wreckage, where they lay for a moment, helpless as landed fish, the waves inflating their clothes like balloons, and then trickling away from their prostrate limbs. The blood ran down Scherff's face.

'What are we to do?' said the Italian then minutes later, as they sat huddled in the shelter of the cliff.

As there was no reply, he appealed to them. 'Look, you are lost. Your friend here is wounded. There is no future for you. Why don't you be sensible and accompany me to the nearest police station? I'll intercede for you, and tell them that you behaved well, if irregularly. The boat, I can say, was leaking anyway, and the storm in no way contributed to its loss. The sentence will be far more lenient than if you try to escape and are captured later.'

There was no reply. Encouraged by the silence which seemed to the Italian to be the outcome of contemplation of the weight of his words, he altered his approach. 'Listen, boys, we were all soldiers together. Irrespective of nationality, soldiers are always open to the same discomfort

and to the same comradeship the world over. I'll
make things easy for you if you make things easy
for me. That is, after all, the unwritten law of
the barracks. I'll get promotion if you come with
me, and you'll get a lighter sentence. Thus we
will all help each other. It seems a very sensible
proposition to me.'

Scherff answered. 'Take off your clothes.'

'*What?*'

'We Germans will always be grateful for what
you have done. You will give us your name, and
perhaps one day we will have the opportunity of
rewarding you properly. Our barrack traditions
seem to be a little difficult, however. Take off
your clothes.'

A quarter of an hour later they parted. The
Italian dressed in underwear under his greatcoat,
blubbering with weariness and the horror of his
situation, left in the direction of La Spezia, while
the Germans walked towards Lerici.

Scherff, who was now dressed in the icy,
clinging clothes of the Carabiniere, had warned
the Italian that if he attempted to follow them
they would tie him up and leave him on the
beach. The threat seemed so awful that the
Italian stumbled off into the dark obediently.
After he had gone a short way, however, realizing
that his tormentors were no longer with him, he
found himself confronted by his sense of dignity
as a sole traveling companion, and promptly lost
his temper again. What to do?

He decided against trying to tail the criminals. It would be too awful to be overpowered and trussed up in such degrading conditions. Instead he broke into a run, and scrambled madly up the little cliff paths he knew so well. The first glimmer of slate-gray light was beginning to penetrate the blackness when he knocked furiously on the door of a small house on the Leghorn-Spezia road. Amid fierce barking, a terrified old lady appeared at a window.

'*Posso telefonare, per favore?*'

VAL DI Sarat was beginning to lose heart. The patrolling had been fruitless, and the men were wet and tired. Cicci cursed the architecture of the town. 'It makes it easy for criminals,' he said.

A relieving Carabiniere had failed to find his friend Chiarelli. The absence had been reported, and the search had been localized in the port. Tempers were running high among the shipping, where sleep had been interrupted by the visit of police launches. The Spanish ship was outside the harbor by now, and nearing the three-mile limit. Radio messages asking it to stop for inspection had been ignored, and Val di Sarat was convinced that the German had boarded it, and was now out of reach.

'The search in the town is just a routine maneuver now,' he said.

Then Chiarelli's phone call came through.

Cicci and Val di Sarat rushed to the police station sharing the same motorcycle.

'One German on the Spanish ship,' said Cicci, breathless. 'The other – what? Speak louder.'

Val di Sarat seized the phone from Cicci.

'What? *Two* Germans, one with a blink! Where? Walking towards Lerici?'

Cicci looked at the map.

'In your clothes?'

Cicci seized the phone back from Val di Sarat.

'How are you dressed?' he roared.

There was a pause.

'Aren't you ashamed of yourself!'

'No time to lose,' snapped Val di Sarat.

Telephones were active. Everyone was shouting. Half an hour later a Carabiniere was arrested at Lerici. Three quarters of an hour later this Carabiniere had successfully proved his authenticity, and was reprimanded by his commander for looking suspect.

AN HOUR before the fresh alarm, Hans and Scherff had reached the main Via Emilia at Avanza, and had thumbed a lift from an American jeep filled with soldiers, who, it appeared, were not going anywhere in particular. Scherff had found a pair of handcuffs in the pocket of his tunic, and now he was ironically linked to Hans as though they were prisoner and escort.

The soldiers were singing of New Orleans in

its heyday, and were past caring about military matters, so they were quite content to run their new-found friends as far as Leghorn, although their essential mission was to deliver a can of kerosene a mile down the road from their starting point.

'Where d'you want to go, bud?' said the grinning sergeant, as they stopped in one of the main thoroughfares.

'*Quì, quì,*' answered Scherff, eager to disappear into the streets before people were out and about. It was only about eight o'clock in the morning.

The word '*quì*' seemed to tickle the fancy of the soldiers, who roared with delight, and set it to jazzy music. Dutifully Scherff joined in the laughter, and got out, followed by Hans. The soldiers implored Scherff not to treat Hans too harshly. 'Hell,' roared the sergeant, 'you only live once in a lifetime, that's what I say, and that once is sheer hell, so why not forget the whole damn thing.'

'What's he done anyway?' cried another one. 'Stayed home overtime with a broad?' And they rocked with renewed laughter, until the arrival of a U.S. military police patrol in the distance sobered them abruptly.

'Brother, this is where we leave,' said the sergeant. He maneuvered the jeep so as to attract the maximum of attention, turning in a wide arc over the pavement, shattering a garbage pail, bouncing back onto the road with a groan of agony from

the springs, and then flashing away to a symphony of whistles from the suspicious MPs.

'Quick,' said Scherff, and the two men, linked
by the handcuffs, ran down a side street. The
MPs began cantering after them. As they turned
first left, then right, Scherff wished he had never
had the overclever idea, which hindered them,
and had fulfilled no purpose, except to excite
the garrulous sympathy of the compassionate
soldiers, and cause them to linger long enough
for the MPs to come into sight.

This headlong flight was precarious to a degree.
No passer-by would call the vision of a policeman
sprinting with a handcuffed culprit natural, and
each new corner held the possibility of a disagreeable surprise.

It had been so stupid to start running. As a
disheveled Italian, he might have bluffed his way
through by pretending to talk no other language,
but then of course the U.S. patrol might have
been hand-picked from men of Italian origin.
Perhaps it had been as well to run.

Instinctively both dashed for cover into one
of the strange gentlemen's conveniences which
add to the comfort if not to the beauty of
Latin cities. Here they hid behind the sheet
of protective metal, their backs leaning on the
central structure, their feet off the ground, tucked
awkwardly behind the metal shield. They waited
and watched through the ornamental design of
punchwork. The Americans soon appeared, and

slowed down to a walk as the empty street baffled them.

They expressed their irritation by shouting at each other. Then one of them, a white-helmeted giant, approached, with the obvious intention of making his burden lighter to bear. Hans and Scherff were unable to move. They felt like statues cruelly infused with life. The American did not enter the convenience, however. He regarded it as a symbol rather than as a reality, and proceeded to relieve himself against the outside, his face only a couple of feet away from theirs. His rhapsodic humming of 'Night and Day' made the tension even more ghastly to the fugitives inside.

When he had finished his pleasurable duty, he stood for a while looking at the ridiculous pagoda with a patronizing affection, inspecting every detail of the architecture, but never catching Hans's or Scherff's eye through the slots.

Eventually he turned away, and called to his friends, 'Say, Don, can you imagine putting up a ***** insanitary thing like that?'

Don called back. 'What d'you say we forget the whole ***** thing?'

'Sure, ***** it,' said the first American, and they resumed their beat as though they had seen or heard nothing untoward.

The two Germans relaxed, their bodies stiff with the strain of maintaining their unnatural positions.

'Where's that damned key?' whispered Scherff, as he fumbled among unfriendly pockets.

At last he found it lurking in the tattered lining, and turned it in the lock.

'18, Via 22 Gennaio,' he said.

'What's that?'

'We'll separate now. Stand a better chance. Go there. Top floor. Ask for Sandbeck.'

'Where is it?'

'One of the roads leading from the harbor. Don't forget. 18, Via 22 Gennaio. You leave first. Good luck.'

Hans left the fetid shelter with some relief, and was soon walking briskly towards the sea. He suddenly felt that sensation of appalling weariness which people in less generous countries experience as they gladly confess to crimes of which they are innocent for the paltry remuneration of a little sleep. The world looked uninviting under the heaviness of his eyelids, and he felt that perhaps the simplest course of action was surrender. For the guilty, the distance is a prison.

It was raining, still raining, with an unrelenting gentleness. The sky had endless reserves. It could go on like this for weeks.

By chance he looked at a street sign. It read 'VIA 22 GENNAIO.' He was not particularly relieved, just obedient to his instructions. He soon found the house he wanted and climbed the stairs, which curled sinuously round a dark courtyard, open to the sky. The rain accompanied him on his journey.

He rang a bell, and a rough voice spoke to him in good Italian, in Italian which was too good. He smiled and realized that he was too tired to remember the name he had been told to mention. Such negligence, such inability to think, warranted surrender.

'Steinbock,' he said.

The voice on the other side of the door was puzzled and suspicious.

'There's no one of that name here.'

'Steinberg. Steinbeck, Salzburg.'

'What do you want with this man?'

Hans threw caution to the winds, and spoke in German.

'Scherff sent me,' he said.

There was a pause.

'I don't understand German,' said the voice.

With a hopeless gesture of supreme irritation at his own stupidity, Hans corrected himself. 'Müller,' he said. 'I come from Müller at La Spezia. Has he arrived yet?'

'What's your name?' said the voice.

'Winterschild, 108th Infantry. And now I remember the other name. Sandbeck. I'm exhausted.'

There was a jangle of chains, and the door was opened by a small, blond, bald man, casually dressed.

'Come in,' he said.

Hans entered the room which was practically unfurnished. There was a camp bed, a gas ring, and a bag full of clothes.

'You really must be more careful,' said the man. 'Such carelessness as yours may cost us all our liberty. My name in Leghorn is Roberti. I am—'

Hans heard no more. He dropped limply onto the camp bed, and fell into a sleep perilously near death, illustrated by deeply mysterious images, undimensional.

HE WOKE twenty hours later with the winter sunlight streaming onto his face. He was on the floor. Sandbeck was on the bed. Of Scherff there was no sign.

As Hans lay on the floor, he shut his eyes again, and could feel the rays of the sun penetrating his pores.

'Good morning.' Scherff came in through a door giving onto the roof. He was dressed in old civilian clothes.

'Where have you been?' asked Hans.

'Out on the tiles, having a cup of coffee.'

'Coffee?'

'Acorns. Want one?'

'I'm starving.'

'Come on.'

Sandbeck grunted in his sleep, sighed, opened one eye, and said, 'Shut up.'

Scherff smiled. 'Dreadful character.'

Sandbeck muttered something, and turned over. It was hard to believe that only recently there had been such excitement. The sky looked newly washed, and the air held a promise of noonday warmth. At the moment it was crisp and bracing. The sounds in the street traveled far, with crystal clarity.

Hans screwed up his face as he looked into the blinding light. The town was very calm. The great bare trees waved gently to and fro, and the stippling on the pavement altered its pattern like a net in clear water. Hans smiled. He was noticing things again.

'You will leave at eleven o'clock,' said Scherff.

'Where for?'

'Rome, as I told you.'

Hans spoke on a sudden impulse. 'I want to go to Florence,' he said.

Scherff looked surprised. 'Florence? Why?'

Oh, what harm was there in it?

'A girl,' said Hans.

'You, with a girl?' said Scherff. 'Incredible' – and then he changed his tone of voice. 'Listen, I didn't do all I have done for you for fun. When you have paid back your debt, you can go wherever you like, but for the moment you will do as you are told.'

'My debt?' asked Hans. 'But I thought this was a patriotic organization, in which there is no thought of remuneration.'

Scherff grinned knowingly. 'It is a patriotic

organization, but it is like all other organizations in that its officials must live.'

'I am not clear about this. Are you referring to a moral or a financial debt?'

'When you reach Rome, you will see that it comes to the same thing.'

Sandbeck came out onto the roof, yawning and unkempt.

Scherff continued. 'You will catch the autobus which reaches Rome at about six or seven this evening. To refresh your memory, you will report at Via dell' Aspromonte 15, where you will say that Müller sent you from Spezia. Tell them that Schneider left on the S.S. *Fernando Po* as per schedule, and that Spezia is closed for the moment. Müller has joined Sandbeck at Leghorn.'

'How long are you staying here?' Sandbeck asked.

'A month, two months.'

'God,' said Sandbeck, 'there's no privacy.'

'To continue, you will travel in clothes which our friend Sandbeck will give you.'

'I only have one overcoat to wear myself,' said Sandbeck angrily.

Scherff smiled. 'Now you have none. Hans, you will be deaf and dumb, and wear dark glasses. I have a hearing aid to fix to your ear. You will carry a map of Rome in your pocket. You will talk to no one.'

He dug into his pocket.

'Here is the bus fare, a thousand lire in Allied military currency as pocket money. A loan, mind you. And I'm afraid you will have to go without documents owing to the fact that Schubert – tell them that Schubert never turned up. They may know more than we, and anyway their guess is as good as ours.'

Hans looked at Scherff with a kind of admiration.

'You know,' he said, 'when you were in the unit I would never have entrusted you with a job requiring such courage and such initiative.'

'And I,' answered Scherff, 'would never have believed that a woman would play a part in your life. There you are. Life is full of surprises, and men are fashioned by circumstances.'

He thought for a moment, and added, 'Even Nazis.'

IX

WHEN THE autobus was passing by Fallonica in the early afternoon, a jeep overtook it at great speed. Val di Sarat, seated by the driver, passed a few feet from Hans. Neither saw the other. It was as though a theatrical company had played La Spezia and Leghorn and was now entering Rome in order to re-enact its drama there.

The police and Carabinieri were intensifying their search of the area south of Spezia when Hans arrived in Rome. He was helped from the vehicle by the other passengers, who were eager to show their gratitude to a '*mutilato della guerra.*' They were in an elevated mood, as they were to a man members of the great drifting population created by the war, and were approaching home after a long night of danger and isolation. They sang '*Stornelli*' and wept as they stood once again on the sacred soil of their mother city. Hans smiled weakly, waved at them, and limped away into the streets.

The buildings were inundated with the liquid evening light, which threw huge shadows recklessly and boldly into the distance. The ocher-tinted walls seemed to have relapsed into a great serenity, pure and noble as music for strings, warm, yet aloof. The angels on the churches smiled, their dimples picked out by the teasing play of light and shade. The lettering on the prophets' scrolls were uncannily legible, each letter grooved deep and true and black on the gray stone. It was a time of day for the eye to rejoice in the minutest subtleties, in the most delicate insinuations of architecture, pervaded as they were with the crystalline atmosphere of youthful twilight. Rome lay like a display of overripe fruit in the dish of hills, and it was worth clinging onto life.

Via dell' Aspromonte was to be found not, as Hans had expected, in some murky trans-Tiber quarter, but right in the heart of the commercial and social district, a stone's throw away from the atrocious Altar of the Nation, that exuberance of dead-white colonnades commonly known to visitors as 'The Wedding Cake.'

It was a tortuous thoroughfare, picking its way cunningly through a network of stubbornly misplaced buildings. Number fifteen was that typically Roman paradox, an ultramodern, neon-lighted shop inserted brutally into the flank of a *quattrocento palazzo*, which in its turn gave way in certain places to mossy stones betraying a pre-Christian origin. At first Hans refused to believe that the address was the right one. He had negotiated so many twisting stairways that he naturally viewed this brazen modernity with some misgiving. Then he thought again.

The shop was a shipping agency called Compagnia Montes y Maier, a Spanish name, but linked to a German one. Incredibly, there were travel posters in the window, and among them a model of a steamship, and a smaller one of a cargo boat. He looked at them casually. The white passenger ship was beautifully made, a creamy, glossy toy which took Hans back to his childhood. It would smell of lacquer. Hans squatted to appreciate it from close to. The master craftsman had inserted real glass in even the most unapproachable port-hole, while the network of tiny ropes was accurate to the most minute detail. Even the planks on the deck were to scale. Hans looked at the bows. The boat was the S.S. *Presidente Padilla Lopez* from Buenos Aires.

He looked at the other ship, the tramp steamer. Not nearly as attractive, and yet somehow more redolent of the sea, more adventurous. The tall funnel, with its bold red and yellow stripes, had all the slightly pathetic dignity of a celebrity living out a grudging retirement. It could grumble, that funnel, and reprimand the squat, silent youngsters of today; it was traditional, it had authority. The ship was called the S.S. *Fernando Po*, Barcelona.

Abruptly Hans looked up, to find a pair of pale blue eyes looking at him from the depths of the shop. There was no mistake. He went in. The man inside did not acknowledge him, but just stood there, gazing. Instead, a small, dark assistant appeared from behind a curtain, and asked Hans whether he needed anything. Hans spoke in his curious Italian, although he had noticed from the accent that the dark man was a foreigner too.

'I come from Signor Müller at La Spezia.'

The dark man looked at him steadily.

'Signor Müller? How is he?'

'He is with Signor Sandbeck at Leghorn.'

The dark man looked at the silent spectator, who opened a door and beckoned Hans through it without saying a word. The dark man disappeared behind his curtain.

Hans and the blue-eyed man climbed up two flights, and then entered a smartly furnished waiting room.

'I'll find out whether he can see you,' said the blue-eyed man in German.

'Who?'

The blue-eyed man smiled, and went out. Hans, left alone, glanced round the room. It was very simple, and yet very comfortable. The lighting was indirect. On the face of it, it was an ideal waiting room for a reputable company on a secure financial footing, and yet there seemed to Hans to be something dishonest, or obscure, about it. All the furniture gave a strange impression of concealing something else. He had no further occasion to reflect, however, because the blue-eyed man returned, and said 'Follow me.'

The door to the next room was thrown open, and Hans found himself in the presence of a man whose personality struck him immediately and forcibly. He was tall and broad, with prematurely white hair lying back romantically along the sides of his head. His skin was tanned to an almost Red Indian hue, and a pair of pure gray eyes of hypnotic intensity stared inhumanly from exceptionally deep sockets. He was a study in the most startling contrasts. His nose was razor-sharp, his lips thin as files, the lines on his face definite and grim. Even when he smiled, which was often, he was unable to lose the look of a startled petrel which proclaimed both his initiative and his capacity for desperate courage. It was a presence which would have lent distinction to the austere, greedy ranks of the Teutonic Order, bearing lightly a title of sonorous splendor. Here was the pith of Germany at its most militant, its most unswerving, its most ancient.

'Here we have no names,' he said, smiling his

humorless, dangerous smile, 'so call me Erhardt
and invent a name for yourself.'

'My name—'

'I don't want to hear it. Sit down.'

They both sat down.

'Well, have you thought of a name?' asked
Erhardt.

'My mother's maiden name was—'

'Nothing too complicated now. Something
very simple. A name to lose in the crowd.'

Hans laughed.

'Schmidt,' he said.

'We already have a Schmidt.'

'Schneider. He's gone.'

'He got off, did he? Good. Yes, you could be
the new Schneider, but we try not to duplicate
names if we can help it. It would be better to
think of something entirely new.'

'Hansen,' suggested Hans.

'Yes. Yes. I don't think we have a Hansen on
the books. Vaguely Danish origin. Yes, it's very
piquant. Good. Fine. Now, Hansen, have you
any news for me?'

'We had trouble at La Spezia. Müller's had to
clear out, and he's with Sandbeck at Leghorn.'

'What sort of trouble?' asked Erhardt keenly.

'My fault, I'm afraid.'

'I'm not concerned with blame. What happened?'

'Schubert's disappeared.'

Erhardt thought, betraying no emotion.

'So Schubert's disappeared,' he said. 'It's almost certainly a capture. If by any chance it isn't, God help him.'

'Schneider lost his head. We had a dreadful time.'

'Good riddance.' Erhardt smiled, lit a pipe, and then said, 'Now I shall explain to you what we do, and roughly how we do it. By the way, why do you blink like that?'

Hans blushed involuntarily.

'Russia,' he said.

Erhardt nodded slightly in understanding. He could ask the most embarrassing questions with the single-mindedness of a doctor. Questions were, to him, not devices of speech to be treated with discretion. They were just the quickest and neatest way of arriving at answers.

'Our job is to get Germans out of Italy—'

'But I don't want to leave Italy—'

'Just a minute, just a minute. Nor do I.' Erhardt laughed. 'That is only part of our work. There are those who wish to go to the Argentine, or to Central America. Countries like Guatcmala badly need German technicians. They dislike the Americans. Enforced familiarity has led to the logical outcome. Also we have large German minorities in all Latin American countries. It is very convenient. What I have done is to approach this company, Montes y Maier, whose representatives I knew intimately in Hamburg before the war, and I suggested to them an arrangement whereby I collect Germans and send them to Latin America once specific jobs have been found for them, and then, once they are there, they pay a percentage of their earnings to the parent office in Buenos Aires or Montevideo, or in whatever area they happen to be. I am paid a salary here, with a variable percentage according to the quantity of men I send across. You are frowning. Why?'

Hans answered with a little feeling. 'It sounds like white slave traffic to me.'

Erhardt laughed. 'Perhaps. But think for a moment of the alternative. What future would a man like Schneider have in Germany? Not very intelligent, not very clever, rather stupid in fact. The Wehrmacht trained him to mend the most intricate tank engines, and now he has a job in Asunción as a technician in one of the largest garages in Paraguay. He will be paid over twice as much as he would be in Germany, where such people can be found anywhere. Even if he pays ten per cent of his salary away all his life, are you going to tell me that he will not be better off than if he had stayed in Europe?'

'What if he refused to fulfill his bargain once he is safely there?'

Erhardt shrugged his shoulders. 'None of us have passports or papers of any sort. We have to rely on our benefactors. With friendly money on our side, anything is possible, but if we are disobedient – you understand?'

'But, as time goes by—'

Erhardt laughed again. 'I am not suggesting that this state of affairs will last forever. But until we begin to be courted by both West and East – in other words, until the hypocrisy of the forced hatred of war is replaced by the hypocrisy of the forced affection of peace – we must survive by our wits.'

'Why are you telling me all this?'

Erhardt looked ruthless. 'Because I want my activities to be understood. I am working for the benefit of the German soldiers, and only incidentally earning my living. I work secretly, but only in so far as the Italian officials are concerned. Here, everything is, and must be, aboveboard.'

Hans rose and walked to the window. Erhardt watched him, and then asked, quietly, 'Are you satisfied so far?'

Hans turned. 'Just as a matter of interest, what would be your reaction if I said I wanted no part of this business?'

'Are you going to say that?'

'Not necessarily.'

'Exactly. If you had said so, I would have considered you a fool, first of all because you hadn't bothered to hear me out, and secondly because you haven't a chance alone. That, don't you see, is my main strength.'

'No, I don't see that,' said Hans. 'I could give you away.'

'Why would you do that?'

Hans reflected. 'I want you to tell me more.'

Erhardt continued in a tone of slightly weary magnificence. He was used to qualms, and to pep talks. 'I have explained to you about our work in the New World, which I deal with personally. Now there is another aspect to our activities. The Levant. The department run by Fromm, whom you have met briefly downstairs. He is an airman. The Levant is mainly attractive to airmen, you see. The Jews will be supported by the United States. Not officially, of course. It will all be unofficial, and, in its way, quite amusing. Shortly you will find American pleasure yachts plying the Mediterranean, filled with war material supplied by wealthy Jews. The Russians will also wish to help the Palestinians, but will be embarrassed to find themselves on the same side as the Americans. Still, the Jews will be well supplied. This is what I prophesy.

'Now, I thought, what contributions can we Germans make? To cut a long story short, owing to my initiative in certain quarters, we are now supplying the Lebanese and other Arab states with ex-Luftwaffe personnel. In these transactions, I receive a cash payment for each qualified man I deliver according to their merit, so many thousand lire for a pilot, a little less for an observer, a little more again for a radio engineer, considerably less for ground staff, and so on. Their salary, once they reach their destinations, is their own. That is that story. Now, coming from the general to the particular, what is your personal aim in all this? You don't want to leave Italy?'

'No,' said Hans vigorously.

'Are you absolutely sure? I never ask about the past, because it is none of my business, but if there should be any reason why further residence here would be unwise, nothing could be easier than to fly you to Beirut, or preferably, to ship you to B.A.'

'Why would it be preferable to ship me to B.A.?'

Erhardt laughed softly.

'I believe in long-term investments.'

'I see. The fact remains, I want to stay here.'

'A prolonged stay in Italy must be of a permanently temporary nature, if you understand me,' said Erhardt.

'I don't.'

'Italy is not as attractive a proposition to me as the others, for the simple reason that it does not offer prospects to compare with more unexploited countries. My local business here cannot last forever.'

'You mean you will eventually run out of Germans.'

'No, I don't mean entirely what you think,' said Erhardt. 'I visualized a situation whereby the Allies, in a fit of vindictiveness, mingled with a kind of misplaced pacific urge, would destroy all our captured war equipment as a symbol of their victory. I have never forgotten what they did to our fleet the last time. Well, I salvaged what equipment I could. Stole it from dumps. Rebuilt it.'

'What on earth for?' asked Hans. 'Surely you're not going to reopen the Italian campaign by yourself?'

'No.' Erhardt was smiling keenly. 'No, but the Italians have started making films about their blessed partisans. Now the first Americans are coming over to immortalize their ephemeral successes in celluloid. The British will follow. Do you understand?'

'No.'

'You surprise me. In order to win a battle, it is necessary to have an enemy, even in the cinema. Correct?'

'Correct.'

'Very well, but if you destroy all his equipment, he is hardly a worthy enemy, and detracts from the splendor of your successes, even in the cinema. Correct?'

'I suppose so.'

'It stands to reason that if the Italians blow up a German tank made of cardboard, they are not particularly heroic, even in the cinema. Correct?'

'No.'

'The idiots didn't foresee the situation, and now they come crawling to me, and hire what equipment they can, in order to blow it up.

My mechanics repair it. Then it is ready to be blown up in another film. As there is very little competition, I can ask what I like.'

'Fantastic,' said Hans.

'Common sense,' answered Erhardt. 'Do you wish to work for me in Italy?'

Hans shrugged his shoulders. 'Yes,' he said.

'Any particular requests?'

'I would like to go to Florence.'

'Florence?'

'Yes, because—'

'I want no reason,' interrupted Erhardt. 'So long as you play fair with me, I don't want any explanations. All I expect is good work and loyalty.'

Then he seemed to remember something. 'I will see what I can do about Florence,' he added, 'meanwhile, you will sleep tonight at the Hotel Brioni-Excellent, a third-rate place, but clean. Here is ten thousand lire in advance of your eventual salary. It will be repaid me out of your commission. Call in at ten o'clock tomorrow, when my photographer Bergmann will take a portrait for your identity card. Any other questions?'

'No,' said Hans, 'not at the moment. Where is the Hotel Brioni-Excellent?'

Erhardt chuckled, and rose from his desk.

'We have a traditional manner of welcoming new friends,' he said. 'I'll run you over in my car.'

'Your car?' asked Hans. 'How did you get a car?'

'Better ask me how I got the petrol. It's far harder to come by than a car. But if you do ask me, it will be the one question I won't answer.'

AT ABOUT the same time, Val di Sarat was dining with his uncle at Alfredo's Restaurant in the Via della Scrofa, not many streets distant. Colonel Ubaldini insisted on ordering his favorite dishes of *fettucini* and breast of turkey done in batter before he thrashed out the problem of his nephew's failure. The bottle of white Cinqueterre was dull with cold, but still it had not reached the requisite temperature, and was sent back.

'One must be able to appreciate that slightly floral bouquet to the full,' he said to the waiter, in the gently admonishing tone of a fallen angel philosophically acclimatized to the dismal temperature on earth. 'And that can only be achieved when the liquid stabs the tongue senseless. It is at the moment of the tongue's revival from the shock that the glorious aroma, vitalized by the natural warmth of the mouth, first declares itself. One can feel it lingering at the base of the nasal passages, and one can breathe it out, like an ephemeral perfume briefly and irretrievably sensed on a country ramble. At this temperature, which is somewhere near boiling point, the wine tastes like a heavy Bordeaux, which sits on the tongue like an old lady, and belabors the palate with her parasol.'

The waiter, thoroughly confused, declared that the bottle had been on ice all day.

'All day is far too long,' shouted Ubaldini, outraged. 'Cinqueterre is a delicate wine, a wine which cannot and must not travel. It is like a rare tropical bird, which wilts and dies in captivity, its plumage faded, its mating call a croak. Open that bottle now, and all we will taste is freezing water redolent of cork. Take it right away, and give it to that American general I see sitting over there. Tell him it is a rare specialty, and charge him double. Keep the profit yourself. He will be delighted, because Americans enjoy things which are inordinately expensive, even if they are thoroughly unenjoyable. I will be pleased to watch him, because I never tire of the entertainment afforded by human idiocy. It is the reason I love my work. Before you do that, however, bring me a bottle of your best Lacrima Cristi. A pity, for I had set my heart on Cinqueterre, but it will be quite a change to sip the nectar of the grape fed from the bowels of the planet, the cream of the lava which destroyed Pompeii. The wine has a splendidly robust tang of iron and ashes, the quality of a great caricature. What are you standing there for? Go and get it.'

The waiter, his mouth open with admiration at such compelling yet incomprehensible loquacity, gazed stupidly at the colonel before returning abruptly to earth and his functions.

Ubaldini shrugged his shoulders. 'And they talk of educating the masses!' he said. 'I don't believe that fellow understood a word I said.'

'May I begin?' asked Val di Sarat.

'But you have not yet been served,' observed his uncle.

'I'm referring to my story.'

'Ah, yes. Your story. How was the weather up there on the coast? Deplorable? I heard it was.'

Val di Sarat, remembering his sacrifices of several nights' sleep, to say nothing of a slight temporary deafness occasioned by Ottoni's irrepressible siren song, began to allow a little annoyance to penetrate his manner.

'I thought you regarded the matter as urgent?' he said.

'No. Not a bit. Nothing is ever as urgent as you imagine. Urgency is the hallmark of a subordinate. A real chief is never in a hurry, and is only surprised by the expected.'

'Even in a matter of life and death?'

'My dear boy, the ambulance, packed with subordinates, rushes through the streets at the public peril in order to reach the hospital with the invalid. At the hospital, the great surgeon takes his time.'

'And what if the patient dies?'

'It is an act of God. I am a fatalist in these matters.'

'Well, then, I won't tell you what I have to.'

'Don't be silly, my dear chap, a suitable interval has now elapsed for you to impart your message without appearing to be unduly servile – only don't rush with the narrative.'

There was silence. Ubaldini looked keenly at his nephew.

'Now you are sulking. That is even worse than eagerness. You must not mind it, my lad, if I teach you your job in an indirect way. I trust in your intelligence, and know that you will learn many valuable lessons in being irritated by me.'

Val di Sarat burst out. 'Once and for all, I am not in the least interested in your job. When this particular chore is over, I will go to sea. It's all settled in my mind, so do let's catch this fellow quickly.'

'All in good time,' said the uncle, attacking the breast of turkey which had just been placed before him. 'This impatience does so betray your inexperience. Think of the businessmen who casually buy and sell the world to each other. When two of them meet in order to discuss ruining a third, they have lunch together. Over their aperitif, they discuss golf. Over their hors d'oeuvres, they discuss the stock market. Over their meat they discuss women. Over their cheese, they malign mutual acquaintances. Over their brandy, they tell dirty stories, and just as one of them rises to go to another appointment they formulate a plan of diabolical intricacy in a very few words, and the fate of their absent rival is sealed undemonstratively and efficiently.

'It is the same with statesmen. When they meet to negotiate a treaty, they spend ninety per cent of the time at banquets or at the opera, getting to dislike one another. Only on the last day of a week's ritual do they dip their pens into the ink and sign the document which would have taken lesser men five minutes to sign and seal. But they know that to be important a man must bask publicly in a luxury of wasted time. The turkey is delicious, and the wine, although a little on the young side, has an exuberance and an impatience which is particularly appropriate tonight. Tell me, do red-headed women attract or repel you?'

It was only when the colonel was lying back in his chair, spasmodically and noisily sipping a black coffee laced with some digestive liqueur, and puffing greedily at the twisted rope of an Italian cigar, that he consented at last to talk of the fruitless chase.

'You failed to catch Winterschild,' he said, slowly, 'but you caught a man called Schubert, carrying on his person a quantity of forged personal documents. Congratulations. He may have a special value.'

'Cross-examination has extracted nothing from him.'

'I am not thinking of information,' said Ubaldini. 'I am thinking of the fact that we hold him in custody. You look puzzled. Never mind. Go on with your story.'

'I am convinced,' Val di Sarat said, with passion, 'that the Germans have some sort of organization in Italy for helping each other.'

Ubaldini smiled.

'You don't believe me?'

'Of course,' answered Ubaldini. 'I am sure they have.'

'And what is more,' Val di Sarat went on, 'they are being smuggled out of the country by a Spanish ship, the *Fernando Po*. If one Spanish ship does it, I don't see why all the ships of that particular shipping line couldn't do it. The first step is to find out, tomorrow morning, the names of other ships of the Spanish companies plying between Spain and Italian harbors.'

'The *Fernando Po*, the *Conquistador*, the *Hidalgo*, the *Almendralejo*, and the *Juan José Llossas*,' said the colonel, grinning, self-satisfied.

'You know them—?'

'My dear boy, the trade is not confined to the Spanish shipping lines. The company in question is the Compañia Oriental y Nacional of Barcelona. It is linked commercially to an Argentine group called the Atlantica La Plata, S.A., which is, in its turn, the parent company of a Panamanian shipping line, a handful of factories engaged in light industry, various obscure nitrate interests, a chain of garages, a host of other activities, and a shipping agency called Montes y Maier.'

'D'you mean to say you know about it?'

'Naturally.'

'And you don't stop it?!'

Val di Sarat was really angry. Had he been wasting his time? Was anybody above suspicion?

The uncle looked at the drifting smoke of his cigar as though trying to hypnotize it.

'Why should I try to stop it?' he said, very softly.

Val di Sarat slapped the table, vehemently.

'Because it is your duty!'

The uncle looked at him quickly, and said, 'Listen, dear fellow.' The colonel leant forward, and talked quietly to his dense nephew. 'We are traditionally the most hospitable nation in the world. It is a tradition of which I am proud. The country is still full of Germans on the run, without papers, or with forged papers. They are escaping on ships, and occasionally by plane. As you say, they are organized; very well organized, being Germans. Consequently, their attempts to evade us are invariably successful. But then, of course, I make no real effort to prevent them from going, except when an incident like this case of Major Winterschild occurs, and our paths cross by accident.'

He smiled at Val di Sarat's intensely concentrated, incredulous face, and continued. 'Italy has enough internal problems to occupy the

Carabinieri all the time. There are bandits in the Abruzzi, bandits in Sicily, bandits in Calabria, and Communists everywhere in the north and center. We have no time, no men and no inclination to torment these fugitives, who, until so recently, were our comrades in arms. Why should I go out of my way to obstruct with a lot of silly officialdom the men who are doing the job I have to do, but more efficiently than I could? You look surprised.'

'But what guarantee have you that they are in fact clearing out of the country at a consistent rate? I mean we may have lighted on an isolated case.'

'Dear nephew, I watch them. Oh yes, I watch them. Occasionally I even make an arrest, just to keep them on their toes.'

'But who are they?' insisted the perplexed Val di Sarat. 'Who is at the head of it? And how do we catch this fellow Winterschild, and prevent him from leaving the country?'

'One question at a time,' said the uncle, smiling. 'The head of it is a charming but intensely disagreeable fellow who calls himself Erhardt. The paradox amuses you? I am glad, it was intended to be funny. The case of Winterschild will be reopened tomorrow, and it will not be difficult to catch him now, you mark my words.'

'But what are you going to do?'

'Eat, my dear child, eat. I shall eat another breast of turkey, because mine is an inordinately large frame to uphold. With it we will share another bottle of Lacrima Cristi. Will you join me? By the way, it was silly of you to force all this information out of me during our first dinner. Now we will have nothing to talk about during the second.'

THE NEXT morning, Hans reported to Montes y Maier at the time appointed, had his photograph taken, and then went to see Erhardt. He found him in an ebullient mood.

'Things have turned out well,' he said. 'Go next door. You will find a row of men in there. Join that row. It is a little bit like an identity parade, but it need not frighten you. Don't ask me any questions. I am superstitious, and talking about it may ruin our chances.'

As Hans reached the door, Erhardt called after him. 'By the way, Hansen, you may have to leave Rome today, without waiting for the identity papers. It all depends—'

Hans, who had slept well and who felt ready for any new adventure, asked no questions but went obediently to the next room. Here he found a line of men being segregated into two sections. They were all unmistakably German. At one end of the room sat the blue-eyed man from the shop, and a gnarled fellow whose otherwise sober dress was enlivened by a tie which was covered with pineapples and words of love in Hawaiian.

Hans saw all eyes turn towards him, and

heard the gnarled man say, 'That's not a very brutal face.'

'But it is a very characteristic German type,' said the blue-eyed man.

The gnarled man considered the problem importantly. 'Yeah, I like that blink. That's good. That's very good for the guy that breaks down, the guy with the Jewish mother.' The gnarled man studied Hans with the expert eye of a surveyor.

'How tall are you?' he asked at length.

'One meter ninety-six,' said Hans, puzzled.

'A good height. I like that height,' said the gnarled man as though someone had had the temerity to contradict him.

'Is he in?' inquired the blue-eyed man.

'He's in,' said the gnarled man.

The blue-eyed man looked at Hans. 'Kindly join the left-hand group,' he said.

Three hours later, Hans found himself sealed in the back of a heavy diesel truck with ten others. It was pitch dark, and most uncomfortable. The acrid fumes of oil rose through the floor. Hans asked his colleagues if they knew where they were all going. Rumor had it that they were going to be film stars.

Two Hours after the departure of the truck, a police officer appeared at Montes y Maier, and asked to see Signor Erhardt. He was asked to sit down, and Erhardt came down the stairs smiling from ear to ear, betraying no misgivings.

'Can I help you, *Tenente?*' he asked.

'I come from Colonello Ubaldini,' said the officer. 'He presents his compliments, and requests you to join him for a drink at Rosati's at six o'clock tonight.'

Erhardt thought for a moment, and then said regretfully, 'Oh, do tell him that I am most touched by his invitation, but unfortunately I have a prior engagement with a business associate.'

The police officer smiled. 'A refusal will be treated as a deliberate evasion,' he said.

Erhardt smiled back. He, too, was a master at the game. 'I would rather disappoint my business associate than Colonel Ubaldini.'

The police officer saluted, and left. It was just after twelve.

Peeping through a small keyhole at the back of the slow-moving truck, Hans recognized those curious moss-laden honey-combs, the Etruscan tombs near Sutri.

'We're going north,' he told the others.

'On which road?' they asked.

'The Flaminia. Towards Siena and Florence.'

At two o'clock, the truck stopped. The back was opened, and a number of strangely drawling civilians appeared carrying plates of sandwiches and bottles of wine. Hans recognized their accents as being unmistakably American. As the Germans sat and ate their lunch, the sunlight streaming into their prison, one of them asked an American where they were.

'Place called Aquapendente,' he said.

'And where are we going?'

'Don't ask me, brother. I only just hit Rome. I'm not the driver. All I know is that we get where we're going after dark.'

At a few minutes before three they were incarcerated once again, and the truck left. Hans knew this road well from his memory of the maps. Later, when the gasping and groaning of the engine announced that they were climbing, Hans was able to furnish the information that they had reached the rugged flanks of the Radicofani hill, and that their panting progress up the twisting highway would be followed by an equally precipitate descent.

At six o'clock Hans guessed from the fairly unrestricted motion of the truck that they were approaching Siena. The texture of the road still felt good, which meant that they could not have launched out onto a secondary artery. At one point he thought he felt the shape of the weird sweeping bridge which spirals out of San Quirico d'Orcia. Basing his calculations on that, he reckoned that they would be in Siena at about seven.

And then what? He closed his eyes. Could they indeed be going towards Florence? Erhardt had known his eagerness to return there, and had said things that morning which could have been taken as hints. 'Things have turned out well. Don't ask me any questions. I am superstitious, and talking about it may ruin our chances.' What had he meant by 'our'? Did he mean it in the sense of his organization, or just in the sense of himself and Hans? Was he, behind that forbidding, aquiline façade, really an exceptionally considerate and generous man?

Florence and Teresa. He felt a special, urgent warmth, a bursting of floodgates, as he examined the gallery of fragmentary memories stored in his mind, untouched for so long in the bustle of escape. He played over these visions as a miser plays over his hoard, the ecstasy heightened by his abstinence.

While he was thus lost in abstractions, a couple of painfully real forces were converging in the city he had just left, in order to do battle over him.

Erhardt knew Ubaldini's philosophy, and consequently arrived at Rosati's a quarter of an hour late, only to find that Ubaldini had not yet arrived. He sat down at the only vacant table, and waited, already slightly annoyed.

Rosati's is one of the places where Rome meets after office hours in order to readjust its public relations. It is here that reputations go like a puff of air; it is here that rumor is born and that crises are precipitated, all among the gushing soda fountains, the clink of glasses, the smell of rich pastry and of heavy perfume.

Erhardt studied the faces of the crowd, who were so tightly packed that they seemed to be governed by some sort of tide, as weeds are in water. Over there he saw Benedetti, the famous film director, to whom he had lent a couple of armored cars and twenty men for the making of the world-shattering reconstruction of the German occupation of Naples, *Vesuvio Trema*. Benedetti, caught in the violent cadences of an aesthetic debate, greeted Erhardt amicably, and then returned to his tone of virulent scorn without effort. In the distance, Erhardt saw the conical gray head of the honorable deputy Alderighi-Moroni, who had asked such awkward questions about the Germans on the run in the Chamber of Deputies, while, seated at another table, the wife of the actor Sgombini sat, her fingers entwined with those of the actor Taglia. Their appearance together was tantamount to an announcement of official infidelity. Commiseration with Sgombini quickly gave way to ruthless laughter about his cuckoldom.

Then Ubaldini arrived. He at once apologized for being late. 'Unavoidably detained.'

'Old hypocrite,' thought Erhardt, and said, 'What will you drink?'

'No, no, dear fellow, the invitation came from me. As the party may not be entirely agreeable, I should ask for the most expensive item of the menu. After all, it is paid for by the state.'

When they were served, Ubaldini with an

alpine liqueur tasting of mothballs, Erhardt with
a beer, Ubaldini said, 'I always like coming here,
owing to the noise. Nobody can hear what you're
saying, and it guarantees absolute privacy.'

'Do you see who I see over there?' asked
Erhardt.

'You refer to Alderighi-Moroni? Yes, he's always
here, finding new things to complain about.
He's the complete politician, without conviction, without scruple, without imagination. He
knows that a politician must talk. The sound
of the voice is important in the Chamber, not
the words the voice uses. After a time, when
the timbre has impressed itself sufficiently on
the political cognoscenti, people begin to ask
themselves whether the great owner of that
particular voice will deign to use it in attacking
this, that, or the other issue.'

'A cynical philosophy,' said Erhardt, who had
no use for Latin acidity, the quality the French
so proudly call logic.

'I am used to that accusation,' replied Ubaldini,
somewhat flattered, 'but nevertheless what I have
said is entirely true. At all events it is true in
Italy, where a debate in the Chamber requires a
voice which will stand out, like the soloist in a
concerto, above the orchestral accompaniment of
senatorial censure. The important thing is to talk,
to shout, to roar. An ambitious and tireless man
like Alderighi-Moroni comes here in the hopeful
search of scandals.'

'You don't think we ought to move to another café?' asked Erhardt.

'Why?'

'After all those awkward questions he asked in the Chamber.'

Ubaldini laughed. 'I am a man with a career requiring qualifications and intelligence. What have I to fear from a man belonging to a profession where the only qualification is volume, and where intelligence is an embarrassment?'

At that moment, the terrible bearded parliamentarian, on the scent like a terrier in springtime, arrived at their table and looked imperiously at Ubaldini.

'I trust, *Colonello*, that you did not flinch unduly at my scathing words in the Chamber regarding the escape of those German prisoners from custody,' he said, with an affectation of mildness.

Ubaldini did not rise. 'What words?' he asked. 'I didn't read them.'

Alderighi-Moroni looked as though someone had spat in his face.

'You are not going to pretend that you didn't read my speech of last Monday on irrigation in Sardinia?'

'What on earth has the escape of a few German prisoners to do with irrigation in Sardinia?' asked Ubaldini ingenuously.

Alderighi-Moroni was excessively irritated by such a simple observation, and said, 'My speech

was, as always, extremely catholic in conception. Very all-embracing. Very universal, I might
almost say. My attack on your handling of the
situation came near the end of my address, and
was greeted with full-blooded applause from all
sections of the Chamber.'

'Did you mention my name?'

The way was wide open for one of Alderighi-
Moroni's celebrated sarcasms, so widely feared
in Rome.

'I mentioned General Calzoletti, and certain
of his less significant flunkeys,' he said.

Ubaldini smiled good-naturedly. 'In the debased
language of politics, that is quite a compliment,
I believe. After all, the names you call each other
are far worse than flunkey.'

'You do not seem to mind,' replied Alderighi-
Moroni, his eyes narrowed, 'but allow me to
warn you that one more piece of carelessness,
and I shall expose you before the nation. Your
past is not so untainted that you can afford too
much publicity.'

Ubaldini lost his smile, but not his composure.
'Is that a threat?' he asked.

'Take it as you will,' Alderighi-Moroni answered.
'The fact is that I, of all the Italian politicians,
am entirely incorruptible. I give no quarter, and
I ask for none. Take your choice. Do your job,
or be exposed. There are only two alternatives,
efficiency or degradation.'

The time was ripe for the counterattack.

Ubaldini said, 'You have just rashly threatened me with exposure. Before I answer your charge, I must introduce you to my friend, Herr Wehrli, a journalist from Switzerland, who is here to study Italian democratic procedure.'

Alderighi-Moroni was immediately charming to Erhardt, and told him how many delightful holidays he had spent in the Alps. Erhardt, amused, told Alderighi-Moroni how many delightful holidays he had spent in Capri.

Ubaldini interrupted this exchange when he said, 'You also saw fit, *Onorevole*' (He took care to use the full title of a dignitary before he felled him to the ground – thus the victim had further to fall) 'to make an unfortunate aspersion about my past. I think it only fair to inform you, now we are dabbling in the past, that I have a large collection at home – not of butterflies, or stamps, or color prints, nothing as picturesque as that – I have a large collection of Fascist party cards belonging to various people, some of them nonentities, others of them upstarts, a few of them in the Chamber. I will refrain from elaborating on the coincidence, and ask you for five thousand lire.'

'You wouldn't dare!' sputtered Alderighi-Moroni, white as a sheet.

'Wouldn't dare what?'

'Have you stooped to blackmail?'

Ubaldini laughed. 'My dear *Onorevole*, if I ever blackmailed you, I wouldn't do it for a

mere five thousand lire, which is, as you must
know, chickenfeed. In any case, you could easily
counter-blackmail me. You have even vaguely
hinted at such a possibility. No, no, this five
thousand lire is the penalty for leaving your
car with one wheel over a pedestrian crossing.
You can either pay me now, or if that is
too embarrassing, you will find a very angry
Carabiniere standing by it.'

'What are you talking about!' blurted Alderighi-
Moroni. 'I left my car miles away from the
pedestrian crossing!'

'In that case, the car must be as ambitious as
its master, and able to travel forward by itself,
thereby, like its master, making of itself a damned
nuisance.'

Alderighi-Moroni purpled, opened his mouth,
and stamped out. To add to his humiliation, the
people at the two next tables clapped Ubaldini's
victory, having listened unashamedly.

'Is his wheel really over a pedestrian crossing?'
Erhardt asked softly.

'It wasn't,' answered Ubaldini with a smile,
'but I gave instructions for it to be pushed when
I saw it there. I guessed he'd single me out for an
insult if he saw me, so I prepared my last word.'

Erhardt clicked his teeth with a kind of
admiration, the white colonist's appreciation of
the witch doctor's power over his own people.

'Yes,' continued Ubaldini, 'I am fairly experienced in turning disastrous situations to my own

advantage. Perhaps you will have noticed what a lot of trouble our agreement to let those Germans of yours escape from captivity at Ancona has caused me. By the way, are they out of the country yet?'

'Two of them. The other leaves by air on Friday.'

'Middle East?'

Erhardt nodded.

Ubaldini smiled. 'It is really an exquisite revenge for all our miseries to act the part of host to nations which are preparing to cut each other's throat with all the abandon of enthusiasm and inexperience. My dear Erhardt, I am the butler who holds the coats of the Arabs and Jews as they train to knock each other out. You were right in your prophecy about the future. It was very shrewd of you. There are one or two American pilots here already, looping the loop for the benefit of the young fanatics from Palestine who want to lay their lives on the altar of their reconstituted land. I tell you this because I have carelessly dropped a hint to them about the presence of German pilots in Italy, destined to go to the assistance of the Arabs.'

'You never do anything careless,' said Erhardt.

'Maybe not. It amuses me, however, to see their righteous fury, which boiled and bubbled merrily until I reminded them just how illegal their activities were, and explained that I never indulge in favoritism where my toleration of illegalities is concerned. All the same,' he added darkly, 'I have helped you enormously.'

'I admit that,' answered Erhardt, 'and I am doing my best to fulfill my part of the bargain.'

There was a pause, while Ubaldini looked steadily at Erhardt.

'Good,' he said at length, 'I hope you will go on in the same manner.'

'I hope you will.'

The conversation entered a morass, and there was silence until Ubaldini, toying irritatedly with a fork, eventually said, 'I have arrested Schubert.'

Erhardt expressed no surprise. 'He is already replaced.'

'It is dangerous work, dabbling in false identity papers.'

'Living is fairly dangerous nowadays.'

Ubaldini pouted. 'Do you want Schubert back?'

Erhardt was expressionless. 'What are the conditions?'

'Winterschild.'

'What?'

'Perhaps I don't pronounce the name properly,' said Ubaldini, and spelled it out.

'I don't know what you're talking about.'

'Are you sure?'

'Absolutely.'

Ubaldini cleared his throat. 'Let me tell you about this man. I must warn you first of all that he is wanted by the Italian government in connection with war crimes, together with another man called Brehmig, about whom we know less – who may, in fact, be dead for all we know. But Winterschild is very much alive. We chased him as far as La Spezia the other day, but he evaded us ingeniously with the aid of another couple of Germans, one of whom was being smuggled aboard the *Fernando Po*.'

Erhardt's expression in no way changed, although he was quickly realizing of whom they were talking.

'The next thing we heard, he was heading south. He is easy to recognize, my dear Erhardt. I say this in case he has presented himself to you under another name. He has a permanent blink of the right eye.'

Erhardt thought. 'No,' he said at length, his brow lined with concentration. 'I know no such person.'

'You are sure?' Ubaldini prompted softly. 'Because I regret to have to warn you that if I find that you do know this man, and are, in fact, shielding him, then I will come down on your organization with all the power at my disposal. You will all be arrested, and imprisoned.'

Erhardt was stung. 'I don't expect to have my word doubted,' he said.

'Then you are very unimaginative, if I may say so,' replied Ubaldini. 'The fact remains that if you hand over this man Winterschild, you will get Schubert back, and you may even derive some other less concrete benefits. I don't know. It all depends on my mood at the time. On the other hand, if I find you have in any way aided this man, I will smash the organization that you have so ingeniously and painstakingly built up for yourself. It is for you to decide.'

Erhardt was quick to reply. 'I have given my answer. And I want to warn you that if you ever attempt to break my organization, we will resist arrest.'

'How?' Ubaldini laughed.

'The arms we hire out to film companies are not dummies,' he replied, with frigid intensity, 'and we are far better organized than you.'

'Better than the Americans? Better than the British?'

'Yes.'

Ubaldini rocked with laughter, and slapped Erhardt on the back. 'I entirely agree with you,' he said, 'but we have on our side the slight advantage of numbers.'

'You have the advantage of numbers over the successful bandits in the Abruzzi.'

'Admittedly.'

'We would not hesitate,' said Erhardt quietly.

Ubaldini was all smiles.

'My dear, admirable Erhardt, we are both of us far too intelligent to fight with anything but our brains. It has been a most charming meeting. I have made my position clear, and you have issued

a counterthreat that has me quaking in my shoes.
So serious do I consider your threat that I may
even cut off your supply of gasoline. Now I am
afraid I have another appointment. A delightful
little lady who appreciates to the full the power
of the police. Let's meet again soon. *À bientôt*,
Herr Wehrli.'

BACK IN his room, Erhardt sat behind his desk,
and talked rapidly to his deputy.

'Fromm, we must move quickly. You know
Hansen, the new man?'

'Yes.'

'He has a past, a history, whatever you like to
call it — at all events, he is wanted by the Italian
police. They are making it a condition for the
release of Schubert that we hand him over.'

'In that case,' said Fromm, 'I think we should
comply. We can't afford to protect anyone for
sentimental reasons. Our situation is far too
precarious.'

'No,' answered Erhardt, 'the man was an officer. His whole manner declares that fact, and if he
is now blamed for war crimes, in my experience
that only means that he was a good officer. I
refuse to hand people over to the dubious justice
of a course of recrimination simply because they
did their often painful duty well. No.'

And he thought for a moment.

'Listen,' he continued, 'get Redlich off that
plane on Friday. We'll send Hansen.'

'But Hansen is not a technician!' Fromm protested.

'Never mind, we have fulfilled our contract to the letter so far, they will have to accept this single exception. We must get Hansen out of the country. When they see we are speaking the truth, they will release Schubert in any case. Fromm, I will go tomorrow personally, and fetch him back, so that we can rush him to the plane after tomorrow morning.'

The blue-eyed man grimaced. 'And Fromm,' said Erhardt, who hated nothing more than mute criticism, 'if the worst should happen, we must always be prepared to move at a moment's notice. You know our plans. It is your responsibility to see that everything is in a state of readiness. Is that clear?'

X

THE SUN rose early over San Rocco the next morning, and the few high clouds heralded an ideal day, not for the hunter, it was too windy, not for the sightseeing visitor, but for the camera.

Joel Hellstrom, one of the greatest cameramen in the world, looked at the horizon through his clouded glass, and said, 'Not bad.' In point of fact, conditions were perfect, but Mr Hellstrom was so great, and knew it, that he could never afford to admit himself to be more than mildly optimistic about anything.

The director, Luther Tacoo, another early bird, decided, in consultation with the script writer, Bartram Magnus, to shoot the harrowing scene in which the Germans destroy the village.

For this purpose Olympic Pictures had rebuilt

an intact village in wood and plaster not a
hundred yards from San Rocco, having realized,
rather late in the day, that it is extremely
difficult to show a village being destroyed by
false Germans after the job has already been
effectively done by real Germans.

The film in question was, of course, the fruit of
Hooper Boyt's graphic talent. The novel, named
Thus Loud Your Bugles Blow, had turned out to
be a terse, stuttering work, ungenerous in style,
convulsive and commercial. The book's climaxes
were skillfully reduced to lyrical explosions of
telegraphic length, interspersed both with deserts
of dots and tricks of style which transformed
descriptive passages into strings of cogent cap-
tions. *Thus Loud Your Bugles Blow* was selected
by all the literary circles as the book of the day,
week or month.

Olympic had spared no pains to ensure the
success of their pictorial epic by engaging a cast
commanding an astronomic salary. To play the
count, they had engaged a star of the silent
days, who had graduated with the relentless
march of the years into Southern colonels. There
was not a single drama dealing with the dawn
of American history which had not got this
distinguished white-haired man, Durand Dixon,
either surrendering or vanquishing with words of
portentous magnificence on his lips. The count,
as he played the role, would have been present
at Valley Forge. The real count, offended by

his inferred connection with a history so recent, locked himself in his castle, and sulked.

The actor playing Old Plumes was a Mexican, Diego Ramirez, who had ridden howling and lassoing over endless frontiers since the dawn of films. He now adapted his limited if revolutionary technique to the arduous business of delineating an elderly infantry officer. Arduous because Señor Ramirez was, frankly, not as convincing an actor off a horse as on one.

Val di Sarat, Rory Torrance, a great Hollywood profile, tall, seductive, teeth filed to a symmetrical nicety, hair parted by a squadron of specialists to disguise an unfortunate tendency towards baldness, attacked the problem of being Italian by adopting a curiously stilted pronunciation of every twentieth word. Torrance had a highly developed sense of character.

A beautiful Norwegian girl, blonde as sweet corn and not without a certain charming boredom of her own, played Angelica, a gratuitous fantasy of Boyt's imagination, composed ostensibly as a symbol of the dreams and the sufferings of Italian women, but in fact the outcome of an unerring box-office instinct. Far from suggesting the mud and dung of tortuous streets, the endless, automatic pregnancies and the opulent tragedies of the south, her emotional appeal was redolent of disaster in the hospital corridor, the clean, selective, pinched dramas of the snow-drenched north. Still, with the unconscious coaching of a couple of Italian maids (both selected for their ability to speak English), and the conscious guidance of Rory Torrance, Sigrid Tollefsen was determined to make the great effort of characterization. She wore a gold cross round her neck for a start.

Hans, reduced in the scheme of things to a mere cipher of unsupportable tyranny, was played by a scarred specialist in gangster chiefs, a man whose fortune was the shattered left side of his face, and who therefore refrained from expressing anything on the intact right side.

It was natural that Old Plumes was quite as offended as was the count by the gross distortion perpetrated in his name. His feelings when confronted by the hope of immortality after a lifetime of devotion to a set of selfless rules can be imagined, as can his rage when that immortality turned up in the shape of a raucous and guttural Latin American with a flavoring of Aztec blood.

'I have served the Crown for fifty years,' he said bitterly to Buonsignori, 'and now they mock my loyalty by consigning it to a cannibal.'

But Buonsignori was the wrong man to complain to, as his part had been cut out of the story altogether.

'Better a cannibal than nothing,' he replied ruefully.

'I am far from certain,' muttered Old Plumes.

Filigrani, incensed by the presence of American

capitalists in the village, was doing everything he could to make their stay insupportable. Whenever the Americans desired to shoot in a specific direction, Filigrani would hang a red flag on a prominent building or stick one boldly in the center of the field. Invariably the American director would ask for the offending rag to be removed, only to find that the blight had been erected on soil belonging to Filigrani or one of his cronies. As Filigrani had become a Communist only after he had done extremely well out of a more traditional social system, he owned a generous portion of the houses in the village, as well as quite a few of the adjoining olive groves.

Neither the progressive elements, owing allegiance to the visionary caprices of the party, nor the reactionary elements inclining towards an unreasoning glorification of the count's horrid ghosts, could for long tolerate the invasion of these rich barbarians, and therefore did nothing to restrain their children from using the immense chromed cars which were parked in their tasteless profusion in the Piazza as God-given toys.

The children, too young to implement their instinctive dislike with intellectual reasons, contented themselves with abandoned mischief. They scratched vulgar words into the cellulose with knives; they soiled the white-walled tires in the course of their natural functions; they improvised music of the most uncompromising modernity, using the wheel-hubs as instruments of percussion, the radiator grilles as metal harps, the horns as brass.

Tacoo and his adjutants could only shout their annoyance. The children, the skill of centuries of successful brigandage bred in their bones, vanished without a trace whenever a punitive expedition was launched in their direction, only to reappear noiselessly at their gleaming prey when the attention of the Americans was drawn towards yet another red flag which had appeared sneakingly round the angle of some wall.

The Italians, who had fought so bravely and with such a semblance of unity when they were assaulted by the German invader, and who had been so ungenerous in their recollections of their neighbors' heroism when the coming of peace had once again permitted them the luxury of internecine hatred, now began to be forced into the old wartime ways again, for Tacoo, with his relentless pioneering face, touched with the arrogance of a man who has forged his road through a wall of lesser men, was to their sense of easy generosity superficially just as irritating as any Nazi.

Steps had to be taken. Buonsignori talked to Old Plumes. Old Plumes hatched a plot with the count. Buonsignori dropped a hint to Filigrani. Filigrani whispered to Old Plumes. Buonsignori agreed to meet the count. The village was at war again.

Filigrani drove his car a few kilometers to the north, and hid it in some leafless shrubbery. Buonsignori passed, as if by chance, on a cart pulled by a couple of oxen. Pulling his hat over his eyes, Filigrani mounted the cart, and crouched inside, out of sight.

'I can't help asking myself if it's really necessary to take all these precautions,' said Buonsignori, as he whipped up the oxen to increase their pace to one mile per hour.

'For the sake of the party and its high details, I dare not be seen with the count,' said Filigrani. 'Can't you go any faster?'

'We are going all out,' said Buonsignori. 'If I whip them any more, they'll only get annoyed and stop altogether.'

At the same time, Old Plumes met the count at the castle, and they went out into the country together, ostensibly to shoot little birds in the calm of the evening. The elders were converging. They met once again in the ruined abbey, where two servants, near relatives of those who had served the family tree at such sacrifice, were waiting with a picnic meal, spread artistically on collapsible tables before a superb fire.

Filigrani, who affected a Calvinistic disdain for galantine in public, but who was at the mercy of a healthy appetite for it in private, viewed the meal with undisguised animosity, and reminded the count that they were here to work against the Anglo-American exploiters, and not to indulge in dainties which gave every appearance, by their luxury, of having been prepared by sweated labor. The count told Filigrani for the thousandth time that he employed people to do his starving for him, and that he would therefore continue unashamedly to draw the dividends from his investment.

'Times have changed,' he added, with a heartfelt sigh. 'Nowadays, if you do not wish to eat galantine, there is no compulsion for you to do so. In the times of Ermenegildo degli Occhi Bruni, however, refusal would have been impossible. The only choice in those days was between galantine and death, and even then it was often not a choice at all, as the galantine was invariably poisoned.'

Filigrani's conscience was eased by the fact that he had registered his disapproval, and he attacked the meat with voracity. Once again, as he studied his guest, the count had cause to admire his illustrious forefather. 'He would not have failed to poison this meat,' he reflected. 'I have still much to learn.'

Buonsignori opened the proceedings by suggesting that it should be brought to the notice of the invaders from the New World that a meeting of the village fathers had taken place, and that resolutions had been passed deploring the distortions of recent history perpetrated by the film company, complaining of undue noise in the village, and of damage to property occasioned by rostra, arc-lights, cranes, etcetera, etcetera, etcetera.

The count listened to the strings of muttered etceteras with dignified apathy, and then asked to what they referred.

'Nothing in particular,' said Buonsignori, 'but I have noticed that the cumulative effect of etceteras in arguments of a legal nature is considerably more striking than a chain of valid words.'

'Perhaps,' answered the count, 'but historical precedent shows us that it is never advisable to deal with a democratic opponent in a democratic way. If we do that, we exhibit an unjustified courtesy, and will only get a meaningless reply to our meaningless complaint. We have not, unfortunately, a monopoly of etceteras. I beg your pardon, etceterae. How foolish, the word has no plural.'

'The only true democracy is a people's democracy,' said Filigrani.

'The only true democracy is a state like America, where people have the right to criticize, but not to act. Far more humane to take away the right to criticize, once you consign people to forcible inactivity. A prison without a window destroys the yardstick whereby a man may contemplate the extent of his unhappiness, therefore it is less cruel than a prison with a window.'

'What plan have you?' asked Buonsignori of Old Plumes.

Old Plumes cleared his throat. 'I believe,

gentlemen, in the most energetic action within the general framework of prudence,' he said. 'I believe in stating our case, not with the coldness of a diplomatic communication, but with a passion and with an undisguised emotion. Let these Yankees feel ashamed that they are desecrating the name of our sleeping warriors by their distortions!'

'But our complaint is that they are distorting us, not the sleeping warriors! We will sound insincere,' said Buonsignori.

'It needs an explosion or two. An apparent accident. An American wounded. A rumor or two. The town is unsafe. A carefully planned campaign of minor mishaps,' said Filigrani.

'We are not in Russia!' retorted the count.

'Alas!' answered Filigrani, eating the last piece of truffled brisket.

'I have a better idea than any of yours,' said the count quietly, as though it went without saying. The others looked at him skeptically.

'In two days' time the monument to the heroism of our village will be erected in the Piazza Vittorio Emmanuele II, am I correct?'

The others nodded.

'The one to the May Day Shock Brigade will be unveiled next May first, near the washing troughs,' said Filigrani.

'I am not concerned with that,' replied the count. 'In my opinion, the Piazza Vittorio Emmanuele II is far too full of statues already. There is the group of angels dedicated to the victory on the Piave at one end and the ridiculous bust of Carducci in a panama hat at the other end, to say nothing of the little Garibaldi drinking fountain in the middle, and the odious excrescence which is supposed to be Andrea del Sarto seeking inspiration crushed up against the wall of the church. One more statue will make five, and there won't be room for any traffic to move in any direction. Already there have been complaints from the school that recreational football is to all intents and purposes impossible in the main square.'

'But we can't cancel the statue now!' exploded Old Plumes 'It will mean an expropriation of public funds, which were collected in good faith!'

'You are only so indignant because you are mentioned on the inscription,' said Filigrani truculently. 'I am in favor of the abolition of the scheme.'

'I am only suggesting,' went on the count, 'that the statue should be erected not in the village, but instead on the exact spot where the heroism took place.'

There was a pause for reflection.

'Why should that air our grievances with the Americans?' asked Old Plumes.

'Isn't it obvious?' answered the count. 'At the height of the day, when the sun is in its most photographically clement mood, military bands will strike up and ruin their sound tracks, and also, far more important, the location of the statue will be carefully selected so that the shots of the false village they have had the temerity to build so close as to perpetually rub our noses in it, will be invalid. We will place the statue, my friends, at the turning of the road, so that it will be impossible to take any pictures of the plaster village from the southeast without including the statue, which could not have been built, historically speaking, until after the incidents they are depicting.'

Buonsignori was the first to begin laughing, followed by Old Plumes.

'But!' The count interrupted them, with a gesture of caution. 'It is essential to accelerate our preparations, and to install the monument tonight. Val di Sarat must be telegraphed to attend the inauguration. The orchestras must be rehearsed. All must be in a state of readiness.'

They all shook hands. Filigrani pledged his moral support, but insisted on maintaining his independent freedom of action in regard to sabotage. Old Plumes spoke with a quaver in his voice. 'Our methods are different, our cause is the same!'

Then they dispersed, as secretly as they had gathered.

THE MONUMENT consisted of a stone foundation with a copper figure of an Italian soldier confidently striding into space in spite of a certain sinister restraint urged by a ghoulish bat-like figure at his elbow. When the sculptor was challenged about the significance of this highly disturbing symbol, he walked off in a huff, muttering about Philistines and invoking Donatello's shade as a witness of the banality of the times.

The monstrosity now stood, shrouded in dust-sheets, in Old Plumes's stable. That night, however, a group of men broke the stillness of the night by grunting and groaning under its weight. Elsewhere, from the depths of eerie courtyards, the sour notes of brass instruments at practice were heard. The sound of the inexpertly trilling fifes stung the unblinking owls into paroxysms of hooting. The local countryside was secretly alive, while the Americans were mostly in Florence, oblivious to anything but their gnawing home-sickness, and, as ever, charming slaves to their violent generosity.

Not far away, where the ancient truck had finally expired on a twisting hill, Hans and his colleagues were sleeping in a hotel (at least its existence was recorded in the guidebooks, but without comment). Their emotions were dead-ened by the fact that they were all asphyxiated by fumes. It was planned to make an early start the next morning.

Erhardt arrived in Florence that night by train, and broke his journey there, planning to catch a coach to San Rocco at the first light. In

Rome, Val di Sarat received the wire from the
Comitato di Guerra, and reacted like Napoleon
on Elba, the voices of the Old Guard carried on
the wind. He borrowed a car from his uncle's
considerable collection of semi-official vehicles,
and determined to be present at the unveiling
of his monument. The stage was set for the
final act.

'No One's going to tell me that the activities
of the local kids are just the high spirits of
youth,' said Luther Tacoo to his staff over an
early breakfast of blueberry pancakes and syrup.
'I've got kids. The youngest is thirty-four now,
but I can recall what they were like twenty-five
years ago. Sure they liked to destroy things, but
it was never malicious, premeditated destruction.
They destroyed an object in the process of finding
out how it worked. What we're face to face with
here is something utterly different. No kid of
eight is going to scrape "Yankee go home" on
the paintwork of an automobile unless he's been
told to do it, unless he's been indoctrinated by
the commies.'

The staff knew better than to interrupt their
director when he was on a voyage of discovery
into the shallows of the human mind. He was
a fine-looking man, this veteran of the silver
screen, with a mop of the whitest hair obeying
every whim of the breeze atop a leonine head
burnt by sun and wind. His eyes were blue,

frank, and innocent, as though nothing in his long life had shaken the simple convictions he learned when he was young. Like many successful Americans, he had borne his riches well, and had recognized that wealth was a corrupting influence unless a sense of responsibility grew with it. Now he regarded himself as an unofficial ambassador for the way of life which had made him what he was. The physical aspects of the Italian landscape did not really captivate him, since the olive trees were smaller and more stunted than his own Californian ones, and the buildings of the fifteenth century seemed to him unsanitary. His mission was that of an innovator, more daring, more visionary in his early dotage than he had ever been in youth.

'I was talking to Senator Hank Garrity,' he went on, not name-dropping, but sure of his place in the scheme of things, 'a good friend of mine, and I told him that movies on location ought to have the same privileges as ships. Just as a United States ship anchored in the harbor of a foreign port remains U.S. soil, so should the area of foreign territory included in the lens of a U.S. movie camera be regarded as U.S. soil for the duration of each shot. That would automatically give the U.S. jurisdiction over the actors, stand-ins, and townsfolk included in such a shot while the cameras are turning. He expressed great interest in the idea, and told me he'd bring it up at the next session.'

'Great idea,' murmured the assistants.

'Meanwhile,' Tacoo drawled on, 'until such a time as we are protected by legislation, we've got to keep our heads, and prove we mean business by our example. It's okay to give away PX cigarettes and razor blades and tissues and cases of Coke, but these people must never feel that our generosity is the fruit of condescension. If they offer us some of their wine, it's our solemn duty to drink it, and if we feel it wiser from a hygienic angle to drop a Halozone pill into it, this should be done as inconspicuously as possible.'

Just then the second assistant rushed in, breathless.

'What goes on?' asked Tacoo. 'More ripped tires?'

'Worse than that, Mr Tacoo,' he gasped. 'We went out there to set up on the master shot of the village, the way you told us you were going to do it last night – and there's a thing right in front of the camera.'

'A thing?'

'I don't know what it is, Mr Tacoo, because it's wrapped up, but I guess it's a statue, monument of some sort.'

'A monument? You just don't move a monument overnight.'

'That's what they've done.'

'Get it out.'

'I can't.'

'Why not?'

'It's very heavy. It's cemented to its base.'

'They can't do that!' cried Tacoo. 'Sure, we move houses, bridges, power stations overnight, but they just don't have the know-how. What's it doing there anyway?'

He placed a naval cap on his head, because he owned a yacht at La Jolla, and strode out into the obedient sunlight. After rounding the corner from the small hotel which was serving as headquarters to the production unit, he saw, silhouetted against the skyline, in the most prominent and unavoidable position, a piece of voluminous drapery buffeted by the breeze. Before it stood the count in a green hunting outfit, accompanied by a valet, who was holding a shotgun, and a hysterical water spaniel. 'Count, will you please have this thing moved,' said Tacoo, firmly but pleasantly.

'It cannot, will not, and must not be moved,' said the count, and his peremptory attitude was underlined less subtly by the spaniel, whose eyes were so contorted with suspicion one saw the whites and nothing else.

'Listen, Count,' Tacoo implored, 'I've got a job to do just like you have. Why not let us behave like grown men, and make a deal? I'm six days behind schedule already. We're pouring dollars into Italy. Our presence here may not be to your taste, but we're creating employment and, by creating employment, we are helping to fight Communism.'

'There are many ways of fighting Communism,' snapped the count, 'and I am not sure that
the best way is to fight it with its own weapons,
the weapons of mendacity and distortion, because
in those fields the Communists are expert and we
are amateurs.'

'What do you mean by that?'

'I mean that you are using the martyrdom of
our village as a pretext for a piece of gratuitous
and vulgar commercialism. Our glorious women
are being symbolized by a bony lady from the
Arctic Circle. Colonel Garretta, a great soldier
and a gentleman, is being played by an Aztec
desperado whose style on a horse is as conspicuous
as it is vulgar. The role of Captain Val di Sarat, a
Piedmontese soldier of fortune of almost sublime
recklessness, has been consigned to a superannu-
ated gigolo, and his name changed to Puccini,
presumably because it is easier to pronounce.
Buonsignori, a splendid example of my country's
devoted peasantry, has been totally ignored. Even
the Germans, who were adversaries worthy of our
mettle, have been shown as slobbering brutes
without intellect or cunning, which makes a
farce of our victory. As for myself, I will not
even comment on the utter depravity of your
choice of an actor to depict me. Suffice it to
say that the florid face and the plebeian stance
of the gentleman in question may throw light on
the evil conditions in the cotton plantations of
Alabama, but they are a living insult to the few

of us who can trace our origins without difficulty to pre-Christianity.'

'How do you know all this?' asked Tacoo, amazed.

'For centuries we have protected our soil and ourselves against foreign invasion,' answered the count. 'We have wrestled with barbarians, Carthaginians, Spaniards, Austrians, and recently with Germans. Now we defend ourselves against you. The first necessity in battle is to understand your enemy. Hannibal crossed the Alps with elephants. We had to understand the elephant before we could defeat him. At first sight its very size fills you with foreboding. Then, on further acquaintance, you discover that it is a fundamentally tender beast, with elegant manners and a tendency to sleep. No creature with a gestation period of three years can be other than endlessly patient and resigned – it cannot be consistently ferocious. Once we knew this about him, Hannibal was defeatable. Throughout the long chapters of time we have examined our foe before attacking him. An underground movement exists here permanently, against all comers. When you arrived, our first action was to steal a script from your office. This we read, and it is the reason for our opposition to you.'

'It's a damn good script,' cried Tacoo, as the milk of human kindness went rancid.

'The fact that you consider this travesty to be good closes the door to all further argument.'

Tacoo tried to be reasonable for the last time. 'We want you to help us,' he said.

'Help us just by leaving us alone,' replied the count. 'Under these draperies is a statue which pays homage to the real heroes of the battle of San Rocco. It will be unveiled at twelve o'clock next Thursday.'

'Twelve o'clock! We'll be shooting then!'

'With the military band of the Ninth Military District, a contingent of Boy Scouts, His Grace the Bishop of Montalcino, and representatives from the Organization of Ancient Combatants from the African Wars, with their own orchestra, which will play the marches of our Ethiopian regiments simultaneously with the music of the other band. Captain Val di Sarat will be here personally to receive a commemorative medal at the hands of his uncle, Colonel Ubaldini, of the Carabinieri. Professor Zaini, of the University of Siena, will represent the Premier and General of Cavalry Bassarocca will, if his health permits, represent the General Staff.'

'This is a premeditated and coldly calculated attack on us, on what we're trying to do.'

'Call it what you will, it is a patriotic mani- festation. The statue has been erected on my soil. The road belongs to the state, but the village, and in fact the landscape, belong to me.'

'Why wasn't I warned of this?'

'Does justice warn the culprit of its coming?'

It was clearly fruitless to continue this conversation. Tacoo tried to placate the spaniel with a dog-loving and playful gesture, but the loyalties of the animal were established, and it snapped. Tacoo regained his own lines, where his assistants were awaiting him with some anxiety.

'It's no use,' he said bitterly. 'We'll need some diplomatic action on this. Get the Allied Control Commission on the phone. Meanwhile turn the camera round, and we'll concentrate on the reaction shots of the Germans. Close ups. They can't interfere with those.'

Immediately the unit was animated into the most frantic activity. A third assistant called the Allied Control Commission on the phone, but since Signor Virretta, the postmaster, had been a member of the May Day Shock Brigade, and had in fact been responsible for the theft of the script from the film company, the line was mysteriously busy for hours on end. An attempt to send a telegram later in the day fared no better, since Signor Virretta mangled the message.

Meanwhile the Germans were paraded for Tacoo's inspection. To the urgent cries of the assistants, Hans dressed himself somewhat reluctantly as a corporal of artillery, and allowed himself to be made up. Then he left his billet together with the other new arrivals, and lined up in the cold sunlight. There was something familiar about the lie of the land, the curious twist of a mountaintop, which ended not in

a peak, but in a comma; the large cross on a
hill; the sweep of the valley from pastel shades
and the delicate silver of the olive trees into
the darkness of its unlit depths; the cluster of
cypresses around the inevitable cemetery, like the
admonishing fingers of some two-dimensional
Byzantine saint. San Rocco!

Hans felt the flush and tingle of fear creep up
his back, and send a volley of needles into his
cheeks. His eye began blinking uncontrolledly.
He had to escape before he saw more than the
artificial village, before he was marched to the
scene of his crime, and had his nose rubbed
into it, like a puppy. Worse, before he was
recognized.

'Are these the men?' It was Tacoo who had
arrived, and begun his inspection, accompanied
by the man in the loud tie whom Hans had seen
in Erhardt's office.

'Good. No good. Okay. Make him a corporal. He's a good type. Doesn't look German
enough . . .'

Tacoo passed down the line. Perhaps there
was a chance he might be rejected? The director
stopped before Hans.

'That blinking eye may be distracting . . .'
he said.

'I figured it might be interesting, for one shot,'
replied the man in the loud tie.

'Give me the script,' called Tacoo, in the grip
of a sudden inspiration. Feverishly he thumbed

the pages. 'Yeah. Yeah, he could be the guy the officers talk about in the big scene in the old mill, the guy whose nerves are shot, the guy with the Jewish mother, the guy who wanted to be a priest.'

'That's what I figured,' said the man in the loud tie.

They all looked at Hans intensely.

'Can you say a line?'

Hans boiled inwardly. 'My mother was not Jewish. I am not religious.'

'Great. Great,' cried Tacoo, 'he talks English. That's about all he has to say. Take his corporal's stripes away, and give him a script. This guy must be a private, a deserter.'

'I was a major,' snapped Hans.

'No, no,' said Tacoo, for whom films were a reality and fact mere fiction. 'You're a great private, great neurotic private,' and he walked away, while Hans's colleagues congratulated him on his good luck.

'Where are the officers?' called Tacoo from the middle distance. All the assistants began screaming for the officers, and three men dressed as a lieutenant, a captain, and a colonel respectively emerged from the make-up tent. Hans gazed at the colonel, who had a red mustache and powerful glasses, and noticed something curious about the stance of the man.

'The lieutenant's great,' said Tacoo. 'The captain needs a scar or two to make him look more brutal. The colonel's all wrong. Looks like an Englishman. Typical Englishman. Get that mustache off, crop his hair, scrap those glasses, and give him a monocle.'

The colonel remonstrated. 'More German colonels wore mustaches than you think,' he said.

As soon as he heard the voice, Hans knew it was Brehmig.

'Nobody in America knows this,' replied Tacoo. 'Get it off.'

'And the monocle is from 1914 to '18, not from '39 to '45.'

'So you're a veteran,' said Tacoo. 'Now, let's line them up with the men, and see the general effect as they march through the village on their errand of death.'

As the three officers walked toward the men, Hans saw that Brehmig was pale and nervous.

'Bring the finder,' yelled Tacoo, as he knelt in the roadside dust. 'Now advance. Colonel, you give the order.'

'*Vorwärts – marsch*,' said Brehmig in a casual, civilian voice, and the regiment of extras ambled forwards.

'Stop! Not like that – as though you meant it. You're soldiers!'

'*Vorwärts – marsch*,' cried Brehmig, with more vigor, but it made no difference to the lassitude of the extras.

'Halt! For Christ's sake!' yelled Tacoo. 'You're

German soldiers, out to destroy a village for your goddam Führer and Fatherland. You believe in what you're doing. Might is right. You don't know better. I want to see evil written on your faces. Nothing less than the blood of women and children will satisfy you now. You've never had democracy. You advance like a well-oiled machine, indoctrinated in hatred. I'm the village. Come on and get me!'

'*Ich mach's nicht mit,*' said one soldier, falling out.

'*Ich auch nicht,*' said another.

'What the hell's the matter with those guys? Get them back in line,' screamed Tacoo.

'German soldiers were not animals,' shouted the man who had fallen out. 'We were no better, no worse than your soldiers. We killed each other, that's all. Not women, not children.' Tacoo advanced, furious.

'Let's look at the record,' he said, menacingly. 'Are you going to tell me that this village burned down because an Italian was careless with his cigarette? No, sir. It was a calculated military action undertaken by the German High Command, and you guys didn't complain to them. No. You waited until an American movie company got here to complain.'

'I was not here,' the German rebel replied. 'I was in ambulance unit in Viareggio, and we saved the lives of many American airmen. If you

want to show a murder, get the murderer to do
the scene, not us.'

'Are you trying to tell me you weren't a
Nazi?'

'I was a Communist.'

Tacoo stopped in his tracks. 'A Communist?
That's worse. A Communist in the Nazi army?'

'Gerhardt here is a Quaker.'

'A Quaker!'

'One of the very few in Germany. He always
shot his rifle into the air, because he was opposed
to killing.'

'And I suppose,' Tacoo roared, 'the others are
Seventh Day Adventists, Holy Rollers, Buddhists,
Dukhobors, and Zionists, and there isn't a single
goddam Nazi among the lot of them!'

The other Germans, who understood very little
English, looked blank, except for Brehmig, who
turned around casually to see what was going to
happen next, since he was playing colonel and
would be responsible for the next bloodthirsty
attack in the direction of the camera. His mouth
dropped open when he saw Hans. Hans looked
away and blinked.

'Sam,' said Tacoo in despair to the man in
the loud tie, 'didn't I say I wanted indoctrinated Nazis?'

'So they're going to admit it?'

'Christ, Sam, why didn't we just build the
village on the lot in Hollywood? There you've
got real extras to work with, not these lousy

phonies. Authenticity. That's all everybody talks about these days. What's authentic about this? Land-owning capitalism defending the Communists against the hard dollar, Fascism making believe the mammoth war machine was nothing more than the Salvation Army dressed up. I tell you, Sam, the world's gone crazy. You got a great script, four million bucks, a block-busting stellar cast, and you break your head because the values of authenticity are false, corrupted, rotten.' Tacoo sat heavily on a camp stool, and added, pathetically, 'Sam, I'm homesick.'

AN HOUR later, the cameras began turning on those few Germans who were willing to look brutal in close-up. During the intervals in the shooting, Brehmig sidled up to Hans.

'We must get out of here,' he whispered.

'Not so loud.'

'They've threatened to shave my mustache off. Then everyone will recognize me. Turn away quickly. There are some villagers up there on the crest, come to watch the shooting.'

'They're children. They're too young to remember us.'

'There's a man among them.'

'Buonsignori.'

Just then, a well-aimed rock landed square in Brehmig's back. He staggered forward, and was about to turn in anger when Hans restrained him.

'Don't turn,' he muttered, as the assistants drove the nimble children away.

'Did they do that because they knew who I was?' asked Brehmig, pale as a ghost.

'No, because you're the officer,' said Hans. 'Officers are better targets than men.'

'I can't bear it any longer.'

'What?'

'My remorse.'

'Remorse?' Hans looked puzzled.

'Can't you see that it's an instrument of divine justice that we should have been sent back to the scene of our crime?'

'What's happened to you? Are you sick or something?'

'Where did they find you ... the organization?' Brehmig stammered.

'In the north.'

'I escaped eastward ... towards Milan ... up there in the industrial areas, you learned what hatred was. It was nothing, down here, in villages. Just nothing. A few men conspiring in an oasis, with all the desert to escape into. But up there, among the factories, you could see the bullet holes on every wall. Bodies in the streets. The whole city was like a closed room. My God, my God, what have we done? What have we done?'

'Shut up!' said Hans urgently, shaking Brehmig by the arm. After a moment, Brehmig guiltily regained his self-control, and added, 'I went from church to church. There's no shortage of those in Italy. That's how it started. They'll never look for Germans in a church. Whenever I felt I was followed, I'd look up for a telltale church tower, and run for dear life. One night, I almost fell into a trap. They were raiding cafés, Italian, British and American military police. There were jeeps all over the place. I ran to a church, Santa Maria la Immacolata. And I stayed there all night, on my knees, too terrified to move. For the first hour, I just strained my ears to listen – wondering if the police were going to enter.

'Then, as my eyes got accustomed to the dark, I began seeing the effigies of Christ and His apostles as they gazed at me from every corner and from the wall. There were so many of them, and they must have been staring at me for a long time before I could see them. From one side His marble head gazed at me sternly, beating me to my knees, piercing my empty soul with a thin white light, a rapier which found nothing but flesh in its thrust, no spirit, no heart. When I found the strength to turn away, He was smiling at me from a canvas, so sadly that I winced under the scourge of His understanding. There was no escape, He was everywhere except ahead of me, where the altar lay in darkness. I was a boy again, and it was Sunday. I was small in the world of grown men, in a Presence which made even them into children. I understood nothing except that I understood nothing. I was a speck

of dust blown casually into existence. I had no
mind, and as I was on my knees, I was as tall
as I had been when last I went to church. There
was no hand to hold, no looming face bent low
over me to hear whether I knew the words of
the hymns. I was an oprhan. I dared not look
anywhere but forwards, for fear of being impaled
on a glance which said, "You are responsible. You
were a child for a handful of innocent years. The
day you took a rifle in your fingers, you were
old enough to look Me in the eye. And you
did not.'

'I stared, stared, at the darkened altar; the
more I tried to strangle my thoughts, the more
I thought. Then the dawn came. Slowly the
light began to glow, and suddenly, horribly, He
appeared again on stained glass, gazing down at
me from high up and far away, His face moving
from melancholy pallor through the color of life
to a flaming wrath, and He shouted, "There is
no escape. You were born what you are, but you
have become what you have done." And I knew
there would be no more peace.'

Brehmig was shaking convulsively.

'How did the organization find you?' Hans
asked quietly.

Brehmig spoke hesitantly, with a dead voice.
'A man came out of the shadows, and said to
me, "You were clever. You had the same idea as
I did. It was a narrow squeak." So I hadn't been
alone at all. But from then on, I was. Fellow

called Kreipe. SS man on the run. Put me in touch with Erhardt.'

'By the way, what's your name?'

'Dorn.'

'Mine's Hansen.'

Brehmig began laughing hysterically, sadly. 'Who are we trying to fool?' he shouted.

Calling an assistant, Hans told him that Dorn wasn't feeling well, and Brehmig was led off to see the nurse.

JUST BEFORE midday, Erhardt arrived from Florence. He listened calmly while Tacoo complained about the recalcitrant attitude of the German soldiers.

'I hope you have been able to shoot in spite of this incident,' Erhardt said.

'We've shot a few close-ups on those willing to show the necessary spirit,' Tacoo replied, 'but when they're all together, they're no better than a lot of unemployed at a soup kitchen.'

'Leave it to me.'

Erhardt ordered the Germans to line up, and treated them to a long patriotic harangue, in the course of which he berated them roundly for their inability to behave in a soldierly fashion just because this was a mere film and not a real slaughter. He reminded them of the wide diffusion the film would surely enjoy, and told them that this was a unique opportunity to place the military virtues of discipline for which their nation was

famous on the pedestal of immortality. He also
informed them that they were being paid for their
work, and that the consequences of their lethargy
could be disagreeable in the extreme, since they
had no documents of any sort, and labor camps
everywhere were avid for new inmates. As he
talked, his gold tooth flashed like the shields
of a distant army, and so convincing were his
arguments that he was cheered at the end, the
Quaker and the Communist being as vociferous
as any of the others.

That afternoon, the Germans charged the
camera as though it were a ghetto, but before
that, Erhardt had called Hans aside.

'Hansen,' he had said, 'have they shot on
you yet?'

'They took one close-up this morning, Herr
Erhardt.'

'That's unfortunate. Never mind, I will talk
to Mr Tacoo.'

'What's wrong?'

Erhardt smiled. 'As I told you in my office,
we don't ask each other any questions in this
organization. We don't even know each other's
real names. As far as you know, I may have been
a Gestapo colonel, or a latrine-cleaning private
of a holding unit. The same goes for you. Our
work is patriotic, and we are dedicated to the
eternal greatness of Germany as well as to mere
survival. You understand?'

'Yes.'

'Unfortunately our Italian hosts do not have the same interests at heart. They are inclined to be inquisitive about our activities, and possibly in order to mollify their conscience, which can hardly be entirely clear as far as Germany is concerned, they are eager to create heroes for themselves from the ranks of the partisans and other public nuisances. In order to do this, and to insist that they were on the side of the victor in spirit if not in fact, they have an urgent need of not only martyrs but of scapegoats. Do you follow me?'

'Not entirely.'

'That does not surprise me,' said Erhardt, smiling, 'even the simplest things are complicated here. As you must know by now, even if you did not know before, this village of San Rocco was destroyed by German soldiers as a reprisal for a partisan attack, a reprisal I personally consider to be absolutely justified in the light of the underhanded and unofficial quality of the aggression. According to the Italian authorities, the destruction of this village was perpetrated by an officer named Major Winterschild, and the one thing which distinguished this officer was an inability to stop blinking his right eye.'

Hans blinked once or twice rapidly, as he always did when he was nervous. Erhardt glanced at him casually, smiled briefly, and went on.

'Hansen, there are many soldiers who suffered from shock and other traumatic afflictions – there

are many who blink – it would be too tragic if
they made a mistake and got the wrong man. You
are to go at once to the Hotel Belsoggiorno in
Florence. Room 117. Here is thirty thousand lire.
The room is reserved in the name of Dr Cohen of
Zurich. We indulge in little jokes. Here too is a
Swiss passport. You will find your photograph
inside. You will wait for me there. Clear?'

'Yes, but where will I go – eventually?'

'Beirut. You will be Dr Cohen until the day
after tomorrow. Then you become Engineer
Redlich, an expert in jet engines.'

'But I don't know the first thing about jet
engines,' Hans protested.

'I will give you a book to read in the plane,'
Erhardt laughed, 'and by the time you get there,
you will know more than the Lebanese.'

TACOO WAS so delighted with the prowess of the
regenerated Germans that he expressed very little
regret when Erhardt informed him that, owing
to a family bereavement, the man with a blink
in his eye had been removed from the picture.

'It's a pity,' Tacoo said, 'but I got one shot
of that blink, and cut in at the right moment
it can have a whale of an effect. Say, you've got
to find me a new colonel, though.'

Erhardt tensed. 'What happened to Dorn?'

'Guy with a mustache? Got taken ill. Nurse
tells me he was running a fever, and she left him
in the first-aid trailer. When she got back after

lunch, he'd gone. Vamoosed. I told him to take off that mustache, and he wouldn't. The glasses either. Hey, you wouldn't play the colonel for me, would you? Be a great colonel.'

Erhardt smiled uneasily. 'I can't. It is against my policy. I have no time.'

'It's a great pity.'

A little later Erhardt was on the phone to Rome, talking to Fromm from the village. 'Fromm,' he said, 'wire me the moment they release Schubert. I will stay here until I hear from you. If they don't give Schubert back by Thursday, wire me all the same. Say "There will be no music" and sign Lopez. Apart from that? Nothing new. Oh, Dorn has disappeared.'

XI

Night Was closing in when the gasping, asphyxiating bus finally reached Florence. Hans, in civilian clothes once more, was searching the streets for a familiar shape, a familiar walk. He got out at the terminal and walked for a while through the city, ready at any moment to be surprised, and to surprise. The few people in the street were going about their private business as they do anywhere else, weary ants finding their painstaking way around the hill, oblivious to the thought that there's the universe beyond the wall. They seemed unhelpful.

Hans found the Hotel Belsoggiorno, which belied its name, so redolent of grapes and tarantellas, by being an old, disheveled, arthritic building with a glacial entrance hall, a dark tunnel framed by cracked tiles, veined walls, and a ceiling showing its war wounds. At the desk sat a moribund man with the crossed keys of better days on his lapels as the only marks of pride, while behind him stood the Moorish gates of the wooden elevator, the words 'OUT OF ORDER' displayed on yellowed cardboard which must have been there for years.

'Dr Cohen? Room 117,' said the man, with the weary complicity of the venerable brothel-keeper who remembers the time when cabinet ministers still graced the mirrored alcoves. 'Passport?'

Hans gave him the passport, and the man passed him the rusty key with its enormous appendages of chipped enamel.

'This says 86.'

'Room 86 became Room 117 after the redecoration,' said the man. 'It's on the sixth floor. The elevator is out of order.'

Hans climbed the stairs, each one of which reacted as though awakened out of a deep and peaceful slumber. Room 117 was very small and dark. The window gave onto a wall, and a gutter passed by it like a toy river, boats of aged orange peel jostling each other as a sudden narrowing of the duct prevented their further movement into the drainpipe. Hans switched on the light. A bleak bulb crept into life so feebly that Hans could stare at it without distress, and see the tangle of filaments. He shut the light again, and lay down on the bed. The bed took the strain, and yielded perhaps a quarter of an inch to his weight. And he thought.

He had lain on mattresses during the war, on the grass, staring at the sky, but he had been in uniform, ready at a moment's notice to respect himself, and thereby make others respect him. Thoughts had been canalized, restricted by a sense of duty. In any case, he had not the imagination to send them away on wild galloping flights of fancy. They were probably capable of galloping but they had nowhere to go.

Now he was a civilian, a Swiss doctor. His passport was in order. He was no longer on the run. There were two days to wait. To wait and think. The twilight was turning into night. The distant sound of a juke-box playing Neapolitan nonsense, a sweet orgy of grace notes, was a pleasure, not a nuisance, a shaft of ordinary pleasure to take the bitterness out of the solitude.

What had happened to Brehmig, sour unpleasant Brehmig? Could it be that a man of that stamp, never willing to risk his neck playing the game, forever on the sidelines, a man whose very rank, lieutenant, at his age, was indicative of a desire for relative comfort without responsibility, could now collapse under the weight of religious symbols? And remorse, was that the word he had used, remorse? Hans reflected on all the religious symbols he had ever seen. They had left him cold, as they left him cold now. Christmas cards. The sad sweet look of aunts. *Stille Nacht, heilige Nacht* sung a little flat, with a reticent stridency.

He was a man. He had fought, from an early age. His knees, impervious to brambles and to nettles on maneuvers, impervious to barbed wire later on. After shy beginnings, bravery had become a habit. Shouting and counter-shouting were the only coinage of intellectual exchange. That was manhood, maturity, the full, gruff, silent life.

A bed creaked, not his own. It sounded closer than his own. It was next door, downstairs, above, very close. Hans looked at the ceiling. Voices. A rich Italian bass, too sumptuous to be reassuring, the voice of seduction, with the curve of a selfsatisfied smile about it, a cello played with indecent relish, and an eloquent mezzo-soprano, with the sulky cadences which proclaim love to be painful, morose even. Going to bed at this hour, eight o'clock? The woman's voice turned capricious, then plaintive, hard to get. The bass droned on, spattering monosyllables into the evening, sure of itself and wealthy. Suddenly they were both talking at once, clambering over each other to an apex. Then silence again, and a massive groan of bedsprings.

Hans blinked unrestrainedly. Once again the bass began a murmured melody, a psalm. It rose and fell over its governed range, captivating by its aura of security, the tenderness of the very strong. Occasionally she would say a pathetic, reasonable word. He grumbled like a river near a torrent, then subsided again into dark, tremulous whispers, while the bedsprings creaked and squeaked and found no way of making themselves comfortable. The colloquy seemed to go on forever, the pinnacles of passion rising to a higher note every time they were attained, only to subside exasperatingly into secrecy and stillness.

After half an hour, Hans began to feel irritated. He rose and paced the room. Then, when the mezzo-soprano began moaning like a dog locked in, he fell onto his bed again, and listened. The bass never seemed to lose his composure. She was an instrument he could play by ear. Slowly her moans began to flow into each other, raindrops on a window, and she cooed a lullaby to herself, a sound which came from the beginning of time, when the earth was wet and steaming, and creatures left the sulphurous ponds to fill their nascent lungs with air. Louder and louder grew the weird song, stopping, starting again a quarter-tone higher, exploring a scale music had forgotten. Abruptly the cantilena broke to give way to sharp gasps, vaguely negative implorations mingling with exhortations to pursue a fleeing enemy on some vast plain of pleasure. The bass joined in, now a baritone, trumpeting his triumph, whipping his spiraling consciousness into a whirlwind of delirium, where nothing mattered but the liberation, the opening of the floodgates, the shower of doves set free from captivity. The wall bulged, and the small reproduction of the Mona Lisa shivered on its thumb tack. They were next door. A yell from the caverns of antiquity, a dying note of a night bird, vivid breathing, again a complaint of springs, and all was quiet until the sordid sound of a grudging tap, and the asthmatic cough of water urged through old pipes told Hans that all was not beautiful. It was nothing but adultery in a Victorian hotel.

Enervated, he left his room, banging the door as a protest against the lowness of it, but as he walked in the underlit street, he could not free himself from the sounds he had heard. What was there to talk about at such length? He had lain with women, usually in silence, for about five minutes. Certainly the women had sometimes said a thing or two, trite endearments, but conversation had irritated him at those moments. Love was a brief ecstasy, a cleaning of the mind, a physical necessity, like calisthenics. Or there was the hand-in-hand imbibing of the loveliness of nature, the meandering in meadows and along the banks of rivers, the furtive necking, with mother in the next room, the coltish illusion of eternity, but surely the two had nothing in common? How could a man sleep with a woman he respected? The very act of love was selfish, and a negation of the purring into the ear of the beloved.

Like a child who leaves the favorite food
till last on its plate, Hans walked towards the
Uccello Rosso a roundabout way. Would it still
be there at all? It was unlikely. And if it was,
could Teresa still be working there? It was even
more unlikely. Still, he could bask in memories.
She had been the cause of his flight into the
south, never deeply felt, but ever curious. He had
no cause to go elsewhere. His parents were old,
Germany defeated, in spite of his promises. He
could face neither. As for Teresa, he remembered
his reactions with surprise, although his fury with
Grutze seemed almost comical now. Teresa. He
thought of her frequently, in fact he thought
of no one else, and yet, when he remembered
himself at the time, he couldn't recognize the
man who could stand in silence for so long, just
dreaming, just looking holy, at grips with a surge
of inner whiteness. *Amore.* That was the word.

As he rounded the corner, he saw that the
Uccello Rosso was no longer there. In its place
was a new club, as garish as the other had
been discreet, the Club Waikiki. The American
occupation had made its presence felt, and the
wide boys of Florence had searched their dirty
minds to find names which would slake the
homesickness of the overpaid and lonely. Artificial palms stood sentinel at the doors of the
drive, while photographs of the half-undressed
lay under sheets of pink and purple cellophane to
beckon the unattached into a place of communal

sin. The electric guitar could be heard in the
street. A commissionaire in the sarcastic uniform
of a Bosnian archduke hissed and whistled at the
passing trade, 'Hey Johnny, 'ave a good time.
Plenty girls. Strip show in twenny minoots.'

Hans entered, and found it lighter inside than
he had expected. Only the corners of the room
were left in an aquarium gloom, but the center
was as bright as Broadway. A gross woman in a
grass skirt was singing a Hawaiian love song with
Italian words, the bruises on her legs suggesting
that she had a cruel lover. Cautiously he looked
around. The club was full of Americans, nice
boys who were under an obligation to make a
noise because they were in a noisy place, who
drank because they were far from home. A small
group of British sergeants sat at an unprivileged
table, staring at nothing, and sipping beer at a
thousand lire the bottle as though it were some
rare vintage. They occasionally tapped out the
rhythm of the song with idle feet or tough
fingers, just to show they were good sports.

Hans found a dark corner to sit in, and
ordered a brandy from another false Hawaiian
girl, who shed grass on the floor as she moved.
There was no sign of Teresa. He stared at
his enemies. He would be hard put to it to
know behind whose lines he was. The Yanks
were noisier than the Germans, livelier, and yet
their problems were evidently much the same.
They preferred demonstration to reticence. They

preferred to dance crazy, improvised dances in full view of their colleagues to the subversive sinning of old Europe, with its knee-touching under tables, its champagne and flowers and mildewed elegance. The English, turned to stone on contact with the seraglio, were more understandable to him. They were never closer together than when in touch with vice. When bent on pleasure, they would set forth as a group, and sit in silence, blowing their pittance on repulsive beer, and imagine afterwards that they had had a good time.

The lights went orange, and a man, his slick face suffused with good-nature, begged for silence from the podium. His hands held out, his thin mustache curled up into a crescent, he spoke into a microphone which hooted occasionally like a train racing from a tunnel. 'My Yankee frenns,' he said, 'di Cloob Waikiki pressent to you its Cabaret unic in Hitaly. Fest of hall, from Cairo, Egypt, Miss Fatima Luxor.' He led the clapping himself, and then made way for a plump, displeased lady who made some meaningless movements in the air that were supposed to have torrid sexual connotations, while the band of electronic instruments evoked the mystery of a cardboard Orient. Her navel undulated, an angry hornet in perplexity, while she lazily shed one flimsy lilac garment after another, her face remaining as expressionless as the sphinx itself. After five minutes, she was left in a pair of transparent trousers, in which her gigantic buttocks jostled each other in friendly fashion, while her nipples were hidden by bathrobe tassels, swinging like pendulums.

Clapping and whistling accompanied her departure. The master of ceremonies, still applauding himself when the others had left off, then announced from Bergen, Norway, Miss Astrid Olaf. A cavernous blonde rushed from the wings, her cheeks sucked in to indicate the fatality of the vamp, and struck the pose of a flapper of the '20s. Inhaling cigarette smoke from a long holder, she blew it out dangerously into the face of an imaginary victim, then undid her midnight dress, button by button, smiling satanically and breathing hard. The dress fell to reveal the skeleton of a weight-lifter, skin stretched over the frame with not a square inch to spare. Cigarette still in mouth, she performed some acrobatic tricks, bending herself into a series of naval knots, her spine having the pliancy of a sardine. Eventually, as Anitra's Dance swelled to a frantic tempo, she used her gifts to delineate a primitive slave girl dancing before the all-demanding god of the Volcano. The performance ended with her collapsed like a folded deck chair in a pool of purple light, the ultimate submission evidently favored by the god in question.

The third to appear on this international parade of lovelies was heralded as, from Allahabad, India, the Maharanee Indrapura. The orchestra struck up the appropriate piece of Rimsky-Korsakoff, and Teresa sidled onto the podium, bells ringing on her wrists and ankles, caste mark of wet lipstick on her forehead, her breasts and loins swathed in artificial silk. Hans could hardly look at her as some deep resentment began to stir within him. He was unreasonably furious with her, and yet found himself looking at the faces of those wrapped up in her performance with the mingled jealousy of a husband and the outrage of a cuckold. From left to right and left again her eyes traveled, in time with the music, doll-like. Slowly she began to unwind the art silk, and dance her way clumsily out of its voluminous folds. Soon she oscillated listlessly in nothing but a spangled brassière and a sequin-covered *cache sexe* the shape of a heart. Hans stared into his brandy, then looked up again at the humiliation of his dream. She was without talent for anything. Without talent for life.

He sat numbly through the next act, false Brazilian, with bananas and pineapples to discard in stripping, and during it he saw Miss Fatima Luxor enter the club through some curtains, now dressed normally as a hostess, in a red knitted dress more dowdily suggestive of nudity than were all the transparencies. Quickly he drained his brandy, paid for it, and crossed the floor to take his place at a table near the curtains. Here he waited, his eyes fixed to the place where the girls emerged after their performance.

During the fifth number, from Manhattan, Miss Harvest Moon, Astrid Olaf entered the club. She glanced at Hans in an interesting way, but he looked away quickly. Her eyes were dark, her hair dark at the roots. As Italian as all the others. He waited. Then, while from España, Señorita Dolores Alcazar was busy goading a mimed bull with the red rag of her passion, Teresa passed through the curtains. Hans rose, and blinked. She showed no sign of recognition, but sat down beside him.

'You remember,' he said stiffly.

'Remember? No,' she replied.

She had aged. Her dark eyes no longer searched. They knew, and what they knew was ugly. The pores had enlarged as powder had been added to powder over the months, with no breath of air, no touch of the sun. She asked for a cigarette. He bought her a pack of American ones, sea stores, not for sale on the mainland.

'Anything else?' he asked.

'Champagne.'

'Do you mean that?'

'Certainly,' she replied, 'I love it. I live on it. I have it for breakfast. I brush my teeth in it.'

She got her champagne. Italian, at French prices.

'Seriously, you remember me, don't you?'

'In this profession, you have no memory.'

'What profession? Dancer?'

She laughed. 'I can't dance.'

They sipped their champagne in silence. 'D'you want to come home with me?' she asked.

'I remember your room.'

'Many people do.'

'Yes,' he said, 'I'd like to come home with you.'

'D'you want to stay here any longer?'

'No.'

She hesitated for a moment. 'My fee has gone up,' she said. 'I've become very expensive.'

He stared at her, trying to penetrate through the time lost, searching for a trace of softness.

'What's the matter?' she asked flippantly. 'Mascara running?'

As they left, she passed by the table of Miss Fatima Luxor. 'I'll be back in half an hour,' she said.

Miss Fatima Luxor, who was with a drunken top sergeant, looked Hans up and down like a piece of livestock. Out on the pavement, Teresa shuddered.

'It's cold,' she said.

'It's warm.'

'We can walk to my place.'

'I know. I know we can. Wouldn't you prefer to come to my hotel?'

'No,' she said, 'it's too risky. Your wife may turn up. I may be used as a pretext for a divorce. Either you come to me or I don't go at all.'

'I have no wife,' Hans answered hotly, 'you
know that. I have been waiting for this moment
through the long months of war — all my life,
all my life, Teresa.'

'You remember my name? How sweet.'

For a while there was no noise but the patter
of feet on the pavement.

'Shall we go the long way by the river?'

'Why?'

'In memory of the night we spent there, the
two of us.'

'Oh, I spent so many nights there, with so
many people.'

They reached her house in silence. She searched
for her key, found it, opened the door, and they
climbed the stairs.

Her room hadn't changed. There was a sewing
machine by the window, an oleograph of Christ
with a wreath of thorns on the wall, a radio in
a cracked bakelite case by the bedside.

'Ten thousand lire, or twenty thousand lire
for the whole night,' she said.

The illusion of a home. The knickknacks of
the housewife. This might be the room of a
spinster earning a reputable salary in the post
office. He pulled twenty thousand lire from his
pocket, and laid it on the table.

She grimaced, went to her dressing-table, took
a vaporizer, and sprayed the room with a sickly
haze of carnations. Then she wiped her face
hard with a soiled towel, and the caste mark

disappeared. Hans sat heavily in a chair. She smiled at him, but he didn't respond.

'You're very gloomy, *amore*,' she said.

'Don't use that word.'

'Gloomy?'

'*Amore.*'

She began to strip, and this time he made no attempt to stop her. The dress fell off by force of habit. Soon she was naked. The expression on her face was still that of a woman wearing her clothes. And the expression of that other face, the human body, was as grotesque as it always is when one is not in love with the spirit which animates it, the surprised eyes of the breasts, the single nostril of the belly-button, the delighted smile of the pelvis, with its silly little goatee.

Teresa dabbed some perfume into her armpits, and then settled into bed, trying to look inviting. He hated her, but slowly took his clothes off. It was normal to do what he was doing, normal and soldierly. But he wouldn't talk like the bass in the other room, he would be silent again, and swift.

'Turn out the lights,' he said.

He Awoke in the morning, and could remember nothing at first. There were traces of light round the curtain: seven, seven-thirty. For a moment he didn't even know whether he was in his hotel or not. Glancing sideways he saw Teresa, asleep, her hair spread on the pillow. With her eyes shut, she

looked much more like the girl he had carried
with him in his cool heart. The shape of her
face was elusive, hard to recreate in the memory.
Asleep it was gentle and young, with its trace of a
dimple on one side, the left side as you looked at
it, and its mouth, as cunningly fashioned as the
curve of a violin, puckered into a cosy, perverse
smile. She frowned in her sleep, a cloud passed
over her forehead, she was probably dreaming.

Hans examined her face in every detail, and
conjured up a foolish illusion of domesticity.
This was his wife. Surrounding them was their
struggling home. They couldn't afford a new
radio, so they had to make shift with the broken
bakelite one. He mended it himself whenever it
went wrong, which was often. It gave you a
slight shock when you touched it. They needed
new curtains. The oleograph of Christ was a
present from her mother. Dear old soul. New
curtains and a better job.

He shifted to a new position as discreetly as
possible, in order not to wake her. There were
those who spent their whole lives in offices,
whose dreams were the travel posters in the
agency windows. Straight from school, he had
known the frigid majesty of the Russian winter,
the long yawn of nature. It was travel of the
kind unknown to Baedeker. And Italy. Nights
on the freezing floors of monasteries, the towers
of churches erected by velvety noblemen as a
deposit on the fare to heaven, used as a guide

for the artillery. Now he was longing for an office, time to think. He was lying to himself. Thought becomes a habit; a habit must have a beginning. He had never thought deeply in his life, and now he didn't know where to begin. All that passed through his mind was conventional, and yet perhaps it was a little victory to realize it. What could that infernal *basso profondo* have been murmuring to that woman? What kind of fevered poetry could a man produce at such a moment to make the occasion seem different from any other?

'You'll have to go out for your breakfast. I sleep till noon.'

Teresa had woken up, and with the opening of her eyes, the illusion of security evaporated.

'I don't eat breakfast,' said Hans, avoiding her look. He was annoyed.

'It's daylight.'

'You mean my twenty thousand lire's worth is up.'

She grimaced. 'You're easily satisfied,' she said.

'What d'you mean? What happened?'

'What happened? Nothing. You fell asleep.'

Odd, not to remember. Then he was alarmed, since it began to sound like a reflection on his powers.

'You ought to be happy.'

'I am. It gave me a good night's rest, which I badly needed. Good-by.'

'Holiday with pay,' he said, not moving.

She pretended to sleep for a full minute, but the expression on her face lacked innocence. She was awake.

'Since I haven't been very demanding, there is something you can do for me.'

'What?' She was bored.

'Tell me honestly whether you remember me or not.'

She thought it over, her eyes still closed.

'Oh, I remember everyone,' she muttered. 'Photographic memory. Makes me very unhappy. Giovanni, the son of the President of the Banco Popolare di Lavoro, who used to bring me roses, white roses, and who shook like a leaf when we went to bed, but then he was only sixteen – two weeks older than I was. Boys develop slower than girls. There was Captain Pattoni, Pottoni, Pittoni, I can't remember. He had a problem. I promised never to tell. There was a German general, wouldn't tell me his name, afraid of blackmail, many of them are. He gave me chocolates as though I was a child. It seemed to give him pleasure. There was the Canadian officer who couldn't function unless I pretended to beat him with a feather duster, and scolded him for wetting his bed . . .'

Hans leaped out of bed, and started dressing, trembling with anger.

'And do you remember me in all this menagerie of freaks?' he snapped.

'Freaks?' she asked. 'Aren't you one of them? It's not often a fellow gives me twenty thousand lire for the pleasure of going to sleep in my bed.'

Hans put his shoes on without bothering to untie the laces.

'Got a train to catch?' she asked.

'Good-by.'

'Yes, I remember you.' Hans stopped at the door, and stared at her. 'Your name is Hans.'

'Why didn't you admit it before?' he asked, his voice gentle, defenseless.

'Why should I? I can't get sentimental, not at my age, not in my job.'

'Why not?'

She shrugged her shoulders, and closed her eyes.

'Isn't that what some men pay you for, to be sentimental?' he asked, roughly.

'Oh, sure. I know the phrase for "I love you" in sixteen languages.'

'That's what I paid you for, to be sentimental,' he shouted.

She sat up quickly. 'Keep quiet! Think of the neighbors! You'll have me thrown out!'

'I paid you to be sentimental!' Hans whispered ferociously.

'Why didn't you tell me? *Amore.*'

'You do remember!'

'Remember? *Amore* is the Italian word for love. One of the most common in the language.'

'You remember our night together – when I was up here before – you began to take your clothes off – I prevented you – and when we stood all night, hand in hand, in the open air.' He searched her face, leaning forward anxiously, looking first into one eye and then into the other.

She did not flinch. Her face hardened.

'It was the most cruel night of my life,' she said.

'Cruel?' He stepped back, amazed.

She drew the bedclothes over her head, and lay still.

'Teresa. Teresa. *Amore. La bella Fiorentina.*'

He tried to pull the bedclothes away, but she had seized the sheets in her clenched fists.

'You'll stifle,' he said foolishly. 'Is there anything you need? How was it cruel? It was marvelous. I came back to see you. I risked my life. I . . . Teresa.' He fell on his knees beside the bed.

'Do you want to do something for me?' she asked, in a muffled voice, but one which was strangely in control of itself.

'Yes.'

'Go away. Just go away.'

He was taken aback for a moment. 'May I come back tonight? To the club?'

'I can't prevent you. It's a public place.'

He stood up. 'I would like to smash your face in,' he said, slowly.

'That would be another thirty thousand lire,' she replied.

He left, determined never to see her again, his chest tingling with self-righteousness.

AFTER A day spent staring at the patterns of the moisture on the ceiling, he left the hotel at nightfall to go to the Club Waikiki. He had endlessly reconstructed his scene with Teresa, inventing all sorts of mitigating circumstances which might excuse her vile behavior. It was foolish to have gone to her room, more foolish still to have given her money. Money corrupts. A true saying. Once money passed, he was a client, and just as guilty as she, guiltier, since he had searched her out. The strategy was to get her out of the club, and then to force her to walk in the old byways, among the statues. There were women who misunderstood courtesy, who thought of it as weakness. Before, he had been in uniform. There had been that to help him, an enemy uniform, symbolic of enforced order and ruthlessness. He had been too kind altogether, too sensitive. Wrong moves at every turn. He should have shaken her, bent her to his will, frightened her by his unswerving violence. When she hid under the bedclothes, he should have ripped them into shreds. Idiotic to threaten to beat her up. Do it, man, do it. She'll live to be grateful. Women are raw material to thrash into shape, to be broken like horses, and once broken, like horses, they become man's good friend. It's not brutal. It's what they want. They're disappointed in you if you don't.

He entered the club. Nothing had changed, except that it was earlier, and the girls were still seated at the somber tables as the master of ceremonies had not yet summoned them to parade their gifts. As his eyes became accustomed to the darkness, Hans saw Teresa in the distance, drinking with two civilians, sulking to her heart's content as they crooned at her, and told her spicy stories. Bank clerks on a spree. As he walked towards her, Hans saw Miss Fatima Luxor, who shot him a curious look of complicity, as though she knew that twenty thousand lire had been spent to no good purpose, and that his impotence might be hiding some unguessed but exciting perversity of the mind which only someone of her amatory talents could free. Hans put the thought out of his mind as he sat down at the next table to Teresa. The scores would be settled that night, and they would wipe that maddening expression off Miss Luxor's face. Teresa ignored him. If necessary he would create a scandal by kicking the two Italians out. But later, later. There was time.

His determination gave him a sense of well-being he had not enjoyed for years. He even clapped when Miss Fatima Luxor eventually appeared to evoke the Old Nile. There were just nine thousand lire in his pocket, but he wouldn't need them except for brandy. Teresa left her customers to change at the very start of the cabaret, and didn't look at Hans as she left. He ordered another brandy, and sang the melody with the band. Then he became conscious of a figure standing before him. It was Brehmig.

'What the hell are you doing here?' he asked loudly, in German.

'Sh! Sh! May I sit down?'

'Not for long. I have a date.'

'For a moment only.'

Brehmig's eyes were bloodshot. Either he had been drinking, or crying. His overcoat was dilapidated. With his glasses and his farcical whiskers, he looked like a genius, or a tramp.

'What's that, brandy?' he asked.

'Want one?'

'I haven't eaten for two days. Better not.'

'I haven't eaten either. A sandwich.'

'A sandwich!' Brehmig made it sound like eureka.

'What's the matter, why aren't you shooting the film?'

'I couldn't!' Brehmig whispered, horror-struck.

'Why not? What about me without glasses, without a mustache? Are you a coward?'

'Yes . . . yes . . .' moaned Brehmig, the tears gathering uncontrolledly in his eyes. 'I'm afraid, afraid of myself.'

'Afraid of yourself?' Hans became very military as a contrast to the sobbing Brehmig.

'How can you remain so calm? We killed them. Women, children, animals, old men. We did it, the two of us. We drank brandy to give ourselves courage—' and he pointed at Hans's glass with a dirty, shaking finger. Hans moved the glass to the side of the table, away from Brehmig. 'I can see every moment of it now, like a film, the submachine gun in my hand. It made a noise like a typewriter, but there was no little bell to ring when the page was finished. We sang as we marched. There was a lot of smoke, or dust, or something. Perhaps our feet were kicking it up, perhaps it was the bullets, or people falling, I don't know. I can see a child falling like a doll from a balcony. I can see a rocking chair tipping over, spilling an old lady onto the street. I can see a family of geese scudding across the road, a shower of feathers like confetti at a wedding, stupid geese. I can see a dog barking, thinking it was a game, a man advancing with a pitchfork, what hatred! What hatred! Women, all in black, black and red, dry black, wet red, a truck on fire, a lot of broken glass, a panama hat, a shoe, clean linen on the line, underpants and slips, full of holes, why shoot underwear?'

People were beginning to notice Brehmig's gestures, though his voice was drowned by the band.

'For God's sake pull yourself together,' Hans murmured.

'The church on fire. The church. That was

our undoing. The church.' Brehmig clasped his hands, closed his eyes, and let his head rest on the table. 'Oh God,' he said, 'source of all mercies, be unsparing with your chastising rod as with the balm of Your infinite understanding. I killed, I robbed, I desecrated Your altar which is all of nature, drunken on the fumes of wickedness, I forgot You, and I knew not what I did.'

Several soldiers were smiling, believing Brehmig to be a drunk, and they winked at Hans.

'Idiot,' said Hans.

Brehmig looked up, his face wet with tears, his eyes floating in folly.

'Do you mean that you are not haunted by what we did?' he blubbered.

'I don't remember a thing,' Hans replied coldly. 'And keep your voice down.'

'You are either a superman or a monster of wickedness.'

'What do you want with me? And why did you come here?'

'I came here because – don't you remember? – old times – *die schönen alten Zeiten* – the times of irresponsibility – at least you are cursed with a memory, otherwise you wouldn't be here. You are lucky not to be cursed with a conscience, too.'

'But why did you think I'd be in Florence?'

'I knew you'd make a break for it, and where else to go but Florence? Where else to get lost? Pity we couldn't have gone together.'

'I didn't run. I was sent,' said Hans, 'by the organization.'

'The organization?' asked Brehmig, wide-eyed. 'Does it help people, too?'

'I don't know. I was sent,' Hans replied curtly.

'No,' whispered Brehmig, 'the organization is made up of men. Put not your trust in princes. They'll all get caught.'

'You're frightened. Miserably frightened.'

'Yes, I am. The Allies will kill me if they catch me. They'll kill us both. And if I died now, without a chance at earthly redemption, I'd have nothing to say for myself at the bar of Heaven. No fleck of light on my dark record.'

'What do you want?'

'Money,' said Brehmig, with indecent honesty, 'enough for a square meal. Enough to get away. A few thousand lire.'

'You revolt me.'

'I revolt myself.'

Hans toyed with his brandy for a while. Brehmig studied his face for the slightest indication of his intentions.

'Get away?' asked Hans at length. 'Where to?'

'There is a monastery eighteen kilometers away, north of Fiesole. They ask no questions there. You can start from scratch, with a blank sheet, like a newborn child. I trust the justice of God, Winterschild, more than I trust the justice of men.'

'Coward,' Hans spat.

'I deserve that,' answered Brehmig, with a sad, masochistic smile. 'For what it's worth. I wasn't a bad officer.'

There was a silence.

'I have no money,' said Hans.

'One thing the army taught me, and that was loyalty,' Brehmig murmured, 'not loyalty to Fatherland, or flag or Führer, but loyalty to the brothers which fate had given you for the duration of hell on earth.' Quietly he began singing the old German soldiers' song, '*Ich hatt' einen Kameraden.*'

For the first time Hans felt a shiver of emotion shake the roots of his hair and a lump forming in his throat. Violently he took the money out of his pocket, and slapped five thousand lire on the table. 'Take it and get out!'

He had to prevent Brehmig from kissing his hand. 'I am the vilest man that ever lived,' Brehmig stammered, his tears falling onto the table one after another. 'My only hope on this earth is to make myself less vile.'

Hans felt all eyes to be on him after Brehmig walked unsteadily away. He was in no mood for conquest. He had a headache, and four thousand lire. Teresa was on, unwinding her art-silk wrap. She looked ridiculous. He walked out to get some air.

WAS BREHMIG genuine? Wouldn't his marriage

to the church be a marriage of convenience? Hans thought back to the destruction of the village. He remembered it quite well if he bothered to think about it, but that was war! There had been death in Russia, plenty of it, padded legs sticking out of the snow at all angles, upturned palms petrified in positions which were almost laughable, waxworks. He who has been a soldier has a harder heart than most. It was part of the training, damn it. Charging with a bayonet into a sack of straw, left groin, right groin, heart. What was all that for, if not to kill? It isn't surgery they teach in barracks.

Brehmig was a fraud. Fear had pushed him into belief as a last resort. And yet, a night in an empty church might be somewhat eerie, enough to set an unbalanced man off into hallucinations. If it were genuine, he was being unjust. '*Ich hatt' einen Kameraden.*' He deserved the benefit of the doubt, for old times' sake. How could a man make himself cry like that, at will? Brehmig had never displayed a facility for it under fire. You could make your eyes water by yawning internally, but you couldn't produce buckets of the stuff. A medieval bell started beating out a toneless carillon. The faithful were being called to prayer. From the dark and musty pages of the great simplicities came the sound, when hell was a real place with its own flaming geography, horned devils pitching the evil into cauldrons with evident delight; when God the Father sat on clouds to pronounce His awful judgments, and the virtuous, unlike the possessed, were allowed to keep their clothes for their amble in the gardens of Paradise. Hans entered the Piazza, and looked at the church. It was of medium size, and very old, the rough stones revealed now that the stucco had fallen off. The only relief from the rocky bleakness of the wall was a circular window of complicated design. The Piazza was empty.

Slowly Hans went towards the worn steps, a detective on the trail of Brehmig's deceit. The great wooden door was closed, its skin the continent of a race of worms. A small portion of it, a door within the door, gave under Hans's pressure, and he found himself faced by a padded wall, on which church notices were fastened, banns, appeals for charity, solemn edicts, announcement of religious picnics for the orphans. An old man dressed entirely in black held open a glass door for Hans, and he entered the church.

In the distance, distorted by the echo, a voice was burbling monotonously, the responses of a small congregation flowing into the single voice, a water color of sound in which the shades blur and lose themselves in each other. The sweet, admonishing smell of incense pervaded the place. Old women moved soundlessly like black phantoms in the shadows, their faces and their sorrows wrapped in privacy. One of them dipped her fingers in holy water, crossed herself,

curtsied briefly to the altar, and wafted away to
some favorite shrine hidden among the ribs of
the building. Under the baleful and relentless
scrutiny of the old verger, Hans dipped his
fingers in the marble font, and made a quick
fumbling gesture to allay suspicion. Then he
walked quietly in the gloom, but the footfall
of those unused to churches sounds bright and
brittle. The verger followed Hans with his eyes
until he lost him among the pillars.

Hans looked up at the statuary. A *fin-de-
siècle* Virgin Mary, holding a palm branch,
stared sightlessly before her. The dirt had
gathered in the folds of her alabaster gown
and between the leaves of the palms. She
reminded Hans of a friend of the family he
had detested when young. A gigantic Moses
held up the Commandments. An angel stooped
to place a laurel wreath on the dead head of a
medieval lord. St John tended a single sheep
with a look of effeminate docility on his face.
Hans examined the pictures. A martyrdom of
St Sebastian, painted in milky hues in the
Byzantine manner, the body of the victim
foreshortened, arms of simian length, ankles
twisted over each other like coils of rope, the
body punctured by a crazy assortment of arrows
which had been shot from every altitude, and
drawn gallons of blood. In the foreground, no
larger than dwarfs, stood a group of happy
archers, reloading their bows.

'Fellow couldn't paint,' thought Hans. 'Fancy hanging a thing like that up. No perspective. I could do better than that.'

A Christ scourging the moneylenders out of the Temple claimed his attention, but he had no idea of the story, so it seemed to him that an angry and athletic man was ill-treating a group of anxious people who gave every indication of wishing to leave. Hans shook his head. A little farther on, he came across a Last Supper. Christ, indicated by a more elaborate halo than the others, held out his hands in a gesture of supplication, while the apostles whispered and murmured to each other. For a long time Hans stared at the bearded face of the Son of God, trying hard to read into it a fraction of the terror and the compassion which Brehmig had seen there. He found nothing. All he saw was a man, bearded like an orthodox Jew, staring at him with an age-old insolence. Even the gesture began to look like an appeal for clemency, mingled with a shrug of resignation at the ups and downs of a small commercial existence. These extended hands of helplessness, contrasting with the aloofness of the brown eyes, appeared to Hans as symbolical of the feline cunning of Israel, the smoothness of advance or retreat according to the strength and vigilance of the opposition.

'We had the right idea,' he said aloud, and walked noisily out of the church, convinced that Brehmig was not only a fraud, but, in his insignificant way, a traitor. He thought for a moment of returning to the Club Waikiki, but he had no stomach to risk new humiliations. He wished to be alone. It would do Teresa good if he didn't go back this night. She had seen him all right. Let her stew in her doubts and sorrows, and wonder where the hell he was.

Passing a tobacconist's which was open late, Hans bought a postcard of the Pitti Palace, and returned to the hotel. He had not written home for a long time. Now, it would be safe. Soon he would be in the Middle East.

Dear Vaterlein and Mutterli, he wrote, and then thought for a moment. *Yes, I am alive and well. I did not write before because I could not, you understand. What has happened to our homeland has filled me with unutterable sorrow and shame. For life, I shall bear the scars of our failure.* He paused. Perhaps he was being too depressing. *Florence is a beautiful town, but of course, it isn't Nuremberg.* What else? How to give his mother pleasure, she who had borne him in her womb, and suffered so that he might be brought into the world? *I have met a very nice girl, who is unfortunately Italian. Nothing serious, you understand, but who knows? We have just been dancing in the Club Waikiki, a very refined and proper place, where the aristocracy goes. I have also been to church. My love as always. Your son, Hans.*

P.S. When you next hear from me, it will be from an exotic land!

As so often happens, pen and mind tell a different story.

XII

THE SHOOTING of the picture was beginning
to acquire a certain rhythm, when everything
stopped again at midday on Thursday. The
village was out in force, little girls in wool
stockings, men in their best corduroy jackets
with medals from all Italy's recent wars pinned
to their chests, women in funereal black. The
wind was fierce, an enervating squall from the
sea, blowing dust in spirals, gathering hats into
its lap, and sowing them in the fields. The
military band of the 9th Military District had
arrived by coach, and were warming up their
instruments in the café. The other band, that of
the Organization of Ancient Combatants from
the African Wars, were rehearsing assiduously in
the cemetery, using the tombs as their benches,
while their conductor, a one-armed, one-legged

hero of the troubles in Eritrea, plunged them
into the massive diapason of brasses with five
eloquent fingers. Filigrani, wearing the red star
of his convictions in his buttonhole, chose to
dress in his oldest clothes, and walked slowly
to the monument with a great wreath of scarlet
flowers, worked into the shape of a hammer, a
sickle, and heraldic heads of corn. Old Plumes
was already there, in a morning suit, his eyes
fixed onto a distance filled with his own personal
images of glory. The count arrived in a coach and
pair, last used by his father for the coronation of
King Victor Emmanuel. He wore the top hat
dictated by protocol, a Golden Fleece hanging
limply round his neck on a brilliant piece of
silk. The two irritated griffins on the door
of his carriage clawed the air on either side
of the coat of arms, three arrows and three
pawnbrokers' balls, with gorgeous ferocity. The
hour was approaching. With five minutes to go,
a stately Lancia limousine arrived, driven by a
Carabiniere. Colonel Ubaldini was helped from
the back seat by a host of willing hands, and he
walked into the sunlight, a-glitter with orders.
It was a surprise visit, and Val di Sarat was
amazed and slightly touched to see his uncle in
the distance.

As the hour of twelve struck, the film cameras
stopped turning, and a group, including Val di
Sarat, Professor Zaini, an old bent man with
a short, accusing white beard, and General

Bassarocca, also bearded, leaning heavily on a gnarled walking stick, marched slowly and reverently from the ruins of the church, preceded by a soldier of the regular army, carrying a regimental banner, which fussed and flurried in the wind like a puppy on a string. Silence settled over the scene.

The cortege reached the statue as men clutched their hats and women their skirts. The few children who asked loud questions were either shushed or slapped mercilessly. The wind broke the silence, beating fitfully, sighing, whistling, dying only to whistle again. The American film contingent stood in the distance, and were moved. The purring of their personal movie cameras indicated that the scene was being recorded for posterity. A child began bellowing, and had to be rushed away. Innumerable salutes were exchanged, and then *Fratelli d'Italia* filled the air with its optimistic lilt. Both bands played it, and although they began together, the veterans beat the regulars in a photo finish.

Professor Zaini, one of those incredible ancients in which Italy specializes, ascended the podium to address the listening universe. He had been in politics from the dawn of the century, and men as venerable as Orlando and Sonnino had wilted under his virulence. The Fascist era had found in him a peppery and malevolent critic, and now under the new coalition he had emerged from the political wings with his venom refreshed and ready to use. He examined Italy's recent past (recent, by his standards, extended to the days of Garibaldi), speaking without notes as befits a great forensic lawyer, brandishing his arms as he invoked witnesses from the sunlit pastures of Elysium, molding sonorous phrases from the air like a sculptor, barking at the age-old enemies of that deep humanism which, he said, had kept the soil of the Italian mind free from the erosion of prejudice through the centuries. His remarkable lucidity was achieved, however, at the expense of time, and it was quarter to one before his physical exhaustion put a period to his eloquence.

General Bassarocca was mercifully brief by contrast. He had very little voice, and all that the audience knew was that every second word was '*Italia.*' Since the distinguished general had a superb capacity for moving himself, it followed that everyone else took the cue, and wept with him. When he had finished, Val di Sarat stepped forward, and cut a tape with his sword. The draperies sagged, and the statue stood exposed. More salutes, and a minute of silence, Italian silence, the noise of children and their angry mothers, a symphony of distant motor horns, and the braying of a donkey with no sense of occasion.

After Filigrani had formally placed his wreath, and spoken gruffly of the band of brothers, some of whom fell so that the sun might shine red, and after the count had traced the village and

himself back to the paleolithic gloom, and after
Old Plumes had shouted his peremptory orders
to the Fates, telling them to do their worst, San
Rocco would stand forever as a testimony to this,
that, and the other, Val di Sarat spoke to the
assembly. He had not prepared a speech. He
spoke from the heart.

'*Amici*,' he said, 'the occasion is a solemn one,
and yet it is also an intimate one. I am not
especially conscious of our glorious past today,
of our traditions, of our valor, of our sense of
justice. I am always conscious of these things, or
rather am I conscious of our aspirations towards
them, and of our frequent failures, the failure
of men to live up to their ideals. The whole of
our nation is strewn with memorials such as the
one I have just unveiled, and at their myriad
inaugurations, fine and noble sentiments must
have been expressed drawing oceans of tears,
torrents of applause, and then a deep sleep of
forgetfulness. When the Fascists marched on
Rome, they passed by many memorials, but
statues are dumb. They depict only glory. About
death itself, gangrene, pain, amputation, filth,
stupidity, inhumanity, self-preservation, they are
silent. The human mind forgets unpleasantness,
and in doing so it prepares the climate for new
unpleasantness. I cannot forget it. I will not
forget it.

'War is the most stupid of arguments. It is the
ultimate solution, just as the ultimate solution of

the successful criminal would be the destruction
of the courts of law. It occurs when there is no
more intention to obey the rules of debate, which
are the rules of the God-given human mind. It
occurs when the stupid run out of answers, and
it is because of the sudden exasperation with logic
and with beauty on the part of those without the
talent for logic or for beauty that the millions
of innocents perish. There is no other reason.
Fools, bankrupt spirits, express themselves at the
expense of others, and those who think in terms
of war are the most foolish, the most bankrupt
of all, and they too often survive the banquet
of death to which they issued the invitations.'
He paused. 'I have been called a hero. I am
told I fought well. Others fought as well as
I, with less luck. Personally, I consider what
I did the least important event of my life. It
was conceived in levity, in the high spirits of
youth. I enjoyed myself. Yes, like a hardened
and conscienceless warrior, I enjoyed myself. I
killed with a light heart, and I enjoyed myself
at the expense of other people. This was selfish,
thoughtless, irresponsible. And I am a hero. I
would rather have written an immortal line,
fathered a healthy child, planted a growing tree
than stand before you today at this altar to
human folly, accepting your congratulations.'

'Are you mad?' whispered Colonel Ubaldini
afterwards.

'Why?'

'Those are the most dangerous thoughts. Luckily for you the people are too stupid to understand them. They thought it was some new form of patriotism, otherwise you'd be branded a Communist at once.'

'A Communist? Good God. Why?'

'You'll never learn. And you'll never be fit for public office. You are a great disappointment to me.'

'I'm very sorry.'

Ubaldini looked at his nephew ferociously. 'I hate waste,' he said. 'I had to work, painstakingly, to reach my present eminence. You are a hero. A hero doesn't have to open his mouth. You've passed all your exams with flying colors, while I sweated my way up the ladder, rung by rung. There you are, with all the cards in your hands, and you try to throw it all away by acting like a boy of fifteen with the weight of the world suddenly on his shoulders.'

'Are you jealous of me?'

'Of course I am, imbecile!'

'Fifteen's a good age, honest. The world is new and clean.'

'The world is very old and very dirty,' and he added as an afterthought, 'and highly rewarding.'

Val di Sarat's speech hadn't made much impression. On such occasions, the inflections speak more powerfully than the words, and the fact that he had had to project his voice to make himself heard was enough to clear him of all suspicion of subversion.

'The boy has a mind of his own,' said Old Plumes. 'And then, heroes are never sound orators.'

MR TACOO, frustrated at every turn in his efforts to spread his gospel of common sense, had a plan of his own. When he eventually managed to reach the Allied Control Commission, a weary lieutenant-colonel had told him they would do what they could, but warned him that everyone in Europe was morbidly sensitive at the moment, and that the impression must never be given that the Armed Services were seeking to exert pressure on behalf of a mere corporation. This was an admirable excuse to do nothing, and Tacoo knew it. Now he mingled with the garrulous crowd, and sought out Val di Sarat. He had caused his property department to prepare one of those diplomas beloved of Americans, a scroll of parchment inscribed with monastic precision, the first letter illuminated with cymbal-clashes of red, yellow and magenta, beginning with the solemn words, 'Be it known that, whereas—'

Now, introducing himself to the hero, he said he would like to make a presentation on behalf of himself, Olympic Pictures, and, by implication, America. Val di Sarat smiled. He had seen many diplomas in Chicago, and he knew the value placed on testimonials of this nature.

'Be it known that, whereas the aforesaid Captain Val di Sarat fought for democracy, and whereas he actively and heroically did engage the enemy at close quarters, and whereas he did furnish a shining example of gallantry in the field which did so inspire Olympic Pictures of Olympic Boulevard in the City of Los Angeles that they did forthwith decide to delineate and depict this action of heroism by the medium of the art of motion pictures, and whereas the high collaboration of the artists and the hero will serve to strengthen those bonds of amity and freedom which bind the Italian and American peoples in their vigilant struggle against World Communism and the Powers of Darkness and Dictatorship, it is befitting and well that this solemn testimonial be offered in commemoration of this great feat of bravery and of the moving picture which will recreate the act for the edification and entertainment of future generations.' It was signed by Tacoo, and a large wax seal dangled from its lower edge.

Val di Sarat was touched, and extended his hand, which Tacoo shook warmly.

'It's the least we can do,' said Tacoo, as the flashlights of the press department stabbed their eyes. 'I would further like to know if you would care to see some of the stuff we have shot,' Tacoo went on, pressing home his advantage. 'There's not much of it yet, but we've rushed through

some of it, and it came back from the labs in
London this morning.'

Val di Sarat introduced his uncle to Tacoo,
and said they would very much enjoy to see the
first dailies of the film after lunch, since there
was to be a banquet.

'About three o'clock, I'll lay it on,' Tacoo
agreed. 'You see, there's been a lot of rather
silly sabotage going on round here, and I kind
of hoped that if you saw the quality of the
stuff we're turning out you might use your
influence to stop it – like scratching insults on
the paintwork of our cars and so on. It makes
for ill-feeling, and that's not what any of us has
been fighting for.'

Val di Sarat agreed, and left for the banquet.

'There you are,' said his uncle, 'there are
strings attached to every public action in this
world, and there is a degree of what the puritan
will stupidly call corruption everywhere. Whenever you give your wife a present for her birthday,
it is a glaring piece of public relations. You are
buying a few hours of peace and quiet.'

'What are you trying to prove?'

'Nothing. I am trying to make you see things
as they are, not as they might be. Why? Because
I wish you to be happy. If I were in your shoes,
I'd boast a bit more. There are ways of boasting
which are attractively humble, you know. What
you think of yourself doesn't matter to a soul.
What they think of you is everything. A man

only exists in the minds of other people. I am known as a great policeman, ruthless, efficient, and hideously imaginative. I am not. I never lift a finger. I am lazy. Laziness handled with care can look like impassivity, just as a degree of sudden activity, after weeks of lassitude, looks like the most imaginative efficiency.'

As he walked, he saw Erhardt sitting in a café, sipping a drink. Without interrupting his conversation, he bowed cordially. Val di Sarat looked puzzled.

'You see,' his uncle went on, 'the fact that I did not interrupt my conversation, but went on talking, has put Erhardt on the defensive. He saw me coming, and prepared to meet my look of recognition. I saw him too, from afar off, but decided not to notice him until I had almost passed him. When I saw him, I expressed no surprise whatever at seeing him here, which further discountenanced him. I forbid you to turn around! You, on the other hand, betrayed yourself by a look of bewilderment.'

'But what is he doing here?'

'I wish I knew.'

'What's the advantage of these games you play?'

'I train myself never to be surprised by anything. That, in itself, gives one a huge advantage. You never know when it may come in useful.'

'What if I told you that I was going to get married?' asked Val di Sarat.

The uncle smiled benignly. 'I wouldn't be a bit surprised.'

'And what if I told you further that I haven't the faintest idea whom I am going to marry?'

'You surprise me less and less.'

'Yes, it is indeed a remarkable gift,' sighed the nephew.

After the banquet, the colonel and his nephew walked heavily to the local cinema, filled with food, Chianti, and Strega liqueur. Tacoo was waiting at the door for them in person, having deemed the occasion of such importance to the entire future of the film that it justified the loss of half an hour of shooting time. They took their seats, and the lights went down. The first shots they saw were of six Germans advancing leerily through the olive groves.

'Like it?' asked Tacoo.

'It looks very much like six Germans advancing through the olive groves,' said Val di Sarat.

'That's what it is.'

'If that's what it is, it's fine.'

'Is that the way they looked?'

'If you put six Germans in an olive grove, they will invariably look like six Germans in an olive grove.'

'Great, isn't it?'

The next shot showed the Norwegian actress, Miss Tollefsen, bursting into a room and saying the line, 'They've taken my baby.' The line might as well have been 'I've lost the address' for the amount of irritation invested in it.

'Who's that?' asked Val di Sarat.

'She's Vera, the daughter of the village black-smith.'

'You have exactly captured the feeling that she is an Italian blacksmith's daughter,' said the colonel.

'Why, thanks,' Tacoo replied.

Again and again she did it, in twenty takes.

'Who's taken her baby?' Val di Sarat inquired.

'The Germans.'

'I don't remember them having taken any-one's baby.'

'They took many adults as hostages,' the colonel declared. 'It seems to me legitimate license. After all, you couldn't very easily have a baby entering and saying, "They've taken my mother." The acting must be in competent hands.'

'That's right,' said Tacoo, 'that's a great angle.'

After a pause, the colonel permitted himself one small criticism. 'The fairness of the lady's hair, while not typically Italian, is entirely poss-ible, especially up here in Tuscany, or near Milan, but I quarrel with her breasts, which are typical of the Scandinavian North, small, hard, athletic breasts with pale nipples, not the pendulous, veined breasts of Italy which seem to tremble with the promise of milk, nipples dark as violets.'

'You don't see the nipples,' said Tacoo, worried.

'Any man worthy of his salt can guess the nipples,' rasped the colonel.

The next shots showed the hatred on the faces of the Germans in gigantic close-up as they watched the village on fire.

'Good types?'

'Very authentic.'

Suddenly Val di Sarat stood up, his shadow thrown onto the screen. A vast close-up of a man filled the theater, and he was blinking. 'That's him!' cried Val di Sarat. 'Winterschild!'

'Come on,' said the uncle, rising with an effort.

'Who?' asked Tacoo.

'A war criminal. A war criminal we want!'

'War criminal?' roared Tacoo to his assistant. 'Call publicity! What a story!'

'Quiet!' yelled Ubaldini, and then went on quietly. 'Are you sure?'

'Positive,' replied his nephew with some irritation.

'Very well then, don't start running round the streets. You may ruin everything. Let us say the film is over. We are leaving the cinema in the usual manner.'

'Are you going to surround the village?'

'No.'

'Why not?'

'I have a feeling it is too late.'

'Was the war criminal the guy with a blink?' asked Tacoo excitedly.

'Yes.'

'Erhardt told me he had had to leave owing to a family tragedy.'

'I thought so,' smiled the colonel. 'Follow me.'

They emerged into the waning sunlight, and Ubaldini walked slowly to the café. Erhardt was still at his table, asleep, a newspaper over his face. Quietly Ubaldini sat down next to him, beckoning his nephew noiselessly into another chair. Tacoo sat down at a table behind, the light of battle in his eye.

'No message from Fromm yet?' asked the colonel.

Erhardt tore the paper from his face, and looked up sleepily. 'I fell asleep,' he said, smiling, and glancing around, fancied himself surrounded. He no longer smiled.

'What did you say?' he asked.

'I wondered if you had had a message from Fromm yet.'

'Fromm? Who's he?'

'You call him Fromm. We call him Luetze in our files.'

Erhardt frowned. 'What about him?'

'Has he wired you yet about Schubert's release? I presume that that is the reason you spend so much time at this café, pretending to be asleep. It is next door to the post office. Every now and then you go in to ask if a telegram has arrived.'

'I don't know what you're talking about.'

'No? It's easy to establish. Let us ask. Perhaps my dear nephew will be so good as to walk to the post office, and ask just how often you have been in there since lunch.'

'What was this wire supposed to contain?' asked Erhardt.

'The words "There will be no music tonight," or "There will be music tonight" – referring, I presume, to Schubert. The subtlety of you Germans is really most oppressive.'

'So now you tap our telephone conversations,' snapped Erhardt.

Val di Sarat, who had risen, sat down again.

'You amaze me,' purred the colonel. 'During the war you tapped every conversation, but when the system which you perfected is used on you, you don't recognize it as the same simple device, but consider it as something vastly immoral.'

'What do you want?'

'I want to offer you a drink. Cinzano?'

'No, thank you.'

'Mr Tacoo?'

'No.'

'My good nephew?'

'No.'

This was uncle at his most infuriating, his most sadistic. 'With your permission, I will. *Signorina! Un Cinzano, per favore, con un pezzo di limone!* He smiled. 'Where was I? Oh yes. Schubert. I made a deal with you, Erhardt. I hope for your own sake that you remember the terms of it.'

'Yes.'

'Would you remind me of it?'

'You know it as well as I do.'

'Yes,' said the colonel quietly, and he leaned forward. 'I promised to release Schubert when you gave me Winterschild. Why did you expect me to release Schubert before I had Winterschild? Just because I've always been a good sport in the past? Or do you seriously think that you are in a position to intimidate me?'

'I fulfilled my part of the bargain as well as I could,' replied Erhardt. 'I came up here to find Winterschild, but he ran away. I have no idea where he is now.'

'Erhardt, Erhardt, you are slipping,' said the colonel pityingly. 'If we overheard part of your telephone conversation with Fromm, it is really too much to expect us not to have overheard it all. Winterschild is waiting to go to Lebanon. Perhaps he has already gone. I knew this, that is why I did not expect to find Winterschild here, nor did I wish to bring this to your attention before, and spoil your lunch. I will release Schubert, tonight, whatever happens. He is quite inoffensive, and of a low intelligence. His real name is Private Palkowsky. Now, where is Winterschild?'

'I tell you I don't know.'

'Has he left for Lebanon?'

'I don't know.'

The two village Carabinieri arrived, saluted, and sat at the next table. Erhardt looked more uneasy than ever. The colonel smiled, glanced questioningly over his shoulder. The senior Carabiniere nodded briefly.

'If he has left, it means that you have taken a terrible risk in swindling me.'

There was a pause. Two Carabinieri on motorcycles swept into the village, and sat in their saddles alertly, within view.

'Well?'

'For the hundredth time, I tell you I don't know.'

The colonel smiled again, ever so sweetly. 'Since I let myself into your secrets,' he murmured, 'I think it only fair to let you into some of mine. The local police have been watching us. I gave instructions that when I sat down at your table, they were to join me. The two men whom you see on their motorcycles across the street come from the neighboring village. Out of sight there is a van load of reinforcements. Why are they here? Now that they have arrived, I'll tell you. If you don't tell me where Winterschild is, I'll arrest the whole lot of your Germans, all fifteen of them, in exchange for Schubert, as I promised. Now.'

'You can't do that!'

'Why not? They're all in one place, for once. It's too easy.'

The perspiration stood out on Erhardt's forehead. 'Very well,' he said. 'The man you are looking for is in Florence ... at the Hotel Belsoggiorno.'

'And what name does he go under, Mendelssohn?'

'Dr Cohen.'

'How nearly right I was. I just overestimated your love of music.'

Val di Sarat rose, flushed. 'I'll go,' he said.

The colonel smiled. 'I would come with you, but I loathe fast driving. I'll follow in my limousine and meet you there.'

As Val di Sarat sprinted away, Erhardt snapped, 'I hope you are satisfied.'

'Not quite,' said the colonel. 'I dislike being cheated. The Carabinieri will stay in the village until the criminal is captured. That will not be for some two hours. However, I am a good-natured man—'

He was interrupted by a girl from the post office, who delivered a telegram to Erhardt.

'Open it,' said the colonel. 'It will show you just how good-natured I am.'

'There will be music tonight, Lopez,' read the telegram.

'You see?' smiled the colonel. 'In spite of the fact that Winterschild is still at large, I have released Schubert. The telegram arrived before lunch, but I instructed them not to deliver it

until I had been sitting here for five minutes.'
He laughed gaily at Erhardt's perplexity. Then
he grew serious again. 'I hope you don't think,
however, that I am such a fool as to give
you a present without demanding something
in return?'

'What?'

'You,' said the colonel, like the falling blade
of the guillotine.

Erhardt rose. 'Me?'

'I will take you in exchange for Schubert, SS
Colonel Diegelhardt, until such a time as Fromm
can find someone of equal rank and standing
to exchange against you. From now on, there'll
always be one of you in prison, just to remind
you of the existence of the Italian government
and its laws. Fromm is already apprised of the
situation. *Sieg heil*, my friend.'

As Erhardt was led away by the Carabinieri,
Tacoo whistled.

'Jeez, what a story! What a great scene for a
picture!'

The colonel grinned modestly.

'You entertained us. I did my best to entertain
you. Those are the laws of hospitality.'

XIII

'I KNOW, I know perfectly well that you are able to effect the arrest yourself, but I ask you for the sake of our old friendship to allow my nephew to do it. We can easily cook the subsequent reports, and we can distribute the credit where it is due to our hearts' content.' Colonel Ubaldini was on the phone to his old friend and enemy Colonel de Gratiis, Commander of the Carabinieri in Florence.

'I am leaving this instant myself, and I will be in Florence in a matter of two hours. Don't forget, Fulvio, that I have been on this case from the beginning. It is only fair that I am in at the kill ... what? ... Not at all, I am doing it for the boy's sake, he's a kind of problem, a hero as you know, but no sense of *savoir-faire*, no interest in career whatever.

I just hope that the sense of achievement he will derive from a capture of this sort will force him to sit up and take notice of the delightful horizon which is stretched before him for the asking . . . I knew you'd understand . . . if you need any more convincing, may I remind you of a certain time in Albania when you needed my help . . . precisely . . . I saved your bacon on that occasion . . . I don't remind you of it very often, but I would like you to remember it now, in case you are tempted to step in and ruin it all. I trust you implicitly. Of course I do. How's your daughter? A son, is it? How foolish of me. I am delighted to hear it. I wish I were so lucky with my nephew. *Arrivederci.*'

Mopping his brow, he struggled into the comfortable cloth interior of his limousine, and said to his chauffeur, 'To Florence, Alberto. Don't hurry, especially on the corners, since with my weight I get thrown about. Also I like the Tuscan landscape.'

Meanwhile Val di Sarat was driving towards Florence as though leading a race. The little car snaked and bobbed over the tortuous road, its tires squealing like grim echoes from the slaughterhouse. He felt identified with the car, an emotion peculiarly Italian, and seemed to translate all the imponderables of mechanical theory into a poem of motion. He was exhilarated. The little engine sounded healthy, and the moisture in the cold evening air gave raucous punch to the carburetor. This was youth rediscovered.

On a sharp right-hand turn, a red Alfa-Romeo appeared on the wrong side of the road, traveling at eighty or more miles per hour. Val di Sarat caught a glimpse of two white figures as he allowed his instincts for self-preservation to take over the wheel. The two cars passed so close to each other that a crash seemed inevitable. They did touch briefly. A wrench and a clatter, and the rear bumper of the red car fell onto the road in a shower of dry mud. The car itself plunged into a field. Val di Sarat slewed his car sideways as he braked. Then he looked back out of the window. The two occupants of the other car, doubtless scions of some rich and idle house, waved at him, and roared with hysterical laughter. He shouted some of the choicest pieces of invective he could think of, put his car into gear, and motored away. Something at the back was rattling annoyingly, but he didn't bother to get out and examine the damage. The joy was gone. He honked at every bend, and thought.

A few years back he might have joined the laughter, and embroidered on the story shamelessly afterwards. 'I was doing a flat hundred and fifty kilometers in my little Fiat . . . I know it sounds improbable, but I have fitted twin-carbs and a supercharger . . . when all of a sudden, a madman in a twenty-five hundred Alfa Super Sport comes round a curve at two hundred k.p.h. . . .' Now, he was sober. He had reached an age when he knew the value of life. Those two lads were young enough to have missed the war. There was all the difference.

He thought briefly of his life, how useless it had been, and of how his untamed talents had been allowed to cascade hither and thither, losing themselves carelessly, of benefit to neither himself nor anyone else. Oh, he had done good, because his heart was in the right place, but it had been unplanned and casual.

His beginnings had been promising. He had studied bridge engineering, a constructive, painstaking job. At the time of the noisiest reassertions of Fascist power, it had seemed dull however. Impossible to sit in a gloomy office and plot out all the dry problems of cantilever construction while outside in the street the puppies of the regime were barking their allegiance to energy rediscovered and giddy aspirations. He had gone to Ethiopia as a legionary. At the age of nineteen it was thrilling to be dressed in black, ready to court death in a costume macabre enough to proclaim the fact that a contract with immortality had been signed. Old ladies surrendered their seats to him in the streetcars, which gave him opportunities for medieval gallantry. In Ethiopia, however, things were different. First of all it was hot, and secondly, the taste of victory turned sour in the mouth as the weight of a Western military machine was hurled against ill-equipped bands of foragers who earned the admiration of the world. It was no fun to be on the winning side in such an unequal contest.

The campaign instilled in Val di Sarat's young and independent mind not only a deep affection for the enemy, but also grave doubts about the ability of the military mind to engineer victories. He came to the conclusion that the victor was the one who managed to stave off defeat longer than his opponent. The loss of life owing to errors, or even just to mental laziness, alarmed him, and the luxury of entrusting human beings to the arbitrary whims of those encased irrevocably in the prisons of their own foolish prejudice filled him with a spirit of revolt.

Believe, Obey, Fight were the instructions of Mussolini. Val di Sarat, being Italian and not German, could no longer believe, since the black uniforms, once they were draped on corpulence, suddenly looked ridiculous. The insistence of the Duce and of men like De Bono, with his white spade beard, on dressing up in costumes which flattered only the muscular legionnaires, and of placing black toques on their heads, with tassels on them which swung like windshield wipers as they engaged each other in earnest colloquy, and then of running on parade to the infectious rhythm of the *Bersaglieri March*, was offensive to his Italian sense of beauty, his sense of harmony. No man who had stood spellbound before the statues of Cellini and Donatello could consider a half-naked Duce shoveling sand symbolically in the Pontine marshes a thing of inspiration. He could not believe, and therefore he could not obey. He could only fight, but that was because he enjoyed it.

After the Ethiopian war was over, he did not volunteer for Spain, but sought his excitements in more independent activities. He raced motorcycles for a season, to the despair of his uncle, and only retired when he had broken his leg twice simply owing to a radical lack of talent on two wheels. It was merely the joy of the chase which kept him going for so long. He could have raced cars, but this he considered too easy. It wasn't worthy of his most ardent efforts. Sickened by fumes and society, he abruptly determined to seek nature in the raw, and without as much as a note of farewell to his spiritual guardian, the then Major Ubaldini, he went to Canada to cut down trees. After the first thrilling release from the intellectual torments of Europe, this new activity began to pall, since he developed much the same feelings for the majestic trees as he had experienced for the majestic Ethiopians. The damned Italian predilection for humanism, which is not so much a philosophy as an abnormal sensitivity towards the human condition, always overtook him and saddened him. The forests appeared to him as an army of trees, each with their own personality, each with their own silent reproach under the ax.

He went to Chicago to be among men again and spent an exhilarating time as personal bodyguard of Lefty Bonelli, a witty and elegant gangster who was inordinately proud of Mussolini's achievements, at the same time easily resisting any temptation to return and take part in the renascence.

'Dictatorship makes it tough for the Maffia,' he used to say, 'since the Maffia is a democratic institution, and can only operate real good in a democracy.' He listened with interest to the stories of how the Duce was improving the Italian roads, but shook his head sadly all the same. 'Good roads is bad for bandits. The way they're set up in the old country, they need bad roads for their getaways. Put a Sicilian on a freeway, and he's lost. Why, we had to learn an entirely new technique over here . . . cost us many valuable lives.'

After a time, Val di Sarat began to wonder if Lefty Bonelli's body was worth guarding, and his doubts came to an end on December 7, 1937, when, in spite of his vigil, his charge was shot dead by Four-Finger Morella after an argument about a slot-machine.

Determined to combat his increasing restlessness, he settled down as a futurist painter, and his pictures hang to this day in many American homes. The prices he asked were so exorbitant that they had evident quality, and there was even a rumor that there were some false Sarats on the market, but in fact he painted them all, true and false. He soon grew tired of his *vie d'artiste*, since it had come so easily. There were probably some poor bastards shivering in Paris attics with real talent, the dealers hovering over them like vultures, waiting impatiently for their deaths, while he had succeeded by the sheer artistry of his deception, by his half-shut eye and impetuous social comportment, which captivated the ladies with dollars to burn and contemporary houses to furnish.

Again his conscience prevailed upon him to stop, and he drifted into the mysterious world of photography for a while. Here his success was even more scintillating, since he knew next to nothing about it, and therefore became one of the pioneers of the blurred school which is usually attributed to soft lighting, but which in Val di Sarat's case was the result of a series of elementary and unforgivable mistakes. A host of dowagers came to have their portraits done in an ectoplasmic diffusion which erased the marks of time. Although they invariably came out looking like buns soaked in milk, they were eminently satisfied, and spread the conviction that here was a man who had elevated photography to the level of an art.

Fleeing before his soul-destroying facility, he determined to go to the East, the home of divine stillness and profound contemplation. Instead of finding a civilization of jade, gongs, and whispered wisdom, he found war and Western influence, the atmosphere of a third-rate thriller. Having caused the pregnancy of an emotional White Russian nymphomaniac, he studied medicine briefly and was soon established, albeit unofficially, as an expert on birth control and its unexpected byproducts. Over this epoch of his life he drew a veil. It was the time of his most sustained surrender to the temptations inherent in his personality. He caused much unhappiness with his casual love-making, he drank in search of momentary oblivion, he did all the conventional things expected of a self-pitying, handsome, troubled man who knows how to excite a woman's interest. Perhaps, he now thought, he had just been a microcosm of a world addled by a desperate malady, a little fragment of that sickness which was soon to explode into the agony and fever of war. No, he deserved no benefit of any doubt. People alone hardly exist. They exist only in contact with other people. In contact with the foreigners in Shanghai, he existed as a scoundrel.

He greeted the news of war with relief, and left to behave like a patriot. Now he was a hero. The twilight was settling over the landscape, and he switched the lights of the car on. The needle on the illuminated speedometer hovered over 120 kilometers. Why was he driving so fast?

He was involved in a chase, like those he had seen in the movies. Soon he would be in Florence, and then there might be excitement, shooting even. He felt the briefcase by his side. The bulge in it was caused by a small black Beretta pistol. A toothbrush, pajamas, and Winterschild's forage cap were the only articles he carried, the latter as a kind of good luck charm. He tried to remember what this damned German had done. Destroyed a village, walked through it with a submachine gun at his hip, spraying every moving object with bullets, and then set fire to the church. Terrible, he told himself flatly. It was so long ago. Not so long really, but it seemed like an episode from a dream, a previous existence, perhaps something he had read somewhere. He could no longer remember any of it clearly. Perhaps he should have kept a diary, jotted down his impressions. Would they still have preserved their freshness?

He wondered briefly, but then suddenly found himself invaded by the surprising thought that he didn't really care. He had never admitted it before, and now, however shocking it was, he felt a great relief. He had to force himself to take an interest in the chase, as he had already forced himself to concentrate at the unveiling. What had struck him so forcibly during that ceremony was not the solemnity of the occasion, but the glaring paradoxes, the spirit of high farce which had tinged it, mottled with the darkness of inherent tragedy. Men were fools, and they would never learn. The faces they pulled when they believed the moment to call for gravity! They were the same faces they pulled as they caught sight of themselves in a mirror, a look of man to man, of inherent honesty, of straightness – of vanity, the look of men conducting a brief love affair with themselves as they leave the barber's shop. And they put plumes on their heads, to declare their rank in the ladder of incentives, stars on their caps, and exploding grenades, crossed swords, piled rifles, acorns, laurel clusters, washing-lines of medals on their chests, filigrees of braid. Like African tribal chiefs, they exalt themselves away from their naked origins and assume what grandeur they can while life lasts.

Val di Sarat had seen too much during his crowded life not to have his vision impregnated with irony, and now he began to see the perils of a perpetual reflection off other surfaces; at least the pomp around the statue was a positive action, as had been his exhilarating gunplay in the olive groves. In Chicago, Bonelli had been an unselfconscious creature carving out a career in the world as he saw it, a man whose manicured nails, whose brown and white golf shoes, whose perfumed armpits were his badges of rank just as surely as the gold braid was the yardstick of the military. Bonelli's gifts had been fired by his generally low opinion of human nature. Val

di Sarat had shared this view in his youth, and
that made his association with the gangster both
amusing and rewarding for a time. His career as
a painter and as a photographer had been built
on the foundation of public gullibility, and he
had chosen his path through the wilderness with
greater brilliance than Bonelli, since painters are
ignored sometimes by the public, but rarely killed
by their rivals. Val di Sarat was proud of his
cleverness, and yet now this pride had soured.
Were the stupid on the earth solely so that they
could be deceived by the ingenious?

The needle on the speedometer pointed to
a steady 120 kilometers. The Alfa-Romeo had
been traveling at at least 130. They had passed
each other at 250. With what object? The young
aristocrats were probably only testing their toy,
and he was hurrying to Florence to risk death at
the hands of a desperate man. Would everyone
be better off if they just stayed at home? The
roads would certainly be less congested. Ah,
China, contemplation of navels, the truth at
the bottom of limpid pools, unruffled by the
sighs of the lovelorn, peace, peace. Shanghai
was a dreadful place, and China in the throes
of endless wars. That kind of peace existed only
on vases or on silks, or in the mind. The Tuscany
of Piero della Francesca was still there, but for
how long? The olive trees still sparkled silver and
the cypresses still pointed to heaven among the
tombs, but already the neon signs punctured the

nightfall with their ripples of vulgarity, and the electrically aided voices of the popular songsters cut into the age-old silence. The mind was the last strong-hold of balance, of order. It had to be purified, protected.

Like one whose palate has been regaled with the infinite subtleties of wine, the cavernous echoes of great cheeses, and who then, in search of further excitements, laid himself open to the frontal assault of curries, oriental spices, enchiladas, Val di Sarat longed for a return to first impressions. He wished to drink clear water as it bubbled out from the freezing arteries of the earth. He wished for a child's capacity for wonder.

As he drove, he opened the window beside him, and also the one near the passenger seat. The cold sharp air rushed in, carrying with it a scent of charcoal fires. It was a smell he knew well, but tonight he noticed it. He even wondered if he wasn't destined to die in a few hours, so sharply did he seem to feel every detail of the world around him. A distant dog was barking, not maliciously, but with excitement at its master's teasing. He couldn't see the dog, but quite surely he knew all about it. This was the bark of a smiling dog, a dog with sharp features and pointed ears and light energetic eyes. An ass brayed. An ass, Biblical symbol of humility, with its back worn by heavy loads, patches of rough baldness, and long eyelashes drooping over eyes which had seen all they wanted to of conditions on this planet, and which kept to themselves.

A bell rang, dully, unevenly. The man in the belfry was getting too old for his job, but no one had the heart to relieve him of the one activity in which he still believed himself to be indispensable. As he raced through a village, the roar of conversation surged briefly from the café, an impression of sudden light, saturating smoke, and activity. Farmers, with faces hewn from brown rock, voices ragged from tobacco and the dust of the roads, teeth ridged like trees, a sour smell of toil. He could see their freckled hands in his mind, spatulate fingers that always worked together, feeling lost without each other's company, simple jokes, ancient games, a sense of values tempered by the seasons and the clearness of the moon and the ache in the toe meaning rain. The café was their stock exchange, and the sky the changing market.

A sudden smell of manure killed the charcoal, the smell of clay-colored pools in the mud of the farmyard, the burning of wood, the drying of apples in an airless shed. There was a lump in Val di Sarat's throat. The road danced behind his tears. It must mean imminent death; everything was too wonderful, and it had about it the quality of a farewell. The evening was the time for valedictions; after it came night, and sleep.

Soon he was in the outskirts of Florence.

People flitted like shadows on the road, their voices ringing in the winter night. It made driving difficult. Most of the bicycles had no rear-lights; a lantern hung cruelly onto the shorn tail of a dray-horse was merely confusing. The little car stuttered on the cobbles, and swerved drunkenly as its tires wandered into the streetcar tracks. The late buses wheezed and puffed all over the road as their air-brakes and brutal diesel engines obeyed the commands of their drivers with elephantine resentment.

He crossed the Arno, black as ink, and saw the spires and the steeples and the bridges. These were the works of man at their greatest, the repayment of a debt to their creator, a token of gratitude for the privilege of living. Everywhere there was symmetry in detail, and confusion in general effect, like life itself. The individual bridges, the spires, were exquisite in their indefinable harmony, acquiring their grace from a submission to the rules. Like a fugue of Bach, they formed emotion locked in the heart of relentless logic. They proclaimed that although the processes of procreation are the same for man as they are for monkeys and for mice, man is fashioned in the shadow of divinity, and life is as dear as thought itself. The only freedom is to be found in the prison of logic, there is no liberty without order.

Val di Sarat parked a little way away from the Belsoggiorno. There were four Carabinieri

loitering rather obviously in the street. With
the heavy heart of one who is committed to an
unwanted duty by a foolish promise, he took
his portfolio under his arm and walked to the
hotel. As he entered, the four Carabinieri closed
in melodramatically, stopping under a streetlamp
so that anyone could see that they were watching
a building efficiently. A young officer stood up as
Val di Sarat approached the concierge. Clicking
his heels, he said:

'Maggiore Val di Sarat, I am Rosselli, Emilio,
placed at your disposal by Colonello Fulvio de
Gratiis, Commander of the Carabinieri of the
Florence Region.'

'Why?'

'I understand that Colonello Ubaldini, who is
some relation of yours, telephoned and asked us
to furnish you with protection.'

Val di Sarat was angry with his uncle. Still in
the mood of his meditations, here he was again,
suffering the intolerable intrusion of Ubaldini's
orderly and hideously ingenious mind. Young
Rosselli was charming and ambitious. His dark
eyes darted about, eager to please on the path
of personal glory. His smile was ingratiating, of
the kind that changes imperceptibly to a frown
of determination as the mood of a superior
unexpectedly alters.

'First of all, I need no protection,' said Val
di Sarat.

'The criminal may be armed.'

'All the same, I need no protection.'

Rosselli acknowledged with humility the stuff of which heroes are made, and bowed gracefully.

'I stand under orders of Colonello de Gratiis,' he said, 'and you must carry any complaint to him.'

Val di Sarat sighed with frustration, and then said, 'Secondly, if the man is desperate, it doesn't seem the cleverest move to plant your men obviously in the street so that any passing idiot can see that the hotel is under observation.'

Rosselli frowned. 'I told them to stand in the darkness.'

'They are, all of them, brilliantly illuminated by the street lights. Is the man in his room?'

The sad concierge blurted out his excuses:

'No, he's out. We had no idea he was a criminal. The reservation was made by telephone, and he carried a bona fide Swiss passport in the name of Cohen.'

'He's out – he hasn't checked out?'

'No, no, his things are in his room.'

'Cleverer and cleverer,' said Val di Sarat sourly, 'the man comes back to the hotel, sees the Carabinicri, and decides to abandon his belongings, and escapes your net.'

Rosselli ran into the street, and hissed some orders to his sheepish men, who retired into the darkness again.

'Have you another key to his room?' asked
Val di Sarat.

'Here,' said the concierge, holding out a key
with a trembling hand. 'In this hotel, nearly
every key opens nearly every door.'

'I know the kind,' replied Val di Sarat.

'I regret. The lift is not working.'

Val di Sarat, followed by a furious Rosselli,
climbed the cheerless stairs.

At Room 117, Val di Sarat placed the key in
the door, while Rosselli drew his revolver, and
stood flush with the wall.

'What are we now?' asked Val di Sarat. 'Boy
Scouts?'

'The man downstairs is old, confused perhaps.
The criminal may be in after all.'

'Don't rush it. Your moment will come. You
can't manufacture a heroic action. You have to
wait for it with patience.'

They opened the door.

'Better not switch on the lights,' said Rosselli.
'He may see it from the street.'

Val di Sarat switched on the light.

'Very few people bother to identify their
rooms from outside the hotel,' he replied, 'and
if Winterschild should be one of those, he would
assume that the maid is in here. If he happened
to catch the play of a flashlight, he would not
assume the maid is in here, but one of us.'

They looked briefly round the room. The
Swiss passport lay on the table. Val di Sarat

opened it, and saw the photograph of his man. Dr Waldemar Cohen. He grunted.

Then his eye fell on a postcard. The stamp was on it. It was all ready to be sent, addressed to Herr and Frau Oberst Friedrich Winterschild, 18 Falkenhaynweg, Langensalza. Careless.

He read the message.

'Is there a Club Waikiki in Florence?'

'Yes,' replied Rosselli, 'a low dive. We've had our eye on it in connection with narcotics.'

'Is it far? Can one walk?'

'About eight blocks.'

'I'll walk it. I'd rather.'

A quarter of an hour later, Val di Sarat, followed at a respectable distance by two of the Carabinieri, arrived at the door of the club. Before he entered, he summoned the corporal who was following him.

'You are following me against my wishes,' he said softly. 'I can do nothing about it, because you have your orders. However, if you wish our enterprise to succeed, I must ask you to stay outside, and watch.'

Cautiously he entered the club, alone. The place was already fairly full, and he went straight to the bar.

'Don't you want to see the show?' asked the barman. 'It begins in a minute. There's no extra cover charge here. Drinks cost the same at a table. They'll fill up in a moment.'

'Give me a Carpano,' snapped Val di Sarat.

The drinks were lined up against a large, modernistic mirror of bluish glass. Val di Sarat peered into it, and as his eyes became accustomed to the new light, he fancied he saw his quarry in the distance, seated alone at a table near the black velvet curtains which led backstage. Cautiously, he risked a look. Yes, it was Winterschild, glum, looking at his fingers. Quickly Val di Sarat glanced at the rest of the room. He saw a small unoccupied table which was sheltered by a barrier, the ideal place for a flirtation.

'Barman,' he called, 'I'm going to that small table over there, at the back. Have my drink brought over. I don't want to do the waitress out of her tip.'

The barman smiled and nodded as Val di Sarat left a couple of hundred lire on the bar.

Winterschild didn't look up. Val di Sarat passed to his table unobserved, and leaned back.

'Don't you want a better table?' asked the waitress.

'No.'

'There's one nearer the floor.'

'No.'

The girl shrugged and went.

'May I join you?' asked a peroxided blonde.

'No.'

'You're not very sociable.'

'No.'

In spite of himself, Val di Sarat was nervous. Incredible, in a couple of minutes you might be a corpse, and still people annoy you. No sensitivity whatever.

Once or twice, he carefully leaned forward. Winterschild was petrified into a moment of dejection. He was still alone. The lights went orange, and the slippery man with the hotel-room eyes begged for quiet, announcing Miss Fatima Luxor. After the night ride and the aroma of woodsmoke, the spectacle of the mountainous creature undulating to the catcalls of lonely soldiery was a sight of quite especial horror, like a glimpse of Gomorrah. Somewhere, not far away, Noah would be sawing his planks.

Miss Astrid Olaf raced out as usual in a tempest of cheap scent, a powdery stench of jasmine, and was followed by Teresa as the Maharanee Indrapura. Val di Sarat had seen the same kind of performances in the burlesque houses of America, almost defiant in their lack of talent and their mournful insistence on the most athletic aspects of the sexual act. They appeared to him about as beautiful as oil wells, and were evocative only of the most desperate loneliness.

During the exhibition, Fatima Luxor paddled across, pulling at her girdle, and stared at Val di Sarat.

'Lonely?' she asked.

'Very, but I like it.'

The way to get rid of such women was to frighten them. They preferred what they

called healthy emotions. They didn't care for
the talkative or the dangerous. Fatima Luxor
was different, however. She was in her forties,
and men didn't pay for bulk.

'Be nice to me,' she pouted.

'Go away.'

'You're violent. I like violent men. I like to
feel possessed.'

'I live with my mother.'

'Where do you live?'

'In Vatican City.'

'Is your mother a Cardinal?'

'Go away. Get out.' He couldn't stand this
senseless badinage. At this moment, too.

'You're a brute,' said Fatima, sitting down.

'I'm a vampire.'

'I could lose some weight.'

Why did he bother to answer? He was angry
with himself.

'What is thy desire, O master? A little frolic
with thy slave?'

Val di Sarat lit his pipe.

'In Egypt my master there smoked a pipe, but
it was a calabash,' she murmured in her thick
Neapolitan accent. She tried a new approach.
Teresa had finished, and the false Brazilian
hostess was now paying her homage to Saint
Cecilia by rattling a couple of maraccas wildly
in the air.

'You like her? She has vitality, but I'll tell
you a secret about her. She's as Brazilian as my

fanny. She comes from Pisa. D'you notice how she leans to one side?'

'You come from Naples,' said Val di Sarat, hardly able to bear the heavy pall of garlic which now hung in the air.

'Life has no secrets for you,' crooned Fatima, her lower lip as shiny as a runway in the rain, her ugly eyes hooded with voluptuousness, the garlic seeping into the air like poison gas in a death cell.

'You're quite right,' replied Val di Sarat, 'and if you don't go at once, I'll complain to the management.'

'The management never penalizes a girl for going beyond the line of duty. What are all these medals?'

'The management would still remove you from my table if I asked them to.'

'You're inhuman. Impotent.'

'Probably, yes. I'm waiting for my wife.'

'This is no place to bring a wife.'

'We're not married yet.'

'Ah, your mistress! Is she as pretty as I am?'

'Not nearly, but I like ugly women. Ugly, small, thin women.'

'If you change your mind,' said Fatima harshly, 'my fee is thirty thousand lire for the night.'

At last she went away, but sat at a table from where she observed him provocatively, pulling her skirt high over her crossed knees. He buried his head in his hands, and spied through a gap between his fingers. It was like being back at school during an exam. Trigonometry probably.

Winterschild had been joined by Teresa. He was talking volubly. She was bored. He looked very little like a monster now, a man with the blood of women and children on his hands. She lit a cigarette with the careful magnificence of a teenager trying the vice for the first time in a public place. He struck a match for her, but she preferred to use her own lighter. There are no silly humiliations to which a woman will not stoop if she is bent on some stratagem. Effective, if unsubtle. Hans blew the match out, and lost his train of thoughts. He just stared glumly before him, and blinked. She threw him a look which could have expressed disdain, but which could also have been the look of a woman who knows she is being followed, and wants to make sure the pursuer is still there.

An impulse made Val di Sarat glance toward the doorway. One of the Carabinieri had entered, revolver and all, obviously on duty. Idiot. He saw Val di Sarat and made a gesture signifying that he was there if needed. Val di Sarat tried to ignore him, but the fellow evidently thought he hadn't been seen, and so advanced towards the table. Fatima Luxor had noticed the look of complicity, and frowned. Val di Sarat made no further effort to arrest the progress of the man, but let him come right to the table.

'Do you need us?' asked the man.

'My car? I don't think so. What's the number?' asked Val di Sarat in a loud voice.

'I don't understand.'

'Imbecile, once you're here, give me a ticket,' he whispered.

'What for?'

'Can I leave the car there for another five minutes?' he asked again, very loud, livid.

The Carabiniere saluted stiffly, and left again, perplexed.

Val di Sarat caught Fatima Luxor's eye.

'Can't even park a car in Florence any more.'

Fatima Luxor left her table without replying.

Now what? Obviously if the arrest were to be effected, it would have to be done at once, otherwise those inexperienced oafs, surfeited on a diet of bad movies, would ruin it all. He looked at Hans. Nothing had changed. He was saying something self-pitying, and Teresa was shrugging it off, inhaling her cigarette as though it were hashish.

The manager arrived with Fatima Luxor. Val di Sarat leaned back so that he would not be seen.

'I hope everything is to your satisfaction, Your Excellency,' said the manager, beads of sweat trembling on his forehead.

'Absolutely.'

'At all times we stay well within the law.'

'What has that to do with me?'

'Well, Miss Luxor tells me you were visited by the Carabinieri just now. I only wish to reassure myself that there is no raid planned.'

'I was told that I had parked my car in a forbidden zone, that is all.'

'That, surely, is the duty of the regular civic police, Your Excellency. It would be outside the province of the Carabinieri.'

'Are you doubting my word?' Val di Sarat asked, feeling very foolish and trembling with irritation.

'Of course not, sir. Never. The word of an officer?'

'I just happened to be dressed like this because I have been attending a reunion dinner of my regiment. I'm not even an officer any longer. I have no connection with the Carabiniere whatever.'

'I see,' said the manager, quite unconvinced, and smiling sickeningly. 'I just hope you realize that this is an honorable establishment, which caters to the weaknesses of human nature, like any shop.'

'I quite understand, and I am enjoying myself immensely. However, I would like to be left alone.'

The manager retired, bowing, and Fatima Luxor returned to her seat, no happier than before.

Over in the corner, Hans was talking earnestly, thrashing something out. Teresa was overacting her boredom. It was time to put him out of his misery. Val di Sarat opened his briefcase, and summoned the waitress. She came in a rustle of straw. He gave her his visiting card and Winterschild's cap.

'Take this to the gentleman in the corner,' he said, and while she was on her way to her destination, he slipped the little black pistol into his pocket.

Hans looked up bleakly at the waitress, took the cap, and stood up, wide-eyed. He studied the visiting card, and blinked uncontrolledly. Val di Sarat rose and wandered over, casually.

The two men stared at one another, uncertainly, while Teresa, suddenly conscious that something unexpected was occurring, looked years younger.

Hans stretched out his hand.

'May I salute a brave officer,' he said.

At that moment he lost the sympathy of Val di Sarat.

'No.'

Val di Sarat sat down, and Hans grew pale with fury.

'Sit down and listen to me.'

Hans refused tacitly.

'You want to make a scene?'

Hans sat down.

'Have you no imagination at all?' asked Val di Sarat coldly. 'Why do you think I'm here?'

Hans didn't reply. He was struggling with

tears of outrage. To have his hand refused was tantamount to a slap in the face.

'This is the end of the road for you,' said Val di Sarat quietly. 'You are guilty of a war crime, one of the most callous and most revolting of the entire war. You're not even listening. You're still angry that I didn't shake you by the hand.'

After a pause, Hans spoke with a visible effort at self-control.

'That was war,' he said, 'and war is war. There are no rules. But that doesn't prevent officers from behaving like gentlemen, and accepting an honorable handshake.'

'I am not proud of what I did during the war,' Val di Sarat replied, 'and I won't shake a hand offered me in order to commemorate any episode of those infantile high jinks we indulged in. You don't understand me. I should have shot you dead at the time. You would have understood that better.'

'I don't know why you didn't.'

'You would have done so.'

'Yes, I would.'

'Yes, because you have no respect for life.'

'What do you want with him?' asked Teresa, suddenly hostile.

'I came here to arrest him for crimes against the Italian people. He was responsible for the destruction of the village of San Rocco al Monte, in which forty-two men, forty-six women and eighteen children died,' said Val di Sarat, lighting his pipe.

Teresa stared at Hans.

'I'm told that's true,' said Hans, 'but I don't remember clearly. I saw worse things. I saw worse.'

'I saw worse, too,' replied Val di Sarat, 'but this was a deliberate, calculated and useless act of revenge. Because you couldn't catch the partisans, you took your vengeance on whatever was at hand. That was a crime. If I had allowed myself to be captured, I suppose that you would have shot me, and that the women and children would have been spared. Through German eyes, I am therefore very much to blame myself. Unfortunately, however, these criminal excesses are never seen through the eyes of the loser. You killed uselessly, and you must pay the price.'

'You don't seem very upset,' blurted Teresa. 'You speak like a lawyer, not like a man.'

'Perhaps I too am trying to keep calm.'

Hans looked crestfallen.

'I don't feel guilty,' he said.

Val di Sarat frowned.

'I'm not surprised,' he replied softly, 'because even I can hardly remember what happened.' He stared at Hans acutely. 'I only know the facts,' he said, 'because they are documented. I know who died, what was destroyed, and its value. I also know it was wrong, a wrong thing to do,

an ugly and repugnant thing, because I have a
sense of what is right and what is not. Have
you tried to feel guilty?'

'Yes, I have.'

'And?'

'I don't. I can't. It isn't fresh enough. I . . .
can't remember. Perhaps I was ill. Perhaps I am
ill now.'

Val di Sarat puffed at his pipe. For some
absurd reason he was moved.

'What do you remember?' he asked.

'I remember chasing the partisans into the
olive groves. I remember our fight as clearly as
if it was yesterday. Then we went back, and a
general – General Grutze gave us the order to
destroy the village. We were all hysterical, and
drank a lot of brandy. Then we walked through
the village . . . we sang I think . . . and shot
. . . and the church burned – it was fun, like
a bonfire. Then I came to Florence, and met
Teresa here. That I remember well. I think I
must have fallen in love. The retreat came. I had
to go. I said good-by to my comrades in Savona,
and got down to Rome. Then they sent me to
Florence, and here I am.'

'The mind remembers what it wishes to remember. You came here before?' Val di Sarat looked at
Teresa. 'Where do you come from?' he asked.

'San Rocco al Monte,' she said. 'I lost my
mother there.'

'And you can sit with this man?'

'I didn't ask him to sit with me. You know what I am. I can't choose my friends.'

'Is that why you've changed so much?' asked Hans, emotionally.

'Changed?' she replied. 'Changed? I'm older. I didn't like my mother. She beat me. Good riddance. My father was killed in Libya. I agree, war is war. What's the difference how a person's killed, it doesn't make them more alive. I liked my father. He was killed honorably, by a British bullet. I hated my mother. She was burned in the church, and went straight to Heaven because of it. Good luck to them both. I'm still alive, and when I go, I won't blame anyone. I'll just be damned grateful.'

'You've never learned how to feel,' said Val di Sarat, with a sudden intensity, letting his pipe drop into the ash tray with a clatter.

'Feel?'

'Feel. We had a childhood, all of us, and we came of age at the end of it. We had no adolescence. We're like wine, we've got to mature quietly, unshaken, untroubled, if we're to survive. You say you think you fell in love with this girl. You think? You don't know? How should you? Look at her, acting the part of the world-weary courtesan. How old are you, eighteen? You'd be laughable if you weren't so tragic. What sophistication you put into the handling of that cigarette! And you, you went to war so bravely, straight from the nursery,

you discarded your cowboy's uniform for your
soldier's uniform, and off you went with a puny
stunted vineyard in your heart. From pretending
to kill Red Indians in the park you went straight
to killing real men, as though your nurse had
one day given you live bullets for your pop-gun,
flames for your water-pistol. How should you
know how to feel, either of you?'

'Are you any better?' Teresa asked hotly.

'No,' said Val di Sarat, 'not much. I had more
time to think, though. I'm a few years older than
either of you, and therefore I can blame myself
for my own stupidity. You never had a chance,
either of you. You aren't in a position to blame
yourself. You'll have to leave it to society.'

Hans was straining earnestly to understand.
He had a German predilection for philosophical
discussion, and never felt more elated than when
slightly out of his depth.

'You came here to arrest him,' said Teresa.
'Why don't you get it over with?'

'Are you really so hard?' asked Val di Sarat.
'I don't believe it. You're Italian. You're built
like a woman. You've buried your dreams, but
they're still there, somewhere, under the surface.
You don't like other people, because you mistrust
them, and so you wish to deny them your love.
But it's there, I can see it in your eyes.

'We can think we're so different when we're
young, but before long we come back to the simple, unoriginal values we reacted against simply

because they belonged to our parents. Wouldn't you feel any joy in a child? The first stirrings of life in your womb, the sensation that you were part of nature itself, part of the seasons, keeper of a mystery, a person big with two pulses, and then the painful donation, the gift to the free air, a tiny resemblance groping for your immensity, the gush of food, the little hands suddenly tranquil with contentment, the milk-blue eyes closed in the serenity of your sheltering warmth?'

Teresa burst into tears, floods of tears.

Hans stood up stiffly.

'You have upset her,' he announced. Damned Italians, with their fluent talk. Is that how they talk in their bedrooms?'

'Lunatic,' Val di Sarat replied. 'I have made her feel at last. Has she ever felt for you? Did you ever take advantage of her? That's what other humans are for. That's what love is.'

Hans blinked.

Val di Sarat put his pipe in his pocket, and rose.

'I can't arrest you,' he said. 'You were not responsible for your actions. You don't know how to feel for yourself, and therefore you cannot be expected to feel for other people. Perhaps when you said you thought you loved this poor girl, you had your chance, but you certainly didn't take it. Do what you wish. The only emotion I have seen in you is when I refused to shake you by the hand. I imagine that is as deep as it goes. There's no chance for you. Try to escape again from the police and from your responsibilities. You may succeed, you may not. It really doesn't matter.' He made to go.

'I am not in the habit of escaping from my responsibilities,' Hans said.

'In that case, perhaps you should give yourself up. I don't know what they will do to you. Whatever it is, it will be unpleasant. But perhaps you may learn to feel. Colonel Ubaldini, of the Carabinieri, is staying at the Hotel Belsoggiorno, your hotel. He would be most delighted to see you.'

'Just a moment,' Hans said quietly. 'You are very clever with words. You're quite right. I can't feel much. I can feel anger, and annoyance, and frustration. Not much else. I want to be loved and yet I don't think I know how to love. I understand that. But I don't understand all you say. Will you do me a favor?'

'What is it?'

'Tell me in words that I can understand why I should give myself up.'

There was a pause.

Val di Sarat answered quietly, reasonably.

'I will hate myself for what I am about to say. It is quite unlike me, but perhaps I am holding out my hand to a man in need by saying what I do. I speak not for myself, but for public opinion. It is deficient in honor not to give yourself up. It is cowardly.'

'Thank you.'

VAL DI Sarat left the club and walked into the night. The two Carabinieri slavishly followed him at a distance. When he reached the Arno, he took his pistol out of his pocket, and dropped it into the water. The two men caught up with him.

'Where are we going?' the corporal asked.

'I'm going for a walk.'

'Where to, Your Excellency?'

'Siena, Venice, Rome, any ideas?'

'But the criminal?'

'I lost track of him. He wasn't at the club. Good night.'

The bewildered men returned halfheartedly to the city. Soon Val di Sarat was out in the country, the woodsmoke, the dry leaves, the uncertain cough of dogs who hear a footfall but don't know if it's worth a real bark. It was cool, the moon was full, the stars were out, and silence had a sound. He did not know where he was going, but he knew that he would stay upon that soil, which was his, which was home, and build. He had seen too much and felt too little. From now on, each day would be a rebirth, each morning he would see the sky for the first time in his life. He was ripe for love. Someone sleeping at that moment, not too far off, would take his fancy. He would plunge into the delirious pleasures of conventional, bourgeois life, with

meals on time and the screech of children and
the carving knife at the ready, poised over the
abbacchio. He felt in his pocket. He had no
money. He roared with laughter, all alone. It
was a good start.

'STAY WITH me,' implored Teresa, 'don't do
what he told you to do. I need you. I need
you.'

Hans looked at her, at the face which had
haunted his dreams and decreed the pattern of
his Odyssey. Here she was, pleading with him.
Her expression was not one he recognized. Gone
was the mystery, the need for endeavor. Gone
was the torture, the uncertainty. There would
be no bargaining. This was surrender. But it
was hardly a surrender of which he could feel
proud. He had had help with his homework,
not from an expert, but simply from one who
knew what to do with words.

'You need me?' Hans asked. 'You don't need
me, you need a man. Security. Something.'

'I need you,' she said hoarsely, so sincere she
seemed to be lying.

'Listen,' Hans muttered, eager not to attract
attention, 'we couldn't help each other before.
It will happen again. We will run out of words,
because . . . because we don't know how to
communicate. I don't know how to talk to
you . . . or to anyone. I can give orders, and
take them. I'm spoiled.'

'Don't you understand that I am frightened, too?' she asked.

'Frightened? Of what? You treat me as though I disgust you – like a block of ice. One of your own people comes along, talks to you in your own language, and your eyes are suddenly full of tears, you begin to sob, to carry on – I can't move you.'

'I hate being moved. I hate that man who came in. So self-righteous, so cruel. He made fun of me, that's why I cried. You never did that. You led me into temptation by your – politeness. I acted up. I'm only a woman. I've no experience in dealing with people, I just imitate what I see.'

'Who are you?' said Hans, directly.

'What do you mean?'

'Do you know who you are?'

'Who I am? We're different with different people. All of us. That's something my job taught me. With some I'm sophisticated, with some I'm simple. With you – I don't know yet. I only know that I want to find out.'

Hans closed his eyes. 'I've found out what I am with you. That's the trouble. I'm someone trying to forget what he is, and I can't find anything to put in the place of what I try to take away. I try to be tender, I try to be patient. When you were unpleasant to me, it was possible for me to imagine I was succeeding. I was like someone making a sacrifice, someone with a sick wife, someone, perhaps, paying a debt. I don't know. Anyway, I didn't recognize myself, and that in itself was a relief. Now—? God knows. Do you follow me?'

'Yes.'

'Really?'

'Almost.'

Hans smiled slightly, very weary. 'Almost. Yes. I hardly know if I make sense any more. Even when I think, I have my doubts. I'm sick. I believed, you know – I believed in what I was doing. I thought it right. Sometimes I still think it's right. It's very hard to know, because we lost. Those who win never have doubts about whether they were right or not, but those who lose . . .'

'But war is war, you said it yourself.'

'Yes, but my darling, my Teresa' (ridiculous, he felt, to talk so to someone one was bent on leaving) 'my whole life was war . . . from the cradle it was war, and now there's nothing left. I've never been to school. I have to start again with the mind of a small child – I can't. I've seen too much. I am a little mad.'

'You think I know a life away from war? What am I doing now? Exactly what I did then. For me, peace never came.'

'And yet a few words from that Italian officer, and you broke down. You have the capacity to cry. I have not. I can be scared. I can feel fear, other smaller emotions, but I can't cry. If they came in now, and told me that my mother had died under the most horrible circumstances, I wouldn't know how to react. It doesn't mean anything to me. I've seen it all. And when you cried, you became a stranger, someone I no longer could pretend I knew. That's why there's no other way.'

He rose, and walked sharply across the room, not looking back. Somewhere behind him he heard his name shrieked, once, twice, and a flurry of people rushing, but he had half escaped from the obligation and the pain of living. He was running away in order not to be called a coward, and he felt better away from thought, away from illusion, away from the spice, the color, the ultimate glories of existence.

The street was empty. He only heard his own shoes beating against the paving stones. The rhythm was hard and accurate. A regiment of one man was marching to its destiny.

He entered the hotel, and the old man at the desk shook visibly at the sight of him.

'Colonel Ubaldini, please.'

'Room 24, on the next floor, to your left.'

'Thank you.'

Hans climbed the stairs with the confidence of a Gauleiter conducting a house raid. The old man whirled the aged telephone handle, and spoke breathlessly into the silver mouthpiece.

'Colonello Ubaldini, he's here, the murderer. He's on his way to your room.'

The two Carabinieri came in from the street.

'It's him,' whispered the old man, his eyes moist with terror. 'Room 24.'

The Carabinieri drew their revolvers and crept upstairs.

'No shooting here,' implored the old man.

Hans knocked at the door.

'Just a moment,' sang the colonel.

The Carabinieri reached the upper stairs, saw Hans, and stopped in their tracks.

'Come in.'

Hans entered the colonel's room.

The colonel, stripped to the waist and in his shorts, was shaving. A woman in a blouse was sitting on a chair, like a cook being interviewed.

'You chose a bad moment. I have the kind of beard that has to be shaved three times a day. Please sit down. I have been killing time by dictating a few letters to the secretary. That will be all, Signorina.'

'But . . .'

'Oh, yes.' The colonel waddled to his trousers, dug into the pocket, and fumbled secretively with some notes. 'Here is money for the postage stamps,' he said, giving her a handful of them.

She examined them with a thoroughness which was embarrassing for him, and then left with a miserable '*Buona notte.*'

'Now,' said the colonel. 'You gave us quite a runaround.'

A second later the woman was back, and searching on the floor.

'What is the matter now?' asked the colonel testily.

The woman gathered something to her, and muttered, 'I left my stockings,' as she left again.

The colonel smiled warmly at his prisoner and even winked. He was in good form.

'I will take custody of you in a moment. Damn, I cut myself again. People are often afraid of being arrested, but there's really nothing to it. When all parties are sensible, there's never any need of toughness. Did you see my nephew?'

'Who?'

'The one who shot your hat off.'

'Oh . . . yes.'

'What did you do to him?'

'Me? Nothing.'

'Why isn't he here with you?'

'I don't know. He left.'

'Left?' The colonel, his face still half covered with lather, turned and looked at Winterschild. 'What do you mean, left? Just like that?'

'He told me to come here, and left.'

'Oh God,' sighed the colonel, 'more trouble. By the way, are you armed?'

'No.'

'I'm glad to hear it. You don't seem a very desperate character. Why did you give yourself up?'

'I am told I killed some women and children, and I consider it cowardly to evade my responsibility.'

'Quite right. It was a dastardly act. This blade is blunt. Why did you do it?'

'I can't remember.'

'I see. That's a good reason. By the way, if you look in my brief case, the second partition . . .'

Hans stood up obediently, while the colonel followed him in the mirror.

'. . . you'll find a pair of handcuffs.'

'Handcuffs?'

'No, no, forgive me. You're quite right. It was thoughtless of me. There's really no need.'

A FEW weeks later, after a short trial in which Hans made no attempt to defend himself, but conducted himself in a soldierly fashion throughout, the papers announced that he had been executed by a firing squad. He died bravely, with no show of emotion, which was a fitting end for one who had been trained for death, but not for life. The same editions of the newspapers printed the news that Colonel Ubaldini had been promoted to the rank of general of brigade for his brilliance in engineering the capture of a dangerous enemy of the state.

The postcard was never sent, and so the elderly parents of Hans Winterschild were resigned to the loss of their son in the last days of the war. When Friedrich Winterschild was eventually appraised officially of his boy's death before a firing squad, he courageously kept the news from his wife.

It so happened, however, that when the finished film of the destruction of San Rocco was shown in Germany a year and a half later, a piercing scream was heard in a theater when the close-up of a blinking man filled the screen, and an old lady was carried senseless from the auditorium. The old still remember how to feel.